W9-DCN-128

*SHE THOUGHT SHE'D ESCAPED THE TERRORS
OF HER PAST . . .*

LINDA DEVONSHIRE—Witnessing her parents' brutal murder had left her vulnerable to attacks of schizophrenia. She was so certain she'd been cured. Then the fears returned. Someone was pursuing her and meant to kill—again.

ELEANOR DEVONSHIRE—She'd opposed her son's marriage. Now Keith's young widow was back. She'd try to make Linda welcome—for the sake of her grandchild.

THOMAS DEVONSHIRE—A successful banker, he carried on the solid family tradition. But now he'd have one thing in common with his artistic, easygoing brother—Linda.

BEATRICE DAILEY—Her little girl and Linda's were best friends. But she'd never forgive Linda for taking Keith away from her. And never, never forget. . . .

TOBY DEVONSHIRE—She'd seen how Beatrice punished her own daughter and it filled her with terror. But who should she fear most—Beatrice? A mysterious stranger? Or Linda—her own mother?

*BUT NOW EVERY NOISE IN THE NIGHT, EVERY
CREAK ON THE STAIRS, TOLD HER THEY WERE
BACK AND THAT DEATH WAS ABOUT TO
STRIKE FROM . . .*

OUT OF THE SHADOWS

By Duffy Stein

THE OWLSFANE HORROR
GHOST CHILD

OUT
OF THE
SHADOWS

Duffy Stein

A DELL BOOK

Published by
Dell Publishing Co., Inc.
1 Dag Hammarskjold Plaza
New York, New York 10017

Copyright © 1984 by Mel Berger Enterprises, Inc.

All rights reserved. No part of this book may be reproduced
or transmitted in any form or by any means, electronic or mechanical,
including photocopying, recording or by any information storage
and retrieval system, without the written permission of
the Publisher, except where permitted by law.

Dell ® TM 681510, Dell Publishing Co., Inc.

ISBN: 0-440-16826-0

Printed in the United States of America

First printing—October 1984

For my brother, Ed

Acknowledgments

For their guidance and assistance,
my sincere thanks and appreciation to
Coleen O'Shea, Susan Moldow,
and Maggie Lichota.

chapter 1

The night was thick with swirling fog. Rain fell in a fine mist and a cool breeze swept the air, slanting the rain into the face of the young woman walking along the deserted street. Her hurried, anxious footsteps echoed loudly, hollowly, on the pavement, the only sound to break the night.

It was 2 A.M. in Youngstown, Ohio, a half-hour rest stop for the passengers on the Greyhound bus, a fill-up of gas, a change of drivers. Earlier that evening Linda's seven-year-old daughter had complained of a queasy stomach—a combination of the catch-as-catch-can eating over the last three days of traveling and the constant motion of the bus. Toby wasn't feverish, Linda tested, but her face was pale, her eyes liquid, and her hands were folded across her stomach. The drug counter in the terminal was closed, but the cashier at the newsstand suggested a store three blocks away, which was open late. If she hurried, she could catch them.

She barely did. The druggist was just closing and didn't want to let her in. She had to pound on the door and beg him to open up. Grumbling, he sold her the medicine, then with a definitive flick of his wrist locked the store behind her. Linda was again alone on the silent street.

As she hurried back to the terminal the fog engulfed her, filmed her eyes. Above her a streetlamp flickered and pulsed with tentative light, a dim, ghostly beacon. She kept her glance straight ahead and her step purposeful so she wouldn't have to look toward the doorways and alleyways that lined the sidewalk, blackened holes that tauntingly hid lurking, shifting shadows.

From one of which the man must have come.

The muted fluorescent lights of the bus terminal were barely visible when she heard the sounds. The kick of a small rock against the side of a car, the faint splash of water in a puddle, a heavy footstep on the pavement. The street was no longer deserted; she wasn't alone. Nervously she glanced behind her but saw nothing on the darkened sidewalk. She stiffened instinctively and quickened her pace, more than a walk yet not quite a run, and she tried to soften her step so she wouldn't be heard.

She spun around again and saw the man out of the corner of her eye, a slender figure a hundred feet behind her. In the patchwork of darkness and fog he might not have been there at all. Only a residual image of something else, or a cruel trick of the eye. But he was there, stepping into the hazy glow of a streetlamp, momentarily spotlighted against the night. Then he was through the circle of light and into the shadows between two lampposts, out of sight. He probably meant her no harm, Linda considered. Just someone outside in the middle of the night as she was. But still she was caught midway between the safety of the drugstore and the bus terminal. Clutching her purse to her chest, she started to run. Toby's medicine sloshed in its plastic container.

She knew he was chasing her. He was running now too. His footsteps slapped the ground, splashing the puddles as he landed hard in them. A car hurtled past, splattering water from darkened pools, but either the driver didn't see what was happening or didn't want to get involved. *"Help!"* Linda cried, but the car was already past her, its taillights lost to the mist, dimming like closing eyes.

Her stomach weakened but adrenaline coursed through her, pushing her faster, pumping her legs harder. Her breath strained and her heart beat madly with fear. She screamed again, but the sound was trapped by the fog and she knew that no one would hear her. She turned quickly, looked over her shoulder to check the man's progress. He was closing the distance between them, running in and out of the shadows. *"No!"*—the word gurgled; she was so close to the terminal now, so close. Just a few more steps, a few more . . . It was almost within reach. Her footsteps echoed loudly as they pounded against the pavement forming a litany of her thoughts—*a few more steps, a few more steps.* Another car sped by, its rumbling engine and broken muffler blocking out all other sounds. She could no longer hear, but only sense, the man growing closer, gaining on her. She was afraid to turn around again because now he was seemingly right on top of her.

Then she heard him speak, his voice low and gravelly.

"I'm going to kill you," he said, and she heard as well the mocking laughter rise gruffly from deep in his throat.

She shocked to the words, and a helpless squeal escaped her lips. Instinctively she spun around to the voice and saw the man. And even in the dim light of the fog-covered night in this strange city, she knew who was chasing her. She had recognized his words, his voice, and now she was seeing his familiar features too.

He had found her again.

Fine, cold needles prickled her face and neck. Her breath caught high in her throat. The scream started to well involuntarily inside of her, the sound muffled by tight vocal cords, a nightmare shriek that would not break the air.

She wasn't watching her step. There was a dip in the sidewalk that threw her off balance. Her legs slipped out beneath her and she crashed to the ground, skidded across the rough sidewalk, ripping her stockings, skinning her knees. Her purse flew out of her hands, the clasp opened.

A hand touched her shoulder.

He had caught her!

The scream escaped her throat, harsh, rasping, her breath choked with terror, palpating.

The hand withdrew quickly. Linda hunched into herself, skittered across the wet sidewalk, muddying her dress and legs. She pulled herself away from the figure that was looming over her. Something metallic gleamed in the light of the streetlamp. A knife!

"Don't kill me!" she begged, her voice thick.

"Kill you?" The voice filled with surprise. "Are you all right? How can I help you?" And through her haze of fear she thought she recognized the man standing above her. He had been on the bus with her. She dimly remembered that he had offered her and Toby a candy bar earlier in the evening. And she saw the metallic gleam was only his belt buckle, flaring in the light. But

where was . . . ? She turned her head to the dark and lonely
street behind her; it was empty now and silent.

"There was someone chasing me," she gasped.

"There's no one here now," the man said. "You're safe." He
reached out for her. "Here, let me help you up."

Still in shock, Linda pulled away from him, but he did not
withdraw his hand this time and finally she grasped it, tentatively
at first, then tighter. The man saw the furtive look of fear still in
her eyes. He cupped his hand under her arm and helped lift her to
her feet. Then he picked up her pocketbook and carefully gave it
to her so she would see he meant no harm. Then the medicine,
which, protected by its plastic casing, was still intact.

"Someone was chasing me," Linda repeated as if her words
hadn't penetrated. "He wanted to kill me. Didn't you see anyone?"
Her hair, wet from the rain, was matted down across her forehead,
and she pushed it back on top of her head.

The man shook his head. "He probably saw me coming and
darted into one of the alleyways. But it's all right now," he said
soothingly. "He's gone. You're safe." His voice was soft and
reassuring, his face warm and kindly.

He took out a handkerchief. "Here. Let's clean you up."

Dully Linda took the handkerchief and wiped her legs. The
scrapes were bad and she was bleeding. The skin on her palms
was rough. She kept looking around her, twisting her head,
searching the darkness for the attacker. Where was he? Where
did he go? Was he just out of sight, watching, lurking, waiting?
But there was no evidence at all that there had been anybody out
there with her. Except for the two of them the street was again
deserted, the fog seemingly having closed in around them.

Suddenly, she did not feel safe even with this man who had
come to her rescue. She had to get back to the terminal, back on
the bus, away from this street, this town. *And Toby!* She almost
gasped out loud. She needed to go to her daughter, who was
alone on the bus, sick.

"We'd better get away from here," she said, her voice still
thick and filled with fear.

She started walking but her legs trembled. She felt weak and
reached out for the man's arm. "Help me, please," she whispered hoarsely.

"Of course." The man cupped her arm and led her toward the terminal. "Perhaps you should tell the police."

Linda shook her head. "There's no time. The bus will leave soon and my daughter's on it."

"I'll walk you to the ladies' room. You can get cleaned up there."

"I'll do it on the bus," Linda said, wanting to get back to Toby. She needed to see immediately that her daughter was safe. She offered the man his handkerchief back, wet and muddy and streaked with blood.

"You keep it." He smiled, then nodded toward the cafeteria. "I'm just going to get some coffee before the trip starts again. Can I get you anything?"

"No, thank you." Linda forced a smile. "You've done enough already. Thank you again for coming along when you did." She hurried onto the bus and up the aisle to her seat. Toby was hunched next to the window, her eyes closed. Linda touched her daughter's shoulder and Toby turned toward her.

"I've got the medicine," Linda said softly. "Do you want some?"

"Uh-huh."

Linda opened the plastic stopper and held the bottle to her daughter's lips. "Here, take a sip and I'll get you some water."

"I don't need any water, Mommy," Toby said. She sipped from the bottle and let the chalky liquid trickle down her throat. "How much longer?" she asked.

"Just another day, honey, then we'll be there. Now why don't you go back to sleep. It's very late."

"Okay." Toby kissed her mother. Linda took the small blanket out of her travel case, draped it around the little girl, and pulled her close, stroked her head. She hoped the medicine would calm her stomach and let her sleep.

Although she had been restless for the entire trip, Toby had never complained, as if she recognized the seriousness and necessity of the move. A questioning, probing child, usually vocal, she had been unusually quiet, overwhelmed by the never-ending countryside that flew past the bus window at fifty-five miles per hour. A beautiful child, with wide brown eyes and sandy blond hair, she squirmed against Linda, her arm clutching a raggedy doll that she hadn't put down since boarding the bus—a tie to home.

The driver swung the door closed, pulled away from the platform. In a few minutes the bus was back on the highway, the hum of the wet tires soothing, comforting, the slanting rain against the window cleansing, the bus a cocoon of safety. Youngstown was behind her. The man was behind her.

Soon Toby was breathing evenly. Linda carefully took her arm from around the sleeping child. She touched her leg where she had fallen. It had started to bleed again. She dabbed at the raw skin with the handkerchief, but she knew she should clean the wound properly. She made her way up the narrow aisle to the tiny restroom in the rear of the bus, again expressing her thanks to the man who had come to her rescue as she passed his seat. She ran water onto a tissue and gently wiped the blood away, knowing she would have to get a disinfectant at the next stop. She removed her nylons, which were hanging tattered around her knees, and threw them away.

Then she leaned against the sink and inhaled deeply to try to compose herself and regain her strength. Her heart had still not quieted; it thumped painfully, rapidly.

It couldn't have been *him*, she thought. It was only the circumstances that were similar—the flickering streetlamps, the fog-swept night, her fear as she was being chased—all reminders of the other times. And that was why she thought she had seen his face, heard him say what he had. But in all the confusion and noise of the passing cars, she no longer knew what it was she had seen and heard. And she knew it couldn't have been him at all.

She stared into the cracked mirror above the sink. Her face was streaked with dirt, and even in the blur of the smoky glass she could see how pale and tired she was. Her almond-shaped eyes were dull, a fogginess to the crystalline blue, making them almost seem gray and hesitant, distant. The soft wisps of hair that framed her oval face were limp, drab, and lifeless, from the rain tonight and the three days already spent on the bus. She washed her face, took out lipstick and dabbed her mouth, ran a comb through her hair, and decided there was little she could do with it now. Then she heard someone outside the bathroom door. Quickly she closed her pocketbook and went back to her seat where she slid in next to her sleeping daughter and stared out the bus window at the dark factories of Ohio that slipped by, amorphous shapes in the night.

They had been traveling with the storm. It had been raining for three days, ever since they left Los Angeles. Three days on the bus with only rest stops and dinner breaks. One more day and they'd be in New York, then a bus change for West Ledge, Connecticut. Their new home.

The air conditioning was blowing strongly out of the window vents. Linda shivered and ran her hands up and down her arms to warm herself and to wipe away the fear that still layered her skin. Though she yawned, she was still skittish and sleep refused to come. She leaned against her daughter and stared out the window, dully watching the rain strike the tinted glass and race down in slender rivulets to form pools on the outside ledge. She focused on two drops, rooted for a winner, and gave up as they blurred together and dropped out of sight. She closed her eyes to still her thoughts and forget about the night's attack. Now it was all behind her—she tried to tell herself—only an isolated incident, no lasting threat. Yet, with a stitch of mounting panic that rose from her stomach, she knew it would never be all behind her.

On her eleventh birthday, Linda's life had been marred forever by tragedy. The September night had been cool, the clouds thick and low but the rain had held up as if helping out the child in her celebration. Her parents had taken her to a nighttime showing of *The Sound of Music* and then for a sundae at her favorite ice cream parlor. It was almost midnight and they were walking home, holding hands, singing songs from the show, when suddenly a man stepped out of the shadows of an alleyway. His face was craggy, weatherbeaten, with a blond mustache and tight curly hair that covered his ears like cold-weather muffs. He was cradling a knife in his palm. "Your money!" his gravelly voice demanded. Confused and frightened, Linda's father hesitated. "Don't hurt—" he begged, but before he could even reach for his wallet, the man lunged forward and stabbed him, a quick, jabbing blow. Then quickly he withdrew the knife and feinted toward Linda's mother, who stood frozen, too horrified to move. In shock she watched as the knife tore her dress and entered her. Jerking the bloodied knife free, the man then turned to Linda.

"Now you." He leered as he wielded the knife in front of her face. "I'm going to kill you too."

"Run, Linda, run!" her mother gasped as she clutched her stomach and blood ran through her weakening fingers. Wide-eyed, in terror, Linda didn't have time to think, only react to her mother's voice. Summoning speed and adrenaline as she never had before, she ran and ran and didn't stop running until her legs gave out from under her on a dark Chicago doorstep. When the police found her, her arms were locked around her knees, her chin buried in her tightly closed legs, pressed into herself. The man was never caught.

Linda was traumatized by the brutal deaths of her parents and her own narrow escape, and suffered repeatedly from nightmares. They were always the same—the man was chasing her through endless streets and alleyways, waving a knife, red with her parents' blood. He wanted to catch her and kill her as he had her mother and father. As she ran from him, she looked over her shoulder and his face burned into her memory.

She carried her nighttime fears into the daylight hours as well. Strangers frightened her. She screamed at sudden movements, misinterpreted innocent gestures, thought she was hearing threatening words. The man was out there, she was convinced, lurking in the shadows, waiting to kill her too.

Paranoia. Reactive schizophrenia. Linda remembered the doctor's words from when he and her aunt were whispering in the kitchen when they thought Linda was napping. But she was really standing behind the slightly open door listening to words she did not understand, wondering what was happening to her, why she didn't have control over her thoughts and feelings, why she was so afraid.

But the prognosis was good. The schizophrenic episode was acute, a reaction to the terrible stress precipitated by the deaths of her parents, and the symptoms disappeared in a matter of weeks. And, as expected, therapy helped Linda. She accepted that the man couldn't hurt her; he was gone, her illness over. Not over, the doctor warned, but controlled—she would always remain susceptible to another episode. Schizophrenia was unpredictable in recurrence; an acute attack was often a prelude to a chronic pattern. She would always be vulnerable.

As Linda passed through her teenage years it was evident that splinters remained from the incident. She was shy, fearful of meeting strangers, especially men. She didn't date until she was nineteen, then only because her aunt pushed her out of the house. For almost four years she didn't let men get close to her. She was withdrawn, afraid.

Until she met Keith.

She was twenty-three when she bumped into Keith Devonshire on the cashier line at the coffee shop in Westwood, not far from the UCLA campus. She had eaten alone and was paying her check. Her purse slipped out of her hand and change scattered across the floor. He knelt down to help her retrieve her money and when they stood up, he smiled.

It wasn't her habit to let herself be picked up, but Keith Devonshire was the kind of man she had always dreamed she would bump into. He was twenty-four, his eyes were a gentle and winning forest-green that almost seemed to change color in shifting light from green to brown, like the changing seasons. His voice was soft but he exuded maturity and sophistication, unlike many of the other young men who had tried to date her and from whom she had turned away.

They walked and talked for hours. She told him about herself— born in Chicago, daughter of a shopkeeper. Her father had always worked long hours but was never too tired to spend time with her. They never had much, but there was a comfort to their simple life, and they had each other.

After she was orphaned she was raised by her father's sister, who saw her through high school and two years of community college. Three years earlier her aunt had died, leaving her with no living relatives. She went out west to put distance between herself and her past, to try to forget.

Then Keith took over. He was the dark sheep of the family. His father and brother were stuffy bankers in West Ledge, Connecticut. "Almost have to be with a name like Devonshire," he said. He had gone to UCLA, the first of a long line of Devonshires not to go to Harvard and then straight into the family banking business the way his older brother, Thomas, had.

He had watched Thomas grow into adulthood under the very strict, watchful eyes of overbearing, authoritarian parents: Thomas Devonshire, Sr., and Eleanor—cold, distant to each other and their children, unemotional, unable to freely express their feelings.

But perfect bankers—ruthless in business, getting what they wanted.

It wasn't a life for Keith. He refused to play the Devonshire game and grew up on his own, tuned his parents out, sought his own models. His brother was sent off to Harvard for his undergraduate and MBA degrees. There had never been a question about his going and never a complaint. He was molded into his father: stiff, all the humor drained from him. Also the perfect banker. Being the younger son made it easier for Keith. It was Thomas who got the parental attention, the molding. Keith wanted UCLA and they let him go, convinced that soon he would outgrow his rebelliousness and make a commitment to the life he was born to lead. But he refused.

While he was uncertain about his future, the theatrical bug had hit. The closest he had gotten to actual movie making was being a page at Paramount, seating the studio audience for filmings of television shows. He conceded that he had minimal acting talent and so had turned to writing screenplays.

Linda lived for the times she saw Keith; days and weeks flew past like moments. Since her two years of college had prepared her for nothing, she was a gal Friday at an insurance company. But her nights were hers—theirs—and she had never been happier. Shy and reserved, she had been out with only a few other men. Certainly none had been like Keith Devonshire. Though she had grown comfortable with her loneliness, Keith showed her there was a world outside her living-room window. She trusted him— the first man she ever did—relaxed with him, opened up her inner self to him.

They dated, made love, fell in love, swore they invented the emotion. They were floating on air. She was captivated by him. By his gentleness. By his love. He proposed after six months and there was no question of her acceptance.

Then came the problem. Not with Keith, but with his parents. Full of hope and the future, Keith brought her home to Connecticut to meet his family. But Linda wasn't a pure-bred, she had nothing. The elder Devonshires did not approve of her and did nothing to hide their feelings, especially Keith's mother. They would not sanction the wedding so she and Keith eloped, then returned to California to live happily, independent from the

Devonshire family, who had cut them off financially and emotionally.

Keith wrote screenplays during the day and managed a fast-food restaurant at night. Their house was small and crowded with scripts. He felt badly for Linda. They were the first Devonshires to be almost broke. Did she mind? he asked. Should they return to Connecticut? He was certain if he went home and joined the bank, his mother would eventually accept her.

No, Linda said. She wanted Keith to be happy and he never would be in Connecticut in a banker's suit and tie, and she didn't want him to sacrifice his dreams for her. He would soon hit with a screenplay, she knew it, and until then, well, she was used to not having much. Now she had Keith and that was all she needed. Keith and their baby, Toby.

She had never been happier.

Toby was six and a half when the car accident occurred. Keith was killed.

Keith's brother came west without his mother. He offered to fly the body back home to Connecticut for burial next to his father, who had died the previous year, but Linda suspected Keith wouldn't have wanted that. The ceremony was simple, the funeral inexpensive. Linda insisted on paying for everything.

Thomas led Linda away from the gravesite, supporting her with his arm.

"If you ever need anything," he said, looking at her briefly, then averting his eyes as she met his, "call me." Linda felt that he wanted to say more to her, but he didn't. He stayed in California for one night and then left.

There was no insurance, and the little money Linda and Keith had saved was quickly spent. She found hourly part-time work as a gal Friday, but the pay wasn't very much. Other young women in her situation—widowed, divorced—had family to help out, parents to move home to; she and Toby were totally on their own. That winter Toby suffered terrible bronchitis. Linda was fired after she stayed home from work for several days to care for her child.

Keith had been dead for over a year. Life was hard, and Linda and Toby had very little. They lived from paycheck to paycheck—when there were paychecks. They juggled bills when there weren't. Toby was growing and continually needed new clothes. And she

was the only girl in the second grade not to go on the class trips
because Linda couldn't give her the bus fare. Then she remembered Thomas's words.

It took a week for her to build her nerve and make the phone
call. The Devonshire family—what was left of it—still intimidated her. She wouldn't have called, but she needed the help, for
Toby. She wanted more for her daughter than she was able to
give her.

The time she spent on hold as the secretary buzzed her through
to Thomas was interminable. She considered hanging up, then
thought about her child and held on.

Thomas was surprisingly warm and friendly. Not the cold man
she had met only briefly in Connecticut, not the man who had
flown west to bury his brother.

"How are you getting along?" he asked.

She tried to keep her composure but broke down completely.

Thomas listened, then said, "I thought as much. I feel very
badly for not having checked on you, but . . ." He trailed off. "I
have an idea," he said brightly. "We've just foreclosed on a
house in West Ledge. I don't feel any particular pressure to sell it
right away. Why don't you come and live here for a while until
you get back on your feet again? You sound like you need a rest,
and I'm sure the change of scenery will be good for Toby too."
He had been feeling guilty, he added, that he had not reconciled
with Keith before his death, that he had not fought more vigorously against his parents for cutting them off. He really wanted to
help her.

"What do you say?" he asked.

"I don't know," she hedged. It was so much easier to just
borrow money from Thomas and not uproot herself. And she
certainly didn't want to return to a place where she hadn't been
welcome. But a lot of time had passed and there was nothing for
them in California, so when Thomas pressed, she finally relented.

"Good," he said. "Do you need plane fare?"

"No, we'll take the bus," Linda said. "You're doing enough
for me this way. I can't ask you to do more."

She hung up quickly so he wouldn't hear her cry.

Now the rain had stopped. The sun was sneaking into the
morning sky. There was rustling on the bus as the light filtered in

and people twisted in their seats to shield their eyes and prolong their sleep. Twenty-four more hours until New York, three after that until West Ledge. The long night was behind her, her life was ahead of her. Linda stroked Toby's head again and finally drifted into sleep.

chapter 2

The hands on the clock moved agonizingly slowly. The pile of mail lay unread on his desk, letters unsigned, the computer printout unopened. *Get with it*, Thomas Devonshire scolded himself, angered that half the morning had already passed and he had done nothing but look at the clock and try to estimate where Linda and Toby were in relation to West Ledge. It was now eleven and they were an hour from town, undoubtedly tired and nervous.

He was nervous too. He squeezed the handgrip he always kept on his desk to see him through a tedious phone call and to keep himself strong for tennis and golf. But today he worked it nervously, stretching the tendons in the top of his hand. He had a striking physical presence: tall, broad-shouldered, with his father's full head of straight, short-cropped hair, laced now with gray that made him a distinguished-looking man of forty-one. His body was muscular; he kept in shape on the tennis court and golf course and in once-a-week Nautilus workouts at the country club's health spa. He was always strong and in control, although not today. He felt unsettled about Linda and Toby's arrival. Could he face them? he wondered.

The door to his office opened and Jeff Forbes, one of the bank's vice-presidents, burst in. His sleeves were rolled up and he looked harried.

"Have you had a chance yet to look—" Jeff stopped in mid-sentence as he saw the printout sheets. A half-filled cup of coffee was resting on top, staining the report with a brown ring. "I see you haven't," he finished.

"Sorry." Thomas shrugged.

"Anything the matter?" Jeff asked. "This isn't like you."

Thomas shook his head. "No. Just a little distracted today, that's all."

"It is a nice day," Jeff agreed, and automatically glanced out the window at the sunny July morning. There was the slightest hint of a breeze in the air, rustling the leaves. He laughed shortly. "Was even tempted to take the day off myself . . ." But he saw something in Thomas's eyes that told him it wasn't the day that was preoccupying his boss. "Well, no rush," he said, and started for the door. "I'll just leave them here with you. You'll get to them when you have the time. But you know they want our counterproposal by Monday."

"Keith's wife and child are arriving today," Thomas said softly. "I'm picking them up in an hour—less than an hour."

Jeff clucked his tongue. Now he understood. He said nothing.

"Funny," Thomas continued. "I can easily put together multimillion-dollar deals, talk to senators and corporate presidents, but I don't know what to say to my sister-in-law."

"How about 'hello'?" Jeff offered with a weak smile, then embarrassed, he shook his head. "I'm sorry. I didn't mean to be flip."

"Forget it," Thomas said. "I haven't gotten much past 'hello' in my own mind." He smiled wanly. "All she really needed was some money, Jeff. I could just have sent her some to get her going again. I didn't have to invite her here."

"You said this was something you had to do, Thomas. That's never a mistake."

"No, I really don't regret inviting her here. That was the right thing to do." He shrugged helplessly, palms up. "I just can't figure out what to say to her."

"Why don't you ask her to review the printouts and suggest a counteroffer? Hey, can I do anything to help?"

"Thanks, but this is all mine."

"Okay. I'll be on the Johnson merger if you need me."

Jeff closed the door behind him. Thomas was tempted to run after him, ask him to stay with him, but he didn't. The entire bank couldn't grind to a halt, and besides, as he had said, this was all his.

He reached for the cup of coffee, touched it to his lips. Cold. He spilled it into the plant on his window ledge and looked at the clock: 11:15. He wasn't going to do any work that morning, that was clear. Not until after Linda's arrival.

Linda. He closed his eyes and her face filled his vision. He remembered how she looked when he had seen her last—at Keith's funeral. It was a grim day—overcast, a sprinkle of cool rain, but nobody brought umbrellas. Her eyes were puffy from crying, her hair limp, disheveled. She was disoriented, almost in shock. He should have stayed longer in California, should not have left her the way she was. But she had friends closer to her than he was, he rationalized. Yet the real reason, he knew, was that then, as now, he didn't know what to say to her. Words could not make up for her loss, for everything that had happened.

He could just have sent her the money now; that would have been easiest. But not enough. Linda's call had touched a nerve within him. When he explored his emotions, he knew he felt guilty for his actions—for not having stood up to his parents to tell them they were wrong to cut off Keith and Linda, for not having kept up contact with them himself, and for abandoning her after the funeral. His heart also went out to Toby, an innocent child who had suffered because of the Devonshire family. No, money alone was not enough. He wanted himself and his mother to personally care for Linda and Toby. They owed it to them, and to Keith's memory.

The sudden buzz of the intercom made him jump. He depressed the call button. "Yes, Diane?"

"You asked me to remind you when it's eleven thirty," she said brightly. "Well, it is. What's the matter? No clocks in there?"

The problem, Thomas wanted to say to her, is that there are too many clocks in here, and right now all of them are rushing forward. Instead he said, "Thank you, Diane."

She clicked off first and he was left holding the dead phone. A half hour. He looked at his watch again, wishing it were still yesterday, wishing it were tomorrow. Anytime but right now.

The grandfather clock chimed once, sounding the half hour. It seemed unusually loud and drew Eleanor Devonshire's attention from the magazine she was idly thumbing through. But it was no louder than usual; she was tense, susceptible to sound. She hadn't slept well the last several nights, and without makeup the lines that marred her cheeks and webbed around her eyes seemed deeper, more accented by her tiredness. Her hair was steel-gray, brushed high off her forehead with curls fringing the sides of her face. Her eyes were dark and pierced downward over her straight nose and small, narrow mouth. Unconsciously she ran her hand over her neck to try to tighten her skin, which was fleshy and given to age. She stared for an extra second at the antique clockface, hoping that perhaps it was wrong. But the clock had ticked perfectly since being manufactured in 1810 in Watervliet, New York. The face was decorated with lacquered birds in flight. She had never particularly cared for the design, but Keith had always liked it.

Keith. She thought about her son and her eyes grew wet. She suddenly saw him as a boy—thirteen years old, scrawny, freckled—and a sad smile crossed her face as a memory came. Keith had come racing into the house. His friends were all going on an overnight camping trip, could he go too? If he cleaned his room before he left, she said. Yes, he promised, he would, but in his excitement he forgot. Angered that he had broken his agreement, she had driven to the campsite and taken him home in front of all his friends. He had to learn responsibility, she said. Integrity. Humiliated, he didn't speak to her for days, and she let the feud linger as well. Stupid, she thought. What was the difference if the room was clean or not? But back then it did make a difference. He had to learn.

She had always done what she thought was best for her sons. Always.

Her hands felt cold and she rubbed them against each other. Her circulation wasn't good and she knew she was tending toward arthritis. She was getting old; yet her mother had lived to be eighty, and at only sixty-five that gave her quite a few years more. She prayed she could live them free from pain—physical and emotional.

11:35. The tick of the clock was bringing Linda and Toby closer to West Ledge. She hadn't seen Linda in ten years; she had never seen Toby. She had to admit curiosity about her granddaughter, even a desire to meet her. Toby was the last of the Devonshire line, as Thomas had never had any children. Yet the trade-off of having Linda return to West Ledge would be

great, since she would undoubtedly rekindle memories and regrets that were now best forgotten.

But still, there was no way to stop them, no way to turn them
back. Thomas had presented her with a *fait accompli*. "I invited
them, Mother," he had said. "I will not uninvite them." A *fait
accompli*. She couldn't argue with Thomas—he was stubborn, as
she was, as all the Devonshires were.

But she had closed the conversation by saying what she felt.
"You have made a mistake, Thomas," she said. "It's not good
that she's coming here. Not for us. Not for her. Not for her
child." Then she had been silent.

Toby's stomach had calmed and now she was restless. She was
tired of sleeping, tired of playing games. They had picked out red
cars, milemarkers, state borders—even the initial excitement of
crossing state lines had waned, and she was barely keeping up
the list she had started when they crossed into Nevada. They had
played war until Linda couldn't look at cards anymore. Four days
of war and more napping than either of them had ever done in
their lives. But even with all the sleeping they were both tired,
drained from the long trip. Linda checked her watch. Only fifteen
minutes to West Ledge. She was committed; there was no turning
back.

A thought had crossed her mind more than once over the
seemingly endless trip—to just get off the bus somewhere, disappear into oblivion, start a new life. But then she faced the same
problems she had in Los Angeles—no money, no prospects.
No—Thomas's way was the only way. For now. It was just so
painful to return to West Ledge, to see Thomas. And Eleanor.
But she had to go—for Toby's sake. Except for a few friends in
Los Angeles, none of them close, all of them uncomfortable
around her after Keith's death, she had no one. Her parents were
dead. Her aunt. Keith. She was at the mercy of Thomas
Devonshire, and if this was all a cruel joke, only welfare was
left.

But Thomas's offer was genuine, she knew. It had come from
his heart. He had even offered to send her money to fly east, but
she had declined. "You're doing too much for us already," she had
said. But that wasn't the real reason. It would have been too
quick to fly, too fast to leave one life for another. She knew how

long the bus trip would take and she needed the time, a demarcation between her former life and the next. A buffer to sift through memories and to brace herself for what lay ahead.

She took a deep breath as they passed the green and white road sign: "You are entering West Ledge, Connecticut," where she had not been for almost ten years.

Thomas was standing outside the terminal when the bus pulled up. She saw him first, through the tinted glass. He was wearing a gray suit and tie, and she smiled, thinking of the jokes Keith had made a long time ago. Then she frowned and her eyes misted. She knew the memories were inevitable—good ones about Keith, sad ones, bittersweet; and unpleasant ones about her last trip to West Ledge.

"Are we there?" Toby asked. The look on her daughter's face clearly indicated she hoped they were.

"Yes, baby," Linda answered. "You've been a very good girl." She stood up in the aisle and stretched, took her hand luggage from the rack above, and, holding tightly to the only person that mattered to her, she started for the door. This is it, she thought as she exited into the bright sunlight.

"Hello, Linda," Thomas said. There was an awkward moment of indecision—should he kiss her or not? He did, on the cheek. "How are you?"

"Tired." She smiled. "And a little wobbly."

"I'm sure," Thomas said, and smiled warmly.

Linda looked into Thomas's eyes and for a fraction of a second thought she saw Keith. She hadn't noticed it the other times, but the brothers had identical eyes—deep reflecting pools of greenish brown, soft yet probing. His eyes were Keith's for only a moment, then he was Thomas again.

Their eyes were the only features the brothers shared. Thomas's face was more angular than Keith's, his features more defined, his jaw stronger, more set. Harder, Linda thought, but she suspected her impressions of each man were affecting her vision.

"And how are you, Toby?" Thomas asked.

"Fine," the little girl answered shyly, and hid behind Linda's legs.

"You remember Uncle Thomas, don't you?" Linda asked, suspecting that she did not. They had met only at the funeral, and Toby was undoubtedly too numbed by the event to remember

Thomas, who was gone almost as fast as he had arrived. Linda spent part of the trip east telling her about Thomas, and her grandmother, and it was the first time she had shown Toby the few pictures Keith had of his mother and brother.

"Hey—who knocked your teeth out?" Thomas asked. He touched Toby's upper lip. She was missing her two front teeth.

Toby giggled hesitantly. "Nobody. They just fell out."

"Did the tooth fairy leave you money?"

"A quarter."

Thomas looked impressed. "Hmm. The tooth fairy gets hit by inflation too. I only got a dime. Well, you let me know when your next tooth is about to come out. We've got a pretty good tooth fairy around here too."

The driver was opening the luggage compartment under the bus. Toby spotted their suitcases first.

"I'll get those," Thomas said. "Come on. I'm parked over there."

"I'm having the rest of our clothes shipped," Linda said. "I put the furniture into storage."

"Good. We'll deal with that when we have to."

Thomas and Linda settled into the car, Toby between them.

Thomas exhaled. "Welcome to West Ledge. You've been here before, I remember."

"Briefly." Linda smiled uneasily, and both remembered the time Keith had brought her home to meet his family, never to return again.

Thomas started the car and pulled out into the midday traffic, making more out of leaving the parking space than he had to. There was a lull in the conversation. It wasn't coming easily, and neither expected it to. Thomas covered the awkwardness by pretending to study the sideview mirror.

"How have *you* been, Thomas?" Linda asked, though she was bothered by the formality of the question and her wooden tone. Before she left California, she had actually practiced saying things like that in front of the mirror, and felt silly then, as now.

"Good," Thomas said as he stopped at a light. "Busy, as usual. We're financing a new high-rise outside of town." He remembered the printouts on his desk.

"Your mother—?" Linda asked, and Thomas heard a slight breaking when she said the word.

"Fine." And a measure of relief flooded into his voice. *She* had brought it up. "You'll see her tonight. She's asked that you and Toby come to dinner."

"Oh?" Linda asked, surprised, and a nervous smile played across her face.

"It'll be okay," Thomas reassured softly, although he knew what he said had not been entirely truthful. *He* had asked his mother to have them over for dinner. Eleanor had protested at first, said they would all feel uncomfortable, but then had finally agreed.

"How was—?" They both started talking at the same time, broke off, and laughed nervously.

"You go," Thomas said.

"No, you."

Thomas patted Toby on the leg. "We'll let Toby go. Did you help the driver drive the bus at all?"

Toby laughed. This man—Uncle Thomas—was silly.

"What states did you pass through?"

Toby brightened. "I kept a list. Can I read it to you?"

"Of course."

"We started in California . . ." Toby said, and as her voice droned on, Linda used the moment to catch her breath, grateful that Toby was taking up the slack in their conversation. She thought of two old friends, meeting after years of separation, and when they should have so much to say to each other, finding nothing at all to talk about. She and Thomas were hardly old friends, she knew, but in that context, what *were* they? Nothing.

She stared out the car window, eyeing a row of shop windows as they passed through the center of town. Toby's voice was far away. Linda's arm was propped on the rest, her palm supported her face. Her cheek leaned against the glass, fogging it with her breath. Her eyes were distant and glazed. She was nervous, she knew, her stomach jittery. Her life was turned upside down, unsettled, transient. Because she was being led around by Thomas, she felt a little like a child, and she couldn't help but feel somewhat demeaned. But she knew that Thomas in no way meant her to feel that way. Then Toby was finished and Thomas was speaking.

"I've really got to apologize for the way the house looks. I'd have to call it a bit run down."

"Does it have walls and windows?"

"And maybe even a secret entrance and passageway or two, I think someone mentioned."

"Whatever—beggars can't be choosers," Linda said, and the surprised look on Thomas's face made her blush and immediately regret her words. "I'm so sorry. I guess I'm tired right now and a little ashamed of myself."

"No, you shouldn't be ashamed," Thomas said, and turned to her. "If anybody, *I* should be. And am." He met her eyes for a second, then turned away, back to the street. There was a moment's pause, then he said, "Let's make a pact. I know I'll feel better and I'm certain you will too. We're both nervous about each other, aren't we?"

"I'll say."

"So here's the agreement: We can say anything we want to each other without apologizing, without feeling ashamed or awkward."

"That's a deal." Linda smiled.

For the first time Thomas noticed the scrapes on her knees. His eyes narrowed with concern. "What happened?"

Linda sloughed off the question. "A little accident, that's all."

"Do you want a doctor to look at it?"

"No, it's not necessary," she said quickly. "It's nothing." She wanted to get off the subject of the night before last, not be reminded of what had happened on the Ohio street. More so perhaps than the attempted mugging; *who* she thought had been there and what she had heard still prickled at her disturbingly. Even now she could see the man coming out of the shadows, gaining on her, reaching out toward her . . .

"How about lunch?" Thomas asked, and the question snapped Linda back from her blur of thought.

She exhaled. "To be honest with you, all I really want is a long, hot shower. Would you mind terribly just taking us to the house?" Her tongue tripped over the word. She couldn't bring herself to say "my" house, because it wasn't her house. It was Thomas's. The bank's.

"I understand." He smiled and turned onto a pleasant, tree-lined street. Some boys were playing ball and stepped aside to let the car pass. There was a mix of houses—old, new, Cape, Colonial. Thomas pulled into their driveway and they all took in the house. It was Victorian, three stories high, with a screened veranda raised off the ground by bricks and latticework. Squared wooden posts supported a sloping roof up to the second floor. Some paint was peeling from the clapboard walls and one dormer window in the attic was broken and boarded up, but otherwise it was a perfectly livable house, not at all run-down.

Thomas unloaded the trunk. "There's still some furniture left inside," he said. "And I've added a few things. Oh—here's your key. All the locks are changed so you have complete security. Just the bell doesn't work. I noticed it only yesterday and didn't have time to get it fixed."

Linda shook her head; it didn't matter.

As soon as they entered, Linda saw that he had really gone out of his way. The house was spotlessly clean, and anticipating her tastes, he had added little touches to remove the depressing quality. The living-room furniture was old and gray and somewhat dreary—an overstuffed couch and Morris chairs on clawed feet—but there were new brocade throw pillows to lend color to the room, airy curtains, and a bouquet of fresh flowers. Thomas had also stocked the refrigerator and cupboard.

There were three bedrooms on the second floor, two to the left of the central staircase and the master to the right. Toby found hers immediately by the pink coverlet and a toy chest filled with dolls. Linda suspected Thomas had bought everything new, and was touched, appreciative. Funny, she thought for a second, if only the family had been this thoughtful and considerate when she was last there . . .

"Linens," Thomas said, opening a closet and sounding something like a real estate broker. "And blankets. And towels. There's soap in the medicine chest. Also medicine—aspirins and such." He opened another door into the master bedroom.

It was a large room that ran the length of the house, from front to back. The windows were open and a light cross breeze blew into the room, rustling the curtains, giving the room the sweet smell of summer. Linda looked outside to the back and saw the yard—a large plot with a vegetable garden and flowerbed, although not kept up, overrun with weeds. But what potential! In the corner of the yard was an old-fashioned well and water bucket. "It's really wonderful, Thomas," she said warmly.

"And now I think I'd better leave you," Thomas said. "You're tired and I'm sure you want to rest. I'll pick you up at eight for dinner—oh, there's an alarm clock next to your bed." He took Linda's hands in his. "You have my number at the bank. Anything at all, just buzz me, okay?"

"There won't—"

"Promise," he said firmly.

"I promise."

She walked Thomas downstairs, then out to the porch.

"Here's some cash too." He squeezed the bills into her hand.

"Thomas!" She protested when she saw the money.

"Don't worry about it. There's lots more down at the bank. I just take what I want." He winked. "I've got the key." He stopped her before she could say anything else. "Please don't thank me." Then he squeezed her hands and walked down the porch stairs. "See you later," he called, waving.

As the car backed out of the driveway, Linda and Toby waved good-bye. Toby said, "I like Uncle Thomas. He's nice."

"Yes," Linda agreed. "He is."

chapter 3

Feeling refreshed, Linda awakened before the alarm. The nap had been surprisingly reviving. She threw off the covers and climbed out of bed, pulling her bathrobe around her. Toby's breathing told Linda she was still asleep. Linda decided to let her rest another hour. She would have preferred that Toby sleep through the night, but she couldn't miss dinner with Thomas and Eleanor.

She stretched. It was too early to dress so she wandered downstairs. There was a can of V-8 juice in the refrigerator so she poured herself a glass and settled into one of the wing chairs in the living room. The sun was dipping below the houses to the west and the room was darkening. She curled her feet under her and hunched into the deep chair, looked out the window.

She felt an odd prickliness on her neck. As if fingers had lightly, almost imperceptibly drummed across her. She shook off the feeling but still she let her eyes dart rapidly about her, searching out the dark corners of the unfamiliar room. Of course no one was there, but still she had the unmistakable feeling that something was wrong. The other night . . . She rubbed her hand over the back of her neck to remove the crawling feeling that had slithered over her. The other night was over, forgotten, and she resolved to think only about her future—*their* future, hers and Toby's—which, while still uncertain, at least seemed somewhat secure. Thomas had gone out of his way to show her that.

But still, she wasn't happy that her life, her destiny, was out of her control, in the hands of the Devonshires. That would have to change. Thomas had given her relief, a breather, but she didn't want to be dependent on him. She would have to get a job, pay Thomas back, be on her own.

Linda struggled to smile as she willed a veil of calm to settle over her. She knew she had made the right move by coming east. Everything was going to work out just fine. But her smile faded as she thought about the dinner with Eleanor. She still had to face that. She hadn't seen her mother-in-law in ten years. Linda would never forget her first visit.

From her first glance at the Devonshire family house, Linda had been overwhelmed. Estate, perhaps, was a more appropriate term. It was two stories high with a brick facade and white columns that made it almost look like a southern plantation house. It was situated on a rise above a country stream that bubbled and meandered behind. As the cab slipped through a gate formed by overhanging leaves, up the circular drive, Linda was able to see a swimming pool and a landscaped tennis court in the back. For a second she questioned why Keith would ever have given all of this up.

Eleanor Devonshire had met them at the door, and Linda had watched as mother and son kissed each other—politely on the cheek. All that Keith had said about his family was summed up in that one moment.

"And this is Linda," Keith had said, extending his arm toward her to draw her closer to his mother.

"Welcome," Eleanor had said formally, and had shaken Linda's hand. "Keith has told us so much about you."

Linda had felt Eleanor inspect her critically, and she'd tried to remain composed and face the woman as an equal. But they weren't equal, Linda had known. She was poor, unassuming, a commoner compared to the older woman who exuded formality, elegance, self-assurance. Eleanor was tall, regal. Her light wavy hair was pulled back away from her face, her forehead was high, austere. Her glance was sharp, her eyes dark and piercing, almost charged with electricity, and from the start she'd frightened Linda.

Keith hadn't been home in almost a year, but there was stiffness to the dinner conversation, polite small talk about Keith's writing. It was evident that the family didn't think much about the film industry. "A terrible financial risk," Thomas, Sr., had said, and ticked off all the motion picture disasters in recent years. Linda had wanted to rush to Keith's aid, defend his creativity, but she felt intimidated by the surroundings, by his parents, and offered little. Once off the subject of making movies there was more money talk between father and older son. The bank was financing a new shopping mall and they were evaluating risk and potential. "That's where the money is, Keith," his father had lectured. "Land. Real assets. Real returns. Not paper dreams." Keith had nodded respectfully, tried to pretend interest in what was being discussed, but underneath the table he rubbed his leg against Linda's, telegraphing with his eyes: I don't take them seriously and you shouldn't either. We live, we feel, and they can't possibly know what they're missing.

After dinner Eleanor had asked Thomas, Jr., to entertain Linda in the living room while she and her husband spoke with Keith in private in the den.

They had little to say to each other. Linda was still overwhelmed by the opulence of the house, and Thomas was unable to put her at ease. He spoke briefly about how much he admired his younger brother's freedom and attitude, how he often wondered if he would be happy living that kind of uncertain life. But then, almost as if he seemed afraid of having said too much, he grew silent, thoughtful. She was very pretty, he said, much prettier than his wife had been. He was married for three years, divorced now for two. "It didn't work out," he had said, and he did not elaborate.

Later Keith told her what had been talked about in the den. His father was president of the bank, but his mother was the stronger partner at home. She ruled the roost and led the conversation.

"She's a charming girl but isn't right for you," Eleanor had said bluntly.

"How can you say that, Mother?" Keith had answered patiently, although tightly. He stared out the window. The house was on the outskirts of the town, and beneath him were the rolling hills and farmlands of western Connecticut. He had always loved the view from this window as the land sloped downward past the tennis court. But he had never liked the room, his father's den, filled with mahogany, leather, and imported cigars. And even today it conjured up memories of childhood. It had been this room in which he had been disciplined, lectured to, taught the meaning of money, position, the manners of a Devonshire.

"Don't make it harder than it is, Keith, please," Eleanor had said.

"Oh, I intend to, Mother," Keith had snapped in response. "It's because she doesn't have a pedigree, right? You don't even know her. You just don't think she's wealthy enough to bear the Devonshire name, right?" He'd turned to his father. "What do you have to say about this?" he'd asked.

"We only want what's best for you, Keith," Thomas, Sr., had said.

"What you *think* is best for me," Keith had snapped in response.

"We know all about her," Eleanor had said, taking out a report in a manila folder, slapping it against the mahogany desk. "Where she is from, who her parents are—were—"

"You ran a check on her!" Keith had exclaimed, horrified.

"She has nothing, Keith!"

"She has what I want. Tenderness. Honesty. Life! More than all of you put together."

"There is another thing," Eleanor had said, raising her chin slightly. Her superior position, Keith always called it, and it made him bristle that she was using it on him. "Perhaps there is something you know nothing about. I wouldn't have expected her to tell you any of it."

"What is that, Mother?" he'd asked dryly.

"I must question how stable she is."

"Stable?" he'd asked angrily. "You mean like in center of gravity?"

"I mean as in mental health," Eleanor had said brusquely. "And you know exactly what I mean!" She'd calmed herself, regained her composure. "After her parents' untimely deaths she was scarred by the incident. There was a period of her life when she was sick and sought psychiatric help. She was under a doctor's care for more than a year suffering from"—her mouth had turned downward with revulsion—"schizophrenia. And the report shows she still remains troubled by dreams and paranoia. Did you know any of this, Keith?"

There was a long moment before Keith answered. He looked slowly from his mother to his father, then to his mother again, because what she had said hadn't fully registered. Then he had asked incredulously, "You mean you had nothing better to do than hire an investigator to check out the girl I want to marry?"

"We just made some discreet inquiries," Eleanor had answered.

Keith's eyes had narrowed in disbelief. It was as if he were seeing his mother for the first time. He knew who his parents were, what they believed in, what they were like and capable of, but this had gone beyond all borders of decency and trust.

"We were only thinking of you, Keith."

"How?" he had asked, his voice rising with his mounting emotion. He was no longer incredulous; he was outraged at what his parents had done.

"We thought perhaps you didn't know," Eleanor had snapped. "But I see you did."

Keith had looked at his hands. They were shaking in his fury at his parents. He had clenched his fists to absorb his anger, tried to quiet his pounding heart. He had steadied his voice so not to betray his emotion when he answered. "Yes, Mother. Linda told me all about it. She was sick then but she's cured now, and I love her and that's all that matters. But you can't understand that, I know," he'd added with a ring of pity in his voice.

"It doesn't matter what I understand or not," Eleanor had said. "Your father and I have talked and we both feel it is time for you to stop this California foolishness, return home, and take your place at the bank along with your brother."

Keith had absorbed what his mother said, then he spoke slowly, pausing between each word. "That's not what I want, Mother. I want to live in California and I want to marry Linda."

"We talked about that too," Eleanor had said. She glanced at Thomas, Sr., who'd nodded that she should continue. "You have always been rebellious, not at all grateful for what we have done for you, for what we can offer you. We suspected you might say something like that. Therefore our response is—" Eleanor had paused, taken a breath, then stared at Keith piercingly. "If you marry that girl, we will cut off your money, cease to send you your stipend each month, cross you out of your inheritance. Is that understood?"

Keith had nodded slowly. "Perfectly, Mother, Father."

"We are thinking only of you, Keith," Eleanor had said quickly. "You must believe me."

"I do," Keith had said sadly. The next morning he and Linda drove to Vermont, where they were married by a justice of the peace.

Linda still remembered the stony look on Eleanor's face when they returned after the wedding ceremony and told her what they had done. And the last words she had said to her son in her fervent hope he might come to his senses and call the marriage off.

"Read the psychiatrist's report, Keith. She isn't stable, I tell you . . . isn't stable."

Linda winced with remembered pain and pushed deeper into the Morris chair as if trying to escape from the words that echoed loudly within her, conjuring haunting memories that she knew would always remain a distant part of her, no matter how much she wanted to believe the traumas were all lost in her past.

Because they weren't. They would never be. The night before last was proof of that.

". . . Mommy?" Toby's voice distracted her, and Linda looked up. Her daughter stood in front of her, rubbing her eyes. Linda checked her watch. It was almost seven, time to get ready. Thomas would be coming by for them soon.

"Did you sleep well?" Linda asked, pulling Toby between her legs and wrapping her arms around her child.

"Uh-huh."

"Feeling better?"

"Uh-huh."

"Come on. Let's go and pick out something pretty to wear, okay?"

On the way upstairs, Linda decided to wear pants. She would have preferred to dress more formally, but her knees were badly scraped and she just didn't feel like having to explain anything to Eleanor.

chapter 4

Thomas turned his Mercedes into Linda's street, pulled up in front of her house, and shut off the engine. He straightened his tie, checked his hair in the rearview mirror, and took a deep breath, readying himself for the evening. He hoped it would all go well.

Linda opened the door, and Thomas smiled when he saw her. She had been tired that afternoon, her face weary from the bus travel. But now with rest, there was a sparkling lightness to her eyes and a youthful sheen to her skin. He immediately saw the beauty that must have first attracted Keith. And how many others? he wondered briefly, then said, "You look lovely."

Linda lowered her eyes shyly. "Thank you."

Thomas knelt down and kissed Toby's cheek. "And you too."

The night breeze tickled Linda's bare arms. "Chilly."

"Yes. The evenings here are a little cooler than what you're used to, I'm sure."

She reached for sweaters for both of them. "I'm glad I remembered to pack these. Back in California we hardly ever wore them. You know, Toby doesn't even have a winter coat. We're going to have to—" She broke off, embarrassed. Winter was months away, and who knew where they would be when the first snow started to fall?

"Why don't we solve that problem when we come to it?" Thomas suggested gently, understanding her discomfort. Then he smiled and said, "It's funny. This morning this was just an empty house. Now only hours later it already feels lived in, homey. . . ."

"Thomas, I've got to thank you again for every—"

He held up his hand; cut her off. "I'm not fishing for thank-
yous, Linda, okay?"

She nodded, smiled, agreed. "Okay."

"Another deal between us—to go with the one we made
earlier." He pointed a finger at her, pretended sternness, enunci-
ated each word. "No more thank-yous!"

Before she could say anything, he took her arm. "Shall we
go?" He also took Toby by the hand and walked them to the car.

The evening was clear and bright, the sky filled with the
pleasing scent of pine. And no smog, Linda thought, after years
of choking Los Angeles nights.

"Breathe deeply, Toby," she said. "This is air."

"Huh?" Toby questioned, and both adults laughed.

They drove up to the Devonshire house through the long,
circular driveway and immediately Linda was thrown back years.

"It hasn't changed," she breathed, and Thomas understood
what she meant. He touched her arm supportively.

"She's older now," he said.

She still frightens me, Linda said to herself. She entwined her
fingers in Toby's as they got out of the car and walked toward
the house. Returning to where she had not been for ten years.

When the door opened, Eleanor stood framed in the hallway
light. Involuntarily Linda stiffened as if she had seen a spectre,
hesitated, and clasped her daughter's hand tighter. Toby looked
up questioningly at her mother. Thomas noticed, took Linda's
arm, and guided her forward. Eleanor's dress was black silk with
a high mandarin collar. She was wearing a Cartier watch, a star
sapphire surrounded by diamonds, and a cabochon ruby ring. As
Eleanor extended her hand, Linda saw the ruby ring on the older
woman's thin and bony finger. Steeling herself, she raised her
eyes and looked at Eleanor. She was surprised. The last time
Eleanor's eyes had glowed red, like burning embers; now they
seemed softer.

"Hello," Eleanor said, and smiled. She took Linda's hand and
ushered her into the house. Then she knelt down. "This must be
Toby. My, what a lovely, lovely child. She looks just like her
father, with that strong Devonshire face. You can see it
immediately. You're going to be my little girl, Toby." She
beamed. "Would you like that?"

Toby blushed and smiled tentatively, then Eleanor urged, "Come in, come in." On a small table next to the door there was a gift-wrapped package. "This is for you, Toby."

The little girl's eyes widened in pleasure. She hadn't been expecting a present. "Thank you."

"Grandma—" Eleanor prompted.

"Grandma," Toby repeated, trying to be comfortable with the word.

"Why don't you open it?" Eleanor suggested.

Toby searched her mother's face. Linda smiled and Toby went at the wrapping paper. Above her, Linda and Eleanor exchanged glances. Linda tried to read the older woman's face and hoped she was seeing genuine pleasure written across it, a melting. She exhaled a breath of tension. She prayed that these moments would set the tone for the entire evening and for however long she was in West Ledge.

The gift was an antique doll in colonial costume. It was wearing a flowing blue-and-white patchwork dress of gingham, and a ruffled petticoat beneath. There was a shawl of white linen and a blue silk tie.

"She's so pretty!" Toby squealed happily.

"It was mine," Eleanor said. "I recently found it up in the attic. I loved it as a little girl and thought it would be nice for Toby to have to love too. I never had a daughter of my own to give it to, and, well, a granddaughter is the next best thing. The clothing was a little torn so I had it redressed, although I tried to be faithful to the original costume. It's over two hundred years old."

"I love it!" Toby hugged the doll to her chest. Linda was surprised and pleased that Eleanor had gone to the effort to have the doll readied for Toby.

"Does she have a name?" Toby asked.

"Oh, she must," Eleanor said. "But by now I've long forgotten. Why don't you give her a name of your own?" She leaned in toward Toby. "Whisper it to me. It'll be our secret, something just the two of us can share."

"Okay." Toby nodded eagerly and studied the doll. She put her mouth next to Eleanor's ear and whispered in a voice that carried to the others, but Linda and Thomas pretended not to hear. "Patricia."

"Aren't you forgetting something, Toby?" Linda asked. With her eyes she motioned toward Eleanor.

Toby blushed and said again, "Thank you, Grandma." She went over to her. Eleanor knelt down and let the girl kiss her cheek. Then she straightened up.

"Good. Now that all the formalities are over, come in, come in, please."

The hallway was tiled in a black-and-white diamond pattern. A curving staircase faced the double front doors and wide archways opened into the rooms off the center hall. There were potted plants scattered throughout, only a few that Linda was able to identify. Thomas saw her admiring them and said, "Mother has the greenest thumb on the block."

"Oh, Thomas," Eleanor said, then shrugged. "Although actually it's true. I love plants, love to watch them grow, blossom, thrive. It's more than a hobby—call it an obsession. I have a greenhouse out back with some more exotic plants which you'll have to see—"

"I'd like that," Linda said, and suddenly remembered what Keith had said on one of the rare nights he talked about his parents: *She spends more time with those plants than with Thomas or me. Maybe if I had been born green she would have loved me as much as her god damned rhododendrons.*

"Why don't you sit next to me, Toby?" Eleanor said, patting the couch. She passed a glass of wine to Linda and apple juice to Toby. As Thomas poured himself a drink at the bar, she smiled. "It's been a long time, hasn't it, Linda? Although I must honestly say that when Thomas told me you were coming to West Ledge, I was certainly uneasy. And then to my house for dinner tonight! Good heavens! But then I said to myself, 'Of course, they should come, I should get to know them. They're Keith's family.' Although I must confess that I'm a nervous wreck." She looked directly at Linda. "If you can believe that of me." Linda smiled feebly and looked away, embarrassed for both of them.

She took in the room. The walls were papered with a delicate floral print, and against the far wall was a stone fireplace with an Italian marble mantel. The house was just as she remembered it from ten years before, and it still overwhelmed her. She swallowed nervously and realized she had barely spoken since they arrived, but she didn't know what to say. Not after all these years.

She fingered the stem of the glass. There was a slight tremor in her hand and she watched the surface of the liquid shimmer. Afraid of dropping the delicate Orrefors crystal and breaking it, she gently put it down on the coffee table.

Eleanor watched her; recognized her uneasiness. "Drink," she prompted. "Please."

Linda stole a glance at Thomas, who shot her silent support. He knew how hard the evening was for her.

"So," Eleanor said broadly. "Tell me all about the trip. I have been over the country many times, but never across it. What was it like?"

Thomas cleared his throat; drew their attention. "I think that's Toby's domain," he said. "Toby, why don't you tell your grandmother all about the trip?"

As Toby started talking, Thomas nodded to Linda. She knew he was giving her a minute to compose herself. Grateful, she picked up her glass and sipped the cool and refreshing wine.

When Toby finished answering questions, Eleanor reached for Linda's glass. "Here, let me top that off for you." As she went to the sideboard to refill the glass, Linda took in the older woman's profile. Her face seemed to have a softer line, her voice seemed gentler, than she remembered from last time. But perhaps the way Eleanor was treating her now was altering her impressions of the woman.

She flashed back on the other Eleanor—the woman who had tried to take Keith away from her. By all rights she knew she should hate this woman, but she couldn't. Too much time had passed, too much anguish, heartache. She was desensitized to her emotions. She had never really felt anything toward Eleanor except perhaps pity. She had had too much love for Keith for hatred to cloud her feelings, and only had hated Eleanor for the way she had treated her son. Linda knew that the woman had never owed *her* anything, except perhaps courtesy, civility.

But tonight it seemed that Eleanor had truly mellowed and was doing what she could to make her and Toby feel at ease. And in that one minute it became terribly important to Linda that Eleanor like her. There was a bond between them now, created by time, by death, by the man they had both loved in their different ways.

Sensing her look, Eleanor turned toward Linda and smiled. Linda returned the smile and flooded with warmth and acceptance. That was why Thomas had wanted them to get together tonight—because Eleanor had changed.

Then Eleanor said, "You must be hungry. Shall we go in to eat?"

Dinner was stuffed cornish hen, wild rice, and glazed carrots, skillfully prepared by Eleanor's cook and housekeeper, a middle-aged woman who lived on the outskirts of West Ledge and worked days at the Devonshire house.

The oak table was covered with Italian linen. Eleanor sat at the head. Thomas was opposite her, and Linda and Toby along the sides, all of them dwarfed by the size of the table.

Glass doors covered with ruffled blue curtains dominated the far end behind Eleanor's chair, and beyond the doors was a patio that overlooked the pool and tennis court. There was another fireplace in the room and on top of the mantel was a menagerie of Lalique glass figurines.

During the meal Thomas talked about things that happened at the bank, people who tried to take out money they didn't have and the ridiculous promises of repayment they made. Linda's laughter turned into a yawn and her eyes threatened to close. She suddenly felt very tired. She had thought she was rested from the nap that afternoon but the trip was still catching up with her and the wine on an empty stomach was making her feel light-headed, woozy. She stiffened her jaw and tried to stifle another yawn so not to appear impolite, but it broke through, although thankfully nobody saw her. She blinked tightly, then rubbed her eyes and tried to shake off the effect of the liquor. But she only felt worse.

As they were finishing the main course, Eleanor said to Thomas, "Why don't you show Toby around the house while I stack the dishes and spend a few private minutes with Linda. Then we can have dessert."

Thomas took his cue and nodded. He extended his arm to Toby. "Shall we go exploring?"

Hazily Linda watched them leave the room. Her eyelids fluttered heavily and she shook her head in an attempt to clear it. Then she tried to focus and pay attention to Eleanor, who was removing the dishes to a sideboard, perhaps making more noise than she had to.

"I wanted a few private moments with you, Linda, to tell you how regretful I am that I hadn't gotten to know you better ten years ago," Eleanor said. "I should have trusted Keith's judgment more than I did, and what resulted from my error, as we both know, was tragic for everyone. . . ."

Linda knew that Eleanor was truly reaching out to her and recognized how difficult it must be for her to say what she was. But because of how the wine was making her feel, the older woman's words tingled and blurred in her ear and became harder to follow. Linda grew more and more dizzy and grasped the table to steady herself, regain her equilibrium.

"Eleanor, I—" Linda struggled against her disorientation to speak, but then she broke off completely when she heard the new words whipcrack suddenly inside of her, shocking her with their impact.

She isn't stable, Keith.

"What?" Linda asked sharply and looked up, confused, not certain what it was she had just heard. Her eyes opened wide although they were still dull and liquidy, and Eleanor seemed out of focus. "What did you say?" she asked, trying to see through the film, praying that she hadn't heard what she thought she had.

Eleanor frowned and peered at Linda. "I said that perhaps I was too hasty in prejudging you. I never got to know you the way Keith did. He tried to tell me but I wouldn't listen. Something I should have done before so unceremoniously asking you to leave my son's life. . . ."

She isn't stable, Keith.

Linda jumped. She was no longer hearing what Eleanor was saying now, rather Eleanor's voice from years ago, etched into her memory, mournful, desperate.

She isn't—

"Don't—" Linda cried painfully and shook her head to free it of what she was hearing.

—stable

"No!" She thought she had left those words long behind her.

"Are you all right?" Eleanor asked, alarmed, and moved closer to Linda.

Isn't stable . . . isn't stable . . . The words echoed inside her mercilessly. Linda grew panicky. She didn't know why her memory was punishing her like this. Desperate to escape what she was hearing, she put her hands to her ears to try to blot out the words, but still the voice persisted inside her. In her heady state she had no control over herself. She moaned plaintively and lunged out. Her hand swept across the table and knocked into the Orrefors glass, almost empty of wine, her palm crashing down on top of it as the crystal shattered against the tablecloth. Linda yelped in surprise and pain and grabbed her bleeding hand, all sound stopping inside of her as she shocked to the injury.

Eleanor screamed at the sight of the blood dripping onto the tablecloth and was instantly at Linda's side. "Thomas!" she called. She took Linda's hand. The glass had just nicked the fleshy part and it wasn't bleeding badly, although it aggravated her earlier scrape, which was still red and raw.

"I'm so sorry," Linda sputtered, and shook her head to free it of the gray cloud that was slowly lifting from her as she sobered. "I—" she started, confused, searching for explanation. She couldn't look straight at Eleanor. She tried to pick up the larger pieces of glass.

Thomas rushed back into the room followed by a frightened Toby. He pulled Linda's hand away from the table. "Leave that," he ordered, then asked, "What happened?"

"I don't know," Eleanor said nervously, as if hoping Thomas wouldn't think her to blame. "I was just talking when she—" She looked closely at Linda. "Maybe she should lie down," she suggested, concerned.

"No, I'm fine now," Linda said. She pressed her napkin against her hand to stop the blood and tightened her eyes to try to will away the residual wooziness she still felt. "I must have had too much to drink. Liquor doesn't usually affect me this way but I guess I'm still so tired from the trip. And from—"*what happened the other night*, she almost said, but stopped. She hadn't told Thomas about the mugging and didn't want to tell them now.

Thomas brought over a bandage and piece of gauze. "Let me wrap that."

"Thank you," Linda said, and gave him her hand.

"And I think I'd better take you home."

"Of course," Eleanor agreed. She hurriedly got their sweaters and saw them to the door.

"I'm so sorry," Linda mumbled again, embarrassed.

"Nonsense," Eleanor assured her. "It was a long bus ride and I can appreciate how tired and unsettled you still are." Over Linda's head, Eleanor glanced at Thomas, who then took Linda and Toby's hands and led them outside. The cool air was refreshing and Linda took in deep gulps. From the doorway Eleanor called after them, "We'll get together again soon, yes?"

Linda turned and nodded weakly. "Yes, I'd like that. Thank you."

chapter 5

They didn't talk on the way home. From the driver's seat Thomas stole glances at Linda, who was staring blankly out at the night. The window was open and the cool breeze blew in past her, reviving her. She was still feeling a little dizzy, but even more, she was embarrassed by what had just happened. She had let the wine go to her head, had broken an expensive crystal glass, made a fool of herself! And after Eleanor had done so much to make her feel welcome. She had been nervous about the dinner, she reasoned, jittery, and that was why she had recalled Eleanor's parting words. Although thankfully tonight she had seen how the years had softened Eleanor and knew the older woman would never frighten her again. And, despite the embarrassment, that brought a smile to her lips.

"I'm feeling better now," she said as they neared the house. She felt she was being truthful with both Thomas and herself.

"That's good," Thomas answered. "Is there anything else I can do for you?"

"No, nothing. Thank you." She laughed shortly, critically. "Look at me. My legs. My hand. I'm a complete wreck."

"A lovely wreck," Thomas said, and didn't wait for her to respond before he continued, "Now, you get a good night's sleep and I'll call you in the morning. *Late* in the morning," he corrected, and they both smiled. "You've got a lot of sleep to catch up on, I'm sure."

Toby had fallen asleep in the back seat, and Thomas carried her upstairs and put her to bed.

Linda saw him to the door, closed up behind him, and flipped off the downstairs lights. Climbing back up the stairs suddenly reminded her again of how tired she was. She looked in quickly on Toby, who hadn't moved since Thomas had laid her down. She kissed her daughter lightly on the forehead, pulled the covers tightly under her chin, and tiptoed out of the room. Then she slipped off her clothes and got into bed, expecting to fall asleep instantly, but she was overtired and could not find a comfortable position.

She had tossed and turned for what seemed like hours when she heard the sounds, and despite the warmth of the covers her body chilled. Her eyes flew open. Alarmed, she searched the darkness of the bedroom—*what was she hearing?*

Again! a squealing noise, a painful moan, and the sounds were suddenly recognizable—the slight give of wooden slats warped and weakened by time, the wheeze of compression, resistance, the result of pressure, *weight!*

Her chest swelled with a gasp of breath. *Was there someone in the house? Walking up the stairs?*

Had he followed her again? Found her?

No! She choked back the thought. That wasn't possible. She stiffened her body so not even the sheets or blanket would make a rustling noise as she strained to listen.

Another stairboard groaned. Higher now. Closer.

Someone *was* there!

She swallowed tightly, painfully. Her lips moved. *Who is it?* But the words remained thoughts. Her mouth was open but fear had stolen her voice.

Again. Another sound. A spiraling moan as the house was disturbed.

"Who's there?" she called. Barely a whisper through her dry lips.

And then suddenly there were no more sounds. Only silence, but an ominous silence that comes from the unknown. The split-anticipated-second before the explosion of a thunderclap. The instinctive tensing, waiting . . .

The creak was sudden. A pinprick of sound. A rush of pain.

Like the game she played as a child when you opened your mouth to mimic a slowly opening door straining on ancient hinges—short, guttural choking sounds from deep in your throat. Singular. Discreet.

A door! That's what she had heard.

But not her door, not the front door—

Toby's door!

"My God!" she gasped. There was someone in Toby's room.

In one motion she threw the covers off her, jumped to the floor. "Who's there?" she croaked again. Her breath was coming fast now, irregular, rasping.

In the hallway, she glanced down the staircase. A passing car threw circles of light along the wallpaper, like twin spotlights in a horror play. Shadows darted in and out of the lights—maybe tree limbs whisking at windows, maybe arms retreating down the stairs. Maybe nothing at all because he was still upstairs.

She didn't know what she expected to find when she opened Toby's door, but she didn't stop to think about it—her child was in danger. She flipped the switch. Light flooded the bedroom. In her deep sleep Toby shifted from the light. Catlike, Linda took in the room. Nobody was there. The room was as it had been when she and Thomas had put Toby to sleep hours before. The window was shut to keep out the breeze, the curtains drawn against the night. All the same.

Not the same.

Something was different.

The closet door.

It wasn't fully closed now. A thin sliver of darkness led the way into the closet where it did not fully mesh with the jamb. Now, had it been shut all the way earlier? She couldn't remember. Had the clasp caught? Was it broken?

She had to know. She grabbed the doorknob, steeled herself, and pulled. She gasped as the figure fell out at her feet, its arms and legs collapsed in a heap, looking up at her with unblinking button eyes. It was only Patricia, the doll Eleanor had given Toby. Thomas must have put it in the closet.

But there was no person in the closet. Nobody at all in Toby's room.

She went back into the hallway and turned on the light. She looked in her bedroom—nobody. In the two other bedrooms on the second floor—nobody. She ran downstairs, turning on lights as she passed switches. Nobody. In the living room—nobody. The kitchen. The dining room.

The door to the cellar remained locked, the front door and

kitchen door as well. Apparently nobody had been in the house, which was now brightly lit and mercifully silent.

Linda exhaled sharply, dropped her arms to her sides, then breathed deeply, evenly, composing herself, and let the tension drain from her. But even though there was no danger, she shuddered coldly and suddenly felt very small and very alone. There was a faint throbbing in her knees from where she had fallen. She quickly went back upstairs, threw water on her face, and took two aspirins to try to relax. Then, after leaving the hallway light on, she climbed back into bed. But she couldn't sleep. Her heart was still racing and her eyes roamed the shadowed room, her ears tuned for sound. *House sounds*, she now knew—moans and groans and creaks and wheezes as the old Victorian house shifted and settled and strained with age. Outside her window the dark outlines of tree branches waved ominously in the night breeze, tentacled arms brushing the glass. She turned on her side, away from the taunting shadows behind the window, and wished to God that Keith were there with her. How she missed him, needed him; how frightened she still was.

But then she shivered again as she remembered—even when Keith had been with her, *lying right next to her*, her fears had still overwhelmed her. And while tonight she knew that she had only scared herself, *that no one was chasing her*, she hadn't always known that.

She remembered a summer night in Los Angeles when she and Toby had finished shopping. It was after dark and she was parked in a far corner of the mall lot. A dying fluorescent tube pulsed on and off above her. The man must have been hiding between parked cars, out of sight. She had been fumbling with her car keys when he came up behind them. She heard only a rushing sound—that was all. And then Toby's gasp of surprise. When she looked up she saw the man's hand on her daughter and the flat of a knife pressed against Toby's neck, their faces alternately in light and shadow as the fluorescent bulb sputtered and groaned with fading life. The slightest movement by either of them and her baby would be killed.

"Give me your money," he had said, and she immediately handed him her purse. But before he let go of Toby he had made an exaggerated cutting motion with his hand, drawing the sharp edge of the knife across Toby's neck, and grunted gutturally, pantomiming slitting her throat. Then he had gone, disappearing into the shadows. Linda had grabbed her daughter, clutched her to her chest, and screamed and screamed.

Toby survived the incident unharmed, but for Linda the aftermath was a horror. Her childhood memories came flooding back and she was once again haunted by terrible nightmares. She had thought it was all behind her, but it wasn't. The man who killed her parents had returned to her mind again, this time to kill her daughter. It was Toby the man was chasing down darkened streets, and Linda woke up terrified and drenched in perspiration. And while she knew they were only dreams, she still had to run into her daughter's room to see that she was sleeping undisturbed. Only when satisfied that nothing was wrong could she return to bed again.

Then she started to see him outside as well—peering at her through a car window, from across the street or from a closing elevator door. Always just out of touch. She cried out his presence but Keith didn't believe her. He felt she was regressing to her schizophrenic state, only imagining the man, and took her to a psychiatrist.

But one day on a busy street, out of the corner of her eye, someone brushed past her and she heard him speak. "I'm going to kill you, Linda . . . and Toby . . ." he said in a gravelly voice.

"No!" she gasped, and covered her ears with her hands to blot out the awful words.

The man turned to her and she saw his leering, familiar face. She screamed and fainted. When people revived her, she looked around frantically for the man. "Where did he go? Did anybody see him?" A policeman helped her home.

That night she couldn't sleep. She replayed in her mind the events of the afternoon. As Keith and the psychiatrist told her, she *had* probably misheard something, mistaken the man, but again she saw him brush past her; heard the terrible words he uttered.

She jammed her eyes closed to erase the sight. Then she got out of bed quietly so not to disturb Keith, went across the hall to Toby's room. She just wanted to see her daughter, that was all.

She flipped on the carousel lamp next to Toby's bed and saw the face. There for only a second, illuminated by the lamplight like a ghostly figure, then gone. He was outside the window, standing on the roof of the attached garage, looking into her little girl's bedroom. It took Linda a fraction of a second to react, then she screamed.

Frightened, Toby burst awake. Keith came racing into the room. Cradling Toby, her hands running frantically all over the child's face, Linda told him what she saw.

"Come," Keith said softly, and reached out for his wife's hand.

"No—" She didn't want to let go of her child.

Gently Keith pried Toby loose from Linda and laid the questioning girl back on the bed, covered her up, and switched off the lamp.

"I want to stay here," Linda said.

"Let her sleep," Keith said. "I'll come back, check on her. She'll be all right."

Linda let herself be led back to their bedroom. Keith sat her on the edge of the bed. Her fists were balled in her lap, rubbing against each other. Keith sat down next to her; covered her hands with his; warmed them.

"I wasn't sleeping, Keith," she said almost desperately. "It wasn't a dream and don't tell me it was."

"I won't," he said softly. "I know it wasn't a dream." He looked deeply into her eyes. "What it might have been, Linda, was your own reflection. When you went into the room, you turned on the light."

"Yes." Her breathing was still heavy, like a frightened animal.

"Look outside now, Linda." He lifted her chin, directing her to look out the bedroom window. "Look. Do you see your own reflection?"

She saw her face in the window like a darkened mirror, her image, contoured in lights and shadows, whipped by tree branches that brushed against the glass in the night wind.

But it hadn't been her reflection she had seen in Toby's window.

"I saw him, Keith, I swear it," she protested. "He's playing with us. He could have gotten in if he wanted to."

Paranoia. Reactive schizophrenia. Words that had passed between her aunt and the doctor when she was only a child.

She remembered what the psychiatrist had said to her during

her therapy. They were looking for reasons for her delusions: They were out celebrating her birthday when her parents were killed. If they hadn't been, the tragedy would not have occurred, and that was very intense guilt for a child to live with. *She was at fault for her parents' deaths!* So, he analyzed, when she started having the nightmares of the man coming to kill her, it was only a subconscious wish that she had been killed too, because if she were dead, she wouldn't have these terrible feelings of guilt.

She told all of this to the psychiatrist Keith sent her to, who pieced together that the guilt returned with the mugging in the parking lot and brought on the hallucinations. Something could have happened to Toby, and it would have been her fault because she created the circumstances. She had parked in the far corner; stayed in the store until after the sun went down. She had to understand her fears, the doctor said to her, address her feelings of guilt, and they would go away.

"I don't feel guilty," Linda responded weakly. "I feel cold, and I feel terror. I didn't imagine anything, misinterpret anything, mistake my own reflection . . ."

Without telling anyone, she slept with a sharp knife under the bed.

Keith was working the midnight shift at the restaurant the night Linda woke up and heard the sounds—faint at first, seemingly coming from far away, if at all—the tap-tapping of smooth leather on polished hardwood, the whining creak of a sagging stairboard. Startled, Linda raised her head off the pillow and strained to listen. Was there someone in the house? she wondered, but almost immediately there was no question, because she heard the voice, low, guttural, an animal snarl. "I'm going to kill you, Linda . . . and Toby . . ." And this time she knew he wasn't playing!

Reacting automatically, she jumped out of bed, grabbed the knife, and raced out into the hall. She fumbled for the light switch but it did not respond. Then she saw him—only a shadow at the top of the stairs, but there! and walking toward Toby's room. This was no hallucination. Hysterical, she lunged after him and stabbed him again and again. Then she ran screaming into the street.

The police arrived at the same time Keith was coming home from work.

"I killed him, Keith! He's in there!" she cried in hysterical triumph.

First the police went in, then Keith, then finally they called for Linda.

"Is that the body?" the policeman asked and Linda followed his pointing finger.

There was no body. But there was her knife, stuck into the newel post of the banister at the top of the stairs, which in the dark could have looked deceptively like someone's head.

She let herself be hospitalized voluntarily. God forbid something like that happened again; she might have harmed Keith or Toby.

"Isn't stable . . . isn't stable . . ." Eleanor's words followed her, haunted her. There was no man in the house, only her reaction to the stress of the mugging. She was hospitalized for three months and then they told her she was cured.

Again.

Now she was feeling better, groggy, ready to sleep. She squinted and looked at her watch on the night table. It was just after midnight; she had been asleep for less than an hour when the house had awakened her. Midnight—the end of her first day in West Ledge. It had been a very long day, filled with confused memories and resurfacing fears, voices from the past, sounds in the night. As well as reminders: of when things were better for her. And when they weren't.

From somewhere in the distance Linda heard a dull click. It could have been the sound of a door closing. But she knew it wasn't.

chapter 6

Linda slept through the night and wakened briefly at nine when Toby whispered in her ear. "Mommy, there's a girl who lives across the street. Can she come over and play? We'll be quiet."

Mumbling her assent, Linda turned over and went back to sleep, then awakened about eleven and luxuriated in bed, finally feeling she was free of the last two days. The phone rang.

"How are you today?" Thomas asked.

Linda smiled. "I'm really feeling good this morning." She flexed her hand and looked beneath the bandage; the cut had already started to heal. Her legs as well.

"Can I come over and pick you up?" he asked. "I want to find a good used car for you."

"What?" Linda asked, surprised.

"You'll need a car. Public transportation is almost nonexistent and you'll have to be able to get around."

"Thomas, I can't let you buy me a car."

"I insist."

"Thomas, that really isn't necessary," she pressed, but he cut her off.

"Let me decide what is or is not necessary, okay?"

"Okay," she said reluctantly. "But I think we have to talk about things. I can't continue to just accept—"

"A half hour. Is that good for you?"

"We'll be ready," Linda said resignedly.

She put on her makeup, then poked her head out the front door and saw the children playing on the porch.

"This is Carol Ann!" Toby said excitedly. "We're going to be best friends."

Carol Ann had a moon face and dark hair twisted into braids. A beautiful child, but to Linda's glance, she looked sad.

"And Shana!" Toby's arm was draped around a golden retriever, as large as she was, but as tame and friendly as could be.

"Carol Ann!"

The woman's voice was sudden and sharp, and everyone looked up. A woman was coming up the porch carrying a package. She was slightly overweight, with short, dirty-blond hair pulled back from her face. She was about the same age as Linda, but her weight added years to her appearance. Her face was round and Linda immediately saw the resemblance to Carol Ann.

"Carol Ann, what did I tell you about talking to strangers?" the woman asked. "I left you in front of the house to go shopping and find you here!"

Linda couldn't help but notice the sudden fear that flashed across Carol Ann's face, draining it of color.

"But, Mommy—" she protested.

"No 'but mommys'! What did I tell you?" Then she turned to Linda. "And you should know better too!" Unconsciously Linda took a step backward. There was a harshness to the woman's voice, a shrillness, almost frightening on its own.

"Th-they were just playing," Linda stammered, but then she gained her strength; she had done nothing wrong. "Please don't be too hard on Carol Ann. She just wanted to play, that's all. I've taught Toby the same thing about not talking to strangers, but we live here and aren't really strangers, are we?"

The woman hesitated. "I suppose not. I'm Beatrice Dailey."

"Linda Devonshire."

"Devonshire?" Her eyebrows went up in surprise. "Any relation to Thomas Devonshire?"

"Yes, he's my brother-in-law. I was married to his brother, Keith."

"I see," Beatrice said coolly.

"Won't you come in?" Linda asked. "I'll put on coffee."

"I don't think so," Beatrice answered shortly. "Come, Carol Ann, we have to go now."

The honking car turning into the driveway called their attention. Then Thomas bounded up the porch stairs. Linda was surprised when she saw him. His tie was off and his shirt was open at the neck, and instead of the Brooks Brothers suit he had worn the day before, he was wearing a casual sports jacket over light-colored summer pants. Certainly not the staid, proper banker image of him she had tucked away.

"I see you two have met," he said.

"We were just leaving, Thomas," Beatrice said, and let her glance linger on Linda for an extra second. Then she said, "Come on, Carol Ann." She reached out her hand toward her daughter, and Linda saw the momentary reluctance of the girl to go with her mother. Beatrice noticed it, too, because she repeated more sharply, "Carol Ann!" and tightened her hold on her daughter.

"I'll see you tomorrow," Toby said.

The little girls waved good-bye to each other as Beatrice and Carol Ann strode down the porch stairs, followed by a tail-wagging Shana. From the doorway Linda and Thomas heard Beatrice say to her daughter, "What did I teach you about talking to strangers? You were a bad girl, Carol Ann."

And the little girl protesting fearfully, "No, Mommy, I wasn't."

"A bad girl," Beatrice repeated, and then they were out of earshot.

"I think you should know something," Thomas said. "Beatrice and Keith dated through high school."

Linda closed her lips and nodded. "That explains her reaction to my name. Was it serious?" Somehow she couldn't see Keith with Beatrice.

"Not by adult standards, I guess," Thomas answered, "but about as serious as anyone can get in high school. She was more serious than Keith was, I'm sure. When Keith left for UCLA, I really think she expected him to come back for her."

Linda shrugged; there was nothing else to say. A lot of years had intervened, a lot had happened.

As they drove to the used-car dealer, Thomas told her more about Beatrice. She had been married to a real estate developer who did some work with Thomas Devonshire, Sr. He was much older than Beatrice, but still was relatively young when he died. That's when she put on the extra weight.

"Beatrice is a bit reclusive now," he said. "But I do hope you'll be able to become friends. You have some things in common."

"I'd like to be friendly," Linda said, wondering if the other woman would give it a chance.

The dealer led them through the car lot to a green late-model Ford with power everything. There was very little sales pitch, only a description of the extras and a passing hand over the freshly shined chrome. Obviously it had all been prearranged. Linda couldn't help feeling trapped. It had been building up since Thomas's phone call. Inwardly she bristled, as she felt control being taken from her, but she said nothing except "It's a lovely car and I'm pleased to receive it."

The day was warm and sunny. For lunch they picked up Big Macs and French fries and settled into a small park tucked back from the main street. Linda barely touched her food. When Thomas asked her why she wasn't eating, she finally voiced her thoughts.

"I don't want to give the impression that I don't appreciate all you're doing for me, Thomas. I do. But I can't help but feel a little cramped by everything, demeaned even. Decisions are being made for me. Believe me, I am so grateful to you, but I'm not the kind of person who can just keep taking things."

"But I want you to, Linda," Thomas said, his eyes wide, honest.

"Thomas! Cars! Houses!" She threw her hands up in the air. "It's making me feel almost like—" she faltered.

Thomas filled in. "Little Orphan Annie?"

"Yes," she whispered hoarsely, and turned away from him.

Thomas nodded slowly, knowingly, and tucked in his lips thoughtfully. "I have to admit to enjoying playing Daddy Warbucks and I'm afraid I've been completely insensitive to how you might feel. I want to help you, Linda, and perhaps like everything else I tackle I've thrown myself whole hog into the 'save Linda Devonshire' campaign." He laughed shortly, critically. "And like everyone else in my family, it seems, I've been a little blind to the consequences of my actions. I'm glad you're a proud woman and feel the way you do. I think more of you because of it."

"I'm going to get a job," Linda said, "and I want you to keep a tab on everything you give me because I intend to pay you back fully."

"Deal," Thomas said. Then he looked forlornly at the half-eaten hamburger in her hand. "Don't I at least get to pick up lunch?"

After they finished, Thomas went back to the bank. Linda drove slowly through the center of West Ledge. She parked the car, then window-shopped with Toby for an hour and identified the stores where she would be doing her shopping. Then Toby yawned and Linda drove back home.

No sooner had Linda poured Toby a glass of milk and put some water on to boil than there was a knock on the door. Linda was surprised to see Eleanor standing on the porch.

"Come in, come in, please," she said. "I was meaning to call you and thank you for such a wonderful dinner last night." Her voice lowered as she flushed in embarrassment. "And also to apologize again for my dreadful behavior. I don't know what happened to me."

Eleanor waved her off. "It doesn't matter, dear. I understood."

"Can I offer you something?" Linda asked. "I was just making some coffee for myself—" The look on Eleanor's face stopped her from saying more. Her face was long, her eyes distant. "Is anything the matter?" she asked.

Eleanor nodded and indicated Toby.

"Honey," Linda said to Toby, "why don't you go upstairs and lie down for a little while, okay? I'll be up in a few minutes."

"Okay, Mommy."

They waited until Toby was up the stairs, then Eleanor said, "Yes, dear, I'm afraid something is the matter. And it's rather difficult to say."

Linda felt her face redden. "Please—"

Eleanor squeezed her eyes shut, then spoke. "After you left last night, I went through the old photo albums I had taken down for us to look at. I had planned on it for after dinner but of course you had to leave." She cleared her throat and they looked away from each other, embarrassed. "It was something I hadn't done in quite some time," Eleanor continued. "There were pictures of Keith, of course—as a child, a young man, before he left for California. The pictures triggered memories inside of me. *Painful* memories," she stressed, and her voice cracked. "I cried late into last night. I'm afraid I wasn't able to sleep very well."

"It was hard for me too, Mrs. Devonshire," Linda said softly, suddenly aware that this was the first time she had addressed her directly. "Mrs. Devonshire" was so formal, but nothing else seemed appropriate.

"I've done a lot of things in my life I'm not particularly proud of," Eleanor said. "Things that are now, I fear, coming back to haunt me." Her eyes flicked away from Linda, but not before Linda caught the regret in them. Then Eleanor seemed to gain new inner strength. "Let me be very direct with you. It's going to be too difficult for me for you to be here in West Ledge—a constant reminder of my son and what we did to each other, what *I* did to him . . ."

Surprised, Linda said, "You were so gracious to me last night. I thought you were glad to see me."

"I was open to you, dear," Eleanor corrected. "And I tried . . ." She looked down at her hands, folded in her lap. "Look at me. My hands are shaking. They have been since you left last evening." She took a deep breath; said what she had come to say. "I made a very grave mistake ten years ago. I should have approached things totally differently. But I didn't, for many reasons, none of which are important now." She raised her eyes, looked directly at Linda, a pained expression across her face. Her voice started to break as she said, "I would prefer you didn't remain here. It's too . . . too . . . I can't—" She finished in a whisper.

"I'm sorry," Linda said, suddenly feeling weak. "I had no idea." Her mouth grew dry.

Eleanor reached into her pocketbook. First she removed a handkerchief, wiped the corners of her eyes, which were tearing, then a piece of paper. "Here. Please take this." It was a check. Linda started when she saw the amount.

"There is nothing to tie you here, Linda. You have no roots, no family. You can go anywhere with your child, meet new people, friends, start a new life. It doesn't have to be in West Ledge. But for me, West Ledge is all I have. And Thomas. That's all." She tried to smile, kindly, maternally. "Take it," she said. "I owe you." And behind the sad smile, Linda saw the anguish in Eleanor's eyes. Her heart suddenly went out to the older woman who had driven her son from her side, then lost him entirely, and had never reconciled with him before his death. She tried to imagine how it might be to be separated from Toby and inwardly shuddered at the terrible thought.

"I don't know," she said, and looked at the check. But perhaps it might be better if she did—for everyone. She had nothing to hold her there. And she was certain she was already causing Thomas more bother than she was worth. With Eleanor's check she and Toby could make a fresh start somewhere else. And she'd be away from the inevitable memories that being in West Ledge would rekindle for her as well.

"Let me think," she said. Everything was happening too fast. Her emotions were being twisted, stretched taut. There was so much to consider—Thomas, Toby, the car . . .

"Please," Eleanor implored. Now, since her neck was no longer covered by a high collar as it had been last night, Linda could see the looseness of the older woman's skin. She was no longer the Eleanor Devonshire who had once frightened her and driven her out of West Ledge; she was a frail, old woman.

And for this frail, old woman who had never done anything except cause her heartache and shame, Linda slowly nodded her head yes. "Yes, Eleanor," she said softly. "We will go."

"Thank you, dear," Eleanor said, and stood. "You are very kind to do this for me." She made her way to the door. "You'll kiss Toby for me, please, and tell her I love her."

"Of course," Linda said, her voice thick, wondering how much Eleanor could really love her grandchild if she was so willing to send her away. But there was a lot about her mother-in-law she would never understand, she knew.

She closed the door behind Eleanor and leaned against it. The check was pressed between her palm and the plasterboard, her world again turned upside down.

Leaving West Ledge made the most sense, although she didn't know where to go. She couldn't return to Los Angeles—there was nothing for her there—nor to Chicago, where she had been raised. She could look up a few friends from school, but she hadn't kept up closely with anybody and she really didn't want to return there with all its painful memories. She preferred a small town over a large city—it would be safer for Toby and wherever she went she would have to find a job.

She decided she would drive north—somewhere in Massachusetts or Vermont—the Berkshires, perhaps, or a town in the

White Mountains. Eleanor's money would see her through the next several months, certainly enough to get started again, and she was very fortunate to have it.

She smiled and felt an odd rush of relief. The last decision had been made and it was her own!

"Toby," she called. "Come down here, will you?"

"Yes, Mommy?" Toby walked down the stairs, holding Patricia.

Linda settled her on the couch, where Eleanor had been sitting only moments before.

"What do you say if we leave this house and go someplace else?" she asked.

Toby screwed up her face in a questioning look. "I like it here."

"What if we found another place that you liked as much, or even better? Would that be okay?"

Toby nodded slowly, uncertainly, the mouth still curved downward in a frown. "I guess. Would Uncle Thomas be there too? And Grandma?"

"No, honey, they wouldn't. It would be just you and me. Like before."

"But we could still write to Grandma and talk to her, can't we?"

Linda smiled. "Sure we can."

"Okay." Toby nodded. All the points were ironed out.

"Good," Linda said, and moved to the phone, thinking: Now for the hard part—telling Thomas.

His secretary put her through right away.

"How's the car?" he asked. "Any problems? The dealer will take care of them for you."

"Thomas, your mother was just here."

"That was nice of her to come," Thomas said, pleased.

Linda's throat closed and she swallowed. "She gave me some money," she said hurriedly, wanting to get all of her thoughts out in one breath before Thomas cut her off. "She asked me to leave West Ledge, said it was too painful for her. . . ." Linda's words were lost to her in a swirling mist, and she felt somewhat detached from herself. ". . . still pay you back for the car, I'm going to need it." She broke off. She had said everything there was to say. Then Thomas spoke. "I'm coming over."

"Thomas, please, don't make it any harder—"

"Don't leave until I've gotten there."

"What's the point?"

His voice was suddenly sharper than she had ever heard it. "Linda, you owe me this!" he said. Then he hung up. She stared at the dead phone. Toby eyed her cautiously.

"Is Uncle Thomas mad at us?"

Linda tried to smile. "No, dear, he's not."

"Are we still moving?"

Linda hung up the phone and said with resolve, "Yes. Yes, we are."

Thomas arrived in twenty minutes. His tie was now on, but slightly askew, as if he had been tugging at it. Linda nudged Toby upstairs so she could speak with Thomas alone.

"My mother had no right to do what she did," he said, and Linda saw how upset he was.

"Don't be angry with her, Thomas. It's *I* who didn't have the right to just come to West Ledge, disregard her feelings, intrude on her life. I should have called her first, should have suspected . . ."

"I invited you here. You are not intruding on her or anybody's life."

"I don't want to hurt her," she implored.

Thomas's eyes narrowed. "She's my mother, but after what she did to you, why do you care about her feelings?"

Linda looked thoughtful for a moment. "Because I'm not like her. Because I can't hurt anyone else."

A brooding look crossed Thomas's face. "Yet you don't seem to mind hurting me."

"Thomas, no!" she said, startled. "I didn't say that."

"By leaving you will."

"Please don't say that to me," she begged.

He took her hands. "Do you *want* to leave, Linda? That's the question. Nothing else. Because if you do, you can walk right out that door, take Mother's money, the car, anything you want, and I won't stop you. That decision is yours alone." He dropped her hands and stepped toward the door, showing her a clear path.

She didn't move. Her eyes were wide and she let them roam the house he had so graciously given her to live in.

"I don't know," she said. She was feeling twisted again. "I thought I did. I felt I had made my decision. I didn't want to cause your mother any pain. I didn't want to be a burden on you. And I wanted to retain some dignity for myself."

She ran her hand through her hair, curled it behind her ears, then shook her head limply. "I don't want to go, Thomas, but I feel I should. For everyone." Her eyes were wet, her vision blurred. Embarrassed, she smiled and tried to catch the tears before they trickled down her face. "I'm making a spectacle of myself, aren't I? I *am* more trouble than I'm worth."

"Never," he said, and pulled her close to him; embraced her comfortingly. "And believe me when I say I don't want you to go."

"Thomas, I just know it's best." But her voice wavered and he read into it and smiled.

Linda closed her eyes tightly to stop the tears, but now she didn't know if they were tears of sorrow or relief. She dangled the check.

"What do I do with this?"

Thomas smiled slyly. "I would suggest cashing it. I'll vouch for the signature and I happen to know personally that there are enough funds to cover it."

"I couldn't."

"I didn't think so." He held out his hand to take it. "Here, I'll give it back to her."

Linda was suddenly nervous. "What are you going to say to her, Thomas?"

"I'm going to say," he said simply, "that you've changed your mind and are staying in West Ledge." Then he lowered his voice. "And I promise, Linda, I'll respect all your wishes and won't push myself on you anymore."

"I don't want to hurt her," Linda repeated, almost wavering again. She turned away from Thomas, stared out the window. A boy was riding by on a scooter, followed by a small dog at his heels. West Ledge was a lovely town to live in and she wanted to stay. Then she frowned and asked, "Just why do you want me to stay here, Thomas? And please give me an honest answer."

Without any hesitation, Thomas answered, "Because you're my sister-in-law and I want to take care of you, because you were treated badly and I want to make amends, but mostly, Linda, because I like you."

* * *

Thomas stood in the doorway of the greenhouse and watched his mother in silence, her bent form leaning over her plants, dusting them, watering them, caring for them. Almost lovingly, it seemed. She was so good with *plants*, he thought a bit ruefully. She was repotting a spider plant and her fingers worked the soil, packing it down around the roots of the plant. Then he saw her stop and rub one hand against the other. Her arthritis was bothering her, he knew, and he pitied her for her pain. But right now that was all he pitied her for. He coughed and called attention to himself.

"Thomas," Eleanor said pleasantly, waving hello. She sprayed a bug killer on the schefflera and stood back to admire the patterned shades of green on the leaves. "We almost lost this one, but I was able to bring it back. It gives me such a good feeling." She looked admiringly around the greenhouse—at vegetable bushes, common philodendrons, exotic plants, roses. "They're all such beautiful things, aren't they?"

"I just came from Linda's house, Mother."

"Then you know she's decided to leave West Ledge, I presume. We agreed it was best for her. She couldn't possibly be comfortable here after all that happened. And you don't really have the time to—"

"She's staying, Mother." A tiredness had crept into his voice.

Eleanor stiffened. "That isn't what she told me."

Thomas's lips curled slightly in disdain. "She was only going because she cared about you. I admire her for that. But now—" He took the check out of his pocket; handed it back to her. "She's changed her mind."

"She can't!" Eleanor said sharply. "What did you say to her?"

"It doesn't matter. You can't send them away. She's your daughter-in-law, Toby is your only grandchild." His eyes narrowed pityingly at her. "That's got to mean something. . . ."

Eleanor's head seemed to wobble fragilely on her slender neck as she absorbed what he had said.

"It does, Thomas. It most certainly does. But I can't have her here . . . I . . ." She faltered and turned away from him, having trouble saying what she wanted. Then she said quickly, almost spitting the words out, "I'm afraid of her, Thomas."

"Afraid?" Thomas asked, surprised. "What is there for you to be afraid of her?"

"Her past," Eleanor whispered hoarsely, as if afraid even to voice the words. "She was sick. She was paranoid. Schizophrenic."

"But that was all so many years ago."

"No, not so many years ago. Not at all. It happened to her again recently. She had another attack only three years ago. A bad regression. She thought someone wanted to kill her child and became violent. She had to be hospitalized."

Thomas was startled. "I had no idea."

"It was never important to tell you. I wanted to when you first told me she was coming, but like you I thought she was better. But you saw her behavior last night!"

"She had a little too much to drink, that's all."

"She was . . . unsettled, Thomas. Confused. I had no idea what she thought she was hearing when I was speaking to her. I was afraid."

"How did you know all about this, Mother?" he asked. "Did you have her followed again?"

"No, of course not," Eleanor snapped. "I did it that one time for Keith and that was all." She softened her voice as she remembered. "Keith told me when he was here for your father's funeral. It had just happened and he was very upset. She was in the hospital even then and a neighbor was watching the child."

"He mentioned none of this to me," Thomas said blankly, disturbed by what he was hearing. "I had no idea . . ."

"That's why I'm afraid," Eleanor said. "What happens if one day she regresses again and decides I am responsible for all of the bad things that have happened to her in her life and she comes after me? What if she hears voices ordering her to do this?"

"That's not going to happen, Mother."

"You can't guarantee that, Thomas. No one can." Then she turned away from him and spoke softly. "I was wrong. What I did was wrong. To Keith. To her. And till now it's all been in the past, almost forgotten—as much as a mother can forget a son. But please, Thomas, please don't make us relive it all over again."

She broke off, and Thomas looked at his mother curiously.

Her words moved him; he felt her pain. Perhaps for the first time
in her life, he thought, she was feeling something—regret?—her
Devonshire mask of cold strength crumbling. "Don't be afraid,
Mother," he said gently, appreciating her moment of vulnerability.
"Nothing is going to happen because she's here. I will help her
so she will never become sick again. But I must care for her
here. Please understand that this is something I have to do." He
pulled his mother close to him, felt her body shudder. "And I
promise I won't let anything happen to you."

"I love you, Thomas," Eleanor said, her voice thick. In need,
he thought.

"I love you too, Mother," but their words sounded foreign.
He and his parents had so very rarely traded words of endearment,
now or in years past. He tried to summon up more feeling for her
than he could, patted her back comfortingly. "I love you too,
Mother," he repeated, and tried to erase the strangeness from his
words and feelings. "And no harm will come from her being
here, I promise you."

Eleanor's chin rested on his shoulder, her eyes wide, liquid, as
she looked past him at the plants in the greenhouse, full of the
life she had given them.

"Keith used to love gardening when he was young," she said.
"Your father thought it was all a waste of time, time that could
have been put to better use, but he loved it and I encouraged him.
He had such a green thumb. Do you remember that one tomato
he grew? It was the largest one any of us had ever seen and we
joked that it was one of the outer space tomato people coming to
take over the earth. He didn't want to pick that tomato. Only
when it started to go soft did he finally do it. We took a picture
of it. I saw that picture last night and thought about the night we
all ate the tomato." She tried to laugh. "It was almost like eating
a pet."

"I remember," Thomas said, his eyes distant, an image of his
younger brother and the incident forming. Keith was nine and he
was twenty, home from Harvard for the summer, with no time to
be bothered with gardens or tomatoes. As his father had said, he
had better things to do with his time.

Then Eleanor pushed away from Thomas; searched his eyes
anxiously. "I will accept her, Thomas. For you."

She didn't want to anger her son. He was all she had left.

*   *   *

Carol Ann was playing in her room when her mother pushed open the door and strode in.

"You were a bad girl today," Beatrice said.

"No, Mommy, I wasn't," Carol Ann cried, her eyes widening in fear.

"Yes, you were, Carol Ann, and for the life of me I just don't know what to do with you sometimes."

In one motion Beatrice cupped the girl under her arm and dragged her across the floor. When Carol Ann saw where her mother was taking her, she begged, "No, Mommy, please. I won't be bad anymore."

"You were bad, Carol Ann, and you know what happens to bad girls."

"I promise!" she cried, but with a sinking heart the girl knew she was going to be punished. She hadn't done anything wrong, but there was no stopping her mother when she got in one of these moods. Beatrice tightened her hold on her daughter, pulled her into the bathroom, and set the drain plug in the sink. "Not the water, please. Please don't." Carol Ann's voice filled with frightened tears. "I won't be bad anymore."

Beatrice turned the water on and let it fill the sink. "This will teach you to obey me." She pulled a stool out from under the sink, roughly stood her daughter on it. Then she pushed the little girl's face under the water and held her down as the running water cascaded over her head.

chapter 7

Linda dressed carefully in a suit and ruffled white blouse. She took a last look at herself in the bathroom mirror, pleased with her appearance. Elegant but not ostentatious. Conservative enough to interview for a job with a century-old Connecticut law firm, she decided. She affixed an antique half-moon brooch to her lapel. Her aunt had given it to her as a good luck charm; she had used it over the years. She had been wearing it the day she met Keith. Although the day she met Eleanor its magic had failed her, she would give it another try today. Perhaps if nothing else it would curb the butterflies in her stomach.

Toby came out of the bedroom, also dressed in her best. She, too, was nervous about what the day might bring and the other children she would meet, but was eager to make new friends. The special nature and crafts programs the school offered through July seemed an ideal way to do it.

It was a little past 8:30 when Linda drove up to the school. Other children were arriving by foot or bike, and a small bus disgorged others. Toby held tightly to Linda's hand as they went up to the office. After the forms were filled out, Linda kissed her daughter.

"I'll be here when school lets out, okay? Just wait for me in front of the building."

Though she drove slowly through West Ledge, she still arrived early for her interview. She found a parking space down the street from the office building that housed the law firm of Erskine, Robinson & Howell. Thomas had arranged the appointment for her, and others for later in the week if this one didn't work out.

She readied herself, took a deep breath, and rode the elevator to the second floor and entered the office through the glass doors. The reception desk was empty—that was the position they were looking to fill. Three women in their late twenties sat behind electric typewriters at desks covered with legal pads. Linda caught the eye of one.

"I have an appointment with Mr. Robinson. My name is Linda Devonshire."

"I'll tell him you're here," she said, and disappeared into the back.

Linda took a seat and picked up a magazine. She felt the eyes of one of the secretaries on her and smiled at the woman, thinking she was lending support. But instead the woman sneered at her and turned away. Surprised at the abrupt gesture, Linda flushed a deep red. Then another woman came out and ushered her into Mr. Robinson's office.

The senior partner was a little older than Thomas, a little chunkier, and more than a little balder. He wore a three-piece suit and a watch fob that went well with his girth, and sat behind a desk half the size of the office. Linda recognized her résumé on the top of a pile of others.

He told her about the firm—three partners, four junior associates, three secretaries, and a receptionist who was also responsible for filing and mailing. The girl who last had the job had made a grievous error and jeopardized a major case. They couldn't tolerate that kind of sloppiness and had to let her go. "How is your typing?" he asked.

"Could be better," she admitted. "But I intend to practice."

"The job doesn't usually require that much, but if we get backed up one day you'd be expected to help out."

"Of course."

"The pay isn't all that much," he continued. "Not quite two fifty a week. The secretaries get more but they're skilled in taking legal shorthand and drafting contracts. But whenever you want, and feel ready for it, we can try you out and—well, see what happens. Can you start next Monday?"

"What?" Linda asked blankly.

"Can you start next Monday?" Robinson repeated, enjoying the expression on her face.

Then it sunk in. She got the job. "Why—" she sputtered. "Yes, yes, of course!"

Linda couldn't hide her smile as she walked through the secretary's area. When she passed the desk of the girl who had glanced at her while she was waiting, she said happily, "I got the job. I start Monday."

And she was more than surprised when the girl answered, "How naive can you be? We all knew that last week when Thomas Devonshire called."

Linda felt her face burn. She looked around the room. The other secretaries were staring at her. The interview was a sham, a formality; she had the job before she even came in. She felt a surge of irritation toward Thomas. Why didn't he understand she wanted to do things for herself!

She turned around and walked back to Mr. Robinson's office, hesitated, then rapped on the door with her fist.

"Yes? Come in."

"Mr. Robinson—may I ask you a question?"

"Yes, of course."

"Did you hire me because of Thomas?"

"I see," he said. "We tend to have a gossipy little bunch out there, don't we? Well, I guess interoffice politics is interoffice politics whether it's New York City or West Ledge, Connecticut. The answer to your question, Mrs. Devonshire, is no." He lifted a pile of résumés on his desk, separated hers. "It is true that Thomas is a client of this firm. An important client. He gave me your résumé and asked that I consider it, which I have. You are qualified, more mature than most of the other applicants, and I feel I can count on you to do a good job. But to answer your question—Thomas Devonshire does not hire or fire in this law firm."

Linda smiled sheepishly, looked at the floor, shook her head in self-condemnation. "I'm sorry, Mr. Robinson. I very happily accept your job offer. Can we forget this conversation ever took place?"

"What conversation?" he asked, and escorted her out of the office. "Ladies," he announced from the center of the secretary area. "Please meet Linda Devonshire. She'll be starting next week." He motioned to the woman who had spoken to her. "Nancy, you will please give her every assistance."

"Yes, Mr. Robinson," the woman said.

Linda caught Nancy's eye. The other woman held her glance

coolly for only a second, then looked away. *The hell with her!* Linda fumed. *The hell with all of them. I got the job.* She had taken the first important step in her new life.

She called Thomas from a pay phone in the lobby. "I got it!" she said happily.

"That's great. Congratulations. Hey—how about a little celebration lunch? Are you free?"

"Why, yes," Linda answered, pleased. "I don't have to pick up Toby for two hours."

"Come meet me at the bank. Then we can go to the restaurant."

"I'll be there in ten minutes."

The thrill of a moment ago returned as Linda left the office building and skipped down the steps. Outside she looked up at the windows of the law firm. Nancy was staring down at her. Then she lost her in the glare of the sun as it ducked out from behind shifting clouds. The sudden breeze made her shiver. She just hoped that none of them would resent her for being Thomas Devonshire's sister-in-law.

At the bank, she was ushered into Thomas's office immediately. He was finishing up a call and motioned for her to make herself comfortable on the couch. When he hung up he went over to her and kissed her on the cheek. "I'm so happy things worked out," he said.

"I-I want to thank you again for all your help," Linda stammered. "I probably couldn't have gotten it without—"

Thomas waved off the remark. "I'm sure you'll be running the place in no time."

"I'm going to do my best," she promised.

"How about a drink?"

"Do you have any diet soda? I think that's about all I can handle this early in the day."

Thomas poured two Tabs and they sat on opposite ends of the couch. "So are you all settled into the house?" he asked.

"Well, settling. It's a lot of house for just the two of us. Not that I'm complaining," she added quickly.

"I know you're not."

"I just love the backyard. Toby and I had a picnic out by the well yesterday." Then she asked worriedly, "The water's safe to drink, isn't it?" And added in a small voice, "Because we did."

"I'm sure." Thomas smiled.

There was a silent moment between them and Linda let her eyes roam around the large office. "So this is where it all happens?" she asked, a note of admiration in her voice, yet a tremor of nervousness as well. She was still buoyed by getting the job, but suddenly she felt a little uneasy being in Thomas's office, which represented all the power and wealth of the Devonshire family.

"Well, some of it," Thomas answered, watching her. "I have a lot of executives I rely on. If I wasn't here, they wouldn't even miss me."

"Hardly," Linda said. On the wall was a portrait of Thomas, Sr., and Eleanor. Linda lowered her eyes. "How's your mother?" she asked quietly. She hadn't spoken to Eleanor since she had offered her the money to leave West Ledge.

"Stronger than either of us." Thomas smiled. "Perhaps I made a mistake and thrust you two together too soon, but she'll be all right."

"I don't want to cause her any—"

Thomas held up his hand. "She'll be all right," he repeated. "Your being here is just something she's going to have to live with, and I don't want you concerned about it at all. If there's a problem, it's not yours, all right?"

"All right." She nodded, but Thomas saw the hesitation flicker across her face, the sudden distance and unease. She put her soda down on the coffee table and looked away from him, at the original Botello lithograph hanging behind his desk of a woman's face, fractured by a slanted line from forehead to chin. Perhaps as Linda's past had been, he considered—fractured, troubled. He knew she was still disturbed by what had happened with his mother and for a second he hated Eleanor for all she had done to Linda, who had never meant her any harm. Then as Linda turned back toward him, her face caught the midday sun and he saw the gentleness of her features. She was so attractive, yet so frail and vulnerable and had been through so much. He knew why her actions were so tentative. He had thought it had been because of her uprooting and moving east; now he knew there was much more than that. Now he understood the sadness in her eyes, the catlike wariness that paved the way to her inner self. And suddenly he wanted her to know that he knew and it was all right. He wanted to help her, protect her. Her past shouldn't remain unspoken between them; perhaps it would make her more relaxed, less afraid.

"Linda," he started softly. "I know about what happened to you in Los Angeles and—"

Linda blushed a bright crimson. Thomas immediately saw he had made a mistake and wished he could take back what he had started to say.

"What happened in Los Angeles is over!" she flared. "I was sick then but I'm not anymore. Do you and your mother think I still am?" He saw her hands form fists and tremble as she seemed to fight for control. He reached over to her, touched her closed hands, steadied them, loosened them.

"Linda, I only wanted to say to you that if you ever need any help at all, for anything, I want you to feel free to call on me without hesitation. And that's all."

A long silent moment passed between them. Then Linda exhaled and closed her eyes, embarrassed by her outburst. "I'm sorry," she muttered. "I'm—" She shook her head.

"Look at me, Linda," Thomas prompted, and she turned toward him. "It's all right."

"No, Thomas," she said. "It isn't." She opened her eyes round and wide and looked about. "I'm very defensive about what happened to me and I apologize for snapping the way I did just now. I had no right." She smiled derisively. "I guess you could say that that was a rather paranoid way to react."

"No, I'm not going to say any such thing," he said softly. "I'm just going to repeat my offer of help. And my mother— believe it or not—sends the same offer."

"Thomas, that's kind," she said. "But why do I get the impression the only help your mother wants to give me is to help me out of town?" She waved her hand loosely. "No, don't answer that. That was fresh and not very fair. I understand her. And if I were in her position, perhaps I'd feel the same way."

"Give her time, okay?" His eyes were owlish and she nodded.

He rose. "Shall we go to lunch? There's a phenomenal little French restaurant around the corner. Believe me, if you told me thirty-five years ago I was going to grow up to love to eat snails and frogs, I would have told you you were crazy."

Then he laughed, because she laughed.

chapter 8

Beatrice Daily was giving her closet a thorough cleaning—pulling everything out, taking inventory, and piling up items that she would never wear again to give away. She was taking out dresses, modeling some in front of the full-length mirror, when she saw the dress. It was in the far corner of the closet, flush with the wall. She recognized it immediately. That was odd—she thought she had thrown it out years before. It was her mother's favorite summer dress, a bright floral pattern over a white background marred by a big ugly grape-juice stain in the front that had never come out.

Beatrice sat down on her bed, held the dress in front of her, and remembered the day it had been stained.

She was only a child, eight years old, going on nine. She and her friends were playing dress-up. She knew this dress was her mother's favorite and that was why she wanted to put it on. She wanted to be like her mother.

First the girls made themselves up with her mother's cosmetics—lipsticks, rouge, eyeshadow. Then they pulled the dresses on and high heels and paraded in front of the mirror.

It was Jane's idea to have wine. Her parents always had wine when they got dressed in their good clothes and wine would make the children feel more grown up. But they knew they weren't allowed to have wine. Beatrice remembered there was grape juice in the refrigerator that was almost like wine, so in their high heels they trooped down to the kitchen, pulled goblets out of the cabinet above the sink, and filled them with grape juice. Beatrice was holding her glass, toasting the others, when her foot slipped and her heel broke. She stumbled and the glass of juice spilled all over the light-colored dress.

Then her mother walked in and saw the purple stain. Beatrice still remembered the red look of fury on her face when she assessed the damage.

"It was an ac-accident—" Beatrice stammered, but her mother's rough tug on her arm silenced her. In one motion, she pulled the dress off her, then led her daughter into the bathroom.

"I'm sorry, Mommy," Beatrice cried. "Don't—please."

"That stain will never come out. That dress is completely ruined. You've been a very bad girl," her mother said angrily.

"It was an accident," Beatrice cried louder, hoping her friends would somehow come to her rescue. But they were still in the kitchen, too frightened to move.

"Oh, Beatrice, stop it," her mother said as she pulled the stepstool out from under the sink. "You always yell and cry and make promises hoping you won't be punished. But it's too late for any of that now. You should have thought of that before you were bad. That was the time to consider the consequences of your actions." She stood Beatrice on the stool, turned the water on full force.

"Mommy!" Beatrice pleaded again as she stared down into the sink filling with water.

"I'm not listening to you, Beatrice. You were a bad girl and have to punished."

Her movement was sudden, sharp. Without even a moment to take in a deep breath, Beatrice found herself suddenly pushed under the water, her mother's hand clamping tightly to the back of her neck.

"Let the water punish you! The water punishes bad girls."

From almost the start she had no air. She tried to flail her arms but her mother had a tight hold on them. Her legs were wedged against the sink. She wasn't aware that her eyes bulged wide in terror, or of the rush of water through her ears, as she strained for one more second, one more second . . .

It was a miracle she didn't drown. When her mother released her, Beatrice shot straight out of the water, banging her head against the faucet, but not feeling the burst of pain in her desperation to take in air. She sputtered; coughed; almost gagged. She tried to bolt away but her mother grabbed her again, this time lovingly, covered her with a towel, and dried her hair. Then she cradled her in her arms, rocked the child back and forth.

"I'm sorry, baby. Really I am. But when you're a bad girl you have to be punished. You know that, don't you?"

"Yes, Mommy."

"Were you a bad girl today?"

"Yes."

"Never be bad again and I'll never have to punish you again, okay?"

"Yes, Mommy," Beatrice said to her mother.

Carol Ann came into her mother's bedroom. She was all bathed and ready for bed. Beatrice held out her arms to her daughter.

"Never be bad, Carol Ann," Beatrice said, her eyes distant as she recalled the water raging over her head, burning her eyes and her lungs, about to drown her. "You know I don't like to punish you, but when you're bad I have to. So promise you'll never be a bad girl so I'll never have to punish you."

"I promise," Carol Ann said nervously.

It seemed that lately her mother was getting more and more this way.

Thomas worked late, then drove home and parked in his indoor space. His apartment building, financed by the bank, was one of the few luxury high-rises in West Ledge. The bank had made millions from selling the expensive units, and he had taken the choice penthouse for himself. There were two bedrooms, living room, dining room, kitchen, and study, all professionally decorated, color coordinated. A magazine photograph, a showplace, but sterile, with few personal touches.

He made himself a sandwich and spread out reports on his desk to review for a breakfast meeting the next morning. It was a preliminary meeting for the financing of a new movie sixplex, a profitable venture.

But he couldn't concentrate. He went to the mirrored bar, poured himself a drink, and stared out the window. The glass extended from floor to ceiling. The apartment was on a rise, offering a panoramic view of West Ledge and the valleys beyond. Dotting the landscape below him were the lights of private homes. Behind many of the windows were, he imagined, a husband, a wife—a family.

He closed his eyes and leaned his head back against the couch. Suddenly he felt oddly lonely. He shook off the feeling. He was usually too busy to feel this way. There was always a report to review, a meeting to chair, a reception to attend. Never time to think about himself or experience loneliness. At least not since the years following the divorce.

He had been married for three years, divorced now for ten.

His parents had adored Sandra. She was a Swenson. Her father owned an electrical company and played golf with Thomas, Sr. Thomas and Sandra had bought a house not far from his parents. He was being groomed to run the bank, always occupied, his mind constantly on business. Sandra wanted more time and attention than he was able to give her. More love. More openness. He was the unemotional man, she the opposite. The marriage teetered, then collapsed, his parents' life a role model that failed him.

He had thought he had loved her, but perhaps he never did, perhaps he had only married her because that was what his parents wanted. He did not know why Sandra married him; perhaps she really loved him.

After the divorce he dated extensively, was considered one of the most eligible bachelors in the county, but the women left him feeling cold; there was an emptiness to the affairs. He suspected he would never marry again, and he didn't know how he felt about that.

He opened his eyes and his glance fell on the reports that beckoned to him almost mockingly. He dragged himself over to the desk, feeling tired, drained. Suddenly Thomas realized he wanted something more.

After lunch with Thomas Linda had stopped at a hardware store and made an extra key for Toby. They spent the afternoon practicing working the lock and dialing Linda's office number to report that Toby was safely home. That would be the routine. Then they both had a special dinner to celebrate their self-sufficiency.

Linda put Toby to sleep but she was still too keyed up to read or watch television. It had been a good day. First getting the job, then having lunch with Thomas. She had really enjoyed herself. Her impression of Thomas from the last two weeks had been completely different from what she had expected. He had been generous and gentle with her; she had seen none of the ruthless banker Keith talked about. She really liked him.

She decided to get some fresh air. She pulled on her sweater and stepped outside, sat down on the porch steps, and let the night fold itself around her. There were lights on in the house diagonally across the street, movement behind the curtains. Beatrice Dailey was still awake. In a way Linda did have a lot in common with the woman. They both had seven-year-old daughters and both had husbands who had died too young. Beatrice's husband had been dead for years. She had drawn into herself, watched her daughter overprotectively, neurotically, Linda imagined. She had never remarried, and Linda wondered if she dated at all. Then she thought about herself; wondered if she would ever remarry and when she might start dating again.

The sound stopped her thoughts and startled her—a rustling in the bushes to the side of the house. "Hello?" she called and strained to see, but there was only darkness, shadows, outlines of trees and hedges.

It probably was only an animal, she decided, a raccoon looking for food, but still the sounds were making her uneasy and, suddenly chilled by the night air, she felt uncomfortable sitting outside. Quickly she got up to go back inside and was more than surprised to find the door was locked. She had locked herself out and the key was inside. She jiggled the doorknob for an extra second—perhaps it would engage—but her fingers turned uselessly around the knob, which refused to move. Off in the distance a dog barked, raw and threatening.

She shivered nervously. The brushing sounds of leaves and twigs made perspiration break out on her chilled skin. She whirled around to face the darkness. "Is anybody there? Who is it?" she demanded. But there was no response. Only a car speeding by.

She had to get into the house. But the back door was also locked, as were all the windows on the ground floor. After her first night in the house she had made certain to keep everything locked. That was for peace of mind, she thought ironically. She rang the bell but heard nothing inside, then remembered that

Thomas had said it was broken. She tried knocking, but Toby was a sound sleeper and would never hear her.

The breeze picked up and blew through the hole in the attic window, making a whistling sound. *Linda*, she thought it said, but she knew it was only her imagination. Pinpricks dotted her back.

That was when she heard the footsteps. Real footsteps—not her imagination. A man's step, coming from down the block, even, unhurried, a steady, flat echo against the concrete, loud in the otherwise silent country air. The streetlight swept over her, exposed her to the night. She didn't want to be seen by the man and shrank back into the shadows of the porch. The footsteps grew louder as the man approached, then he was silhouetted in the light, visible from where Linda was standing.

Instead of walking through the light, the man stopped in front of the house and looked up at it for an extended moment. His eyes seemed to peer straight at her, although the light was dim and she couldn't make out his features. Linda tried to make herself smaller and knew that in the dark he couldn't see her—but only if she didn't catch light, didn't move! A bird, disturbed by something, sounded harshly from a tree above her. Startled, Linda sucked in her breath, almost gave herself away, but she remained frozen where she was until the man started walking again, his footsteps growing fainter, then disappearing altogether. Why was he looking at her? she puzzled. Her heart was beating rapidly and her breath exploded from her, even though there was nothing to be afraid of, she told herself. But still she fought a growing panic—she needed to get inside the house *right then*.

She had an idea. If she could ring the phone, Toby would awaken. But the only neighbor she knew was Beatrice Dailey. She hesitated to go to the woman but she had no choice. She crossed the street and knocked on the Dailey door, a tentative rap. There was no response and she rang the doorbell. She heard steps inside and then through the door the rasping voice. "Who is it?"

"Mrs. Dailey, it's Linda Devonshire." Her voice was dry. "I locked myself out and want to call my daughter to let me in. Can I use your phone?"

She heard the latch being removed and then Beatrice was opening the door. Linda started in surprise when she saw what

Beatrice was wearing. The dress was old-fashioned, a style that was popular a generation ago, with a floral pattern. But what was most striking was the stain on the front of the dress.

"I shouldn't let you in," Beatrice said. "I never let people in at night."

"Just for a moment, please. I just want to call Toby."

Beatrice scowled. "Just for a moment."

A sleepy Toby answered on the fourth ring. Linda explained what had happened and told her daughter to go downstairs to open the door when she knocked. She hung up the phone and thanked Beatrice for letting her into the house, then apologized for disturbing her evening.

As Linda passed her at the door, Beatrice said in a low voice, "I loved Keith. You were wrong to take him from me."

"No!" Linda gasped, but Beatrice had already closed the door behind her. She wanted to ring the bell again, tell the woman she hadn't taken Keith from her, but Toby would be downstairs waiting.

She was hurrying back across the street when suddenly she inhaled sharply and stopped short in the middle of the road. The man was back, standing under the streetlamp at the edge of her property, a slender figure, motionless in the dim glow of the light. He was almost invisible, his shadow angled and hidden by the tall hedges of the house next door. Was he watching her? She chilled. Waiting for her?

And because of her shock, too late did she see the car careening toward her, its brights turned on, blinding her, freezing her like a frightened deer in the oncoming headlights. She didn't know which way to jump as it skidded back and forth wildly across the width of the street, its horn blasting warning. At the last moment she leaped out of the way as the car flew past, the teenage driver yelling out the window, "Are you crazy, lady?" Panting, she raced up the porch steps, knocked on the door, and slipped quickly inside.

"Back to sleep now," she said breathlessly to Toby. Her heart was still pounding wildly from her scare. She kissed her daughter good night and scooted her up the stairs. Then, huddled in the protective darkness of the living room, she peered out through the shade. In her panic she had run right past the man. Now he was gone.

Nice going, Linda, she thought. Now you almost succeeded in getting yourself killed.

chapter **9**

It was the first day of her new job and Linda didn't want to be late. She dressed carefully in a white blouse and new charcoal-gray suit she had bought for work and affixed her half-moon brooch. The office was only twenty minutes from the house and when she arrived, nobody was there yet. The reception doors were locked, the office dark. Rather than wait in the outer hallway, she decided to dart across the street and grab a cup of coffee.

It was two minutes after nine when she returned upstairs and the office was operating. The first face she saw was Nancy Stone's, standing at the coffeepot. Nancy was a plain-looking woman in her late twenties with a long, narrow face carried forward on her neck. She eyed Linda and glanced upward at the clock on the wall.

"We start on time in this office," she said with a grunt.

"I was here early," Linda said. "But nobody else was. I only went downstairs for a cup of coffee." Then she thought angrily, Good heavens, why am I apologizing to this girl? I was here at eight thirty and even now I'm only two minutes late—and Mr. Robinson was just coming in.

"Good morning, ladies," he said to the secretaries. "Ah, Linda, right on time. Come into my office, please."

Linda dared not turn around to look at Nancy as she followed Don Robinson into his office. She couldn't figure out why the woman didn't like her from the start.

Robinson took off his suit jacket and draped it over the back of his chair. He pulled some forms out of his desk. "Fill these out sometime today. You'll have plenty of time at the desk.

I'll get Nancy to show you around, how to operate the switchboard console. I'm sure you'll be ready for more responsibility
within the week." He buzzed his intercom. "Nancy, please
come in here."

Moments later the door opened. Linda looked up expectantly,
but Nancy stared right through her without even a guise of
warmth as she approached her boss's desk.

"Get Linda settled, will you? Introduce her to the others."

"Yes, Mr. Robinson," she said formally, and motioned for
Linda to follow her. She led her to the reception desk, where she
mechanically took her through the steps of operating the
switchboard—how to hold calls, transfer them, set up conference
calls. She answered questions asked of her, volunteered no
information. She pointed out the other secretaries, mumbled their
names. She showed Linda the contents of her desk drawers—
message pads, sharpened pencils. There was a typewriter at the
front desk.

"Can I practice typing while I sit here?" Linda asked.

"Why?"

"I don't want to be just a receptionist." Linda smiled. "I'd
like to work up to a legal secretary."

"So you can take my job the same way you took Suzanne's? Is
that it?" Nancy said evenly.

Linda flushed deep red and stammered, "I-I didn't mean that—"

Nancy gave her a no-nonsense look. "What exactly *did* you
mean?" she demanded. "Are you hoping Mr. Robinson will fire
one of us too?" Her voice carried and there was a sudden silence
in the room, office machinery stopping. The other secretaries
were watching, listening.

"I don't want to take any of your jobs," Linda said, raising
her voice as well. "I don't know why you would say that. If I'm
ready to move up and there isn't any opening here, I'll look
elsewhere. As any of you would."

"None of us have Thomas Devonshire calling the boss,"
Nancy said spitefully.

"That's enough, Nancy." Another secretary came over. Linda
remembered her name was Helen, a black woman with golden
skin and a short Afro. "Nancy and Suzanne were very good
friends," she explained. "Suzanne had your job. She was fired

two weeks ago for making a mistake. Something any of us could
have done. We thought she got a raw deal—"

"And then *you* waltzed in like you owned the place. If it
hadn't been for you, Suzanne wouldn't have been fired."

"We don't know that, Nancy," Helen said sharply. "Do
we?"

"No," Nancy grumbled and went back to her desk.

Helen smiled tentatively but Linda could see she didn't want to
be too friendly. Her loyalties were still with the other women.
Linda felt badly for Suzanne, but it hadn't been her fault she was
fired. Well, there was nothing she could do except try to win the
friendship of the others.

Nobody spoke to her the rest of the morning, but then there
didn't seem to be that much conversation among the other secretaries either. Everybody was busy at work, the recent firing
having put fear into all of them. The switchboard kept her pretty
busy, and soon she had memorized everybody's extension. She
was able to steal only a few moments to practice typing and
hadn't had a chance yet to grow bored. At twelve thirty Helen
came over to her.

"This is when you go to lunch. I sit here until one thirty, then I
go out, so don't be late getting back or it cuts into my time."

"No, of course not," Linda said.

She pulled her purse out of the bottom desk drawer. Around
her the other secretaries were preparing to leave. Nancy leaned
over her desk and, in a voice loud enough for Linda to hear,
pointedly asked the others to join her. They quickly agreed and
the three of them slipped out past Linda, talking animatedly,
leaving her alone, obviously so. Linda imagined that Suzanne
used to go to lunch with them as well.

"Where is a good place to get a sandwich around here?" she
asked Helen, who had taken a magazine out of her tote bag.

"Sammy's, around the corner. They're good and fast."

Nancy, Louise, and Rhoda were at a booth large enough for
four people when Linda got there. There was an empty space,
room for her. For a second she met their eyes, hoping they might
ask her to join them. But they glanced at her without inviting her
to sit down and she chose a seat at the counter. She ordered a
hamburger and tried to tune out the conversation of the other
women but found it impossible. Nancy had visited Suzanne over

the weekend; she hadn't found a job yet. With her husband also out of work and two young children, it was going to be tough on them.

They're trying to make me feel bad, Linda said to herself. But I won't let them. I didn't do anything to hurt that woman, she repeated, but as much as she tried, she couldn't taste her lunch and ended up not eating half of it.

About three o'clock Don Robinson came out of his office. "Everything okay, Linda?" he asked.

"Yes, fine," she said, trying to inject enthusiasm into her voice. "I've mastered the switchboard and I'm ready for anything else you can give me."

"I'm just running out for a quick bite. Give my calls to Nancy, will you?"

As Robinson left through the reception doors the phone rang.

"Law Offices. Erskine, Howell & Robinson."

"Well, that's a mouthful."

"Thomas!" she said happily. Finally, a friendly voice. But she froze as she said his name, aware that Nancy was passing on her way to the ladies' room. Nancy's back stiffened for only a second, then she pushed open the door.

"I tried to break away to take you to lunch but I was stuck in a meeting all morning."

"Oh, I'm glad we didn't today."

"Oh?" He sounded hurt.

"Don't get me wrong. I would have loved it, but I only get an hour and we might not have had enough time."

"Well, anyway, are you free for dinner tonight? Just the two of us?"

"Tonight?" Linda hesitated. "I don't know." Another phone line rang. "Thomas, I'm sorry. Please—"

"Answer it."

She put a client through to Mr. Erskine, fumbled with the board for a moment, thought she had disconnected Thomas, but then clicked him back on.

"I really couldn't," she said.

Nancy came out of the ladies' room, walked slowly across the reception area, with one ear obviously on Linda's conversation.

"Why not?" Thomas prodded.

"It's such short notice."

"It is not. You've got—let's see—five hours."

Linda smiled. "But Toby," she said, not wanting to use the word babysitter in front of Nancy.

"There's a woman at the bank who loves to babysit," Thomas said. "That's not a problem. In fact, since I told her about Toby she hasn't left me alone about meeting her. You don't want to disappoint Mrs. Green, do you?"

"No," Linda said, distracted by Nancy, who was smiling coyly at her. Linda suspected she knew what was transpiring. And then she wasn't sure if it was because Nancy knew what was going on, or because she didn't, that she said pointedly to Thomas, "Dinner will be fine." She glanced up at Nancy, having decided to play the other woman's game, although she felt somewhat ashamed of her childish actions. She hung up the phone, annoyed with herself for using Thomas as she had. But she hadn't used him; she wanted to go out to dinner with him.

The rest of the afternoon passed faster. When five o'clock came she said a pleasant good night to each of the secretaries and left them to talk among themselves. By now they all knew she was going to dinner with Thomas Devonshire.

As she left the office the rush-hour streets were crowded with cars and pedestrians. Linda maneuvered through the people briskly; she had to get home, feed Toby, then ready herself to go out with Thomas. She was looking forward to the evening, mentally preparing what she was going to wear, so she barely saw the man sprinting across the busy street.

He was just another person on the edge of Linda's peripheral vision. Just another person dodging the heavy traffic, half lost to the glare of the late-afternoon sun as it glinted off the glass and steel of the downtown buildings. There was no reason to look twice at the man as he jumped a puddle at the edge of the curb and landed on the sidewalk next to her.

No reason at all.

But there was. And that was what stopped her.

Because as the man passed close by, the sun slipped behind a cloud and he was suddenly free of the glare. Linda was able to see him clearly and inside of her something clicked.

Her eyes narrowed in tentative recognition, then her mouth rounded in surprise and confirmation. She inhaled sharply and a squeal croaked deep in her throat, vibrating painfully through her windpipe and up into the roof of her mouth. An invisible hand gripped her spine, inhuman and deathly cold. The shock was intense.

The moment was suspended in time as Linda and the man looked at each other. All other sights and sounds ceased, a picture on a photographic plate, captured forever. The man's features were familiar. His mouth was curled upward in a cruel smile. His mustache was sandy, his hair bushy and curly. It was a face from her past that had been chiseled into her memory as if on granite. A face she had tucked away long ago, although never forgotten. Then with a whoosh of sound and perception time speeded up again and he was past her, gone, swallowed up by the rush-hour crowds as if he had never been there.

But he had been there.

He had been! She grappled spastically as she filled with a terror she hadn't known in years. Involuntarily she whimpered mournfully, a sound with no beginning or end, a caged animal sensing impending doom. Her knees weakened and she grabbed at the car nearest her, braced her palm on the cold metal for support.

A man reached for her arm. "Are you all right, miss? Are you sick? Can I help you?"

Linda's mouth moved before words came out. She felt a tingling in her fingers, a cool numbness. She squeezed her eyes shut, took a deep breath. "I'm all right," she sputtered. But she wasn't. There was an icy weakness in her stomach, and she could barely straighten up. "There was a man . . ." She gasped, not recognizing the voice as her own, then she stopped. There was nothing to say. The man was gone, a block away by now, a lifetime away she had thought.

But he wasn't. He was there.

She lurched away from the man and staggered to her car, fumbled for the right key. With trembling hands she was finally able to insert it in the lock. Then she slammed the door shut behind her and pushed the latch down with the meaty part of her palm. Tenuously safe inside the locked car, she sat breathing heavily, fearfully, her nostrils flaring catlike as she watched people hurry by. *Was he coming back?*

And in that one confused moment, it all came together and made sense. The man *was* there in West Ledge. He had followed her across the country, stalked her in Ohio, was in her house that first night! When she thought it was only the sounds of the old Victorian house she was hearing, she had really heard him, his footsteps on the stairs. When she was almost hit by the car, he had really been in front of her house. Watching her. Toying with her as he had before, laughing at her. Just waiting for the time he would kill her and Toby. The thoughts raged through her head, which was fogged now with fear. The car keys fell through her weakened fingers to the floor. Her hands twisted against each other in her lap. She was barely aware of the people passing by; her mind was turned inward. Fighting panic. Losing. *He was there.* She gagged. Her mouth was open and her breath came pantingly.

But suddenly a voice sounded from somewhere deep inside of her: Stop!

Dr. Valleau's voice. The psychiatrist she had seen in Los Angeles when she was hospitalized, then as an outpatient afterward. She had called him after Keith's death and he had seen her through the trauma. He had died shortly after her last visit.

She inhaled sharply, tried to calm herself, reached for Dr. Valleau. She needed him now, knew he would help her as he had before. She closed her eyes and tried to see him. He was sitting across his desk looking at her wisely. Behind him the Venetian blinds were slanted upward so only a soft, restful light filtered into the room. He was leaning back in his chair making steeples with his fingers, his compassionate eyes peering gently over his narrow nose and jowly face. She heard his voice, soft, almost hypnotic, as he reasoned with her, took her through her fears until she understood them, overcame them. And she could even imagine what he would say to her now.

She had been under terrible stress of late—Keith's death, then the struggle over the past year, the ride across country—*the mugging in Ohio*—all had taken their toll on her. She had been on edge, susceptible; that was why she was feeling panicky now. But she was in no danger.

Then she heard him question her as he had so many times. *How did she feel when she saw the man just now?*

"I felt afraid," she said out loud, her voice sounding strangely flat and hollow, stripped by fear. Her mouth was dry and gummy and she was starting to perspire in the stuffy car. But she recognized the importance of what she was doing. "At first I thought it was really him," she reasoned, "but then when I thought about it, I knew it couldn't have been, because from my therapy I know I'm in no danger now. As I was in no danger last time."

She was in complete control of herself, he would say to her. She had identified the sounds she had heard the first night as just house sounds, and undoubtedly that's what they were. No threat. The man she saw in the streetlight was just a man out enjoying the evening air as she was. No threat. And now the man she had seen was just a stranger with curly hair and a mustache. No threat. Her fear had come only from the shock of seeing a face that was so familiar. *But she was in no danger.*

There was a long moment of silence as she absorbed her thoughts, rolled them over in her mouth. Then she exhaled slowly and felt calmer, because that was what she wanted to believe.

She picked up the keys, started the car, and drove home slowly, cautiously, ignoring the honking of impatient motorists behind her. She was remaining in control of her emotions; her fear was in check.

Almost.

Because when she dressed and prepared to go out, she still couldn't help the undefined feeling of jeopardy that pricked at her, a sense of danger that while unconfirmed still seemed to exist—just out of sight, just out of touch.

And Dr. Valleau was dead.

Thomas arrived with Mrs. Green, an older woman with hair pulled back into a bun and a round face, seemingly frozen into a smile. Linda liked her immediately, and she and Toby took to each other like fish and water.

"Didn't I tell you so?" Thomas asked as they walked out to the car.

Linda tried to recall if she had heard Mrs. Green flip the door lock and was tempted to go back and check for herself, but she wiped the thought from her mind. Mrs. Green was responsible, and she wasn't going to be paranoid.

"How was your day?" Thomas asked as they rode along the outskirts of town, houses giving way to wooded fields. The sun had just set and the sky was a deep royal blue. "Did Don treat you well?"

"I didn't see much of him," she answered quietly. "He was tied up in meetings all day."

"I keep telling him he works too hard. How about the others?"

Linda made a face. "Did you have to ruin a perfectly lovely evening?" Then she told him about the secretaries.

"I can speak to Don about them," Thomas said, frowning.

"No, please don't. Let me handle it. I have to work with them. Their attitude toward me will soften in time, but not if I get them in trouble." She could almost see the smug look on Nancy's face if Thomas Devonshire called Don Robinson on her behalf.

"Okay. Play it your way for as long as you want, but call me if you need me."

"I promise," Linda said, knowing that that was a call she would never make.

The restaurant was across the state line, in New York. The parking lot was only partially filled; few people went out to dinner on a Monday night. Candles danced in glass holders, throwing shadows across the walls. A waiter came to ask about their drinks and Linda demurred, remembering what had happened at Eleanor's house.

Instead they ordered dinner, and then, after the waiter left, Thomas leaned across the table. The candle flame dazzled playfully across Linda's face, caressing her in a netting of shadow and light, giving her smooth skin almost a golden sheen in the flickering red-orange glow. Thomas was drawn to her softness and beauty and fought the impulse to touch her cheek. This wasn't a date, he reminded himself; she was his brother's wife. So instead he took a sip of water and over the rim of the glass looked at her with interested and probing eyes. "Well, Linda Devonshire," he said. "I really know very little about you except the fact that we share the same last name. So, clichéd as it might sound, why don't you tell me about yourself? I want all the vital statistics."

"What is it you'd like to know?" she asked, suddenly feeling shy and a little defensive. Being with her brother-in-law didn't make her feel uncomfortable, but she still felt she had to be a little guarded in what she said. While it was true that they shared the same last name, that was about all. Their lives had been so totally different. While hers had been simple, still it had been good and she was proud of it. She wanted to be careful not to denigrate in any way the life she had had with Keith.

They talked about their childhoods, Linda a street kid from urban Chicago, Thomas, born with a silver spoon in uppercrust Connecticut. He laughed when he told her about the private schools he attended, where everyone looked and acted as he did. "Upper-class clones." He grinned, denigrating his own life, as if embarrassed to be born into wealth. Then he complained that he could never get his hair to stay down as much as he greased and combed it, and Linda laughed, trying to picture him with his little preppy cowlick.

But behind her smile was unease. What she really wanted to talk about was what she was feeling, because she still remained troubled by all that had happened. She needed to talk to someone about it, but Dr. Valleau was dead and she was alone.

She couldn't say anything to Thomas. Not when he knew so much about her. He would think she was just being paranoid, unstable. Perhaps he and Eleanor would even try to put her in a hospital again. And if that occurred, what would become of Toby? She knew she ran the risk of losing her little girl.

So she decided to say nothing to Thomas, just endure her uneasiness on her own, overcome her fears herself. And if she needed to, she could always call another therapist.

Just making her decision made her feel more in control.

During dinner they talked about Keith. "My parents tried to make him into another me," Thomas said. "And that was a carbon copy of themselves. They should have let him live the way he wanted to, not try to make him into something he wasn't."

"Are you happy, Thomas?" Linda asked, and then, embarrassed, tried to take the question back. "I'm sorry. I didn't mean to ask. I—"

He waved her off. "I can answer that." He pursed his lips, searched for the right words. "Yes. My job is satisfying to me. I like the deal making, the thrill of the hunt, the legal shenanigans, the besting of my opponents. Probably in medieval days I would have been a champion jouster." Linda smiled and knew that he would have been.

Thomas studied his wineglass, absently playing with the stem. His fingers were long and slender. They could have belonged to a piano player, Linda noted.

"I do enjoy what I do and can't see myself doing anything else," he said. "I'm also very aware that it's all I do, and maybe that's something I don't like very much." Then he looked up at her and asked, "And you, Linda? Are you happy?"

The question caught her by surprise. She tightened her lips thoughtfully. "It's not been easy for me since Keith's death. And in a way I still feel like I'm in mourning and I don't know how happy I can allow myself to be."

"That doesn't sound healthy."

"Probably not," she agreed.

"I'm sure Keith wouldn't want you to feel this way. He'd want you to pick up and go on with your life." Thomas smiled. "From the little I knew Keith, I would say he would demand it."

The shadows in the room hid the blush from Linda's face. Talking about Keith was making her feel prickly. She didn't want to voice her feelings about her husband. They were private and not to be shared with anyone, not even his brother. "I know that," she said softly, and felt a lump forming in her throat. "And I'm working at my feelings. But it's hard sometimes. Especially at night. Sometimes I reach out for him—forgetting. I had a lot of myself invested in him." The other night in the new house she had taken a shower and become disoriented in the steam of the hot water. And suddenly the clock was turned back. Keith wasn't dead and they were all together in West Ledge, as a family.

Her eyes flicked away, toward the decorative gas lamps that lined the walls of the restaurant. Thomas saw how uncomfortable she was and turned the conversation to more inconsequential subjects. He watched Linda visibly relax after they stopped talking about Keith. But he was curious about his younger brother. There was something almost romantic about the life-style he had led—so different from that of the rest of the Devonshire family. And of course there was the woman he had chosen.

After they finished eating, a small band started to play. Thomas extended his hand across the table. "Shall we?" he asked and Linda accepted with a smile.

As he led her across the floor, Linda leaned her cheek against his shoulder. Involuntarily she closed her eyes, drew closer to

him. It was the first time she had been held by a man since
Keith's death, and it felt good. She thought she felt Thomas's
body shimmer. She was enjoying herself too, lost to the music
and the mood.

When the set was over they took their seats and ordered second
cups of coffee.

After a third cup Linda leaned back in her chair. There was a
lull in the conversation, and she looked at her watch and was
surprised.

"It's almost twelve, Thomas. I had no idea!"

He was surprised as well. "It seems as if we just sat down."
He signaled for the check. "I'd better get you home. Tomorrow
is a workday."

Linda groaned. "Don't remind me." She hadn't thought about
Nancy for hours. And she had also forgotten, at least for the
moment, about being afraid. "I think I could sit here all night."

"It was fun, wasn't it?" he asked her and smiled.

Few cars were out that late and the ride home was too fast.
The radio played soft music, and Linda rested her head against
the window. Low-hanging tree branches framed the road like a
protective canopy, and a small apple orchard spread out on both
sides of them. She let her eyes close. She felt comfortable, at
ease. Safe. When they pulled into her driveway, Thomas shut off
the engine. The living-room lamp was on and they saw the wavy,
changing patterns of television lights. Thomas looked at the clock
on the dashboard. "I'd better get Mrs. Green home so she can
get up tomorrow."

He held Linda's arm as they walked up the steps. The night
breeze played in her hair, the air so fresh and clear it was almost
sinful to go inside and waste it. She could make a fortune
bottling it and shipping it back to Los Angeles.

Mrs. Green opened the door and beamed. "Toby was such a
delight. I'll sit with her anytime."

Thomas reached for his wallet to pay Mrs. Green, but immediately understood when Linda touched his arm and stopped him.
She wanted to be independent and not rely on him for help.

"Thank you again," the older woman said, then Thomas
asked her to wait in the car so he could say good night to Linda.

When Mrs. Green was out of earshot, he hesitated. "Can we
do this again?" he asked. "I'd like to."

Linda smiled. "So would I."

"I have to be out of town until Saturday, when my mother is having a barbecue. Would you and Toby like to come with me?"

Linda hesitated. "I don't know."

"Mother insisted I bring a date, and I've decided it's going to be the two of you." Then he smiled broadly. "Actually, she told me I'd better bring you and Toby or else. It's an annual social event and she really wants you to come, Linda."

Linda smiled. "Then I'd be delighted to."

There was an awkward moment between them. Finally Linda tilted her head up toward Thomas and kissed him on the lips. Briefly. But it had sealed the evening.

She climbed the stairs to the second floor. She was feeling relaxed and was certain she would sleep soundly.

First she checked on Toby; stood in the doorway as the hall light flooded in; saw the gentle rise and fall of the covers. Her child was asleep and safe.

Then she whispered the distant fear she had felt all evening. "I'll never go away again, baby, I promise."

"Hello . . ." Thomas picked up the phone. There was a pause and click. Whoever it was had hung up. Luckily he hadn't been asleep yet. He always had trouble falling back to sleep when awakened in the middle of the night. But now he didn't know if he'd even be able to get to sleep. With three cups of coffee sloshing around inside of him, he expected to be awake for hours. But it was more than that.

He glanced at his desk. He had brought work home earlier, not expecting the dinner to run half as long as it had, but even though he was wide awake now, he didn't feel like doing any. Usually he was such a master of time, but tonight he had completely lost control of it. The realization both pleased him and frightened him. He hadn't so enjoyed the company of a woman in a very long time, since—Sandra? he wondered, and felt no, before Sandra, a fling in college, a girl he never could have brought home to his parents. Now there was Linda—so charming, easy to talk to, pleasurable to be with. Not at all like the women he usually dated. She was unpretentious, lovely in her simplicity. Pretty. He couldn't pinpoint the first moment he felt attracted to her, but it had happened. It was just too bad that she was his sister-in-law.

And also, he smiled ruefully, someone he couldn't bring home to his mother.

Eleanor replaced the phone. He was home. She glanced at the clock, noted the late hour.

And she supposed *she* was home too.

She had guessed when she called Thomas earlier in the evening and no one was home that they were somewhere together. On impulse she had called Linda's house and was not surprised when a babysitter answered. She was out, the woman said, could she take a message? No, Eleanor had answered. She would call again tomorrow.

She went upstairs and climbed into bed, unable to remember now why she had wanted to reach Thomas before.

Beatrice Dailey couldn't sleep; she was feeling troubled, itchy, something was disturbing her. She flipped on the bedroom light, opened her night-table drawer, and took out the picture. It was a faded snapshot, fingerprinted and wrinkled from being held too much. It had been taken at a ski club in Mt. Snow, Vermont. The high school class had gone together. It was supposed to be boys sharing rooms with boys, girls with girls, but it wasn't that way.

A sad smile appeared on Beatrice's face as she thought about the weekend. It was the first time she had made love, and the memory of every beautiful moment had stayed with her since. With a heavy sigh of remembrance and loss, she brought the picture to her mouth and brushed Keith Devonshire's lips with hers.

Then she frowned. She now knew the woman who had taken Keith away from her.

chapter 10

Even when Linda had worked for temporary employment agencies and was sent from company to company, she still had more human contact than she was getting now. Although she suspected that Helen was slowly softening to her and in time might even become her friend, there was no change to the lunchtime clique; they still treated her as if she were the enemy.

Friday morning Linda looked at her hand and ticked off fingers. Only the pinky remained. She had survived four days and only this one loomed ahead of her until the weekend. Eight more hours. Thankfully Thomas had called every day to see how she was; he was a friendly voice that was definitely needed. So! she announced to herself. I have Thomas, I have Toby, and I have me. I'll just grit my teeth and tough out the day. And next week. And the following. And I won't let Nancy or Louise or Rhoda or the late Suzanne get to me.

Nancy arrived late that morning, twirling and parading like a fashion model. The other secretaries soon gathered at the front of the office. Rhoda whistled appreciatively. "New outfit, Nancy?"

"Everything!" She beamed. "Designer suit—" She unbuttoned the jacket and casually swung it over her shoulder. "Blouse. And boots!" She lifted her skirt to model the knee-high boots. "Two hundred dollars."

"You must have been saving for quite some time for clothes like that," Helen said, a bit awed.

"No," Nancy said breezily. "Not at all. And I've got a new jacket at home too. And some other things."

"What did you do—knock over a liquor store?" Louise joked. "Or win the lottery?"

"Let's just say I came into a little unexpected money," Nancy said cryptically.

"A little unexpected money." Louise turned the phrase over. "I got it. She killed her boyfriend and made off with the insurance."

"Maybe," Nancy said casually over the laughter, and glanced at Linda. She walked past her to the hallway and over her shoulder shot her a passing smile. Not a warm smile, Linda noticed, but why would she expect one?

Nor did she really expect to be included later that morning when Nancy announced, "Lunch is on me." And the three regulars walked past her and out the reception doors.

The children were scattered across the grassy schoolyard, tossing balls, jumping ropes, flipping baseball cards, and trading sandwiches. Carol Ann and Toby were late in coming out to lunch, wanting to finish a nature project they were working on together—a special display of pressed and mounted leaves.

Carol Ann pointed to the corner of the yard where three boys were eating lunch, gesticulating in animated conversation. Toby had met Petey, Eric, and Mitchell the first day of the summer program. They lived on the same block as the girls and had readily accepted Toby as a friend.

Toby and Carol Ann joined the boys and opened their lunch bags. Mitchell was talking about a movie he had stayed up late to see on television. "It was about someone who got killed," he said excitedly. "But he came back to life again as someone else to get revenge on the guy who killed him."

"I know all about that stuff," Eric interrupted knowledgeably. "It's called reincarnation. They got people in India who come back as cows and stuff. Sometimes insects and spiders."

"I don't believe any of that," Petey said definitively. "Dead is dead." He turned to the girls. "Did your fathers ever come back?"

Both girls shook their heads.

"See!" he said triumphantly.

"That doesn't prove anything." Eric pointed to a tree limb where a sparrow had perched and was pecking at something. "For all they know that could be one of their fathers now."

"My mother would probably come back as a fish," Carol Ann said. "Given how much she likes water."

"I think you might be part right, Eric," Mitchell said sagely. "I think I once heard that when people die they only come back as people. Not cows or anything. But nobody ever remembers their past lives, so you can't really prove anything."

His words hung over the table. The concept was so interesting that nobody had any comment to offer.

"That's only good people," Eric said, having mulled over the question and arrived at a conclusion. "Bad people can come back as pigs or snakes. Hey, I got an idea!" He snapped his fingers. "Let's make a pact—all of us." His finger went around the table, rested for an extended moment on each of them, and his voice grew low and mysterious as he slowly said their names. "Whichever one of us dies first—whoever it is—he or she has to come back and contact the others." He paused to let the import of his words sink in.

Petey reacted first. "I think the whole idea is dumb." He tried to rally support at the table, but Eric cut him off.

"That's because you're afraid."

"Who's afraid?"

"So make the pact." Eric shrugged.

"Sure. How?"

Eric thought fast. "We all touch each other's hands and swear," he said, and there was a sudden spark in his eyes that the others couldn't miss. He extended his hand. "Look, I'm in," he said with a cloud of mystery.

"This is dumb," Petey said, "but here—" And he put his hand on top of Eric's. Mitchell followed, and the boys turned to the girls. Carol Ann and Toby exchanged glances, then together they put their hands in.

"Now swear," Eric said. Toby and Carol Ann suddenly were nervous about what they were swearing to. It all seemed so forbidden, so dangerous, so spooky. As if just talking about dying could make it happen.

At five o'clock Linda felt free. She covered her typewriter, said good night to the others, and sailed out of the building. On the way home she picked up a pizza and an apple pie. It was the weekend and they were celebrating.

Then she went to the cleaners. When the rest of their clothes had arrived from California, they had been wrinkled after being in a trunk for two weeks. The cleaner got her order off the rack and draped it across the counter. "That's thirty even," he said.

As Linda gave him the money, she saw her good cream-colored dress—and her eyes widened in surprise. The dress had a row of coral buttons running the length, and half of them were missing.

"Excuse me," she said, "but where are the rest of the buttons?"

The cleaner rang up the bill and put the money into the cash register. He looked briefly at the dress. "That's the way it was brought in."

Linda startled. "That is certainly *not* the way it was brought in."

The cleaner produced his ticket. "Here. Read." Linda looked at the buff-colored slip of paper and saw the scrawl: missing buttons.

She felt a flush of red cover her face. She tried to remain calm but felt a tension spawning within her, a tightness in her stomach, and unconsciously her fists were clenching.

"I'm sorry, but I know that the dress had all the buttons when I brought it in."

"Yeah?" the man challenged. "And this says it didn't."

"I don't care what it says," Linda flared.

"Can't help you, lady," the cleaner snapped, and turned his attention to the drive-in window, where someone was dropping off a load. Stiffly, Linda waited until he was free.

"I won't accept this dress the way it is," she said in a shaky voice laced with forming tears. She struggled for control.

"Look, lady, I don't know what you want me to do."

"I want you to repair the dress. It had all the buttons!" Her closed fist pounded against the counter.

The cleaner considered her for a moment. Then he picked up the clothes and practically threw them at her. "I don't want your business, okay? Just take it somewhere else and don't come back here again."

Linda didn't move. She tried calming herself and fought tears of frustration that were welling inside of her.

"I won't accept this dress," she repeated, her voice thick. "I want those missing buttons replaced."

"And I want you out of my store—"

"I'll sue you," she threatened. "I work for a law firm and it won't cost me anything—"

She held the cleaner's eye for a long moment and prayed for the strength not to break. Then the man grabbed the dress, pulled it out from underneath the plastic, and heaved it across the counter so it fell to the floor.

"I'll do what I can," he said gruffly, angrily. "I'll call you when it's done. Now get out of here!"

Linda grabbed up her other clothes and stormed out of the store, only to realize that she hadn't taken back her receipt. Now the cleaner could claim she picked up everything, and she had no proof to the contrary. But she didn't want to go back in again and face another confrontation.

When she got home the pizza was cold and she had to reheat it. She was still bristling from what had happened and found herself snapping at Toby for no cause. She knew she couldn't take her frustrations out on the little girl so she tried to improve her mood. They watched *Family Feud*, then played a spirited game of dominoes, Linda watching as Toby pulled a double-six out of nowhere and walked off with the prize.

Later, Toby got into her pajamas and slipped under the covers. When Linda flipped off the light and plunged the room into darkness, the little girl suddenly remembered the lunchtime conversation and the possibility of her own mortality. The darkness seemed to accent the forbidden nature of what they had sworn to.

"Mommy, wait."

"Yes, dear?" Linda came back and sat down on the edge of Toby's bed. A triangle of light from the hallway streamed into the room.

Toby shrugged, embarrassed suddenly by her fears but needing to voice them nonetheless. "Some of the kids were talking about dying today."

"Dying?" Linda raised her eyebrows. "That's not a very *lively* topic of conversation now, is it?"

Toby smiled at the pun but continued to work her thoughts, and told her mother about the reincarnation discussion and the oath they had taken. "Do people come back after they're dead?" she asked. "Did Daddy come back anywhere?"

Linda immediately saw what was troubling her daughter. "I

don't want you to worry about that silly pact you made, honey. God knows that children do that sort of thing all the time, and it doesn't mean anything at all.''

Toby smiled, relieved. That was all she wanted to hear. She held her arms out. "Good night, Mommy."

Linda kissed her forehead. "Good night, baby. Sleep well." She watched Toby close her eyes and twist onto her side. And as she slipped out of the door she heard her daughter's soft voice. "Good night, Daddy." Almost a prayer.

After the door was closed, Toby lay awake in her bed, comforted by her mother's words. God knew the pact wasn't real and she was glad. She figured dying was probably frightening enough; she didn't want to have God angry at her too. But still she couldn't fall asleep. She watched shadows play across her wall, and listened to the sounds of the night outside her window—crickets chirping, frogs croaking. And she vowed she would never make vows like that again.

Linda went into her room and flopped down on the bed. It was still too early to go to sleep, so she thumbed idly through a magazine. Evenings had always been her least favorite time of day. Toby was put to bed and Keith was out working and she was all alone in the quiet house. She should have counted her blessings back then, she thought. At least then Keith was home at midnight. Now . . .

She was too tired to read. She put the magazine down on the bed and stared blankly at the opposite wall. Paint was peeling in spots and there was a stain of water damage near the ceiling, but it was nothing that had to be attended to.

At nine o'clock the ringing phone shattered the silence and made her jump. She reached across the bed and picked it up.

"I've been thinking about you."

"Thomas!" Her mood changed immediately. "How's business?"

"All wrapped up. We had the celebration dinner tonight. A bunch of lonely businessmen drinking too much and pretending they're having a good time." He paused, then said, "The dinner wasn't half as much fun as if you had been here too."

Linda laughed, flattered by his words.

"How was your day?" Thomas asked. Linda resolved to say

nothing about the incident with the cleaners unless she ended up not getting satisfaction the following week.

"Guess what!" she exclaimed. "I got a paycheck today." She thought about the take-home check of $193. Not much, but certainly a start. "You know a good bank where I can open an account?"

"Oh, I might. And you get your choice of personalized checks. I happen to have a form right here. Would you like Scenes from Americana? Animals of the World? Or basic gray? You don't have to answer right away."

"Nope, that's an easy one," Linda said. "Basic gray-itude. And don't forget, ten percent off the top goes to pay back what I owe you. Or rather, I should say, to start paying back."

"Whatever," Thomas said, embarrassed by the conversation. Then he asked, "How were the girls today?"

"I think there might be a breakthrough with one of them," Linda joked. "She calls me by my name. But I still eat alone. It's not too bad, but could be better. Nancy—she's the ringleader—paraded around in a whole new wardrobe today. None of the others could figure out where she got the money to buy it. I think she's just trying to get to me, prove that she's better or something." A shrug. "But I'm not going to let it bother me."

"We can always get you new clothes too."

"No. I don't want to stoop to her game. Nor would that endear me to the others. No," she said easily. "I think I'll just go on being Linda Devonshire, the girl from the wrong side of the tracks."

"Don't say that," Thomas said, almost sharply. "Don't ever say that. Don't let what my parents did to you in the past affect how you see yourself now. You have more style and charm than women with loads more money." Then his intensity calmed and he yawned.

"Tired?" Linda asked.

"Beyond belief. Being charming with computer salesmen takes a lot out of you. I am going to sleep now. I'll pick you guys up tomorrow for the barbecue."

"Good night, Thomas," Linda said. Smiling, she replaced the phone, then spun around on one foot, did a high kick—extending her leg as far as it would go, trying to bring it level with her shoulder—and almost made it. The strain in her calf and hamstring made her groan. She bent at the waist and touched her toes a half dozen times, then reached above her and stretched to the ceiling. She twirled around the room and inhaled deeply. She felt good, buoyed by talking with Thomas. No longer lonely.

And now she was dreamily tired. She stretched again, yawned, and unzipped her dress. She slipped out of it in front of the open window, let the breeze play against her. She rubbed the smoothness of her slip, teased her nipples. Then she realized the light was on and she was visible from the street. She quickly switched off the lamp. The sudden darkness was comforting. She turned her head, looked out the window.

She saw the man under the streetlamp for only a second. His shadow was long and bisected the circle of light. Then he stepped out of the light and was swallowed up by the night. He had been looking up at her, she knew.

Suddenly she felt exposed. Only a thin slip covered her nakedness. How long had he been watching her? How much had he seen?

Stupid! She scolded herself for having been in front of the window with the light on. Then she pulled down the shade, but it was like shutting the barn door after the horses had escaped.

It wasn't paranoia; he had been looking at her. He had walked out of the splash of light only after she had turned her light off. Was he still out there? Hiding behind a hedge? Watching? Waiting? With the shade drawn, she turned the lamp back on. The window shade was opaque; he wouldn't be able to see in at all.

Stop it. She was being ridiculous. There was no one there anymore. It was just a passerby, attracted to the light, to the woman undressing. Then, embarrassed by being caught, he had ducked away. Or even nothing at all—her eyes playing tricks on her. No man in the streetlight, only the streetlight's own shadow in its circle of light.

The sudden sound made her heart freeze and the feathery hairs on her neck prickle. A faint play of metal. A grating sound. The jiggling of a twisting doorknob turning a quarter inch in each direction and no more, stopped by the lock mechanism.

She held her breath, traced the sound.

Someone was trying to open the kitchen door!

At first she stood frozen. "No," she moaned. "Please no—" The door was locked, she knew that. He couldn't get in through there. The house was secured, protected, unless he broke a window. She grabbed for the phone, dialed the operator. At first it didn't ring through. "Come on, come on—" She hit her fist against her leg.

The jiggling stopped.

Thank God, she breathed.

The pounding began—angry, sharp raps against the door.

He was trying to break in!

"Please hurry," she croaked into the ringing phone.

The operator wasn't finished speaking before Linda gasped. "I need the police." She was put through right away. She reported her name, her location, that there was an intruder, someone was trying to break in. He was there now! "Hurry, please!"

It was as if he knew she had called the police. The pounding stopped. He was gone. She was safe.

She wasn't.

She still felt him, *smelled* him. He was somewhere outside, watching her.

Toying with her.

A strangled moan escaped her lips as if someone was choking her from the inside, because she knew he could get in any time he wanted; he had been in the house before!

Hurriedly she threw on her long terry robe. Within seconds she heard the screech of police sirens as they turned into her block. She raced downstairs, flung open the front door.

She saw the familiar face and inhaled sharply, deeply, an intake of surprise. But her gasp was cut off as the night breeze gusted and a cleaner's plastic clothing bag was caught by the sudden swirl. Ballooned by the wind, it whipped into the room, touched Linda's face, clung to her skin like sticky paper, molded to her features. She didn't realize what it was; she thought the man was trying to strangle her. Startled, terrified, she tried to scream, but only sucked the plastic into her open mouth. Unable to breathe, she grew panicky and clawed at the bag, ripped it off her, dashed it to the porch, then stepped back and squealed from her pent-up terror.

The cleaner with whom she had had the confrontation was staring at her and behind him two uniformed policemen were hurrying up the front walk. Linda's eyes went from the cleaner to the policemen to the porch floor where her cream-colored dress was lying in a crumpled heap in a tattered plastic bag, having been yanked from the cleaner's grasp. Her glance told her all the buttons had been sewed back on the dress.

One of the policemen spoke first. "What's going on here?"

The cleaner growled. "Nothing's going on. I just delivered this to her." A sour look crossed his face and he spat out contemptuously, "I did her a favor, that's all." Then he pointed to the dress on the floor, his scowl suddenly turning into an amused expression. "Now you did this, lady, and we both have witnesses, so don't bring it back to me tomorrow and say that *I* wrinkled it."

Linda still hadn't caught her breath. "Was that you before?" she barked to the cleaner. "At the kitchen door." She looked helplessly toward the policemen. "Someone—"

The cleaner interrupted. His face furrowed exasperatedly and he circled his temple with his forefinger. "You're crazy, lady, you know." Then he turned to the officers and shrugged again. "I only tried to do her a favor . . ."

One of the policemen touched her arm. She yanked it away, then composed herself, tried to show them she was in control, but her face was still drained of color.

"Are you all right?" the policeman asked. He was peering at her.

She nodded because she couldn't find her voice. "Yes, yes, I am," she finally said. "I didn't know it was him," she explained blankly. "I thought—" She shook her head as she looked from one man to the next. "I'm sorry I called you."

The policeman smiled kindly. "There's no danger, Mrs. Devonshire. You were just confused. Don't be afraid anymore, okay?"

"Okay." Linda nodded numbly. "Thank you, Officer—"

"Saul. Lock up behind us now, will you?"

"Yes. Thank you again for coming."

She locked the door, flipped the bolt, then turned and leaned against the door for several minutes catching her breath.

Finally the color returned to her face, although the worried thought still pricked at her: The cleaner hadn't answered her question. Had it been him *before*? When she had heard the kitchen doorknob?

She quickly answered herself. Of course it had been. People in the country always use the back doors. When no one answered, he had gone around to the front. She had taken the sound, twisted it, created danger when there wasn't any.

But why didn't he knock the first time? Why did he try to open the door?

When there wasn't any.

She knelt down and picked up the dress, draped it over the couch, tried to smooth out the wrinkles. It would have to be repressed, but she would deal with that later.

She swallowed as the feeling passed over her. She was being watched. *The house was watching her.* She turned around and faced the empty room, mockingly still, seemingly *interested.* As if asking: What's going to happen next?

Nothing, she said to herself. Nothing at all. The scare was over.

Exhausted suddenly, she turned off the downstairs lights and started up the steps.

First she checked on Toby. The child, a heavy sleeper, had mercifully slept through everything. She watched her daughter in sleep, her knees tucked toward her chin, her blond hair splayed across her face.

She had to be strong for Toby. She knew that if she ever lost her control and they took her away to a hospital again, she might lose her little girl. God, she couldn't even think of living without her.

She went into her own bedroom. The light was harsh and, even with the shade drawn, made her feel exposed. She switched it off, welcomed the darkness. Then she stole a glance behind the shades, steeled herself to meet a face outside the window.

There was nobody. No face on the other side of the glass. No figure standing in the streetlight. *Nobody at the top of the stairs.*

"No!" she said out loud and wiped the disturbing thought from her mind. *She was in control!*

Even though it was still early, she slid under the covers and pulled them up to her chin, trying to lose herself to the oblivion of sleep. But she lay awake in bed, eyes open, heart pounding, listening, as her daughter had, to the sounds of the night—crickets, frogs, and the jiggling of a doorknob, footsteps on the stairs, and the hollow thud of a knife as it was embedded into a wooden post.

chapter 11

It was going to be a glorious day: the temperature in the sixties, the sun high and strong. Perfect weather for a barbecue.

But after the scare last night, Linda didn't feel up to spending the afternoon with Eleanor and meeting a lot of people from the town. Yet she didn't want to disappoint Thomas and not go.

She languished in bed. There was security with the covers around her. But she knew she couldn't hide forever. Finally she stepped into the shower and turned it on as hot as she could stand it, let the water rage over her to try to cleanse herself of what had happened last night. She had mistaken an innocent knock on the door for something ominous, had again felt threatened when there was no threat.

But as she dried herself and brushed her hair, she couldn't escape the slithering feeling that there was still something wrong, someone out there who really wanted to hurt her. She shook her head sadly—*paranoia*. That was the only word for it. She had reason enough to know there was no threat. That's what therapy had taught her. Still, she wanted to tell Thomas how she was feeling, if only for them both to laugh and stem her fears. That was all she really needed, but she knew she couldn't risk his reaction.

She announced to Toby's applause that there would be a special Saturday morning breakfast at the Pancake House. Perhaps her daughter's favorite breakfast would lift her spirits as well.

When they returned home, their stomachs full, Carol Ann was sitting on her front step. Her knees were drawn forlornly up to

her chin. The boys had all gone off somewhere without her. It
was Saturday and she had no one to play with.

"You can play with us," Linda said. "We had nothing special
planned."

Carol Ann brightened. "I'll ask my mother."

Moments later Beatrice Dailey appeared in the doorway, fitting
a wide brim hat on her head. "I was just going shopping," she
said. "I planned on taking Carol Ann with me. But she tells me
she'd rather stay here and play with Toby."

"I'm happy to watch her," Linda said. "We don't have to be
anywhere until three."

"I'll be back before then." Beatrice looked critically at Linda.
"I suppose it's all right."

"Of course it is," Linda said in a hale, too-friendly voice. "I
have experience in watching children, believe me."

"Yes, all right. Thank you." Beatrice started for her car,
turned back toward Carol Ann. "Now don't you give Mrs.
Devonshire any trouble, okay? I'll be back in several hours."

They watched her back down the driveway and turn into the
street. Linda eyed Carol Ann; the child seemed to grow happier
as her mother drove out of sight. It saddened her to think the
little girl felt that way about her mother, but what contact she had
had with Beatrice confirmed Carol Ann's reaction to her.

After the girls played jacks and hopscotch, Linda served cook-
ies and milk. The two girls ate hungrily on the front steps. When
Linda went inside, Carol Ann said, "Your mother is very nice."

"Yes," Toby agreed.

"Does she ever punish you?"

Toby shook her head. "No."

"Mine does," Carol Ann said. "She punishes me a lot." And
she proceeded to tell Toby all about her mother's method of
punishment. Toby listened, horrified. All the kids had once
compared punishments, Carol Ann said, and after a vote was
taken, they unanimously agreed that hers was the worst.
"Sometimes I wish that someone would come and just take my
mother away," she said. "I know I shouldn't be saying that but I
do."

Toby nodded in tentative agreement. She understood how her
friend felt, but her words were unsettling. She remembered the

time *her* mother was away, and that was certainly nothing she ever wanted to have happen again.

"Do you ever skate?" she asked Carol Ann, to change the subject. "All the kids in California do."

"My mother is afraid I'd get hurt," Carol Ann said glumly. "How do you stop anyway?"

"It's easy," Toby said. She went inside and got her skates, attached them to her shoes. Then she skated to the next house, dragged the wheels against the sidewalk, and rolled to a gentle stop. "See? Let's race to that house on the corner."

Carol Ann took off on foot and Toby gathered speed and momentum and crossed the finish line first. Then they walked back to Toby's house. The front door was open and Toby saw her mother inside, dusting the furniture.

"Can I try the skates?" Carol Ann asked.

"Sure." Toby took them off and showed Carol Ann how to attach them to her shoes. Up on the wheels, Carol Ann lost her balance and flopped forward. The girls laughed. Toby took her hand and started to pull her up the sidewalk, Carol Ann flailing her other arm like a tightrope walker.

"That's it!" Toby said triumphantly, as she let go and Carol Ann rolled up the street. Then she practiced stopping and starting and had a grand time.

"It *is* easy!" Carol Ann said, wondering why her mother thought skates were dangerous. "Race you to the corner house. Like before," she said. "Let's go!"

Toby got off first. Carol Ann tried to catch her, took running steps, churned the wheels faster and faster. The finish line was looming and she was gaining, both children laughing wildly.

"I win!" Carol Ann said as she sailed across the line. Then she realized she was in trouble. She was rolling too fast and couldn't stop herself. The corner was fast approaching.

Toby saw the danger. "Stop!" she screamed. "Fall down!"

But Carol Ann couldn't bring herself to drop to the concrete sidewalk.

A delivery truck was trying to beat the impending red light. The driver was watching for cars on the cross street. Only out of the corner of his eye did he see the little girl on skates, careening out of control toward the curb and into his path.

At the same time Beatrice Daily rounded the corner to see

Carol Ann skating into the path of the truck. "Carol Ann!" she yelled, but time seemed suspended. She was helpless to do anything except watch and wait for the inevitable.

The driver slammed on the brakes, swerved, skidded, and stopped short as the girl sailed over the curb and inches in front of him. Then she fell in a heap as her skates caught in a dip in the street.

Beatrice and the driver jumped out of their vehicles. Carol Ann was picking herself up. Her knees were skinned and she was badly shaken, aware of what almost had happened. "Mommy," she cried.

"She just skated out in front of me," the driver said. "You saw her. Thank God I stopped in time." Since everything was all right, he climbed back into his truck, shaking his head angrily, and sped off.

Linda came running up the street, alerted by Toby's screams and the squeal of the truck's tires. In a flash she took in the scene, ascertained that Carol Ann was all right, then saw the look on Beatrice's face.

"Is this how you watch my daughter!" Beatrice screamed at her. "She's lucky she wasn't killed!"

"I was inside," Linda said. "They were playing right out in front . . ."

"It was an accident," Carol Ann said. "We were racing on the skates."

"Where did you get those skates?" Beatrice demanded.

Toby was frightened by the incident, by Beatrice's fury. "T-they're mine," she stammered in a tiny voice. "I lent them to her."

"And who gave you permission?"

Linda protectively pulled Toby close to her. "I will not have you yell at my child."

"I will yell at you!" Beatrice said. "I left you responsible for Carol Ann and she was almost killed because you weren't attentive to her. You were negligent!"

"I wasn't hurt, Mommy," Carol Ann cried, trying to protect her new friend and her mother.

"By the grace of God," Beatrice said. "By the grace of God." She turned back to Linda, pointed a finger at her. "And you thank God, too, that nothing happened to my child." She grabbed Carol Ann by the elbow. "Take off those skates this second. You knew how I felt about skates yet you deliberately . . ." She shook the child's arm and Linda watched helplessly as Carol Ann's entire body seemed to go limp.

"I'm going to punish you, Carol Ann," Beatrice said.

Linda and Toby walked slowly back to the house, the two roller skates clanging against each other as Toby held their straps. They watched Beatrice swing into her driveway, then roughly pull Carol Ann out of the car and toward the house. Beatrice was bobbing her head and shaking her free finger, obviously yelling, although they couldn't hear what she was saying. There was no missing Carol Ann's fear and reluctance to go with her mother, as she tried to hold back and stand her ground outside. But Beatrice's strength prevailed and soon they were up the porch stairs and inside the house, the door slamming shut behind them.

"I got her into trouble," Toby said. Tears started to roll down her face as the little girl felt the pain of her friend.

"It was all an accident, baby," Linda said, and tried to pick up her daughter's spirits. Later when Thomas arrived, even the new beaded sweater he brought for the girl couldn't elicit more than a grim thank you.

"Hey—where's that famous Devonshire smile?" he asked, widening his own with his fingers to make a funny face.

Toby tried, but her smile came out lopsided. Linda told him what had happened. Thomas knelt down and spoke to Toby. "It wasn't your fault, okay? You didn't know she was going to have trouble." He coaxed the corners of her mouth upward. "So come on now—let's put on a happy face for Grandma." Thomas poked her in the belly to make her laugh. But her smile fell as they pulled out of the driveway and she saw Carol Ann's house, and wondered what was happening now to her friend inside.

The Devonshire house was bathed in warm sunlight and touched by shadows of shade trees that ringed it on three sides. As they rode up the circular drive, the house didn't seem as imposing as it once had. Still Linda had no real sense of welcome—either from the house or from its owner—and she wondered why Eleanor had invited her.

Eleanor's hair was piled high on her head and a high lace

collar hugged her neck. She knelt down and kissed Toby.
"How's Patricia?" she whispered.

"Fine."

"You take good care of her and one day you can pass her on
to your little girl too." She patted her granddaughter's hand
affectionately as Toby giggled at the thought of a child of her
own. Then Eleanor straightened up and extended her hand to
Linda. "Hello, dear, how are you? I'm so glad you could come
today."

"I wouldn't have missed it," Linda answered. "Thank you for
inviting us."

"Well, as long as you've decided to stay in West Ledge, I
couldn't very well have my annual barbecue without the two of
you, could I?" She smiled, and Linda suspected that that would
be the only reference she would make to what had transpired
between them last. "Come," Eleanor prompted, grasping Toby's
hand.

Thomas linked arms with Linda and they followed Eleanor and
Toby onto the patio. The pool water was a deep blue, and in the
windless air its surface was almost glasslike. The grounds were
perfectly banked and manicured and not a stray leaf dotted the
grass. A tent had been erected, under which uniformed bartend-
ers were setting up. A gas grill was already aflame, waiting for
the trays full of marinated steaks. A dozen tables were scattered
around the yard, with china, silver, and floral centerpieces. This
was a social *event,* Linda saw.

"I asked you to come a little earlier than the others so we
could spend a few minutes together," Eleanor said. "Would you
like a drink? Some lemonade? Or perhaps something stronger?"

"Lemonade is fine for us," Linda said.

"Tell me, dear," Eleanor said as she poured the glasses.
"Thomas said you were having some difficulties at the office
with one of the secretaries. Is that true? Can I do anything to help
you? I've known Don Robinson and the other partners for quite a
few years. I could say something if you'd like me to. It can be
rather unpleasant in a work environment if your associates are
unkind."

"Oh, no," Linda said. "Everything's changed from the first
day. I just had to show I was a permanent fixture around that
place and nothing was going to shake me loose." She could see

Nancy's face—Thomas Devonshire's *mother* calling to complain about her. "Nothing I can't handle." She dismissed it.

Toby was quietly sipping the lemonade and peering at a squirrel frozen in the yard, gnawing on a nut.

"What a lovely, lovely child," Eleanor said. "I can't get over it. You know, I always wanted a little girl. To take shopping with me. To dress up. I was blessed with two fine sons, but I always felt something was missing by not having a daughter. Will you be my little girl, Toby?"

Toby nodded hesitantly and worked the troubling thought through. "Would you ever punish me?"

"Punish you! Good heavens! Never!"

"Carol Ann gets punished a lot," Toby said, and then everything that Carol Ann told her came tumbling out. "Her mother punishes her by putting her head in the sink, under the water!"

"No!" Linda said, shocked. "Someone should report it or something. There have got to be laws—"

"Whoa," Thomas said, holding up his hand to stop her. "Let's calm down. First off, Beatrice Dailey is a well-respected woman in this community. Second, there are no marks on Carol Ann. And third, different parents have different methods of disciplining a child. Maybe Carol Ann was only exaggerating anyway. In any event, I don't think you'll be able to accomplish anything by calling attention to the matter."

"Well, it still seems a bit cruel," Eleanor said. "But I think you're right in that it is none of our affair." Then she turned to Toby. "Would you like to come with me for a second, dear? I want to show you my private greenhouse." She reached for the little girl's hand and Toby took it eagerly. She felt close to her grandmother; she liked her.

Thomas and Linda watched them walk down the slated path. "I think they've each found a new friend." Thomas smiled.

"I'm glad," Linda said, although she couldn't help but feel a prickle of unease watching her daughter disappear into the greenhouse with Eleanor. She had a strange feeling of finality as Toby passed through the door.

Inside, Eleanor opened up a gated section. "My prize roses," she said proudly, sweeping her hand across the array of reds and pinks. "Every year I enter them in a competition. I won first place five years in a row. Aren't they lovely?" Toby nodded and watched a bee dance from flower to flower. "Maybe you'll come here and help me tend them some time. Would you like that?"

"Yes, Grandma."

Eleanor knelt down and took Toby's hands in hers and looked at her smilingly. "I can't get over how much you resemble Keith. I can see him in you when he was your age. The same nose and eyes—" She touched Toby's mouth lightly and made her giggle again. "The same smile." She tightened her lips and shook her head with a sense of loss and regret. "There is so much you should have, Toby. What a shame it is that you are a Devonshire and have never lived as one. All the result of my one tragic mistake." Her eyes narrowed thoughtfully and she smiled warmly at Toby. "But maybe one day you will be my little girl at that." Then without waiting for Toby's response, she stood and led her from the greenhouse. "Come, let's go back. I think I hear the guests."

Within an hour all one hundred guests had arrived; Eleanor Devonshire's barbecue was not to be missed. Waiters circulated with hors d'oeuvres and drinks. There was a hum of conversation, the clinking sound of plates and silver, fragrances from different perfumes, all intermingling with the delicious odors of the grilling steaks. Linda couldn't help but realize that this might have been the life she would have led if only Eleanor had approved of her marriage to Keith. Yet she had no regrets. Their life together, though simple, was more dear than a thousand parties like this.

She also couldn't help but feel a little uneasy around all of these well-dressed, wealthy strangers and, even in her best casual outfit, underdressed. She had never felt comfortable in crowds and grabbed onto Thomas's arm. He put his hand over hers, patted her protectively, and flitted from guest to guest, introducing Linda, complimenting the ladies, trading goodnatured small talk with the men, joking about their golf games, demeaning his own. Linda watched many expressions change from expectation to surprise and sometimes disappointment as he identified her as his sister-in-law and not his date. Or wife! And she quickly gave up trying to remember the names of the people she met.

Some of the guests wanted to talk about Keith, express their belated condolences, tell her how much they had liked him, how sorry they were to hear of his death. Though they were polite and meant no harm—and probably were feeling as awkward as she was, Linda imagined—she was troubled by all the reminders of Keith, saddened by the memories evoked.

When she and Thomas were alone for a second, he whispered to her. "How are you holding up?"

"I don't know," she answered truthfully. "There's so much going on. So many people."

"And every one with a story." Thomas smiled. "I'll tell you later. Remember who you want to gossip about." He squeezed her hand. "I'm glad my mother invited you."

"Yes," Linda agreed, but she still felt vaguely troubled about the afternoon. As she watched Eleanor circulate among her guests, she was filled with an odd sense of mistrust toward the older woman. Had she invited her today to be reminded of Keith? To show her how painful it would be to remain in West Ledge?

Toby scooted underfoot with steak sauce across her face. "Let me wipe that," Linda said. Then Toby was off in a corner of the yard with the other children.

Later in the afternoon Linda sensed someone looking at her. She had seen the man several times during the party. He was tall with wavy hair and a light-brown beard shaved at the jawline. He appeared to be in his late thirties and carried a Sherlockian pipe. It might only have been her imagination, but she had felt him looking at her before from the shadows. Once she had seen Eleanor standing with him and seemingly both had glanced in her direction. She had tried to shake off the feeling that he was watching her, but now he was eyeing her again.

She asked Thomas who the man was but he didn't know. Though he thought he knew all of his mother's acquaintances who would merit invitation, this man was a stranger. They were on their way to introduce themselves when Thomas was called into the house to take a phone call and Linda was left on her own. That's when the man started through the crowd toward her. Linda glanced nervously toward the house, but Thomas was out of sight and she had no alternative but to meet him.

"Hello." He smiled. "My name is Ira Perdue."

"Linda Devonshire."

"Yes, I know," he said easily. "Your mother-in-law told me."

"You've been staring at me," Linda challenged. "Why?"

"Because you're a very attractive woman."

Eleanor came bustling over and joined them. "Ah, I see you two have met each other. Good. Good." She touched the man's arm, leaned against him flirtatiously. "If I were twenty years younger I would make a play for this man. All right—thirty years younger." She nodded confidentially to Linda and winked. "Take good care of Ira. He's a doctor." Then she saw another guest she wanted to talk to and was gone into the crowd.

"Do you live in West Ledge?" Linda asked politely, hoping Thomas would come back and rescue her.

"Milltown. Just on the other side of the river."

"I don't know where that is. I've just gotten here from Los Angeles."

"Yes. So Eleanor told me."

"I see," Linda said. "What else did Eleanor tell you about me?"

"Oh, that you were married to her son—"

Linda narrowed her eyes and interrupted. "What kind of a doctor are you, Dr. Perdue?"

"A psychiatrist. And call me Ira, please."

"A psychiatrist," she repeated slowly, starting to bristle inwardly. "I guess I should have known." She tightened her lips. "Well, it was nice meeting you, but if you'll excuse me, I want to see if my daughter has had her dinner yet." She started away from him, but Dr. Perdue touched her arm, stopped her.

"Do you have anything against psychiatrists?" he asked.

"No, not at all," Linda said archly. She was annoyed at what was happening. She now knew what he wanted and it wasn't that he was attracted to her. "In fact, several have helped me greatly. But I suspect you know that already."

"No, not at all," Perdue protested. "Why would I know any of that?"

"Just exactly what is your interest in me, Dr. Perdue?" she asked stiffly.

"To get to know you."

"Clinically?"

"Of course not."

"Good, because I don't feel like being examined right now. Or watched from across the lawn like you've been doing." Her voice was rising; two people passing by took notice, but she didn't care. Her annoyance had blossomed into anger at what they were doing to her.

"Believe me, Linda, I—" Dr. Perdue sputtered.

She pulled away from him brusquely as her tears started to form. "I'm sorry, but I just don't date psychiatrists."

"Linda, whatever you're thinking about me, you're wrong," he called after her, his voice filled with concern, professionalism. Hearing his tone, she stopped and turned to him. Their eyes met and the twinge in his made her know she had been mistaken, misinterpreted his advances. But it was too late to change what had happened.

Her eyes still on his, she took a step backward, lost her balance. She stumbled into a woman and knocked the plate out of her hands. Steak sauce splattered down the front of her off-white dress. Horrified, Linda gasped, "I'm sorry, I—" But Dr. Perdue was still there, and now Eleanor was coming toward them, and she had to get away.

Thomas found her at the edge of the property. Her back was to the crowd, her shoulders stiff. "I've been looking all over for you." She tensed to his touch. "What's the matter, Linda?" he asked, alarmed.

She turned to him and he saw the tears that dotted her cheeks. "What is it?"

She collapsed into his arms. "Oh, Thomas," she moaned. "I've just done something terrible. But I didn't know what else to think—"

"What, Linda?" he pressed.

"That man was a psychiatrist. I thought—" She swallowed tightly to choke back her tears. "He had been looking at me like I told you. I thought your mother had asked him to observe me. It had seemed so set up between them." A look of horror flashed across her face. "What must he think of me? And what is he going to say to your mother about me? And that dress? I ruined it."

"Linda, are you all right?" he asked strongly.

"I was so rude to him, and I didn't have to be."

"Let's get you out of here. We can sneak out through there." He pointed through a break in the hedges. "I'll get Toby."

Eleanor was hurrying over to them. "What is it, dear? Ira said you seemed very upset."

"Not now, Mother," Thomas warned. "Linda isn't feeling well and I'm going to take her home."

"I hope it's nothing serious."

"Mother, please, I'll call you later, okay?"

"Of course, Thomas," Eleanor said, then looked at Linda. "I hope you feel better, dear, and if there's anything I can do—"

"No, thank you, Mrs. Devonshire," Linda said. "I'm all right. And sorry. Please tell Dr. Perdue." Then, embarrassed, she turned away from Eleanor.

Thomas made light conversation on the way home and talked about people who had been at the party, giving her all the local "Peyton Place gossip," as he liked to call it. Linda laughed politely and tried to be responsive, but Thomas saw how distant she still was. Out of the corner of his eye he watched her for a moment, then said, "I know it's going to be hard, Linda, but please try to forget about what happened. It doesn't matter. Nobody is going to think anything bad of you, I promise."

"I made a fool out of myself, Thomas."

"Come on," he prompted. "Perdue's probably an arrogant jerk anyway, deserves to be taken down a peg or two. And my mother will take care of that dress. Besides, I've never seen a white anything that hasn't been improved by steak sauce."

He was satisfied with just getting her to smile.

Once home, Toby went upstairs to read and Linda opened the door for Thomas. He hung back. "Hey, what are you doing? Pushing me out?"

"No, not at all." Linda was flustered. "I thought you'd want to get back to the party."

"What? With all those stuffed shirts? I'd rather stay here with you. If you want me to."

"If you'd like," she said, and smiled.

The sun was setting and the temperature had dipped into the fifties. The house was cooling off.

"How about a fire?" he suggested.

"In the summer?" Linda asked, amused.

"Just a little one," he answered as he stacked the logs. "For some good old New England atmosphere. It's also relaxing and I think that's what you can use right now."

She shot him a lopsided grin. "I'd have to agree with that."

After the fire was started he poured them each an amaretto.

They sipped the after-dinner drinks and silently watched the flames lap at the top of the hearth.

"Almost hypnotizing, isn't it?" Thomas asked. There were no other lights in the room and he watched Linda's face, dazzled and shadowed by the flickering flames.

"Mmm-hmm," she said softly, distantly, her eyes straight ahead, mesmerized by the firelight. The fire conjured pleasant memories of the few times she and Keith had gone skiing in Heavenly Valley and sat in front of roaring ski lodge fires, their arms around each other, sipping hot apple cider and swizzling cinnamon sticks. She hadn't been very good at the sport, but after the sun went down and the mountain nights were theirs, it no longer mattered that she had spent more time on her bottom than on her feet. Keith was always there to pick her up, as he had done so many other times as well.

"I love to lose myself to the fire," she said, "and imagine the flames are forming patterns. Sometimes they look like beckoning fingers, tempting you to come closer. Like an alluring siren call." She sighed. "I don't think there's anything as restful as watching a fire."

"Only if you're with someone special. It's not half as much fun if you're alone," Thomas said. His words surprised her and made her look at him.

"No," Linda agreed, then laughed. "I'll bet Dr. Perdue had visions of being with me tonight. I guess I should be flattered, but I don't think I'm ready to go out with anyone just yet."

She turned back to stare into the fire and Thomas sensed a confusion in her.

"You can't withdraw from the world, Linda," he said softly. When he saw her stiffen, he wished he could pull back the words.

"Please don't say such things to me, Thomas," she said chokingly. "You don't know what I've been through . . ." Then she bit her lip sharply. "I'm sorry," she said. "I didn't mean to snap at you like that." She added ruefully, "But that seems to be my pattern today."

He shook his head. He had hurt her and was sorry. "No, I was completely out of line. It wasn't my place to say what I did. There are lots of things I don't understand because I have never suffered a loss as great as yours." When Sandra left him, he had really felt nothing. He accepted it, didn't chase after her, and thus identified his true feelings.

Linda regretted the way she had spoken to him. He was only trying to help her, and she knew her sharp reaction was defensive. He had touched a nerve, one she wasn't ready yet to admit to herself. "Don't apologize, Thomas," she said softly, reminding him of their pact.

There was a long silence between them. The only sound in the room was the snapping of the sparks and the shifting of the logs in the hearth.

Thomas put his drink down on the coffee table and stood up. "I'd better go now," he said.

"Please don't," Linda said quickly. She reached up and grasped his hand. She didn't want him to go. She didn't want to be left alone for the evening. And perhaps for the first time since Keith's death she wanted something more than a solitary evening with a magazine and her memories. "There's still so much fire left to enjoy, and you're right. It really is no fun if you're alone." Their eyes locked on each other's and he slowly sat back down on the couch.

"Maybe a few minutes," he said.

"It's early, and it's Saturday night. You're not going to work tonight, are you?"

"No." He smiled. "Actually I was going to go home, put on a movie, and think about how much I would prefer being here with you."

She smiled. "So why not stay here?" And then she added jokingly, "At least until the fire is out."

"I think there's about a cord and a half of wood out in back. That should last about three months," he said lightly, but behind her laughter he noticed a troubled face. Her glass was empty. "More amaretto?" he asked.

"Just a little. I'm really feeling it."

He poured half a glass and topped off his own. Linda leaned her head back restfully against the couch. Her dark hair splayed out loosely on both sides like an Oriental fan. The amaretto was making her tired, and her eyes were half closed as she watched the parading flames form almost human fingers—dancers embraced in fiery passion or trapped in hellish pain.

Thomas watched her. Her neck was swanlike, graceful, her

lips moist from the liqueur, sensuous, inviting in the glow of the flames. There was a sadness and vulnerability to her eyes. They had seen pain, they had been hurt, they were afraid. And in that one moment when the shadows of the flames bathed her face in a warm blush he understood his feelings and knew why Keith had given away everything for her.

Suddenly he regretted not having gotten to know her better as Keith's wife, but if he had, it would probably have dulled the attraction he was feeling toward her now, the excitement at being close to her.

"What are you thinking about?" he asked.

She tilted her head to face him. "Oh, nothing . . ."

"There must be something up there," he prodded. "Come on—first thing to come to mind."

"First thing to come to mind?" Her eyes searched the ceiling. She followed a snakelike crack until it blurred out of sight. "I guess, how relaxed I feel right now. How comfortable." *How safe with you,* she almost said, because that was how she was feeling.

She had never been a strong person. Her childhood traumas had left her weak, afraid. When Keith first spoke to her in the restaurant, she had been tempted not to talk to him, to just thank him for helping her pick up her money and then walk away, as she had from so many others. Her beauty attracted them, her fear drove them away. And that would have been the most tragic mistake she ever could have made. Keith was strong, self-assured, and when she was with him, she never felt alone. And perhaps now for the first time since his death she wasn't feeling alone any more. Because of Thomas.

"I feel very comfortable too," Thomas said softly. He stretched his arm across the back of the couch, touched her shoulder gently. Surprised, she stiffened and he quickly drew his hand back.

He resisted the urge to apologize and instead he said, "You're very pretty, Linda."

"Thank you." She blushed crimson.

"Maybe I didn't know Keith very well, but I can see he had exceptional taste."

She turned to look at him, a half smile of contentment on her face. For a moment she watched Thomas watch her, his eyes a

warm brown and filled with attraction. And there was something
about the moment, the fire, the closeness to him, that made her
stomach ripple as well.

Thomas reached out toward her, his palm up, and with two
fingers lightly touched her neck. He sensed her trembling and for
a fraction of a second froze, but when she did not move away he
took the glass from her and set it down next to his. Then he
teased his hand along the line of her neck, all the while holding
her almost hypnotically with his eyes so not to lose the spell of
the moment. She purred softly, stretched her chin higher to
longer enjoy his touch, and let her eyes close. Thomas drew her
face up to his and tentatively kissed her. Her lips opened to him,
their tongues touched, and a tingling played up and down her
spine. When he drew back from her, her eyes opened slowly and
he saw the change in them immediately, the hesitation, as she
seemed to withdraw from him. She exhaled and looked away,
toward the fire.

"I'm sorry, Thomas," she said, her eyes clouded with confusion.
She licked her lips, which were suddenly dry. "But I don't know
what I want just now."

"I understand," he said, then added, "It would be easier for
you if I wasn't Keith's brother, wouldn't it?"

"Probably," she admitted. "Although I don't even know right
now . . ."

"You take your time. However much you need. And then you
tell me." She nodded. "Shall we watch some television?"

"Yes."

They sat stiffly on the couch. Thomas's arm was across the
back, his hand only inches from Linda's shoulders. He wanted to
touch her, to pull her close to him, but he made no further move.
Nor did she invite him to put his arm around her. She excused
herself to go to the bathroom and when she returned she sat down
in the armchair and curled her legs protectively underneath her.

That night she couldn't sleep. She tossed in bed restlessly,
unable to find a comfortable position. She had wanted Thomas to
kiss her; her emotions called for it, her body craved it. In only
moments he had reawakened her, made her feel alive again, and
she should have known the guilt was inevitable. She had kissed
another man with passion, with need. She had betrayed her
husband.

Guilt—such a useless, destructive emotion, the doctors had always told her, and then, as now, she knew she was making a tragic mistake in allowing it to shadow her like a constant dread companion, to seize her, control her. But hadn't that always been the pattern?

It wasn't until the morning grayness started to fill the room that a measure of relief flooded through her and she understood that Keith wasn't going to come down from wherever he was to tell her she had mourned long enough. It wasn't Keith's approval that she needed, it was her own. If her emotions dictated, she had to be brave enough to reach out toward someone else and not hide behind a crumbling wall of grief, because that was false protection. She would have to trust her feelings to give her her answers.

She fell into a sleep that comes only from peace of mind and woke at noon feeling she had taken a first giant step toward letting go of an old life and stepping into a new.

She hoped.

Sunday afternoon Thomas went to his mother's house. Eleanor served coffee in the den.

"A lovely party, wouldn't you say, Thomas?" she asked.

"As usual," he agreed. "And you were a lovely hostess. Exquisite in that dress."

"Did you like it?" Eleanor smiled, pleased. She sipped her coffee, then looked at her son over the rim of the cup sadly, knowledgeably. "You saw what happened yesterday, didn't you, Thomas?"

"Yes," he said quietly. "And she was very embarrassed."

"Ira Perdue only tried to make conversation with her—'pick her up,' if that's the vernacular—and she caused a scene in front of all those people."

"Mother, she did no such thing. Don't blow this out of proportion." He stood up, walked to the window, and looked out over the pool and tennis court, the insulated world he had grown up in. "Perdue's being a psychiatrist flustered her. I think you have to appreciate her sensitivity more than you do. She's a very fragile person who's already been through more in her lifetime than anyone should ever have to. She knows you don't want her here in West Ledge, she remembers what you did to her once before, and when a psychiatrist confronted her, at your introduction, she got very nervous."

"Thomas, if I had any idea she was going to react as she did, I never would have suggested Ira meet her. I was only thinking of her, believe me. Ira is recently divorced and the perfect age for her. I thought I was doing something nice." She waved her hand as if trying to be finished with the whole matter. "Thomas, I know how you feel about her, but she frightens me. There is something wrong with her. There will always be. I was afraid for Keith and only tried to warn him that something could happen. And you know something did. My God! She could have killed him or the child. Oh, Thomas, I believe something bad will happen because she's here. To you. To me. To her. To somebody. I feel it."

"I'm not going to let her go away by herself," Thomas said softly, hoping his voice would calm his mother. "I will not leave her alone."

"She was alone in California. You have no responsibility for her."

"Mother," Thomas said firmly. "I've assumed the responsibility, and there is nothing more to talk about."

"Perhaps you've assumed too much responsibility. If something should happen to her because she was here, it would be your doing, Thomas. What if you even caused the problem? Could you live with that?"

Thomas faltered a moment, then said, "Nothing is going to happen to her, and I don't even want to talk about the possibility. Mother, please don't make this harder than it is. I just have to ask you again to accept her being in West Ledge."

"I can't, Thomas. For your sake. And for that little girl. How I feel for her! How wrong it is for my grandchild to be raised by that woman who lives under a cloud of sickness, when at any moment something terrible might happen. We have to do something, Thomas. We can't just let her—"

"Mother, I'm sorry!" Thomas said forcefully, interrupting, "but this is the way it's going to be and I don't want to talk about it anymore." He shook his head from side to side wanting to be free of the discussion. Then he pursed his lips, weighed his words, and added, "And I have to say that if you do anything to hurt Linda again, I won't ever forgive you."

"But I would never harm her!" Eleanor said quickly, urgently. "Don't even think that. And don't be angry with me, Thomas, please. I swear to you that I mean her no harm. None. I was only considering what might be best."

Thomas exhaled, looked at his mother. Her eyes were plaintive, her face sad, hurt. He had been wrong to say what he had. "I'm not angry with you, Mother," he said softly. "Just be more sensitive to her. That's all I ask."

"I will," Eleanor said to him. "I promise."

chapter 12

There was an amusement park in a neighboring city and Linda, Thomas, and Toby spent the following Saturday afternoon on the roller coaster and Ferris wheel. They threw baseballs at milk bottles, dunked the clown in the pool, and ate hot dogs until Linda felt they were all going to explode. Thomas confessed the fun he was having and smilingly complained that Linda was bringing out a part of him he didn't even know existed. "Scratch a Devonshire and deep below the surface I think you might even find a human being," he joked. At the end of the day, when Toby was riding the merry-go-round, Thomas took Linda's hand in his and their fingers entwined.

Linda began seeing Thomas during the week and both weekend days. On Saturday and Sunday Toby joined in and the three went to the movies, played miniature golf, spent evenings watching television and playing board games. They went hiking, bike riding, picnicking in the local woods, and drove to Boston to see the circus. One weekend they went to New York, where Thomas escorted both his ladies around Manhattan. They went to museums and matinees, dined out in expensive restaurants, and took a hansom cab for a sunset ride through Central Park. Toby took well to her uncle Thomas and recognized that something special had happened in their lives. She felt her mother's energy, her new lust for living after a year of mourning as they got over her father's death.

And as Linda grew to trust Thomas, she found herself relaxing, feeling safe for the first time since Keith's death. She was no longer as jittery as she had been, no longer spooked by noises in the night or men coming out of the shadows. *No longer afraid.* Because she knew there was no threat.

Toby turned eight at the end of August. Her birthday party was scheduled for Sunday afternoon, and all Saturday night Thomas blew up balloons and strung linked ribbon decorations across the ceiling.

Thomas arrived late, with a basket under his arm. When he handed Toby her birthday present, a wobbly Lhasa apso with long gray hair and the saddest eyes yelped up at her. The dog stopped the party. All the children had to pet and hold it. "What are you going to call it?" they shouted. Toby thought hard for a minute, then decided. "Princess."

"She's gorgeous," Linda said, then asked under her breath, "She is a *Princess*, isn't she?"

"That's what the breeder told me. Here're her papers, shots, list of instructions of what has to be done when, and—" Thomas reached into his pocket and pulled out a small felt-covered box. "This is for you."

"But it's not my birthday," Linda said coyly.

Thomas reached for the box. "So I'll wait."

"Not on your life." Linda's excitement matched her daughter's as she held her new dog.

"Exquisite," she breathed as she opened the box. The earrings were diamond and gold. "Oh, Thomas . . ."

"Put them on. Let me see you." And when they were in place he smiled widely. "Lovely. Just like you." Then he asked, "Am I being too corny?"

"Never," she answered.

That night a very happy, very tired Toby cradled her new pet in her arms and fell into a blissful sleep with the dog resting against her neck.

Toby and Princess became inseparable. The dog accompanied Toby wherever the child went, except for school, and to Linda, tears seemed to form in all four eyes when Toby left to catch the bus. But the dog was waiting by the door every afternoon, knowing that the key in the lock meant her young master was home.

Princess was a scooter, a slippery devil, who could dart in front of you at breakneck speeds. Sometimes you didn't even know the dog was passing underfoot until you tripped over the

little ball of fur. That happened to Thomas one night as he was
carrying two bowls of soup to the dining-room table; Princess
decided to squeeze herself between his legs. Toby, Thomas, and
Linda had a grand time mopping up the mess, and Princess sat in
the corner, tail wagging happily, lapping at the soup.

During family dinners, Eleanor went out of her way to welcome Linda and Toby. The incident at the barbecue was never
mentioned. Thomas appreciated what his mother was doing and
thanked her for extending herself, but Eleanor just waved it off,
saying it was the very least she could do to make up so much to
Linda. Toby always recounted the adventures she had had with
her mother and uncle, and while Linda suspected the older
woman did not approve of the time Thomas was spending with
them, her glances were only sideways, as if she were trying
subtly to glean something from Linda's eyes, to silently transmit
reproach. And because nothing was ever said, and because of the
fun she was having with Thomas, Linda dismissed her suspicions
and enjoyed her mother-in-law's newfound friendship.

Linda and Thomas held hands when they walked down the
street, Thomas put his around her shoulder when they watched
television, he kissed her good night at the door. And as his touch
began to linger, there was no denying the tension that was slowly
developing between them.

One Friday night in September Toby was upstairs in bed. The
week had been a raw and rainy one, and Thomas was struggling
to build a fire with the wet wood. After using two books of
matches and half the Sunday paper, he finally succeeded in
getting the starter sticks to burn. Satisfied, he stood back to
watch the rest of the wood catch.

"I told you I could do it," he said proudly. He took a poker
and artfully adjusted a log for maximum exposure to the fledgling
flame. "There," he said when satisfied with the arrangement.
"A masterpiece. What do you say?"

Linda studied the pyramidal structure from several angles,
squinted, and drew on her chin thoughtfully. "It looks a little
crooked to me. That log over there."

"Crooked, huh?" Thomas scowled.

"A little."

"I'll give you crooked," he challenged and dove down next to
her on the couch. His fingers found her soft spots and he tickled

her. They giggled and rolled over in each other's arms while behind them the fire crackled and sputtered and rose high in the hearth. Then suddenly, as if a bell had sounded, the laughter fell from their faces, their breath caught, and everything changed.

"My little woodsman." Linda mugged, sticking her tongue out to try to recapture the humor, but the moment was suspended, their eyes locked on each other huskily, knowingly. "I could have built that fire in half the time. . . ." She tried again. But Thomas didn't smile. He touched his tongue to his lips to moisten them and reached out toward her.

"You're so very lovely," he said.

"Don't—" she wanted to say, but her mouth refused to open, and Thomas touched her shoulder. A light touch. A romantic touch as his fingers swirled and curved teasingly. A tremor passed through her body, but Linda didn't know if she was trembling from excitement or pressing guilt. She should have known this moment had to come! And while part of her ached to have Thomas next to her, inside of her, another part of her—the part beset with guilt and fear—screamed that now was the moment to end what they had started. Before it went further, before it became too late to recapture their casual relationship that had never really been casual. It had all been a prelude.

His fingertips played against the tender skin of her neck and eased downward toward her chest, and she had to stop him. She covered his hand with hers and his eyes searched her face questioningly.

"It's wrong, Thomas," she said, her voice barely audible.

"Only if you let it be, Linda," he breathed, his face inches from hers, his brandied breath sweet. "We're doing nothing wrong." In the red-orange firelight his eyes seemed to glow. He took her hands in his, closed them into fists, and brought them to his lips. "On the surface you know that. But in your soul you still harbor guilt about what you want right now, and I understand you would feel this way. But we were thrust together in innocence, Linda. I had no motive in inviting you to West Ledge except to assuage my guilt. You had no motive to come except your concern for Toby."

"You assuaged your guilt," she said distantly. "I deepened mine."

"No, Linda," he begged. "Keith's been dead more than a

year now. A very long time, yet a very short time when you loved someone.''

He pushed her hair high off her face, kissed her forehead, trailed two fingers down her face, looked deep into her eyes, wide and searching. ''Your skin is so soft,'' he whispered. ''Your eyes so winning, so enticing. Deep pools in which I can see myself look at you.''

And suddenly all of their talk was over and she saw in his face what she had been feeling but didn't want to admit. Desire. Need. He opened his arms to her and she entered them. He wrapped himself tightly around her, kissed her tenderly on the forehead, the eyes, the cheeks. He caressed her neck softly, brushed her lips lightly with his, then more and more hungrily, and then both hands lifted her face to him. His touch thrilled her, excited her. She took his tongue inside her mouth, played with it with her lips. Then he pushed forward and covered her mouth with a ferocity that frightened her and made her push him away.

''Thomas, I can't,'' she said. ''It's wrong. Awkward. Incestuous, even. You're my brother-in-law and I just can't.''

She tried to move away from him, but he grabbed her arm above the elbow, stopped her.

''Linda, I don't feel like your brother-in-law right now and I no longer look at you as Keith's wife. We're just two people on the verge of a marvelous relationship.''

''With everything going against us. A dead husband lurking in the shadows of my mind, a mother who doesn't approve . . .'' She shook her head. ''We're making a mistake, Thomas.''

''No, Linda, we're not,'' he said intensely. ''Anything that feels this good can't be a mistake.'' His face was warm, kindly, but she saw the wanting behind his eyes, deepened by the firelight. ''Don't hold an accident of birth against me. Even though I'm Keith's brother, I'm just a man, no different from any other man. It's so very important for you to accept that.''

He couldn't crowd her anymore. He let go of her arm and was pleased that she didn't pull away from him. Perhaps his words had gotten to her. She stared off into the fireplace. She had thought it would all be easier, but she guessed she hadn't fully resolved her feelings of release. But even if it wasn't Thomas Devonshire beside her now, in her thoughts, would her inner feelings be any different? Would she still be feeling unfaithful to Keith? When would it end? She didn't know.

Thomas touched her thigh lightly, trailed his finger up and down her leg. He sensed her squirm at his touch but not move away, and he did not remove his hand.

"I want to make love to you, Linda," he whispered. "But only if it's right for you. I don't want to do anything that's going to cause you pain or regret. Because if it's right, it's going to be wonderful." He paused, licked his lips, and carefully watched her reaction as he asked, "Will you make love to me, Linda?"

The directness of the question surprised her. But it was no longer a question and she knew she wanted what he wanted. He had touched a nerve inside of her, made her feel like a woman again. He had rekindled emotions and needs dormant for a year. She wanted to feel his flesh pressed against hers, his mouth covering her own, his lips against her cheek, her sex. She ached to feel him inside of her. And then she could no longer deny him, deny herself.

They fell into each other's arms and she breathed into his ear. "I want to, Thomas. Please—"

He lifted her off the couch and carried her upstairs to her bedroom. He closed the door and put it on the chain. He slowly, sensuously removed their clothes, let them drop to the floor. He kissed her gently at first, her eyelids, her ears, but then hungrily he smothered her with kisses. While a small part of her mind was still screaming no, her body was alive with a million prickles and raging yes! And then he was inside her and she forgot about Keith, about Thomas being her brother-in-law, about his mother who did not approve, and she let herself be taken by him to plateaus of pleasure she hadn't experienced in more than a year. And it wasn't incest, it wasn't awkward, it wasn't a mistake. It was heaven.

When their lips finally parted they lay snuggled, facing each other. The room was dimly lit from the light of the full moon. A slight breeze ruffled the shade as it stole in and blew across the bed. Linda's eyes were closed, her breathing soft. Thomas studied her, the light fluttering of her eyelids, the line of her red lips, her hair as it fell in wisps across her cheek. In the quiet moments after their lovemaking he was enjoying the sight of her, the smell of her body, the exquisite pleasure of having her next to him. She

looked so sweet in sleep, so innocent. . . . What Keith had gazed
at every night of his life with her. He touched his finger to her
cheek, whisked back her hair, felt the softness of her skin. She
stirred and her eyes opened.

"I fell asleep," she said. "I'm sorry."

Thomas covered her lips with his. Involuntarily she shifted
closer to him as she tried to touch her entire body to his.

"That was so wonderful," she whispered. "I had almost
forgotten." She had been frightened, overwhelmed by Thomas's
closeness, his intensity, not knowing what to expect from him,
from herself. But for all his need, Thomas was a caring lover. He
had tenderly kissed the length of her body and made her cry out
for him before he entered her. "What time is it?"

"Not too late, but I think I should go."

"No," she said, but then realized he was right. Toby shouldn't
find him here in the morning. "Not yet," she whispered.
"Please—" She wasn't yet ready to give up the security she felt
of his lying next to her, the comfortable warmth of his body in
the cool evening. She wrapped her arms around his neck and
kissed him, held him for an extra second, and only then released
him and let him slip out of bed.

From underneath the covers she watched him as he dressed. In
the quarter light of the room his outline was almost that of a
dancer gracefully performing for her benefit alone. And she
reveled in the thrill that he had just been in her arms. When he
was finished she got out of bed and pulled on her robe. He curled
his arm around her waist as they tiptoed downstairs.

At the door he held her and kissed her again. Lingeringly.
Tenderly.

"I'll be home in a few minutes. Call me if you want."

"I'll be asleep." She stretched, fulfilled. "I feel like I can
sleep for a month."

Once back in bed and all alone, she lay stiffly and waited for
the guilt to pass over her. She didn't want to feel guilty about
what she had done tonight. She had made an adult decision to
sleep with Thomas. Keith was dead; she had done nothing wrong.
Making love to Thomas wasn't a sin and God wasn't going to
send down a lightning bolt to strike her dead.

She was a big girl. And a good girl.

That thought made her feel better.

Almost, she accepted, as if she had been forgiven.

Almost.

Early one evening Eleanor and the man sat across from each other at the Country Kettle restaurant. Their table was in a corner of the room, near a brick hearth decorated with pewter dishes and colonial artifacts. Eleanor's eyebrows arched as she scanned the piece of paper just handed her, her lips drawn tight, in a thin line, her expression grim.

"There is no question, then," she stated more than asked. Her voice was tired, flat. The drink in front of her was barely touched.

"None."

She nodded feebly. "Thank you."

The man waited silently, but Eleanor said, "Would you leave me please."

Alone at the table, Eleanor again read the report, but by now she had memorized its contents. It was all there. Times. Places. The man had been thorough. She had suspected and now had her confirmation. Boston. New York. Evenings until midnight. She took a match from the table, lit it and put it to the report, held the paper between her fingers as it started to flame, then quickly dashed it into the fireplace. She watched as the paper fully caught the flames, blackened and twisted into itself like a soul in anguish, and then turned to mottled gray dust with the other ashes at the bottom of the hearth, indistinguishable.

A tear slipped down her cheek. She flicked it away with her index finger.

It was what Thomas wanted.

chapter 13

Work was hectic. The secretaries were putting in evening hours and Linda took proofreading and typing home on a portable machine. She was being given more responsibilities and was really feeling she was accomplishing something.

One morning it seemed that each attorney was involved in a deal bigger than the next. The phones were ringing constantly and Linda was routing calls from the board to the secretaries, taking messages when all the lines were busy. The pile of pink message slips grew and she passed them in batches back to the attorneys' secretaries.

Mr. Robinson came out of his office. His sleeves were rolled up and he looked harried. "Nancy," he said. "I've been waiting for a call from Mr. Donnelly. Has he phoned yet?"

"No, Mr. Robinson. I'll put him right through when he does."

"If I'm busy, tell him I'll call right back. *Right back.* And take his number. I don't know where he is today."

Mr. Donnelly? Linda furrowed her brow. She might have taken two dozen messages that morning but the name stuck out. Unlike many other callers or their secretaries who had been rushed and short with her, Mr. Donnelly had been very polite, spelled his name, even wished her a good day. She remembered having taken the message and, she thought, given it to Nancy. "I think he did call, Mr. Robinson. Didn't you get my message?"

"Nancy?" Robinson questioned.

Nancy shook her head blankly. "I never got it."

"I'm certain I gave it to you," Linda said.

"Obviously you're mistaken."

"What is it, ladies?" Robinson asked impatiently. "Did he call, Linda, or didn't he? Nancy?"

"I don't know whether he called or not," Nancy said definitively. "But I never got a message." She rose and approached Linda's desk, plainly annoyed that Linda had contradicted her in front of her boss. "Maybe you lost the message."

"I didn't lose the message," Linda protested. The phone rang. She broke away from her conversation to pick it up. Nancy reached under Linda's desk and pulled out her wastepaper basket. "What are you doing?" Linda asked, then turned her attention back to the caller.

"It's here," Nancy said as she fished a folded piece of pink message paper out of the wastebasket. "Mr. Robinson—I found it."

Linda hung up the phone. "What?" she asked.

"It was here," Nancy said, with so-there triumph. "I was right. You *did* lose it. You threw it away. See? There are coffee stains on the paper. It probably got stuck to the bottom of your cup this morning."

"It didn't. I wouldn't have made that mistake."

"It doesn't matter now," Robinson said. "Nancy, get him for me." He turned to Linda. "Look, you've got to be more careful."

"Mr. Robinson," Linda said, "I didn't throw that paper away." Her eyes filled with tears, her face flushed bright crimson.

"We'll talk about it later. Nancy—please get him, it's crucial." Annoyed, he checked his watch and disappeared into his office, slamming the door shut.

"Yes, Mr. Robinson," Nancy said, smiling, reveling in her discomfort, Linda knew. She hated the smug expression that crossed the other woman's face. But how else would the message have gotten in the basket if she hadn't thrown it away by accident? She suddenly felt cramped and her head started to hurt with a tense pounding behind her eyes. Except for brief trips to the coffee machine, she had been sitting at the desk fielding calls nonstop all morning. "Helen?" she called.

The woman walked over to her. "Yes?"

"Could you sit here for a minute? I have to get up."

"Of course. But don't be too long. I have a lot of work."

"No," Linda promised.

She pushed open the door to the ladies' room. The silence was welcome. There were no ringing phones or pounding typewriters. It was a two-minute break she needed. At the sink she turned the cold tap on, splashed water on her face, into her eyes, and she shivered as the water ran down her neck. But it felt good. There was a vinyl chair in the lounge area. She was certain Helen wouldn't mind if she took a few minutes extra to collect herself. The look on Mr. Robinson's face when Nancy found the message in her wastebasket was a mixture of anger and annoyance. She had failed him, made a dumb mistake at a critical moment. She felt as if she was almost going to cry.

A few minutes later there was a sharp rap on the ladies' room door. Helen stuck her head in.

"Are you all right in here? Phone call."

"I'm all right," she said, and got out of the chair. It was Thomas calling her, she knew, and she needed to hear his voice.

"Hello?"

"Linda?" For a moment the voice threw her.

"Yes. How are you?"

"Just fine, dear," Eleanor said. "I'll tell you why I called. I'm just down the street shopping. It's almost lunchtime and I was wondering if you were free. It's the last minute and I'll understand if you have a date."

She didn't have a lunch date. She never did. In the months she'd been at the office, none of the secretaries had yet extended an invitation to join them. And Helen, the only one who spoke civilly to her, was on a different schedule. She was tired of sitting alone at the counter every day and eager for company. But she was uncertain about lunching with Eleanor. She had spent a number of evenings at the Devonshire house, but always surrounded by Thomas and Toby; she and Eleanor had never eaten alone. But, she smiled, there was always a first time.

"Yes, I'm free."

"Fine. I'll meet you at the Country Kettle. Do you know where it is?"

"Yes."

"About twelve thirty?"

"I'll be there." She hung up the phone wondering if she was making a mistake.

Eleanor was waiting, sipping a white wine, when she got to the restaurant.

"I'm glad you could come on such short notice," Eleanor said.

"I'm usually free for lunch." Linda laughed.

"Things are still unpleasant for you at the office?"

A shrug. "I'll manage. They still blame me for that other woman losing her job."

"I'm sure that will eventually settle out," Eleanor said, then asked, "How's Toby?"

"Fine. Today is spelling test day so we went over her list of words last night."

"She's so bright."

"Keith used to read with her at every opportunity . . ." She trailed off, feeling funny about mentioning Keith's name. As if she were creating a void between them, when what she needed right now was a friend.

A waitress came over; handed them menus. Eleanor scanned hers quickly. "I'm going to have the diet plate. They do wonders with cottage cheese and paprika here."

"That sounds good. Make it two."

The waitress disappeared and a silence hung over the table. They had covered work, Toby, and food, Linda thought, their array of small talk.

"How was shopping?" Linda asked, trying to keep the conversation flowing, afraid of silences, suddenly feeling Eleanor's eyes peering at her, making her feel uncomfortable.

"I bought a lovely dress," Eleanor said. "There's a women's club meeting this weekend and I'm going to stun them all." Then she cleared her throat. It was a formal sound and Linda tensed. This is it, she thought. This wasn't purely a social invitation. There's something on her mind: Thomas. She was going to tell her not to see him, confirm her suspicions that Eleanor did not approve. Linda lowered her head and spread butter on a slice of bread, making more of it than was required so she wouldn't have to look at Eleanor. Yet she hung on Eleanor's next words and was more than surprised when she heard her mother-in-law say, "If you wish to date my son, Linda, well, you're both adults, aren't you?"

When Linda looked up, the older woman was smiling at her, her eyes warm, disarming.

*   *   *

After school Eric and Mitchell picked up Petey and Carol Ann and rang Toby's bell. They were going to play in the well in Toby's backyard. She had pointed it out to them the day before. The boys' eyes had widened at the possibilities, but neither Toby nor Carol Ann could understand what the excitement was all about. Condescendingly Petey told them that because they were girls they wouldn't be expected to know that the rope and bucket was a homegrown amusement park ride.

"Why didn't you tell us about this before?" they complained.

Toby shrugged. She had never thought anything of it.

"Girls." Petey dismissed the entire sex in one contemptuous sigh. They had wasted a whole summer not knowing about the well, but better late than never.

Petey had wanted to hop right into the bucket and be the first to ride up and down, but Eric, the more serious and scientific one, suggested some basic testing first. Rocks were piled into the bucket to test the strength of the rope. Soon the boys came to the conclusion that yes, the rope and bucket would support their weight, but no, one guy alone working the crank couldn't pull someone back up. And the girls weren't even considered as lifters and heavers. So it would be one in the bucket and two on the crank and the world would be theirs. But then it was too late to go riding and they put it off until today.

Now they tramped through the tall grass in the backyard, rustled through the first of fallen leaves, and leaned over the smoothed bricks of the well.

"I'm first." Petey stepped bravely forward, then warily asked, "You sure you guys are strong enough to pull me up?"

"No sweat," Eric assured him.

Petey climbed onto the brick wall, reached over the open space, and grabbed the rope that held the bucket. He tugged at it to see if it would support his weight. Satisfied, he pulled the bucket closer to him and seated himself on it. He let the bucket swing freely over the opening of the well. "All right. Let me down slowly."

Eric and Mitchell positioned themselves at the crank handle. Carol Ann flicked up the hook that secured the bucket in place. The boys weren't ready for the sudden deadness of the weight. The handle started to slip through their hands, and Petey and the bucket dropped down the shaft.

"Hey!" Petey yelped.

But Eric and Mitchell gained a firm hold on the crank and were able to stem the bucket's downward motion. Petey hit the water with a gentle splash.

"Hey, it's neat down here," he yelled up. His voice echoed hollowly in the narrow shaft. He kicked the water with his sneakers then yelled, "All right, pull me up."

Eric grinned at Mitchell and called down to his friend. "What's it worth to you if we do?"

Petey's answer came swiftly. "If you don't, when I get out of here, I'm going to break your faces."

That was a good enough response for the boys, and, grunting and grinding in unison, they slowly hauled the bucket up and locked it in place at the top. Petey reached for the brick wall and climbed out, hung for one precarious second over the pit, and then catapulted himself off the bucket and sent it swinging back in the opposite direction.

"What's it like down there?" Eric asked.

Petey made a face. "All dark and creepy, with these big ugly spiders crawling up the wall. And snapping things in the water." He grew more animated. "Monsters! I'm lucky I still have both my feet."

Toby and Carol Ann looked at each other. Eric voiced what they were all thinking. "You're full of it."

"Yeah? You go down there then?"

"I will!"

Eric hoisted himself into the bucket and saluted his friends. "Lower away, guys." As Petey and Mitchell slowly lowered the bucket, Eric said manfully, "Give me liberty or give me—" As if on cue, the boys grinned and let go of the crank. The bucket plummeted to the water, Eric's voice echoing up— "deaaaaaath. . . ."

There was a loud splash as Eric hit bottom, then a strange and total silence.

Concern rippled through the children and they looked at each other. Had there been any danger in dropping Eric too fast? Was he hurt? Toby glanced nervously toward the house. Her mother wouldn't be home from work for some time. What if they needed help?

"Hey, Eric," Petey called down. "You all right?" His voice boomed back at him, louder, eerier.

More silence. The boys pulled on the rope. Eric's weight was still there. He hadn't fallen off the bucket. Leaning over the rim, they saw his limp body.

Then a frantic splashing and an animal cry of terror. And Eric's desperate voice. "Guys, pull me up!" Louder. "Get me out of here!" Another half second then a wail of pain. "Fast!" More splashing, thrashing, a terrified scream.

Petey and Mitchell manned the crank. Throwing all their young strength into their work, they quickly raised the bucket. No one knew what to expect when Eric was brought up.

Eric was dripping wet when he came into view, with a look of frozen horror on his face—his eyes wide, his mouth opened and downward in a strangled scream.

"Hey, man, what is it? What happened? Are you all right?"

Eric groaned as if in hellish pain. He dropped his head to his chest, let his tongue fall out. "The monster spiders got me," he said.

The children looked at each other. They didn't know what to do. Then Eric burst into wild laughter.

It took a full second for the other children to realize that Eric had bested them. Petey and Mitchell looked at each other, smiled, and released the handle, sending Eric wellward again. When they pulled him up again he was grinning broadly. "Hey, that was wild."

Mitchell claimed the bucket next and rode up and down a half dozen times before getting out. By now the boys' arms were growing tired and their wet bodies were chilled from the late-afternoon breeze. Petey was ready to go home but Carol Ann protested. "We haven't gone yet."

Toby, who wasn't really certain about the wisdom of this activity, said quickly, "It's all right. I don't really want to do it anyway."

But Carol Ann said, "Well, I do."

The boys shrugged. It was only fair. She was part of the group.

Watching the fun the boys had had riding up and down, Carol Ann hadn't considered how she might feel once she was actually in the bucket. As Petey and Eric lowered her beneath the rim of the well, the stone walls closed in claustrophobically around her. A sudden rush of panic came over her as she seemingly felt her mother's hand on her head, pushing her underneath the water. But she didn't want to appear chicken in front of her friends and so fought the urge to cry out and have them raise her to the surface. She closed her eyes and tensed herself to ride it out.

But this wasn't the water punishment; it was a carnival ride, and as the bucket touched the surface of the water, Carol Ann opened her eyes and dragged her hand through the cool water in the well, then kicked her feet and splashed the walls. The boys were right. It was fun! There was no danger down here and nothing could happen to her in the well.

"Again!" she cried when they pulled her up to the top.

She had just come up from her third and final ride when they all heard the shrill voice—

"Carol Ann!"

—and jumped. Petey and Eric, working the crank, almost lost their hold on it. But they managed to notch it in place at the top of the shaft before they turned to see a red-faced Beatrice stalking across the yard.

"Carol Ann!" she repeated.

"Hi, Mommy," Carol Ann said weakly. She was sitting in the bucket, suspended over the open shaft. From her mother's tone she knew she was in trouble.

"You get out of there this instant!" Beatrice demanded. "Where do you come to play like that? Any of you? Do you have any idea how dangerous that can be?"

"It isn't," Petey said.

"I don't want to hear it," Beatrice said. "Now you get out of that bucket, Carol Ann!" Her voice was like a whipcrack.

Beatrice helped her daughter out of the bucket, planted her firmly on the ground. She grabbed the girl's upper arm and almost yanked her into the air. Carol Ann yelped out in surprise and pain.

"Leave her alone!" Petey ordered.

Without letting go of Carol Ann, Beatrice took one step toward the children. "Don't you get fresh with me!" she yelled.

Frightened, Petey and the others hung back, respectful of the trouble one of their own was in and wanting to help, but not wanting to tangle with this irate mother.

"Never play like that again!" Beatrice said loudly to her daughter, and then pointed at the children. "I'm going to call each of your parents, tell them what you were doing. How would you like that?" But without waiting for an answer, she started to drag Carol Ann back across the yard. Her eyes fell on Toby, who was trying to make herself as small and invisible as possible. It seemed as if she was always doing something to get her friend in trouble. Although this time, it really hadn't been her fault. It was the boys' idea to play in the well.

"And just wait until I call *your* mother!" she said loudly.

"What are you going to call me for?"

Everyone turned to the new voice. Mesmerized by Beatrice's fury, nobody heard Linda come up. Toby didn't realize they had been playing so long. Happily she ran to her mother, a safe haven.

"What's going on here?" Linda demanded.

"I'll tell you what's going on," Beatrice said. She let go of Carol Ann's arm and the girl rubbed the soreness out where her mother's fingers had pinched her skin. "These children were riding up and down like acrobats in your well. They could have been killed!"

Linda looked at the children. They seemed more frightened now by Beatrice than from a month of riding in the bucket.

"They shouldn't have," Linda said. "It is dangerous, I agree. But nothing happened and now they know not to do it again."

"The well is on your property," Beatrice pushed. "If anything happened, you would have been at fault. You really have no sense of responsibility when it comes to children, do you, Mrs. Devonshire?" She spat out the name. "First Carol Ann could have been killed on your daughter's skates, when you should have been watching her! Now this!"

"Now see here," Linda protested. But she knew it was pointless to argue with the woman. She coolly said, "It won't happen again."

"It better not. And you better put a cap on that well. Cover it over with a board. Anybody can fall in there." She grabbed her daughter's arm again. "Come on, Carol Ann. You've been a very bad girl and I have to punish you."

Linda fumed as she watched Beatrice pull Carol Ann toward the driveway, and her anger got the best of her. She hesitated but decided to voice her thoughts anyway.

"You may think I have no responsibility when it comes to children—which isn't true! But you certainly have no sense of how to punish a child."

Beatrice froze. "What was that?"

Linda hesitated again. Her body was quivering in her anger, rekindled again. She hated herself when she got this way, almost out of control, when confronted with the rudeness of clerks, people who pushed in front of her on lines, tried to take advantage of her. But she had committed herself and had to carry through. She strained to keep her voice steady and not betray her fury.

"I know how you punish your child and I don't approve!"

Beatrice's eyes blazed. "What I do with my child, Mrs. Devonshire, is not any of your concern." And without another word she stalked off with Carol Ann in tow.

It was then that Linda noticed the other children, motionless as they watched the exchange between the two mothers. None of them had ever before witnessed such a fight between two adults. Linda, lost in her anger toward Beatrice, had forgotten about them. She breathed deeply, calmed herself, steadied her voice again, and said, "Okay, you'd better go home now. And don't play in the well again."

"Yes, Mrs. Devonshire," they all promised.

When they were gone, Toby said to her mother in a thick, frightened voice, "I didn't do it, Mommy. I didn't ride in the bucket." Her voice cracked, laced with worried tears that her mother would yell at her as Carol Ann's did, punish her too.

The tension eased from Linda's shoulders, the mask of anger from her face. She felt her blood pressure drop, the pounding behind her eyes subside. That's how people get strokes, she thought. She smiled at her daughter to put her at ease. "That's good, honey. I'm so proud of you. Come on. Let's go inside."

As they went toward the house she thought of how insensitive Beatrice was in how she treated her child. It was more than just insensitivity—it was cruelty. The little girl was terrified of her mother. But Linda realized that she should never have had words with the woman. It would only lead to trouble. For herself. For Toby.

chapter **14**

"You look absolutely stunning tonight, Mother," Thomas said.

Eleanor smiled and blushed like a schoolgirl. She twirled around. "Do you like my dress, Thomas? I just bought it yesterday."

"I do. Your hair as well. Your makeup. Lovely." He bowed and kissed her hand like a Frenchman, and Eleanor giggled.

"I spent half the day in the beauty parlor. What used to take an hour now takes—" She broke off, smiled. "Well, a few minutes more."

"Whatever it takes, the effect is magnificent. But why—surely not just for me?"

"Surely just for you. We haven't had dinner alone, just the two of us, in some time now and I thought to myself—why not make it a special occasion? New dress, new hairstyle, professional makeup. You open the wine, Thomas, I'll check on dinner." She winked. "I asked Marie to make all your favorites."

The table was elegantly set with silver candlesticks, flowers, crystal.

"Delicious," Thomas said as he bit into a sweet-and-sour meatball.

Eleanor beamed. "I missed having these quiet evenings with you, with no one else here to entertain, when I could completely relax with my son and we can be ourselves, talk about business, the bank, gossip about the people in town. Speaking of which, Elvira Chester went to New York for another facelift. That's her third. Pretty soon her chin will be up to her eyes . . ."

Thomas laughed good-naturedly with his mother. As they talked, he realized that what was making her so happy was what was making him unhappy. He missed Linda and Toby being there with them. The fine china and glasses couldn't mask the feeling of emptiness at the table. It was even difficult for him to remember going to his mother's house without them, they had become such a part of him. But his mother had asked for a special evening just with him and he had complied. Besides, he wanted to thank her, and when there was a break in the conversation, he said: "Mother, I was very happy about what you said to Linda at lunch, that you didn't object to our dating each other."

Eleanor waved him off. "As I said to her, you're both adults and you can do whatever pleases you. You don't need approval from your old mother, not like a hundred years ago when there was more formality to these things."

"I'm happy you feel that way."

"I'll be honest and say that at first I was concerned. I was afraid of the gossip, of people talking about your going out with Keith's wife, but then I said to myself, Why should we care about what people say? *We* are the important people around here, you and I who bear the Devonshire name. So let people talk. If this is what you want, Thomas, then the issue is closed. You go out with her, have dinner with her and her child, whatever you want."

"That's very gracious of you, Mother." Inwardly Thomas had to smile. His mother didn't have any idea of what "whatever you want" extended to. But at least now he and Linda could be more open about their relationship.

After dinner they had coffee in the den. Thomas took a packet of pictures out of his pocket. "Here, look what I found in my desk drawer. I had no idea I had them. You can put them in your album. Remember when they were taken?"

Eleanor studied the pictures. A smile broke out on her face. "Yes, of course. When you all entered the swim races at the country club during Olympic Week. Keith was—let's see—only five, and you were seventeen. Oh, look at this one, Thomas— you, Keith, your father, all adopting those he-man poses. God, you were handsome."

"Were?" he asked, pretending to be hurt.

"Oh, you." Eleanor smiled. "Still are, of course. . . . And this picture! Look!" But as she continued to look through the pictures, her voice grew more distant and the smile fell from her lips. Her eyes clouded and a sadness replaced the laughter within them. She had to summon strength to keep flipping through the snapshots. "And this picture, after you came in first. Thomas, Sr., was so proud. How we cheered during that race—" She broke off.

"Mother?"

"You were neck and neck until the end. I remember . . ." But then her lips started to quiver, and she dropped the pictures to her lap. "Oh, Thomas, why did you have to bring these? Why?"

"What is it, Mother? What's wrong?" He was alarmed.

Eleanor's hands were trembling, the jewelry on her wrists jangling with the shaky motion. Private emotions and fears surfaced, and from under her closed eyes tears started to spill down her face, a trail of eye shadow painting her like a circus clown.

"Mother?" Thomas grabbed her hands. They were icy to his touch, as if all the blood had drained from them.

"Oh, Thomas." She sighed heavily and tried to stem her tears.

"Tell me, Mother."

But she just shook her head weakly, unable to voice what she was experiencing. Thomas tightened his hold on her hands; shook them. "Mother!"

"Memories," she said softly, "memories. One more pleasant than the next, more painful than the next. And no matter how hard I try I can't escape the pain." She let go of Thomas's hand, covered her eyes with her fingers, squeezed the bridge of her nose, shook her head to try to free herself. "They're dead, Thomas," she whispered mournfully. "Your father. Keith."

And to Thomas her body suddenly seemed to grow smaller, frailer. A chill spiraled up his spine, and he put his arms around her. This wasn't his mother. His mother was strong. She did not cry. He could count on his hand the times in the past when his mother had cried. He was afraid to see her like this. "Don't . . ." he said soothingly.

"I have done so many things wrong. I drove Keith away from me."

"You can't think about that now," Thomas whispered into her ear.

"And when I wanted him to come back, he wouldn't. I begged him, but he wouldn't. And now he's dead."

"Don't punish yourself, Mother," he implored.

"You're the only one I have left, Thomas. My husband is dead. My youngest son is dead. I don't know what I would do if I didn't have you." She looked around the room, a cornered animal glaze in her eyes. "God, this house is so big."

"You'll always have me, Mother," Thomas said, his voice thick. For a second he was afraid he might cry as well. "You don't have to worry. I'll always be here."

She looked into his eyes searchingly. Her own were rimmed with red, her makeup smudged, her elegant demeanor shattered into a thousand slivers of glass.

"Don't ever leave me, Thomas," she pleaded, her voice brittle, odd-sounding.

"No, Mother, never," he promised, and swayed her back and forth as he might a child, pitying her for her pain. She wrapped her arms around him in a clutching embrace. He shivered. Not because his mother was so upset and tortured by her loss, but because he had seen something else in her face. Heard it in her voice. Fear. His strong, cold-hearted mother was afraid. Of his dying like his father and brother. Of losing him. Of being left without family, alone.

"Never," he repeated again, as an odd emotion he couldn't quite identify flooded over him. He choked back his own tears. Then he understood. His mother was changing, growing softer with age. He never would have expected her to approve so readily of his dating Linda. Not the way she had once treated her. And looking at his mother now—a frail figure, huddled in his arms—he knew that she was capable of loving, of fearing, of expressing emotions she had kept so well hidden throughout her life. Eleanor Devonshire was human! he wanted to yell, and he felt closer to her at that moment than he had in a long, long time. In fact, he knew he loved her.

"I will never leave you," he promised again. "Never."

Toby clung to Linda throughout the evening. She helped set the table, clear it, and do the dishes. She was still bothered, Linda knew, by what had happened at the well with Beatrice and what was surely happening to Carol Ann. After supper, Linda helped her with subtraction problems and they watched television together. At bedtime, Toby promptly changed into her pajamas, her teeth brushed and flossed, the model child.

Linda sat down on the edge of her daughter's bed; stroked her forehead to give her one extra moment of reassurance. Then she kissed Toby good night and closed the door. When she checked on her fifteen minutes later, Toby was sleeping soundly. Her worry had exhausted her.

The run-in with Beatrice had exhausted Linda as well, and she was looking forward to a quiet evening in which she could lose herself in the new romance novel she had bought the day before. But as much as she was enjoying the story, she found it difficult to concentrate. The words blurred and ran into each other.

She suddenly felt prickly, as if Beatrice's eyes were on her. She closed the book and went to the front door, opened it, and shivered slightly as the night air swelled around her. She looked across the street. All the downstairs lights in the Dailey house were out and only one lamp burned on the second floor. Carol Ann was asleep and Beatrice had moved upstairs for the night. For some odd reason Linda was curious about her, wondered what the woman was doing, if she was at all affected by what had transpired that afternoon.

She remembered what Thomas had said about the woman after she had first met her. "She changed after her husband's death. She's reclusive now. Overprotective of her daughter." Overprotective to the point of irrationality, perhaps. Then she considered the new thought: Perhaps the woman would value a friendship. What if she made an overture to her? But she quickly dismissed the idea as irrational as well. Not after all that had happened between them. *Have no contact with her*, instinct warned. Toby and Carol Ann could be friends, their mothers didn't have to. Bringing the woman out of herself was just not Linda's responsibility.

Suddenly she felt uneasy standing in the doorway as the light swept out past her, silhouetting her, making her visible to night eyes, vulnerable. Like a nervous rabbit she glanced furtively around the yard. She could see no one in the shadows of the hedges, not that she expected to. Satisfied there was no one there, she went back inside. But still she double-checked the window and door-locks. The fight with Beatrice had unsettled her more than she had thought.

She picked up the novel, eager to lose herself in another's romance. She found her place and was able to read two pages before worry stole over her again and layered her skin like a fine mist. It was undefined; she could not identify the source. Eleanor was no longer intimidating to her and she had resolved not to let Beatrice bother her. So why did she still feel afraid? There was no reason.

But there was.

Because when she sifted through her mind, she always came back to the image of a man—his hair curly, his mustache full and blond. And she knew that Thomas could smother her with protective kisses and she could lock the doors, pull down the windowshades, turn off the lights and shut out the night, but she would never be free of him. He was inside her, and she knew he would remain there, haunting her, forever.

Eleanor kissed Thomas good night. Seeing the note of concern in his eyes, she said, "I'm all right. You don't have to be afraid to leave me."

"If you need me, Mother, will you call?"

"Yes, of course, of course. Go. Drive safely." She tried to shoo him out the door.

He kissed her on the forehead. "Good night, Mother." And then he was gone. Eleanor heard the start of the car, then the whine of his tires against the pebbled drive as he pulled away from the house.

She closed the door and leaned against it. The house was suddenly deathly still. Set well back from the road, no traffic sounds came to her. Then she heard the ticking of the grandfather clock. A familiar sound, she had so absorbed it that she never really heard it, but tonight its tick was loud—a deep, rich, low-pitched ring. Eleanor chilled to the sound. She had lived in this house for almost forty years, ever since she married Thomas, Sr., but tonight for the first time she felt the house was too large for her. Too many rooms. Too many ghosts and regrets.

She looked at herself in the hallway mirror and cringed at her reflection. The whites of her eyes were tinged with red, and black streaks of eye shadow trailed down her face. She reached for a tissue and wiped away the smudges, the makeup as well, and she saw the tired lines of age that crisscrossed her skin.

She went into the den. The pictures were still on the couch, wedged into the cracks between the cushions where she had let them fall. She stood across the room, stared down at them cautiously, almost as if they were coiled snakes, waiting to spring at her if she came too close.

But then she sat down on the couch, sank deeply into its softness, picked up the pictures, and started to slowly look through them again. Unashamed now, she let the tears fall. Pictures of Keith when he was only a child. One day he was four, the next he was grown and off to college. Never again to return home. Not even after his death. How the time had flown, and she had never used the years to get close to him. To either of her sons. Because it wasn't their way. Was it wrong? It was too late to answer any of that now.

But she knew now she should never have given Keith the ultimatum about Linda. He was a Devonshire, stubborn like all of them. That was a tragic mistake. There could have been other ways to make him see that what he was doing was . . . misguided. Better ways.

And because of that one mistake she had lost her son forever. Now she had to be careful. She couldn't repeat her error, lose Thomas as well. He was her only son now; without him she'd have no one.

She got up from the couch and flipped off the light, went from room to room on the first floor shutting off the other lights. Then without turning around to look at the darkness below her, she slowly, almost painfully, climbed the steps to her bedroom.

She would never do anything to turn Thomas against her as she had Keith. She was afraid she would lose his love, afraid she could die all alone.

The grandfather clock chimed the quarter hour, one low mournful note that echoed within her ears like a cry of pain that refused to go away.

chapter **15**

An Indian summer descended on the northeast and the sun hung high and bright in the cloudless sky. After the cool days of early October and first frost that layered the morning grass like a silken sheet, it was almost as if the natural order of seasons was suddenly and crazily reversed. The days were lazy and hot and even though clothing had already been changed, woolen sweaters taken out of mothballs, shorts and T-shirts became the code of dress. Everyone was happy to hang on to one more week, one more day of warm weather, before giving in to the inevitable chill of New England winter.

Carol Ann had a cold and was grounded to her room. But she hadn't sneezed all day and as the hot Saturday afternoon dragged by, it was more and more difficult to remain indoors. She was lying on her bed, counting the birds on her wallpaper, when the pebble tapped against her window. Looking out, she saw all of her friends downstairs.

"How ya doin'?" Petey called up.

"Shh," Carol Ann cautioned. "My mother will hear you. She's sleeping."

"Can't you come down?"

"No. I have a cold."

"You sound okay," Eric said.

Carol Ann shrugged. She felt okay, too, but her mother thought she should stay in for the weekend and then be all ready for school on Monday. She would have preferred to be outside today and home on Monday.

"It's so hot we were thinking about going down to the stream. Can you sneak out?"

"I don't know," Carol Ann said hesitantly. The invitation was tempting. Petey and Mitchell were wearing bathing suits. Toby had on shorts and Eric his cut-off jeans. They were all set to get wet. "My mother'll get angry."

"How will she know? She's sleeping. Come on—sneak out. Put the pillows under the covers. You know how to do it."

"Yeah," Carol Ann said, remembering the day Petey had instructed them all in stacking the bolsters under the blanket to give the impression there was a sleeping child in the bed. "Let me think. . . ."

But not much thought was required. The day was too tempting, the house too confining, for any other answer. "Be right down," she whispered hoarsely.

She tried to remember exactly how Petey had stacked the bolsters and artfully tucked here and adjusted there. She stood across the room to study her work from every angle. Satisfied, she opened the door a crack and listened. The house was silent, her mother and Shana were asleep. She gently eased her door closed and prayed it wouldn't squeal. Then with only the slightest of clicks the latch caught. She tiptoed down the stairs and was out of the house, racing to her friends.

She found them in Toby's yard, letting Princess chase them in circles. Petey had the idea.

"Why should we have to go down to the stream? That's almost a mile away. Let's play in the well again. There's cool water there and it's fun."

The boys were for the idea immediately, the girls a bit hesitant.

"I'd better not," Carol Ann said, not wanting to get caught by her mother and punished.

"Come on," Petey prodded. "She's sleeping. She'll never know. Just for a few minutes."

Carol Ann shook her head.

"You want us to call you chicken?" Petey mocked, then flapped his arms and clucked around the yard.

"All right," Carol Ann agreed. Her mother was a sound sleeper. "Just for a little while. I have to get back before my mother wakes up." Then she turned to Toby. "And you have to try it."

"I don't know." Toby wavered, remembering her mother's warning.

''Come on. You can't get hurt. It's fun. And Princess can ride too.''

All the boys shouted encouragement and while Toby remained uncertain, she didn't want to seem different from her friends. She decided there really wasn't any danger in riding up and down in the bucket as long as they were careful. Besides, it did look like fun at that, and her mother was out shopping so she would never know. So Toby nodded and made her decision.

As Princess was being lowered for the first ride, Beatrice Dailey woke up dazed. A troubling thought had crossed her mind and raised her too quickly from sleep. Her head felt swathed in filmy gray and her heart pounded with intuitive fear. Something was wrong with Carol Ann. She shook herself awake and opened the door to her daughter's bedroom. There she was, under the blankets. Safe. Sound. But then Shana darted past her into the room, hooked her mouth over the covers, and started to tug.

''Don't,'' Beatrice whispered. ''You'll wake Carol Ann.'' She went to the bed and lifted the covers to pull them back up when she noticed the pillows underneath. She frowned. ''Carol Ann?'' she questioned. Then in one motion she yanked the covers off the bed to see the pillows and bolsters. She nodded knowingly and tightened her lips.

''You're a bad girl, Carol Ann,'' she whispered. ''A bad girl.''

Then she left the bedroom to search for her evil daughter.

At the well, Princess seemed reluctant to get out of the bucket, enjoying the cool dunk in the water, but after three trips up and down, Toby lifted the wet dog out and put her down on the grass. Everyone got sprayed as the dog dried herself off.

Each boy wanted to ride first. Petey claimed it and then the other boys went in turn. Then Carol Ann, and finally Toby knew it was time for her.

''It's easy,'' Carol Ann prompted as she helped Toby up onto the rim of the well. ''The only hard part is getting into the bucket, but after that, it's a snap.''

The top of the well was slippery and Toby's hands and knees skittered along the smooth stones. She reached out for the rope to pull the bucket close enough so she could climb into it. She looked down at the water, fifteen feet below her. Though she was frightened, she managed to grab the rope and swing her body into the bucket.

"Do it slowly, please," she said. Petey shot her a thumbs-up go for it. He and Eric gently lowered the bucket until it touched the surface of the water.

"Always hang onto the rope." Carol Ann leaned over the rim and cautioned. "That way you can't slip out."

It was cool at the bottom and Toby giggled. The children were right—it was fun, and she was glad she had done it. She felt a sudden surge of pride within her—she was growing up.

They took turns for the next fifteen minutes, in rotation. Their bodies were wet but the sun was warm and they knew they'd soon dry off.

"Last ride," Petey announced. He had been doing most of the cranking and his arms were getting tired.

Carol Ann was in the bucket, halfway up the well, when Eric nudged Mitchell. "Look over there."

"Holy shit." He leaned into the well. "It's your mother, Carol Ann. She's coming this way. Keep quiet. We'll pretend you're not here."

From the middle of the shaft came a frightened whisper. "Okay."

They locked the bucket, then rimmed the well to block Beatrice's view. Petey stepped forward to greet her.

"Hello, Mrs. Dailey." He tried to keep his voice even, betray nothing. "We hope Carol Ann is feeling better."

"Where is she?" Beatrice demanded, looking around.

"She's sick. In bed."

"You children are in a lot of trouble. All of you." She pushed past them, stared into the well. "Carol Ann!"

Carol Ann, who had been holding her breath, exhaled at her mother's voice. She looked above her. The jig was up.

"I'm sorry, Mommy. I was hot. And I wasn't sneezing and I thought it would be okay. And everyone was calling me chicken—"

"Bad girl!" Beatrice snapped, and Carol Ann fell silent. Beatrice turned to the children. "You're all bad and should be punished. I want you away from here now." Her voice quivered with anger. They saw her face flush red, veins stand out prominently on her neck. "Or I'll take the strap to each and every one of you."

With that the children broke and ran, Toby scooping up Princess. "To my house!" Petey called. Over his shoulder he yelled back, "Good luck, Carol Ann."

With the children gone, Beatrice glared down into the well. "You promised you would never play here again. I told you it was dangerous. I warned you."

"It's not!" Carol Ann cried.

"And then you sneak out of the house and try to fool me!"

Tears started to stream down Carol Ann's face. She had never seen her mother this angry before. The sun had ducked behind a cloud and a chill riffled the air. In the well, Carol Ann shivered; her clothing clung wetly to her cold body. She sneezed. She was suspended precariously above the water, vulnerable. She tightened her hold on the rope so she wouldn't accidentally fall out of the bucket. "Pull me up, please. I'm sorry, Mommy. I'm sorry—" Her plaintive cry echoed loudly in the narrow shaft.

But Beatrice wasn't hearing her daughter. She was trapped by a thick fog of memory, by other voices.

I'm sorry, Mommy, young Beatrice cried.

That stain will never come out. That dress is completely ruined. You've been a very bad girl, Beatrice, and I have to punish you . . . have to punish you . . . have to punish you. The words sounded inside her.

She had been bad and was punished.

And Carol Ann had been bad.

And had to be punished as well.

Beatrice moved to the crank handle, released the hook. Without any lock or counterweight, the bucket dropped suddenly down the shaft. The spray from the splash soaked the little girl.

It was dark at the bottom of the well. Her mother, leaning over the rim, blocked out the sun. Only a thin shaft of light fought its way around her mother's figure, which was silhouetted in the glare. Dust particles danced in the light. Then her mother moved, directed the shaft of sunlight against the brick wall, and Carol Ann saw them in the cracks and mortar crevices—spiders that she hadn't noticed before when it had been warm and fun. Flying things, like Eric had joked about, but they were real and they sprang from the stone and landed on her.

"Mommy, please," she begged as she pushed the spiders off her. She splashed the water to wash them from the walls. "I won't be bad again. Just take me up. I won't be bad. I won't be bad. I won't be—''

Oh, Beatrice, stop it. You always yell and cry and make promises, hoping you won't be punished.

Mommy, Beatrice begged.

"Mommy, I didn't mean to disobey you and play in the well."

I'm not listening to you, Beatrice. You were a bad girl and have to be punished . . .

"Mommmeeeeeee—''

Carol Ann's wailing voice penetrated a wall. Beatrice heard her daughter.

"Mommmeeeeeeee—''

Beatrice shocked to the voice. She shook her head clear, stared down the well shaft. Her eyes widened in an unbalanced mix of terror and surprise.

"Carol Ann?'' she questioned, confused by what she was seeing—her daughter at the bottom of the well.

"Please crank me up, Mommy.''

"My God!'' Beatrice yelled, her voice shaky with worry. "How did you get down there?''

She grabbed the crank, started to turn it. The progress was slow. Carol Ann was heavier than she had expected. She had gotten the little girl three quarters up the shaft when she lost her footing. The crank jumped from her hands. She didn't have time to lock it in place and stem the downward motion of the bucket. A dead weight, the bucket dropped to the bottom of the shaft again.

Carol Ann had wrapped her arms around herself to keep warm. When the bucket started to drop she wasn't able to grab onto the rope. She wasn't anchored when it hit the water, and she tumbled out backward. Her head cracked against the stone wall.

"Carol Ann!'' Beatrice screamed. Frantically she looked around for someone to help her. But she was deep in the backyard and nobody heard. Carol Ann was sinking under the water.

"Carol Ann!'' she cried again, as if trying to shock the girl back into consciousness.

But Carol Ann would never regain consciousness.

Finally someone had heard Beatrice's screams and called the police. The first policeman on the scene shimmied down the rope, and Carol Ann was raised in the bucket. CPR and mouth-to-mouth resuscitation was applied. An ambulance was summoned.

Throughout the rescue procedure, Beatrice stood off to the side, away from the edge of the well, her hands twisting fearfully against each other. When the policeman wrested Carol Ann from the bucket and laid her on the ground, Beatrice slumped to her knees beside them and watched the officer attempt to revive her child. As long as he was bent over her, trying to force oxygen into her lungs, there was hope. Only when he stood and shrugged helplessly did she know that her daughter was dead. She looked imploringly at the policemen.

"They were only playing in the well," she said blankly, not understanding what could have gone so horribly, horribly wrong. "All the children. I told them it was dangerous and they could get hurt . . ." She grabbed her dead child and smothered her in her arms, cradling her head next to her breast. She looked at them questioningly, searching for answers.

"I was pulling her up. She fell out of the bucket." Tears dripped down her face. "It was dangerous. They could get hurt. . . . But nobody else got hurt. Only my baby."

Hands reached out for Carol Ann. At first Beatrice refused to let go. Then the policeman stroked her forehead and said softly, "Please. Give her to us. We'll take care of her."

"I was pulling her up," Beatrice said numbly as she relinquished her hold on Carol Ann. "It was dangerous," she repeated flatly, as if in explanation.

The children gathered, attracted to the whirring lights and sirens. They stood in a small cluster near the house, watching the officers bending over Carol Ann. An ambulance came roaring up and two paramedics jumped out with a stretcher. They lifted Carol Ann, strapped her onto the stretcher, and covered her head.

Beatrice pointed at the children and screamed. "There they are! They were playing with Carol Ann!"

The children froze. They didn't know where to look—at Beatrice's accusatory finger or at the stretcher that was being wheeled past them toward the ambulance.

Linda came driving up. In a flash she was out of the car and took in the scene. She searched for Toby among the children.

Once she ascertained that it was not her daughter in the ambulance, she approached the policeman. "What happened?" she demanded.

Toby ran up to her, buried herself in her mother's arms. The other children looked as if they wanted to do the same.

"What happened?" she repeated.

Beatrice saw Linda and raged toward her, fury in her eyes. "You didn't cover the well!" Beatrice shrieked madly. "I warned you something was going to happen. I warned you—"

"I—" Linda started.

"I warned you!" Beatrice repeated, and dissolved into hysterical tears. They led her to the waiting patrol car to take her to the hospital.

Toby didn't let go of Linda's hand as they walked into the house. Carol Ann had said riding in the bucket wasn't dangerous, but now she was dead. And it could have been *she* who had slipped out.

Tearfully she confessed to Linda that she had been playing in the well with her friends. She knew it was wrong, she cried, dangerous, but she had done it anyway because she didn't want to be left out. She was now telling her mother the truth so her mother would make it all right, remove her fear, tell her nothing was going to happen to her.

Linda listened to her daughter and together they thanked God that she was safe. Yes, she said as she wiped Toby's teary face, she could have been hurt. But she wasn't, and she should learn a lesson from this. Toby nodded. She certainly had.

She went to bed right after supper but was unable to fall asleep. Images from the afternoon flashed in front of her eyes— the smooth stones of the well wall, the rough texture of the rope, the redness of her hands as she held tightly to it. And getting brave and letting go for a moment when she was being lowered toward the water. Had Carol Ann let go of the rope? Was that why she had fallen?

Then she chilled as she remembered the vow the friends had made that day—whoever died first would try to come back and make contact with the others. A childish vow, her mother told her, a meaningless one. But maybe not so meaningless now because Carol Ann was dead.

With her eyes wide she searched the murky grayness of her

bedroom. It seemed to pulsate, almost as if alive. *Carol Ann was trying to come through to her.* She followed swirling patterns of darkness, imagined them coalescing into human features—Carol Ann's face, her lithe body. She strained to hear sounds.

Frightened, she pulled the blanket up over her eyes, covering them. So she couldn't see what was there. So whatever was there couldn't see her. She dared not peek out.

Her body trembled as she waited tensely for something to happen. Then she sensed eyes on her—Carol Ann's!—searching for her, her dead eyes searing the blanket to make contact with her, to keep the vow they had stupidly made.

Her fear exhausted her and finally put her to sleep.

Linda needed consoling too. Thomas drove over to be with her.

She couldn't sit still. She paced the room anxiously, felt sick to her stomach. What had happened was so disturbing, she didn't know what to do with herself. She ran her hands along her arms, which were layered with goosebumps. When Thomas arrived she threw her arms around him and clung to him in a choking hold. She kept seeing the anguish on Beatrice's face as she was led toward the patrol car. The woman had just lost her only child— Carol Ann, a beautiful little girl who had befriended Toby and made their move here such a success for her, *was dead*. So inconceivable.

She felt a terrible ache of guilt as well.

"I should have covered that well, Thomas. She told me to do it. She warned me." In anguish she ran her hand through her hair, squared her jaw to choke back her tears, and shuddered.

Thomas put his arms around her and tilted her chin so she had to look at him. "Do you do everything that people tell you to?" he asked gently. She didn't answer, only stared out blankly through a curtain of tears. He smiled, tried to ease the moment. He couldn't allow Linda to feel what she was. "Listen to me," he pleaded, hoping to break down the wall of guilt she had created for herself. "You had no part in what happened today. If anything, it's the bank's fault. My fault. We own the house."

"No, Thomas, you didn't know the children were playing there," she said helplessly. She pulled away from him and slapped her fist against her thigh in anger. As if causing herself pain could possibly change what had occurred today. If only she could turn back the clock, close her eyes, and will that the afternoon had never happened.

"Linda, for all we know countless children have ridden up and down in that bucket and nothing happened before. It was an accident, pure and simple."

"Oh, Thomas," she cried. "Don't—don't—"

Saying no more, Thomas cradled her in his arms and let her cry. He looked beyond her, his own eyes wet, his heart wanting so to ease her pain. If only he could find the words that would lift her guilt.

Threatening heavy gray-black clouds hung low in the south-eastern sky. A cool air mass had been coming down from Canada since early the previous evening, meshing ominously with the humid air of the Indian summer, and the haze-fringed moon had been visible only through infrequent breaks in the oncoming storm clouds.

Now, at noon, it was dark. The rain had held back for the morning, giving the clouds more time to compact, coalesce, and build. Electricity crackled in the air even before the first bolts of lightning descended.

A perfect day for a funeral, Linda thought grimly as she eyed the darkened sky. Over Thomas's protests, she had insisted on attending. Thomas and Eleanor accompanied her. They were standing off to the side, under a large tree, observers to the tragedy. Linda did not want to intrude on Beatrice's grief, knowing that her expressions of sympathy would not be accepted. She did not bring Toby along.

The service in the funeral chapel had been brief. The minister's tears had fallen freely. Words were uttered that had been said and said again. Everyone wept openly, unashamedly. In the viewing room Linda had filed past the open casket with the others for one last look at Carol Ann. Her young cheeks were reddened to mask the pallor of death, her eyes seemed only lightly closed. She could have been asleep. But now only pillows and bolsters remained on her bed at home; Beatrice had never removed them.

Two men supported Beatrice during the burial. Linda's body was shaking as well, chilled from the wind that preceded the rain

clouds and from her emotion. Thomas's hand was holding tightly
to her arm, as if sensing she might slump to the ground.

The first drops of rain started to fall. Umbrellas went up. The
low rumble of thunder broke the silence in the cemetery and
disturbed the birds that called anxiously to each other, looking
for shelter to weather the storm. Linda looked above her. Barren
tree branches waved accusatory fingers at her, as if nature and
the heavens knew her guilt.

The minister was finished speaking and Beatrice threw a handful of dirt into the grave. Linda flinched as she sensed it striking
the wooden coffin. Then a crack of lightning split the sky and the
funeral was over.

The two men were helping Beatrice back to the car. The other
mourners stepped aside and made a path for her.

Linda, Thomas, and Eleanor watched as Beatrice approached
where they were standing, on her way toward the limousine. Her
face was streaked, from the rain and her tears. Linda looked with
pity at the grief-struck woman. She had lost Keith, a husband,
but to lose a child who was once part of you was perhaps even
worse.

Beatrice raised her eyes; met Linda's. It was the first time they
had seen each other since the funeral service began. Beatrice's
lower lip began to quiver. Suddenly her eyes blazed, anger
replacing the sorrow within them. As Linda stepped backward,
Thomas tightened his hold on her.

Beatrice shrieked, a primal scream of anguish, of pain and
despair, of a mother whose child was dead. "You killed her!
You killed my baby! You!''

"No!" Linda scarcely breathed. "It was an accident."

"You didn't cover the well! You killed her!"

The moment hung suspended. The crowd was silent, in shock.
Then the men supporting Beatrice started to ease her toward the
limousine, and Eleanor turned Linda away from her. But even as
Beatrice was escorted to the car, her head swiveled back toward
Linda, her eyes still bright with anger.

"You killed her!" she shrieked again. "You killed her!" Then
she was inside the car, the door slammed shut behind her. Linda
remained rooted where she was until the limousine pulled away.

Eleanor put her arm around Linda comfortingly. "There, there," she said soothingly. "She didn't mean it. She's upset. She couldn't possibly believe what she's saying."

"No," Thomas echoed as he helped Linda down the path to where the car was parked.

Eleanor fell in behind them, pausing momentarily to watch Beatrice's limousine as it wound its way down the cemetery lane and through the front gate.

Then the rain broke in full force and everyone scurried for shelter.

Beatrice was sitting in a wing chair, her head resting listlessly against the thick upholstered side. She hadn't changed her clothes since returning from the funeral and the black mourning dress hung loosely around her. She was idly rubbing Shana's head, listening to the rain pound against the windows. The dog was subdued, as if she knew that something was very wrong. She ate her dinner quietly and didn't beg for scraps of leftovers. And there was a lot of food left; Beatrice didn't touch the dinner that neighbors had prepared for her. Nor did she want their company tonight. She was grateful that they cared enough not to want to leave her alone, but it was what she preferred, locked in by the rain and her sorrow.

The house was strangely silent without the shuffle of Carol Ann's slippered feet, the play of her television, or the slam of the bathroom door. A child's sounds that she was home. Safe. Alive. Beatrice was thankful for the rain. Without it there would be no sound at all—something she knew she would have to get used to.

The ringing phone was jarringly loud. A neighbor calling to express condolences. Beatrice didn't want to answer it, but its rings became more insistent, and she struggled out of her chair, picked it up.

"Hello, Mrs. Dailey. This is Mrs. Devonshire." The voice was hesitant, faltering. "I wanted to tell you how sorry I am that—"

Beatrice no longer heard the words. Her breath quickened, her heart raced. She couldn't calm herself; she didn't try.

"Why are you torturing me?" she cried. "Why? Haven't you done enough already?" Blood pounded through her temples. "Don't you ever call me again. Don't you understand—you killed her! You killed my daughter!"

She slammed down the phone, covered her eyes with her palms, and wept.

On the other end, Eleanor hung up after the line was abruptly cut off. Her hands were hurting. Her arthritis had been bad all week, and she took a pain killer before going to bed.

Exhausted by the day and by her outburst, Beatrice went upstairs to the bathroom to prepare for bed. She looked at herself in the mirror. She hadn't put on any makeup since her child's death. Her face was tired and lined, her eyes red and puffy from crying. Afraid she wouldn't be able to relax, she turned on the water and swallowed a sleeping pill. Leaving the water running, she stared dully at it as it filled the sink and remembered what had happened. It had been an accident. She hadn't meant to do it. The dress was ruined, she knew, but she hadn't done it on purpose. She hadn't been a bad girl. Neither she nor Carol Ann had.

Then she thought of Linda Devonshire and her daughter. It was Toby who had brought Carol Ann to play at the well. And even though she had been warned of the danger, Linda hadn't covered it. She had been negligent, responsible for what had happened. She had killed her daughter.

First she had taken Keith away from her, now Carol Ann.

It wasn't right, Beatrice considered solemnly.

Keith and Carol Ann were dead; Linda and Toby were alive.

When they were the ones who were bad.

chapter 16

Carol Ann's death preyed heavily on Linda's mind. She couldn't shake the image of the child's funeral; it was imprinted in her memory—the lowering of the small casket, Beatrice throwing a clump of burial mud into the grave, the dirt slipping loosely through her weakened fingers. As much as she tried to convince herself she was not at fault—the children had all been warned and should have known better—she could not lift the guilt she had assumed as her own: She was responsible for the child's death.

At the office she did her job by rote, for the first time welcoming the ostracism of the others, ignoring Nancy, not letting herself be bothered by rudeness and sarcasm. There was a pall over her evenings with Thomas. Their dinners were subdued, strained, as Thomas tiptoed cautiously around her. He and Toby chatted while Linda listened listlessly. Her eyes were hollow and more distant than he had ever known them, a hazy cloudiness to the normally crystalline blue, outside turned in. As if _she_ were in mourning, Thomas thought, but he did nothing to try to lift her spirits, knowing how much to heart she had taken the death of the neighbor child. He knew how vulnerable she was to her emotions; he'd already seen Keith and loss languish deep in her eyes. She would have to resolve her feelings at her own pace.

Eleanor phoned, wanting to get together for lunch. Linda demurred, preferring to be left alone, but Eleanor said, "Nonsense. Thomas has told me how troubled you are, child, and I want to talk to you about it. I can't have you walking around torturing yourself."

Heartened by Eleanor's words and pleased as well that the older woman was reaching out toward her, they made plans to meet at the Country Kettle.

They made small talk until after they had ordered, then Eleanor leaned across the table and touched Linda's wrist lightly. The gesture was tender. Linda looked into the eyes of her mother-in-law, which were warm, reassuring. Eyes like those Linda had so often shown to Toby.

"I'm not going to try to convince you that you weren't at fault. Neither Thomas, nor I, nor anyone can make you see that. That's something you will have to work out for yourself." She pursed her lips, shook her head sadly. "It was tragic, absolutely tragic—the death of the girl, and of course what Beatrice Dailey said to you at the funeral. I can understand the strain that she must be under because I, too, have lost a child. . . ." She lowered her eyes and flicked them away from Linda, then continued. "But the living must go on. I went on, Beatrice will go on, and of course you have to go on as well."

"Yes," Linda said. "Thank you. And I know I will. It's just so difficult now. I keep seeing, remembering . . ."

Eleanor's smile formed tiny wrinkles around her eyes and mouth. "I know. But perhaps it would make it easier for you if you counted your blessings."

"What?" Linda puzzled. "What good could there possibly be in this?"

"Just be thankful it wasn't Toby," Eleanor said softly.

"Yes," Linda mumbled, not even wanting to be reminded of what she had tried to consign to the back of her mind—the terrifying thought that grasped her with poisoned talons—that it could have been her daughter who had died in the well.

When Linda got home from work, Toby was sitting forlornly on the couch. The little girl's chin was rounded and rested on her fists, elbows on knees. She looked as if she had been crying.

"What's wrong?" Linda asked, alarmed. "Are you sick?" She immediately went to feel the child's forehead.

"Princess is gone," Toby said.

"What do you mean, she's gone?"

"She wasn't here when I got home."

"She has to be here. Did you look everywhere?"

Glumly: "Everywhere."

"Well, she couldn't have gotten out. Come on, let's look together."

Toby let her mother take her hand and lead her through the house, searching corners where she had already been a hundred times—under beds, in closets, behind the refrigerator in case the dog had gotten trapped.

"See?" Toby said when Linda finally admitted defeat. "She must have run away. She probably didn't like the way I took care of her." Then she asked, "But how did she get out, Mommy?"

"She must have found a way," Linda equivocated. The answer satisfied the tearful child, but Linda knew something was wrong.

"She couldn't have gotten out," she said to Thomas when he arrived for dinner. "All the doors and windows are closed. And there are no holes anywhere."

They walked through the house, repeating what Linda and Toby had done earlier.

"I'm sure there's an explanation," Thomas said thoughtfully. "You leave the house after Toby, don't you?"

"Yes. The school bus comes at eight. I don't leave for work until eight thirty."

"And the dog was here when Toby left this morning."

"I saw her kiss Princess good-bye."

"So she probably darted out of the house when you were locking the door."

"I would have seen her," Linda protested.

"Did you see her when she knocked into me holding the plates of soup? Did *I* see her?"

"No," Linda said. "She appeared from nowhere. She's certainly speedy and slippery."

"That's probably what happened today. You were buttoning your coat at the door, fumbling in your purse for your keys, something . . . and you didn't see the dog scoot out between your legs. She was probably down the steps and out of sight before you even locked up."

"Probably." Linda nodded distantly, trying to reconstruct the morning. Had she seen the dog dart past her?

"It's my fault," she said. "I wasn't watching."

"Come on," Thomas prodded gently. "What we don't need around here is any more guilt, okay?"

Linda nodded. "But what do we do about Toby? She's so upset."

"I can get her another dog."

"She was very attached to Princess."

"Well, why don't we just wait a little while? I suspect that Princess wishes she were home, and I wouldn't be surprised if before long a little furry thing came a-scratching at your door, whining to be let back in and forgiven. Tell you what—if she doesn't return by tomorrow, I'll put an ad in the paper."

"Okay," Linda agreed, her tone indicating she didn't expect very much to result. It was disconcerting that the dog had run off so soon after Carol Ann's death.

Thomas had to prepare for a breakfast meeting so he left right after dinner. Linda went upstairs to Toby's room, where the girl was finishing her homework. She stood silently in the doorway, watching her daughter work, hunched over the desk, pencil poised, as she searched for answers. Even from the back, Linda could imagine Toby's high forehead furrowed thoughtfully, her face crinkled with understanding and triumph. She would die, she knew, if anything ever happened to Toby; there would be no purpose to life.

She straddled a chair next to Toby and put her arm tightly around the little girl, not wanting to let the child out of her sight or grasp, almost afraid she might get lost as Princess had. Toby instinctively sensed Linda's fear—the hesitancy in her eye and movement. She remembered that the last time her mother had looked so fragile and tentative she had gone away to the hospital. Her father had taken care of her then, but if anything happened to her mother now, she'd be all alone. She drew close to Linda, rested her head against the crook of her arm. Troubled, mother and child clung to each other, trying to suppress their private fears.

"Wash my hair tonight," Toby said. "I like it when you do that." Linda had always enjoyed the shared moment too, the closeness.

Toby stood at the sink and Linda piled the rich lather onto her hair, curling it around her ears in exotic design. She turned on the tap and was putting Toby's head under the faucet to rinse off the shampoo when suddenly she pulled her hand away as if she had been shocked. Toby straightened up and, with the lather dripping down her face, looked at her mother curiously.

"What's wrong, Mommy?"

Suddenly it was as if Toby also realized for the first time how she had been standing. Her head was in the sink, under the running water, and her mother's hand clamped on the back of her neck.

"Don't be afraid," Toby said softly with wisdom far beyond her years. "I'm not. I know you won't ever hurt me."

"No, dear, of course not," Linda managed to gasp quickly, but they both knew the hair-washing closeness and fun would never be the same. The act would always remind them of Carol Ann's death.

Linda finished washing Toby's hair quickly. All she could see was the image of Beatrice on the ground next to the well, the ambulance peeling away, its siren blasting loudly, announcing the tragedy. And Eleanor's words: "Be thankful it wasn't Toby."

At bedtime, they said a special prayer for Princess, and Linda sat with Toby until she was asleep. When the child's breathing was even and restful, Linda kissed her lightly on the forehead.

"I'm sorry," she whispered ever so slightly, then tiptoed out of the room.

Later, in sleep, Linda heard her daughter's scream. It was faint, shaky, laced with fear, garbled, as if her throat were obstructed.

Help me, Mommy, help me! Toby cried. Linda could hear the tremor in her voice.

Toby?

Help me!

Frightened, she sprang out of bed and raced into her daughter's room, but the child wasn't there.

Where are you? she cried. Then she chilled at her daughter's response.

In the well. You didn't cover it. Help me, I'm drowning.

Twigs snapped beneath Linda's feet as she ran through the backyard, slipping and sliding on piles of wet leaves that formed a soft, uncertain mat under her.

I'm coming, baby.

In breathless panic she reached the well. Toby was at the bottom of the shaft, spotlighted in the full moon, her arms

flailing desperately above her. In horror Linda could only watch
helplessly as Toby disappeared under the surface, her cries becoming weaker as her strength waned and the water possessed
her.

The bucket! Linda cried. *Grab the bucket. I'll pull you up.*

Linda cranked the stiff handle, holding it tightly so it wouldn't
slip uselessly through her fingers. The bucket was heavy, the
crossbar groaned under the weight of the girl, but that meant her
daughter was hanging on. *Hold tight, Toby!* she called again,
triumph in her voice. She had beaten the well, cheated it out of
another death—*her child's!*—but when the bucket was finally
raised to the top of the shaft, her daughter's lifeless body lay
sprawled crosswise on top, her arms dangling limply over the
sides. Her eyes were frozen wide and fixed on Linda in
accusation—she had been responsible!

Panting, Linda fought her way out of the terrible nightmare
that left her skin wet and clammy. She was cold from having
thrown aside the covers, her arms tired from cranking the bucket,
which she must have done in sleep. She rubbed her upper arms to
work out the soreness. Slowly, as the dream fell behind her, her
breathing eased, and her body warmed. She exhaled sharply, the
terror was over.

Toby!

It was only a dream, she knew, but still she got out of bed and
went across the hallway to her daughter.

Toby's room was peaceful, a sudden shift from the fury and
terror of the nightmare. But still Linda had to lean over her,
watch the covers rise and fall, see that her daughter was safe,
alive. And she couldn't escape the thought that she hadn't watched
her daughter precisely this way in quite some time.

She wanted to remain in Toby's room longer, but there was no
danger there. Spent, she returned to her bedroom and slowly
recouped her strength.

The next morning Linda almost slept through the alarm and
was late in waking Toby. She was standing at the bottom of the
stairs holding Toby's lunch bag as the little girl came scooting
down zipping up her jacket.

"Have a good day, baby," Linda said, and kissed her.

"Bye bye, Mommy," Toby said.

Linda opened the door and Toby saw it first, Linda a fraction of a second later. Toby dropped her lunch bag and her eyes rounded in horror. "Mommy!" she screamed, and Linda gasped. "No!" Deep in her mind she had feared the possibility of what she was seeing.

Princess was lying on the porch, seemingly wedged against the jamb. The animal's fur was marred by open wounds coated by dried blood that had already darkened. Her legs were mangled and jutted at odd angles; her back was crushed in, her spine broken. A tiny front paw covered the dog's head as if Princess were trying to hide from her injuries and impending death. Beneath the paw, her eyes were open and dry, pathetically questioning what was it that had happened to her.

Linda slammed the door closed. Toby buried her face in her mother's breast as Linda stroked the child's head. She wished to God Toby hadn't seen the dog.

"She must have been hit by a car, dear," Linda said softly, "and then limped back here to die close to you because she loved you."

"Why?" Toby asked tearfully.

"It was an accident, baby," Linda said chokingly, feeling her daughter's pain. "And nobody can say why accidents happen."

Toby shuddered against her mother, but then seemed to grow stronger. She looked up at Linda with wet, yet suddenly adult, eyes. "We have to bury her," she said.

"Oh, no, dear," Linda said. "We should call the police or the animal shelter. They'll take good care of Princess."

"No, we have to do it," Toby pressed. "She was mine. I want to bury her in the backyard so I know where she is."

"All right," Linda agreed reluctantly, although she didn't relish the idea of handling the dead dog.

They carefully wrapped Princess in an old sheet and carried her to the backyard. With a shovel from the garage, Linda dug a small grave. A grave near the well that, although it had been filled in with dirt and concrete by the police, still stood, its circular sweep of brick mockingly tranquil, deceptively innocent in the morning sunlight.

Gently they laid the shrouded body in the grave. Remembering her father's funeral, Toby picked up a handful of the loose dirt and dropped it into the hole, then solemnly nodded to her mother to do the same. Then they filled in the grave and made a marker with sticks. They didn't speak throughout the burial service.

Linda drove a somber Toby to school, then went to work. She called Thomas to tell him about Princess.

"Oh, Linda, I'm sorry." He sighed. "How's Toby?"

"I think all right."

"And you?"

"I'm okay."

"Good. I'll see you tonight."

"Yes," Linda said. "I need you."

She went back to work but she couldn't concentrate. What had happened that morning was tragic indeed, but it wasn't the only tragedy that Linda was still fighting to overcome. Princess's death had taken her mind from her own feelings and focused them on her daughter. But now that the shock was wearing off, she remembered again last night's disturbing dream—a residual effect of Carol Ann's death, she was certain, and a direct outgrowth of her most terrifying of fears. *It could have been Toby who had drowned in the well and she would have been responsible.* She spent her lunch hour aimlessly walking the streets, looking in shop windows, drawn to her own reflection. Her image, she felt, mirrored her mood; her face was tired, her eyes dull, glazed. Like painted glass. She could still see Toby's body sprawled out limply across the bucket, and jamming her eyes closed to try to escape the sight only intensified the image even more. And she knew she had brought it on herself.

She had to pull herself out of what she was slipping into. If she could only lift her mood, raise herself from her depression, somehow put a stop to the guilt she was feeling, perhaps she could escape further nightmares. And now especially, she'd have to put on a positive front for Toby, who would be mired in her own dual loss—first her best friend and now her pet.

But was it possible to fool her subconscious? Could she pretend to be up-spirited so she wouldn't be punished by dreams? She tried smiling that afternoon, and that simple act seemed to lighten her spirits, lift the gray cloud from over her head. Even Nancy's goading didn't disturb her, and she responded to her nastiness with a Cheshire cat grin that she knew irked the other woman to the core. That in turn made her smile all the more. By the end of the day she realized she was no longer pretending; she really was feeling better.

Thomas brought over Chinese food for dinner and a special stuffed animal for Toby, who even managed a small smile when her fortune cookie predicted good luck for the future.

Thomas was pleased that Linda dug into the meal with gusto, and he watched her approvingly out of the corner of his eye. The trauma of Carol Ann's death seemed to be behind her.

"Welcome back to the world of the living," he said when they had finished and Toby had gone upstairs. He reached out for her and pulled her down next to him on the couch.

"It's good to be back," she breathed.

"I missed you." He kissed her lightly, a brush of his lips against her soft, enticing cheek, a lingering touch.

"I missed you too." She let him fold his arms around her and curled in next to him, tightening his hold on her even more. His lips tickled her neck, warming her, making her laugh.

"Do you want a fire tonight?" he asked.

"No. I don't want you to move. I'm too comfortable like this. Besides, I think I'm too tired to even watch you build one."

"Good, because I'm too tired to build one. What a day at the bank! But I don't want to deny you your fire, so why don't we pretend. Look at that fire," he said expansively. "What do you think?"

Linda frowned thoughtfully. "Well, if you want to know the truth, it's good but not great."

"Not great, huh?"

"Nope. That little log over there. Kinda crooked."

"Really? I'll fix it," Thomas said, not moving. "How about now?"

"A little to the right yet . . . there! Now you've got it. Now it's great. In fact, it's the best fire you've ever made. What's the secret?"

"Can't go wrong with invisible logs. Besides, no fuss, no muss, and no ashes to sweep out in the morning. And they burn cleaner too."

"You're terrific." Linda mugged and stuck out her tongue playfully.

At that moment Thomas became sure of his feelings. He had rarely heard or said the words as a child, had difficulty express-

ing them to Sandra—that was the way he was, he always believed.
But he knew now that that wasn't so; now he had no difficulty in
voicing his emotions, because he was certain of them. And in the
glow of the imaginary fire, light enough to see into Linda's eyes,
open and inviting and all his, he said, "I love you, Linda. Very
much."

She sighed contentedly because she was feeling it as well.
"Yes, Thomas, I love you too. Very much." She was in touch
with her emotions, too, and not at all guilty about being unfaithful
to Keith. Because she wasn't.

"How do you feel?" Thomas asked her.

She smiled dreamily and snuggled close to him, trying to meld
her body with his. "Snug as a bug in a rug," she said. But her
smile fell as a sudden dark thought took hold. Bugs were small,
defenseless. Prey.

chapter 17

The weather turned cooler. Toby was dressed in a jacket that Linda had bought the previous weekend. Her day had been a good one. She had gotten a hundred on a spelling test and had done almost as well on a surprise current events quiz. And now the smell of snow was in the air, something she had never experienced before.

The school bus lurched to a stop in front of her house and she and the boys jumped off. "See you tomorrow." She waved to her friends, who started up the street. When the bus pulled past her she saw Beatrice Dailey standing on her front lawn, her hands deep in the pockets of a long knitted white sweater, looking like a ghost, seemingly appearing from nowhere.

"Hi, Toby," she called to the child, and crossed the street toward her.

As Beatrice approached, Toby took a half step backward.

"I was waiting for you," Beatrice said pleasantly. "You left some dolls in my house and I wanted to see that you got them back."

Toby searched her memory, tried to imagine what she had left in the Dailey house. The inventory of her possessions seemed pretty complete—Patricia, Miss Piggy, the others, but if Mrs. Dailey said there was something, well, she must have overlooked something somewhere. So she let Beatrice take her by the hand and lead her across the street.

All the while Beatrice was talking—about missing Carol Ann and how she was in heaven with her father. *Her* father too, Beatrice told Toby. Then they were inside.

"Would you like some milk?" Beatrice asked. "And I made brownies."

"No, thank you." Toby shook her head. Her eyes went to the phone. She knew her mother was expecting her call and she should get home to make it.

"Carol Ann liked brownies," Beatrice said. "And I always told her she should eat them now because before long she would be at that age when chocolate would make her face break out and . . . Well, none of that really matters right now, does it?" she said softly.

"No," Toby said uncertainly, wanting to hurry along the retrieving of her things, then get home. Beatrice was making her feel uncomfortable.

"Well, why don't we go upstairs and get those things of yours." Beatrice reached for her hand and tightened her fingers around Toby's. Toby winced as her fingers were pinched, and suddenly her palm itched and she couldn't scratch it. She tried to adjust her hand in Beatrice's grip but only managed to hurt herself more. She clutched her schoolbooks in her other hand.

Beatrice led her up the stairs and opened Carol Ann's bedroom door.

"Look around, dear," she said. "I think I remember something of yours being in here. I was in here just the other day talking to Carol Ann. Oh, no, I'm sorry—" She smiled and corrected herself. "I meant to say *thinking* about Carol Ann, when I came across a doll I couldn't quite place. That's why I thought it was yours. Now, where did I put it?"

"I don't know," Toby said, suddenly nervous about being in her friend's room. She looked around the bedroom, not really knowing what she was searching for. Dolls perched on the dresser like cats preening themselves. Birds in flight covered the wallpaper. The closet door was partially open and Toby saw Carol Ann's clothing. A dress was laid out over a chair as if waiting for Carol Ann to put it on. Bolsters were under the covers on the canopied bed, making it look as if a sleeping child lay underneath.

"You see, I thought Carol Ann was a bad girl for what she did," Beatrice said, tightening her hold even more on Toby's hand. The girl's fingers now felt numb, tingly, as if all the blood had drained from them. "But Carol Ann wasn't really bad, was she?"

She's nuts, you know. That's what Petey had said about her the other day. The children were sitting on Toby's porch stairs, not feeling like doing anything, still talking about Carol Ann. Petey had crossed the street, picked up a stone, and thrown it against Beatrice's bedroom window. When Beatrice opened the window, the children had run.

"No, of course not. Carol Ann was a good girl. And it was only because of you that—"

"I want to go home now."

"I'm sure you do. And I'm certain you're thankful you can go home, that you're alive."

Toby didn't answer.

"Aren't you?" Beatrice asked again, a little gruffer, with a slight tug of the child's arm.

Toby nodded her head. "Yes," she managed to say weakly.

"Of course," Beatrice repeated. "You're alive and Carol Ann is dead. And you know, I guess I must have been mistaken about your having left something here. There's nothing here that belongs to you."

"Please let go of my hand," Toby whimpered, tears welling in her eyes.

"I'm sorry, but not quite yet."

Almost roughly, Beatrice yanked Toby's arm and pulled her from the room, then led her—almost dragged her—toward the room at the top of the stairway. The bathroom.

"No, Carol Ann wasn't bad. Of course there was the grape juice stain on the dress, but that was an accident. You remember that day, don't you?"

The bathroom sink was filled with water.

In that one moment, which seemed almost to hang by a thread, a strand of spider webbing, Toby's mistrust blossomed into fear. A look in Beatrice's eyes chilled her—almost, she felt in a singular flash, as if the woman were seeing things she couldn't. She tried to pull away from Beatrice but the hold on her hand was absolute. Beatrice was still talking—something more about grape juice stains and then being punished even though it had been an accident.

Punished. The word leaped up at her.

With her free hand, Beatrice grabbed Toby's arm firmly midway between her wrist and elbow and pulled her closer to the
sink. The child's schoolbooks clattered to the floor. Now she
understood. But it was too late. She was there.

Beatrice's hand touched Toby's head, her fingers tangled in
the blond curls. Toby felt pressure against her neck. She fought it
but Beatrice matched her push. The water in the sink loomed
closer.

"You've been a bad girl." Beatrice's voice was stern now.

"Please, don't—" Toby said.

"The water punishes bad girls."

Toby was close enough to the surface now to see the gleaming
porcelain, the drain at the bottom of the sink, smell the slightly
metallic odor of the water. She closed her eyes and took a gulp of
air, readied herself. Her nose touched the water, which traveled
up her nostrils. She knew she wasn't ready; she was going to
gag, choke. She thrashed her arms, tried to catch Beatrice Dailey,
break her hold. But she wasn't strong enough and she felt herself
being pushed under—

Just then the pebble struck the window. Beatrice and Toby
jumped as a second shower of stones splattered against the glass.

Petey and Eric were running away from the house.

Beatrice let go of Toby's arm to raise the window and yell out
at the boys. "I saw you. I'll—"

It was enough.

Toby seized the moment. In one motion she scooped up her
notebooks, all but a pencil that had slipped out of the spiral ring,
and tore out of the bathroom.

"Come back here!" Beatrice called, starting after her.

Toby did not turn back. She prayed she wouldn't trip as she
raced down the stairs, her feet barely touching them, expecting to
lose her balance at any moment and stumble. And she knew if
she fell she would be caught. As she reached the bottom of the
stairs she almost misstepped but regained her footing. Now she
dared not turn around. She would lose precious seconds. Beatrice
would catch her, punish her as she did Carol Ann.

Her fingers closed frantically around the brass doorknob. She
pulled but the door refused to budge.

She was trapped!

Beatrice Dailey had trapped her!

And she was walking down the stairs.

"You've been a bad girl . . ."

Toby looked over her shoulder. Beatrice was now at the bottom of the staircase, just across the room. And she was moving closer. Once again she tugged at the door with all her young strength and strained, but her arm muscles were weak.

"And you know what happens to bad girls."

Then something within her clicked. The bolt lock! Beatrice had thrown it into place when they came into the house.

"The water punishes bad girls."

She wasn't trapped at all!—a moment of triumph, relief, almost victory. The door was only locked. But still she had to get out.

At the same moment that Beatrice's hand touched her shoulder her fingers found the lock and twisted it. Toby heard the metallic snap, grabbed the knob, and yanked. Beatrice was holding her shoulder, trying to gain a firmer hold on her arm. The child slipped through Beatrice's fingers, wriggled away from her touch, and darted through the open door and down the porch steps, surprised that she was still holding her schoolbooks.

She didn't know if Beatrice was following her. When she got to the curb, she prayed there were no cars coming. She quickly looked both ways and ran across the street. She saw her friends up the block tossing a football back and forth. She thought of running to them but Beatrice Dailey was mad at them, too, for throwing the rocks again. She would be safer in her own house. And only when she was on her own porch did she turn to look for Beatrice.

The Dailey door was closed; Beatrice was nowhere in sight. Toby was out of breath and was having trouble thinking straight. All she wanted to do was sit down. She fumbled for her key, her hand shaking. She couldn't insert the key in the lock. Maybe Mrs. Dailey wasn't in her house. Maybe she was sneaking up on her right now. Maybe she was just beyond the hedges, just out of sight, under the porch stairs. . . .

By luck or accident she found the keyhole. Quickly she worked the latch and burst into the house, slammed the door and locked it, then leaned against it, as if her weight would make a critical difference in keeping Beatrice Dailey out. Slowly her breathing eased and she felt safer. Still in her parka, she sat down on the

couch and jammed her chin into her chest to make herself as
small as possible. If she could have made herself invisible, she
would have.

Beatrice Dailey meant to punish her, she understood.

Just as she had punished Carol Ann.

But she hadn't done anything wrong, at least she didn't think
so. She searched her memory. Maybe because they had thrown
the rock, but that had been Petey, not her. . . .

The sudden pounding on the front door made her jump. Mrs.
Dailey was trying to get in! *Go away!* Toby silently mouthed and
hunched into herself, even afraid to turn around and face the
door.

"Hey, Toby, open up, come on—"

"Go away."

Someone kicked the door. "Toby." It was Petey's voice.

Toby jumped up, ran to the window, gently pushed aside the
curtains. Eric saw her peering out. "Hey, open up!"

Toby opened the door and they burst in, bringing swells of
cold air in on their jackets.

"What were you doing in that house?" they asked. "Wasn't it
creepy?"

Toby nodded, glad her friends were there. There was safety in
numbers. Her experiences tumbled out. "Mrs. Dailey said she
had things of mine, but she didn't. She tried to punish me."

The boys' eyes widened. "Like Carol Ann?"

Toby nodded vigorously. "She tried to put my head in the
sink, under the water."

"She's crazy," Petey observed. "I knew it."

Toby moved to the phone. "I have to tell my mother."

"Now, wait a second," Petey cautioned. "Do you think you
should?"

Toby stopped dialing and replaced the receiver. "Why not?"

"I don't know," he said thoughtfully. "But it seems to me
that she'll get upset and she might even want to move away from
here. What do you guys think?"

Eric and Mitchell mulled the question over and both came to the
same conclusion—it was entirely possible. Likely.

"You don't want to move away, do you?" Eric asked.

"Uh-uh." Toby slowly shook her head. She didn't. Finally
her life had some order and stability, which it didn't have in

California after her father died. And people around her—new friends, her grandmother, Uncle Thomas. Her mother seemed happy again, and Toby didn't want to upset her at all. "Uh-uh," she repeated, resolving not to tell her mother anything, just to stay clear of Mrs. Dailey. Believing she was doing the right thing, she swore her friends to secrecy.

chapter 18

Late that afternoon Nancy inquired about some contracts she had passed along from Mr. Robinson early in the morning.

"I told you this had to get out today. I have the rest of the correspondence all ready and waiting for Mr. Robinson's signature."

"I didn't know it was a rush," Linda protested. "Nobody told me. I would have worked through lunch."

"I did tell you, and besides, you should have known," Nancy challenged. "Now it's not going to get out on time and it's all your fault. Why don't you just give everything back to me and I'll do it myself."

She reached for the pile of papers on Linda's desk. Linda's hand clamped down on her wrist. It was an involuntary gesture, fueled by her frustrations with the other woman.

"Don't you touch those papers," she said sharply. "Mr. Robinson asked me to do the work and I'll do it. I don't need you doing anything for me and nobody told me it was a rush—"

At that moment, Don Robinson and Gene Erskine came through the doors, returning from court.

"Here, here, ladies, what is it?" Robinson asked.

Nancy brusquely pulled her hand away from Linda and spoke first. "Mr. Robinson, I'm sitting with the Higgins closing and Linda doesn't have the mortgage papers ready yet. I told her it had to get out by three—"

"No, you didn't!" Linda flared. "I didn't know that had to get out today!"

She was aware that as she spoke the office ground to a halt, the other secretaries watching the confrontation. She knew she should calm herself, try to get her voice under control, but her eyes fogged in anger and her knees felt rubbery. She grabbed the back of the chair to support herself.

"It's all right, Linda, Nancy," Robinson said in a voice that silenced both of them. "It would have been better if the papers got out this afternoon so Bill could review them over the weekend, but Monday is okay."

"I'll come in tomorrow and finish them up," Nancy volunteered.

"*I'll* come in," Linda said quickly.

"No. It's my fault," Nancy retorted. "I never should have given those important papers to her."

Before Linda could say anything in her own defense, Robinson stepped between them. "There's no reason for anybody to come in tomorrow. It'll hold till Monday. I'll call Bill now. Nancy, get him please."

"I didn't know it was a rush," Linda sputtered. Her heart was still pounding rapidly, her skin flushed. "Nobody told me."

"It's all right, Linda," Robinson said, and Linda recognized the tone as conciliatory. He didn't have time for her or her outbursts. "Don't worry about it."

Without saying anything more, Robinson and Erskine walked toward their offices. Linda and Nancy eyed each other hotly and each silently returned to her desk. Nancy picked up the phone to make the call for her boss.

Thomas was waiting when Linda came out of the building.

"What are you doing here?" she asked.

His smile dropped. "That wasn't exactly the kind of greeting I was hoping for."

"I'm sorry," Linda apologized quickly.

He saw it in her face. "Bad day?"

"Don't ask." But then she proceeded to tell him about the confrontation with Nancy.

"Forget it." He pooh-poohed and put his arm around her. "Those kinds of misunderstandings happen all the time."

Angrily Linda broke away from him. "It wasn't a misunderstanding!" she said loudly, and a passerby turned his head to look at them. "Nobody told me it was a rush assignment or else I would have done it—and why are you taking her side?"

"Whoa!" Thomas said. "Please. I wasn't taking her side. I

love *you*, remember? What I was going to say was that Nancy probably forgot to tell you it was a rush.''

His words stopped Linda. She took a deep breath and shook her head weakly. ''Oh, Thomas, I'm sorry. I thought I was going to be fired. I didn't mean to snap at you. I'm sorry.''

''Let's get away from here. I think you've had enough of this building today.''

''I'll say.'' She exhaled loudly, then smiled and let her arms fall to her sides in a gesture signifying ''it's over.'' She snuggled in next to him as they walked toward the cars, then he followed her home.

As they gave Toby her dinner, Linda calmed down. Things were always going to be that way with Nancy and there would be no changing them. She had to be more wary of the woman, suspicious of anything she said or did—or gave to her. She didn't know if Nancy had really forgotten to tell her about the rush and then covered up for herself, or if she had purposely set her up for a fall. Whatever, she would finish the work the first thing Monday morning and have it on Robinson's desk all typed and proofread by noon; she'd try to redeem herself with the quality of the work. But now it was the weekend. As soon as Mrs. Green arrived to sit with Toby, she and Thomas were going out to dinner.

''Rain tonight and tomorrow,'' she murmured. ''Possibly mixed with sleet and flurries.''

''Of course,'' Thomas said resignedly. ''I have a golf game in the morning.'' He had taken off his tie and was sitting at the kitchen table with his white shirt open at the neck. ''If it were tennis, we could move it indoors. It's a bit harder with golf.''

''Unless there are little windmills and things,'' Linda joked from the sink where she was washing Toby's dishes. She was dressed in a marine-blue blouse and light-colored slacks. She had been busy outfitting Toby for her first real winter and hadn't had time to shop for herself. This weekend, she promised.

''Here it comes now,'' they said together, and laughed, as the first drops of rain started to slant against the house.

''Maybe I should change.'' Linda indicated her slacks. ''If we get splattered, these will stain.''

Thomas reached out for her and pulled her close to him, then closed his knees around her. Her hands were still full of detergent bubbles, which she playfully swathed on his nose. He blew upward and puffed them into the air.

"As long as you leave on that blouse," he ordered. "The color looks so good on you. I love the way it highlights your eyes." They were like deep placid pools, darkened by a filtered sun.

Linda beamed. "So I'll get splattered a little." She frowned as she dried her hands. "Toby seemed a little quiet tonight, down even, don't you think?"

Thomas shrugged. "A little. Maybe something happened at school today. But if it's anything serious she'll tell you."

"I'm sure," Linda agreed. Then Mrs. Green arrived and freed them. Hungry, they quickly drove downtown and darted between the raindrops from the parking lot to the restaurant.

Linda shivered as they burst through the door. "Chilly."

"Fall is definitely upon us," Thomas said, and signaled for a bottle of wine. "You've never been through a New England winter, have you?"

"I think our midwestern winters can rival yours any year," Linda said proudly. "I remember some things: snowdrifts higher than the cars, standing on line to buy milk from the one truck that made it through. Winter and snow from a kid's-eye view is certainly different from an adult's. Even shoveling the snow was fun. I couldn't understand why my father hated it so much. Of course living in California, I haven't been through a winter now in almost ten years."

The sommelier brought their wine. Thomas sampled and approved it. "I can't tell you how much I'm looking forward to playing in the snow with Toby," he said after they had clinked their glasses. "I used to have the best times when I was young. New England town living—nothing beats it. There's a hill not far from my mother's house where all the kids used to bring their sleds."

"Your parents let you have sleds?" Linda asked, then waved off her comment. "I'm sorry. I didn't mean to be catty."

"Sleds were allowed," Thomas said seriously, then a smile tugged at his lips. "I guess they thought all that belly-whopping would build macho character and a fierce sense of competition." Linda watched his eyes light up as he recalled the carefree winter days of his childhood. "One time I had really built up a good deal of speed—we're talking speed-checked-by-radar here—and I took a bump at probably thirty, thirty-five miles an hour. I must have sailed ten feet into the air. Luckily I landed flat on the runners so the jolt was minimized. Otherwise it might have been Keith who was arm-twisted into going to Harvard." Linda laughed with him, then Thomas continued with a twinge of regret in his voice and a mask of sadness on his face. "I hung up the old Flexible Flyer at fourteen and never played with Keith. He came of serious sledding age when I was 'becoming a Devonshire.' And I never had children of my own to play with." Then he added, "Which was just as well, I guess, because I would have made a lousy role model."

"Not at all," Linda protested.

"Or maybe I suspected my marriage wasn't going to last and children were one more complication I didn't need."

There was an awkward pause, as Thomas felt he had said more than he should have.

"Tell me about your wife."

"Oh, Linda, why?"

"Please. I really need to know why she would ever give you up."

"Sandra was right to," he said reflectively. "I wasn't a good husband for her. Yes, I was faithful, yes, I earned a good living, but it wasn't right." He touched his palm gently to Linda's cheek, held her gaze. "But I'm different now. Remember the first night we went out to dinner and you asked me if I was happy?"

"I remember."

"And I answered yes. Well, maybe I wasn't being entirely truthful with you, or especially with myself. But I can be truthful now to both of us and say that I am happy, Linda. I've got my work, which I enjoy, but more important, I've got someone I really love. God." He smiled. "Was that *me* talking? See what you bring out in me? I never would have thought myself capable of saying such things."

Linda touched his leg; lightly traced circles with her fingers. "You're a very special person, Thomas Devonshire. And if you have to ask, I'm happy too."

After dinner they went back to Thomas's apartment and made the most exquisite love to each other, as ethereal as it was physical, as much alive with emotion as with sensation. As it had once been with Keith, although he wasn't in Linda's thoughts that night.

In the rainstorm that night the house padded quietly—caged tiger footsteps, Linda thought on the hazy fringe of consciousness.

She was used to the sounds by now.

chapter 19

The rain continued Saturday morning. It had settled into a steady drizzle, although a second wave of the storm was predicted for later in the day. Linda thought about Thomas out on the golf course in this miserable weather, but she knew that golf fanatics were a different breed of person.

Eleanor phoned. Thomas had told her Linda planned on going shopping for fall clothing and she asked if she could come along, to offer some assistance, advice, or just keep quiet if that was Linda's preference. Linda welcomed her—and her advice. She wanted to get closer to the older woman.

Toby was dropped off at Petey's house, where the children were gathering for Saturday morning cartoons, Monopoly, and lunch, and then Linda went to pick up Eleanor. They spent the morning in a local mall, picking out a winter wardrobe, going from store to store until Linda decided she had bought all she could carry or afford.

"May I buy you lunch?" Eleanor offered.

Linda smiled. The morning with her mother-in-law had been effortless, pleasant, as they chatted about styles and designers and the prices people paid for the privilege of putting someone else's name somewhere on their person. Lunch would be nice, she said.

They went to a health food restaurant on the second floor of the mall, where they ordered yogurt and fruit salads.

While they were eating, Linda saw Eleanor lower her fork, then slip her hands under the table. Although Eleanor didn't want to show her discomfort, Linda knew the dampness was bothering her arthritis. A feeling of serenity came over Linda, laced with an odd sense of power, something she had never before felt in Eleanor's presence. She was stronger than this woman who for years had frightened her. She had her youth, her health, and a life that Eleanor, with all of her money and prestige, couldn't have anymore. It was with a mix of pity and pride that Linda looked across the table at her mother-in-law, and at the same time a wave of love crested over her toward the older woman.

As they walked back to the parking area, Eleanor said, "I was so concerned about your reaction to the death of Carol Ann Dailey. I'm glad you're over it."

"Yes," Linda said. "Thank you. I only wish Beatrice could find some degree of peace."

Eleanor nodded sadly. "And Toby? Is she still bothered by it at all?"

"Just an occasional nightmare. The children were numbed for several days. It certainly was a shock to them, but they've come out of it easily."

"Children are so resilient, aren't they? Not like us adults, who tend to carry tragedy and trauma with us for quite some time."

"Yes," Linda agreed uncomfortably, and recognized the awful truth to Eleanor's words.

As they got into the car Eleanor invited her and Toby to lunch the following Saturday—"just the girls"—and asked if Linda would let Toby spend a weekend with her alone so they could get to know each other better. Linda readily agreed. Grandmother and granddaughter had a lot of catching up to do.

Thomas arrived with a pizza for dinner—"Anchovies held. Guaranteed!" he said. While they ate they went through the newspaper and voted for the movie they wanted to see that night. There was only one Disney picture playing within fifty miles and that took all three votes, though Toby's only reluctantly. She had given thumbs up to films that Linda had exercised her veto on.

In the movie lobby they crowded into a photo booth and smiled as the lights brightened and the cameras clicked. They waited for the pictures to slide out of the slot and grabbed them excitedly. In all but one shot Thomas had made a funny face and enjoyed Toby's laughter. "If my clients could see me now," he whispered to Linda as the theater darkened and the movie started.

"They'd see that you were a hell of a nice guy," she whispered back.

The rain had turned to sleet by the time they got out of the movies. When they reached home, Toby was barely able to stand up, tired from the day and filled now with pizza and popcorn and ice cream and candy drops. She had just enough strength to reach up to kiss Thomas good night, and even there he had to meet her halfway. Then he yawned, too, and begged off staying any later.

"I got up at six this morning and I spent the better part of the day playing on wet grass."

"Oh." Linda pouted, disappointed.

"Do you have a scissors?" Thomas asked. "I want to keep one of those pictures. I don't have any of you, Linda."

She snipped his favorite from the strip. Even in the unflattering light of the tiny photo booth she had never looked lovelier, he said. There was a pastel quality to her face, profiled demurely on her long, slender neck, almost like a Renaissance painting. Thomas slipped the picture into his wallet and pecked Linda on the lips. "I love you," he whispered.

At the door, Linda shivered as the cold rain swept in, then she locked up behind him. She checked the back door as well, then went upstairs and prepared for bed. In her nightgown she looked again at the three remaining photos, smiling at the clowning faces Thomas had made. She kept pictures of Keith in her top dresser drawer, and now she took out her favorite. They had rented bicycles for the day at the beach in Venice, California. Keith was lounging next to his, his sweatshirt tied around his bare chest, a casual tilt to his head, a serious, almost sultry expression on his face as the wind mussed his hair. As she compared the photos, she recognized the brothers and knew that Thomas would always be a constant reminder of his younger brother.

She put Keith's picture back in the drawer. She didn't want to compare the brothers or think of how things might have been if only Keith hadn't died. Nor did she want to compare the love she once had for Keith with what she felt now for Thomas. She had loved Keith deeply and always would, but the love was tempered now by time and absence, bittersweet, passionless, unlike what she was feeling for Thomas. She had let go.

She hadn't wanted Thomas to leave her tonight, but she was comforted by the thought that before long he wouldn't be leaving her at all.

It was very late when Linda awoke, closer to dawn than to midnight, the time when darkness seems denser, the nighttime chill more intense, when familiar objects loom suddenly larger and strangely unfamiliar, and sounds flitter, tease, beguile. . . .

The tapping came from across the hallway, from Toby's room. Linda opened her eyes and heard it—the pat of nails on glass, a scratching against the window, as if a dog or cat had been shut out in the cold and was trying to get back in. Or a person! Someone was trying to get into the house!

In one motion she was out of bed. She sprinted toward the door, stopped, listened. She hadn't misheard—the tapping persisted. But then she slapped her forehead as she identified the sounds; it was only the rain blustering against the window, sounding like a million footsteps. That was all she was hearing. She started back toward her bedroom when she stopped. Her body suddenly felt prickly, flushed with a strange sense of deception.

She stood at the top of the stairs, her hand resting on the newel post, rubbing her fingers anxiously over the fluted surface, outlining features—eyes, a mouth. Beneath her the house was dark and ominously silent; she could even imagine it breathing with a life of its own. Like a cobra, coiled, ready to lunge, waiting for its intended victim.

How different a house felt at night, she thought. Foreboding. Daring you to enter swirling patches of blackness that wait to ensnare you like a sticky webbing from which there is no escape. Different and scary. Especially when you're tired and susceptible to boiler clicks, the whine of contracting wood. House sounds. Night sounds.

She flipped on the hall light, which angled into Toby's room, then beat a hasty path to the window. Rain slanted against the glass—a machine gun tapping. Linda's eyes swept the room. Nothing was out of place, yet still something seemed amiss. She frowned and suddenly knew what was wrong. The shade was blowing into the room, whipped by the breeze. She thought the window had been closed. Hadn't it? Apparently not. She had aired out Toby's room that morning and must have left it open.

She pushed aside the shade to close the window. That's when she saw the figure silhouetted behind the glass. She felt it in her stomach first and on her skin, which immediately roughened and cooled. Her body responded before her conscious mind did, but in a millisecond—less!—her entire being comprehended. Somebody was outside Toby's window. Standing on the roof of the front porch. Looking in.

Later she would be surprised she didn't scream, only brought a hand to her mouth, and gasped inaudibly as her eyes opened to take in the sight. A face—blurred, indistinct in the uncertain light outside the window. A body—formless, draped in shadow, lost below the window line. There for only an instant, then gone, but she had already dropped the shade; she didn't want to see him again. *The person* had been tapping against the glass, her mind told her; it hadn't been the rain after all.

She slammed the window closed before it could be opened more, before a hand or a foot could slip in. Though she flipped the lock, the flimsy metal clamp gave her no feeling of security. She backed away from the window, tripped over Toby's sneakers, fell sprawled across the bed.

"Mommy?"

Linda shook her daughter. "Toby, get out of bed quickly," she whispered hoarsely, glancing fearfully behind her toward the window.

"What is it?" Toby turned; squinted against the sudden light.

Linda slipped her hand under Toby and eased her out of bed. "Quickly. Come on!"

Tensed against a smashing window, shattering glass, Linda took her daughter's hand and led her downstairs, taking each step carefully so as not to trip. "We have to call the police," she said loudly, hoping to scare the man away. Twice her hands slipped from the dial but finally she managed to ring the operator to get the police. "Hurry," she begged as she gave her name and location. "He's breaking in now." She kept looking up to the second floor, waiting for the man to burst into Toby's room and race down the stairs after them. The house moaned in the storm, a labored spiraling sigh of age. Branches swept against the clapboard sides and the wind whistled through the broken window in the attic. Linda shocked to each of the sounds—each represented the intruder, somewhere above them. Her body was suddenly chilled—she was dressed only in a thin nightgown, and the cold air drafted downward through the hearth and settled heavily in the room.

Toby was hunched in a wing chair, wide-eyed, watching her mother, understanding the jeopardy, afraid to move. Linda pushed aside the curtain and peered out into the night. Toby's window faced the front of the house, directly over the porch, and she half expected to see the man, caught in the act of breaking in, stealthily drop to the ground and disappear into the stormy night. But when she didn't see him she knew he still had to be on the roof, trying to get into the house. "Hurry," she breathed and pounded her fist against her leg. Her heart beat loudly, high in her chest. "It's all right, Toby," she whispered. "The police are on their way." Quickly she ran into the kitchen, took a knife from one of the drawers, and returned to guard the bottom of the stairs. Light from the second-floor hallway swept down the stairs. Knife poised, she waited for a figure to step into the light. Was he still trying to get in? her mind raged. Would he get inside before the police arrived?

"I don't hear anything, Mommy," Toby whined, pushing farther back into the chair. The silence was even worse. The silence made them vulnerable from every direction.

"Shh," Linda cautioned, and strained to listen, but like her daughter, all she heard was the sounds of the storm. "I'm going to call Uncle Thomas," she said. Her eyes on the stairway, she went to the phone and started to dial. She broke off as she heard the scream of the patrol car and saw through the curtain the spin of the red siren light. She put down the phone and knife and let the police in, then reached for a raincoat from the downstairs closet to cover herself, and for one for Toby.

Officers Saul and Jamison again responded to the call. Their dark blue raincoats were soaked through, rain dripped off the brims of their hats. Linda told them—calmly this time—what had happened.

Saul stayed with her while Jamison went outside, looked around the house, under the windows, in the bushes, then came back in. Nobody was out there now, he reported. He went upstairs, looked out Toby's window at the porch roof, inspected the clasp, opened and closed the window, checked the other rooms that fronted on the roof. All the windows were locked from the inside. "Nobody." He shrugged to his partner when he returned downstairs.

"I saw somebody," Linda protested.

Jamison's eyes narrowed at Linda. "Just why do you think anybody would be out there, Mrs. Devonshire?" Linda heard his tone as condescending, mocking.

"I don't know," she sputtered. "To break in . . . I guess."

"Are you sure it wasn't your own reflection, distorted by the rain?" Saul asked kindly. Her head swiveled toward him.

"No, it wasn't my own reflection. I know what I saw."

"Can you describe the man?" Jamison asked curtly.

"No, I didn't get a good look."

"Anything. Was he tall? Short? Dark? Blond?" Jamison looked at Linda blankly. "Stop me if you like any of these."

"Stop making fun of me," Linda fumed.

"Bill, please," Saul said to his partner.

"All right. All right. Did you see his face at all?"

"No, it was too dark. I didn't see him." She fought to remain calm.

"So you didn't see anything then?"

"Don't say that! I saw that someone was there! Why are you talking to me like this? I'm not the criminal here."

"Lady, we don't even know if there is a criminal here, do we?"

Linda looked imploringly toward Officer Saul, but before the other policeman could intrude, Jamison turned to Toby.

"Did you see him, little girl?"

"She didn't see anything," Linda answered tightly. "Leave her alone."

Jamison shrugged. "I only thought she could help."

"Just don't ask her anything else." Linda glowered. Then Saul put his hand on her shoulder. Surprised by the touch, she turned to him, desperate to be heard.

"Tell us what you saw," he said softly, wanting to listen to her. "Just take your time."

"Dan!" Jamison scowled in exasperation and spoke to his partner as if Linda weren't there. He was coming down with a cold and was annoyed at having to get out of the patrol car in the storm and stomp around the house on this kind of call. She was just a lonely woman, starved for attention, who was seeing ghosts in the night. "There was nobody up there. The porch roof is slippery, angled. You've got to shimmy up a pole to get there. It's raining cats and dogs." He turned to face Linda. "Look, if a guy wants to get into the house, he breaks a window down here, he pries open a cellar grating, he picks a doorlock. What he doesn't do is grapple up a wooden post in the middle of a rainstorm and play peek-a-boo on the second floor."

"He was there!" Linda flared, feeling more and more helpless. "How can I prove it to you? I know what I saw. I'm not making this up. I'm not—" Her breath caught.

I saw someone, Keith. It wasn't my own reflection in the glass.

"—cra-zy." The word came out in two tentative syllables as if she were just using it for the first time. No longer could she fight off the reason for her growing desperation for Saul to listen to her, *believe her.* If nobody had been at Toby's window, that meant only one thing.

"I didn't imagine it," she finished weakly. Her eyes narrowed painfully and her body chilled further with the impact of the thought. Her knees weakened and she reached out to grab the back of the couch.

"Are you all right?" Saul asked her.

But right now all she wanted was to be alone.

"Maybe you'd better go now," she said distantly in a defeated voice. She swallowed, her throat suddenly dry and tight.. "I appreciate your coming so quickly. You probably frightened him away."

She closed the door to Jamison's parting words. "Broad's crazy if you ask me," and was grateful he was already outside and Toby didn't hear him.

Toby hadn't moved from where she had sat earlier. Her body was rigid, coiled tightly into itself. She knew her mother had thought she'd seen a man at the window and the police hadn't found anyone. She should be feeling good about that, but she wasn't; her skin still crawled with something undefined.

Perspiration dotted Linda's forehead; she wiped it away with her palm. Her eyes were streaked with uncertainty and rabbit fear. She knelt down next to Toby. "Everything's okay, baby," she said, trying to keep her voice from cracking. "The police didn't find anybody. I must have just seen my shadow or something. I'm sorry I scared you. Come on, let's go upstairs."

Linda led the way into Toby's room. The light was still burning brightly but now it seemed strangely cold and harsh against the backdrop of the darkened window where Jamison had left the shade halfway up. As she reached for the ring to pull it down she looked outside and saw herself in the glass—her hair disheveled, her face reflected surreally on the scrimmed surface, surrounded by a halo of color as the raindrops dissipated the light. She was so certain she had seen a man before—dimly shadowed, but nonetheless real, corporeal—where her hazy reflection now was. She shuddered, no longer knowing what she had seen. The fragile line between reality and unreality blurred. Her eyes swept the porch roof and the street below, empty in the predawn hours, silent except for the tapping of the rain. Then she pulled down the shade to shut out the night.

She eased Toby into bed and tucked the covers tightly under her chin. The girl's eyes were wide and searching, liquid, demanding answers. Linda had to turn away from them.

"Do you want me to sit with you?" she asked.

"Uh-huh."

Linda perched on the bed and pushed Toby's hair off her forehead. "One favor, okay?" she said to the girl. "Let's not tell Uncle Thomas about what happened tonight. I don't want him to worry about us, okay?"

"Okay, Mommy," Toby said uncertainly. She wanted to ask why they could not tell, but an intuitive sense of self-preservation warned her to say nothing. Just as she had not said anything about Beatrice Dailey.

"You go to sleep now, baby. And tomorrow we'll do something special."

Linda switched off the light. There was a security to the darkness now. The room was no longer lit up and vulnerable to the night. Leaving Toby's door open, she went back to her room and sat down on the bed, feeling very small and lost, utterly alone. Her cheeks were glazed, her breath quick and shallow, her eyes wild in mounting panic. She tightened her hands into fists, and her nails made half-moon indentations in the fleshy part of her palm as she remembered the last time she thought she saw a man at Toby's window, the last time she thought she heard him coming up the stairs. . . .

But there had been no one then, just as there was no one tonight. No . . . one . . . tonight, she grappled with herself, trying to regain control. In a helpless panic she ran her hand through her hair, then rubbed her eyes hard until she saw spiraling circles of light. She had mistaken her reflection for a stranger, *imagined someone had been at the window.*

Created invisible danger for herself again.

As she had years ago.

Dr. Valleau's therapy analyzed why she had hallucinated the man in Los Angeles; she had established a pattern of assuming responsibility for events over which she had no control, he said. Her parents had been killed randomly the night of her eleventh birthday, and while she hadn't done anything to create the circumstances of their deaths, still she punished herself afterward by her nightmares and paranoia. It was the same after the mugging in the parking lot. Again it had been a random attack, again she did not purposely create the danger to her daughter. Yet subconsciously she needed to be a victim, to assuage guilt and responsibility that were not hers. Therefore she hallucinated the punishing figure.

Now it was happening again. Deep down in her mind she felt responsible for Carol Ann's death—and terror at the possibility that it might have been Toby who had drowned in the well. Holding her emotions tightly, frantically, in check, she searched inwardly, trying to imagine what Dr. Valleau would say to her now, how he would help her help herself.

The children had been warned. He would work the concept through with her from a dozen different angles and approaches, as he had done years before. She could not be responsible for their actions. Just as she could not be responsible for her parents having taken her to the movies. It had been *their* choice, he would stress, as it had been the mugger's choice for having selected them and the children's choice for having played in the well.

Although—the punishing thought stabbed at her mercilessly—hadn't it been her choice not to have covered the well? Her responsibility?

No! She banged the bed with a straining fist, trying to slam a door on her mounting fear. *Not now!* she said to herself. She didn't want this to happen now. Not when everything with

Thomas was so promising. Not when she was experiencing the first happiness since Keith's death. *Not now!* She had control, she could call on Dr. Valleau's therapy, and she wasn't going to be sick anymore!

"I'm not going to let this get to me," she said, and only when she heard the words was she aware that she had spoken them out loud. But the strength of her resolve calmed her. She breathed deeply, relaxed her body, felt shakily better, hoping that the words she had just said could penetrate her subconscious as easily as had her guilt and ghosts from the past.

She shut off the light and lay down, wanting to be covered by the darkness that filled in snugly around her like a protective glove. She closed her eyes, but, frightened, opened them again and let them search above her, where splashes of ever-darker shadows crisscrossed the ceiling like the angel of death. The rain had finally stopped and the room was silent—*too silent.* She strained to make out creaks and whines of the shifting, settling house. But as if sensing the approaching dawn, the house refused to oblige her. A silence heavier than air accompanied Linda downward into her restless sleep.

chapter 20

The alarm was just so much more discordant noise somewhere deep inside of her. The radio dial had drifted off the station and her mind absorbed and made it part of a dream. There were passageways. Dark corridors leading from nowhere to nowhere. There was danger in the corridors, she sensed; her mind was trying to alert her to something, but she didn't know what it meant. Then she swam up from sleep, away from the corridors, which soon became just another lost dream, like so many others.

It was really Toby who responded to the alarm, climbed into bed with Linda, and threw her arms tightly around her mother's warm, secure body, laid her head on Linda's chest.

"Good morning, baby. Did you sleep okay?"

"Uh-huh," Toby answered, her voice muffled in Linda's nightgown. "Did you, Mommy?"

"Yes, dear, I did." Linda stroked Toby's head, twirled her fingers through the sandy waves, felt her daughter shiver as she traced lightly down the back of her neck. *This* was reality, Linda thought; her beautiful ticklish daughter with the wavy, sandy hair and California sun freckles that still dotted her pixie nose. But the morning sun slanting in through the window brought back the other reality, the unreality of what had happened last night, and with it a new, undefined sensation of fear that tingled and played with her even now as she tried to push the feeling away.

When she washed her face she saw how tired she was; her eyes were half closed, her head seemingly swathed in a filmy gray through which everything appeared cloudy, and she felt she could fall back to sleep on her feet. But Thomas was coming over soon and she had to prepare herself. She was covering the shadows beneath her eyes with makeup when she identified the source of the fear. She hadn't felt this tentative about herself since she had first arrived in West Ledge, when she was afraid of telling Thomas how frightened she was by sounds and shadows and men in the street, terrified that he and Eleanor would want to hospitalize her and she would lose her little girl. Now she trusted Thomas and was no longer afraid of him, although in a grave sense she knew she still was—of his reaction to her madness, and that it would drive him away.

Just as she had been afraid of losing Keith during the months she spent in the hospital, afraid he would become impatient with her, hateful of her sickness, take Toby and return to West Ledge without her. But he dutifully visited her twice a week. She did not learn until she was released that his love for her had never lessened, that her fears of his abandoning her were ungrounded—just her own paranoia, the reason she was in the hospital.

Now, watching Toby in the bathroom next to her as she brushed her teeth in up-down motions, Linda clearly remembered the day she was released from the institution. Keith had left four-year-old Toby with a sitter and had come to pick her up. It was a typical warm and cloudless southern California day. They joked on the way home about her finally being sprung, but the jokes were defensive; she was nervous about returning home, away from the safety of Dr. Valleau. But any hesitation dissolved when she stepped out of the car and Toby charged toward her, arms open, smiles from ear to ear. "Mommy!" she squealed, happy to have her mother home again.

"Oh, baby, baby," Linda repeated over and over as she smothered her daughter in her welcoming arms. "I'll never leave you again, I promise. Never."

After dinner she and Keith put a very tired, very excited Toby to sleep and they stretched out on the couch, their legs entwined in each other's, massaging each other's toes. God, how good it felt, how she had missed Keith's touch, the simple pleasure of being together with him. Then he reached over toward her and kissed her, and they made love like newlyweds. And she knew she never should have doubted his love for her. It was genuine. Lasting. Till death finally parted them.

She wondered distantly if she would ever have to be hospitalized again.

And if Thomas would care for Toby as Keith had.

And wait for her.

Thomas brought brunch—cream cheese, smoked salmon, and a variety of bagels still hot from West Ledge's one bagel shop. Linda tried to be attentive to him, laugh at his jokes, but she couldn't clear her mind of last night and Thomas couldn't help but notice the distraction in her eyes. Toby was behaving strangely too—every time he looked toward her, the little girl shied away uncomfortably.

"Are you in there, Linda?" he asked later. She was washing, he was drying, and he watched her soap and resoap a plate, sponging it for longer than necessary as she stared absently out the window.

"What?" she asked and pulled back to him. "I'm sorry, Thomas, I was just thinking."

"About what?"

She shrugged and smiled vacantly. "I guess nothing."

"Is there anything wrong? You've been somewhere else all afternoon."

"No, I'm sorry. I'm here." She opened her arms expansively and sang "Ta Da!" They laughed, but she saddened when she went back to washing the dishes and turned away from him so he wouldn't see that the smile had fallen from her face. She knew she was afraid of losing him, his silken hair, streaked with distinguished gray, so sensuous to her touch, his musk smell now as much a part of her as her own, but mostly his love. *She isn't stable, Keith.* Eleanor's words again came back to haunt her. Thomas had been in the house when his mother had said them. She isn't stable, Keith. She isn't stable, Thomas, she could hear Eleanor saying again. And the truth of the matter was that she wasn't.

"I'll get the garbage," Thomas said.

"No, I will."

They reached for the bag at the same time and the contents went sprawling across the kitchen floor—coffee grounds, bagel crumbs. What should have been a funny moment wasn't. Linda exploded. "Now see what you did!"

Thomas knew it wasn't the garbage that was upsetting her. "What is it, Linda?" he asked. "Tell me."

And she wanted to. She wanted to sit barefoot with him in front of a roaring fire and tell him what she had kept from him, because now she needed his help. But it was too late to confess. Although she ached to hear him say it was all right, it didn't matter, he didn't love her any less because she was still mentally sick, she couldn't take the chance of his reaction. She could not be absolutely certain of another person's feelings. There was just too much to lose, especially when she felt she could fight this herself.

"I think I might be coming down with something," she lied.

"Are you feverish?" he asked, concerned, and reached out toward her forehead. She stopped his hand in midair, closed her own around it, cradled it.

"No, I just feel a little funny, that's all."

Linda swept up the garbage and Thomas took it outside. They played Scrabble. Though Linda tried hard to concentrate on the game, Thomas saw her heart wasn't in it. He pretended to have a heavy workload for the coming week and said he wanted to go into the bank for a couple of hours to get a start on it.

"I'll call you in the morning," he promised. "You get to sleep early and feel better, okay?"

"I love you, Thomas," she said, but her tone was not one of passion or even affection; rather there was a tremulous fear in it as it quavered from deep in her throat, as if she were afraid she loved him more than he did her.

After Thomas left she poured herself a drink and sat in front of the fireplace. Toby was upstairs studying for a test and she was alone with her amaretto, her memories, and her resolve. She would fight this, beat this, get better! She swore to herself. Because she had Thomas's love.

But then she shuddered and remembered. When she had hallucinated in Los Angeles, hadn't she had Keith's love?

Coming on the edge of sleep, the voice shocked through Linda like an electric current. Her breath froze and she felt a tightening in her chest, just above her stomach, a kind of cold nausea brought on by sudden fear. She couldn't remember having been dreaming and knew it had been the sound that had awakened her.

But she had resolved not to be frightened by noises and was already steeling herself to ignore it when she heard the voice again.

You killed my daughter.

It was clearer now, no longer muffled by sleep, filled with accusation and wet with the spittle of hate. And familiar—not just a passerby speaking randomly outside her house. Frowning, Linda reached above her and turned on the lamp.

A metallic snap broke the air, then the whining croak of a hinge, the gentle clasp of a closing door, and the voice again.

I have to kill you. And your daughter.

Now there was no mistaking who was speaking and like icy snakes had slithered their way up her legs and wound around her body, Linda knew that Beatrice Dailey was in the house, a maniac, a crazy woman, wanting to kill both her and Toby. Alert to the danger, Linda jumped out of bed and charged into the hallway, stood hunched on the landing. Her nostrils flared catlike as she searched the air trying to discern Beatrice's presence. Despite the silence that now rose thickly from the first floor, she knew that Beatrice was down there. Waiting.

Hurriedly she went back into her bedroom and dialed the police. She reported the intruder in a hoarse whisper, shaded by her palm, and prayed that the phone would not go dead in her hand, the wires cut. Her eyes were trained on the doorway. She was ready to spring if Beatrice mounted the stairs. She could use the lamp as a weapon if she had to.

When she hung up the phone she coiled the lamp's cord, removed the shade, and hoisted the lamp in her hand. Then she went back out onto the landing. Frightened, her breath came in spurts, high in her chest, caught, as if she'd swallowed something. With her free hand she reached out for the banister and pressed against it for balance and support. Gently she eased herself down the first step. She was exposed on the staircase, backlit by the nightlight that washed out from the bathroom in a muted blue, and at any minute she expected to see Beatrice appear from out of the shadows at the bottom. She knew she should just go into Toby's room, barricade the door, and wait for the police, but she was flushed with a strange sort of victorious relief. This proved she wasn't crazy, that she hadn't hallucinated last night, that it had been Beatrice at Toby's window. Beatrice, out to avenge the death of her daughter.

Her mind abuzz, Linda was barely aware she had reached the bottom of the staircase. Cautiously she peered around the banister. The back of the house was draped in darkness, but it was a living blackness that almost seemed to pulsate.

She reached out for the lightswitch, patted the wall a half-dozen times until she found it, then jumped back to the wall as the light exploded in the room. Unconsciously she had raised the lamp above her, ready to bring it down on the intruder. Her eyes darted frantically in constant motion so not to leave an angle unobserved. But she didn't see Beatrice anywhere. Where was she? Crouched behind the sofa? The wing chair? She rubbed the back of her neck to remove the crawling feeling that slithered over her. *Beatrice was watching her.*

"Please, Beatrice," she begged in a shaky voice she didn't recognize as her own. "I called the police. They're coming now. I'm so sorry your daughter is dead. If I could do anything to bring her back, I would. It was an accident. I was wrong not to cover the well, but I didn't think the children would play there again. Please don't hate us. Please don't hurt us."

But there was no response to her plea. She took another cautious step into the living room, catching her breath, trying to hear the slightest sound the other woman made, to somehow discern her location.

A floorboard squealed and she jumped. Then she realized it was her own step that had caused the wood to give and moan. By now it was apparent that Beatrice wasn't in the room. And a glance told her the cellar door was still latched; she hadn't gone down there. And the front door—still locked; she hadn't gone out there either. She was still in the house. So Linda pressed forward, her heart thumping madly as she started toward the dining room, through the squared archway of sculpted wood, one slow step at a time, trying to take in 360 degrees as she walked. The dining room was clear.

The kitchen. That's where Beatrice had to be hiding.

"I've got a knife, Beatrice," she said, hoping the lie would frighten the woman into coming out and facing her. All she had was the lampbase, but it was heavy and could be an effective weapon.

But the door stared back at her silently, mockingly, daring her to come closer. She swallowed. Beatrice was in there, waiting for her. To kill her! Then the thought hit her madly. While she was down there had Beatrice somehow slipped past her and run up the stairs? Was she with Toby right now? No, she couldn't be. She would have heard something—steps, voices, *screams!* No, if she was still in the house, she was down there, in the kitchen, *baiting her to come through the door.* She inhaled sharply, a deep breath, and silently counted to three. Adrenaline alone made her kick the door open and hold it wide as the dining-room light swept it.

One glance took in the entire room—there were no dark corners for anyone to hide. Nobody was there. She flipped the kitchen switch and checked the back door. It was locked from the inside; Beatrice hadn't been in there at all!

She experienced an odd moment of detachment—confusion, fear, but most of all pathetic understanding. *She knew what she had heard,* but she had really heard nothing. As frightening as it was to think Beatrice was inside the house, it was even more frightening now to know she hadn't been there at all.

She covered her eyes with her hands to stem the welling tears and maddening frustration, and pushed her forehead tightly against her palm as if to realign whatever was inside of her that was making her the way she was.

God, she prayed, when was it going to end?

Her heart pumping, Toby escaped from a nightmare.

But it had only been a dream, and she knew dreams couldn't hurt her. She was calming herself when she heard the sounds. They seemed to form a pattern, and she identified them—footsteps. She burrowed deeply under the blankets, afraid to move. There was a small degree of safety gained by remaining in bed, under the covers. Just as if you hid real quiet and didn't move, and couldn't see the danger, then it couldn't see you either. Couldn't get you. Black shadows would pass over you, the night demons would go somewhere else. A child's protective netting. But when she heard the slam of a door the net threatened to slip from beneath her and let her fall. Someone was in the house. Maybe her mother didn't know. She had to warn her. But her mother was *out there*, where the footsteps were. A toss-up. Fear was equally balanced. Should she stay in bed, or go to her mother? Here she was alone, vulnerable. At least with her mother she'd be safe. So cautiously she threw off her covers, wiggled into her slippers, and opened the door to her room and peered out. Something was definitely wrong. The lights were on downstairs. It was the middle of the night; they shouldn't be.

She tiptoed to her mother's bedroom, but she wasn't there. Nor was she in the bathroom. Toby relaxed. The mystery was solved. For whatever the reason, her mother had gone downstairs. Toby decided to go down as well.

Linda's head was hurting, a tension pounding behind her temples, a desperation. She had hallucinated Beatrice's voice tonight. Her sickness was closing in on her, tightening around her like hardening wax, getting worse. She poured a glass of water, gulped two aspirins. Her hand rested on the kitchen counter and slipped downward against the silverware drawer. She slid it open.

The knives gleamed. She picked up one she used for carving meats, turned it over in her hand, rubbed her finger lengthwise along the flat of the blade. She touched the tip, let the sharpness prick at her. She weighted the knife in her hand. The feel was familiar. It was exactly like the knife she had kept under her bed in Los Angeles, and in staccato flashes she remembered the night she had heard the footsteps on the stairs and the threatening voice of the curly-haired man who had come to kill both her and her daughter. And how she had raged after him and stabbed him again and again.

But she hadn't really, she knew, and her own breath threatened to choke her with the realization that on that night, just like tonight, the sounds, the voices, had existed only in her mind.

"Only in her mind," she repeated, banging her fist against the counter in endless frustration and helplessness.

Toby didn't like being downstairs at night, she realized as she reached the bottom of the steps. She held tightly to the banister, afraid to give up the security of her hold on it. She didn't like the furniture; it was old, depressing, with heavy squared-off arms, shading places for people to hide, *things* to hide. She also didn't like the way the fall wind brought life to the tree branches outside the windows and waved spidery shadows behind the curtains, seemingly reaching out for her. But if she didn't look when she went past, they couldn't trap her, couldn't hurt her!

The sudden pounding startled the little girl and her head swiveled to the sound. But she knew it was only her mother in the kitchen and happily she started for the door, away from the hulking furniture and monster tentacles that lurked behind the windows. But then she stopped. Her mother thought she was asleep; she didn't want to burst through the door and frighten her. She should enter the kitchen nice and easily and whisper to her mother that she was there. So tentatively Toby put her palm against the wood and started to push.

Linda stared at her own reflection in the kitchen window, her eyes dull, glazed over, half expecting that at any moment her features would become distorted, shimmer, and wave like a soap-bubble flashback and dissolve into someone else—the curly-haired man, Beatrice Dailey, she didn't know who. The well-crafted line between reality and unreality had shaded and blurred indistinguishibly.

Behind her she heard the squeal of rusty hinges, a tentative sound, *an imaginary sound*, she was sure. Turning dispassionately toward it, she accepted the sound as a hallucination. And was more than surprised when she saw movement. A hesitant opening of the kitchen door, a thin band of light trickling in from the dining room. And in the clear kitchen light she knew this was no hallucination. There was danger!

Beatrice Dailey was creeping up on her. She had been hiding in the house all along, waiting for Linda to be lulled into complacency. Now was not the time to glory in her vindication. Linda grabbed the knife and sprang into a waiting position behind the kitchen door. She had to protect herself and her daughter. Her heart was exploding. Her hand quivered but she steadied the knife above her head, her fingers stiff around the handle, cramped from tension and fear. Poised. Ready. The kitchen light glinted off the blade, making it seem to flare with life. The door slowly opened, but Beatrice was not yet visible. At the first shadow, Linda started to bring down her arm in a smooth, unbroken arc.

As she sensed Linda's presence behind her, Toby involuntarily jumped, away from the opening, away from her mother. Her tiny gasp as she inhaled sharply alerted one unconscious part of

Linda's brain that sent a signal to her arm to stop a fraction of a
second before gravity and momentum brought her elbow to full
extension and made everything else too late.

Her hand wanted to open and drop the knife to the floor, but
her fingers remained frozen around the handle. God, Linda
thought. What if she had swung downward with the knife. *What if
she had actually swung downward!* Quickly she crossed the
kitchen and put the knife down on the counter as the most
indescribable chill coursed through her.

"Mommy?" Toby questioned. She wasn't certain what had
just happened, why her mother was hiding behind the door to
frighten her, but now there was no danger and she felt safe again.

Linda ran back to her daughter, who was still standing in the
doorway. She fell to her knees and cradled the girl in her arms,
as much a gesture of comfort as supplication. *What had she
almost done?* It was what they had put her away for last time!

"Baby!" she cried, her face buried in her little girl's chest.
"I'm sorry . . . I'm sorry . . ."

"You didn't scare me, Mommy," Toby said. "I wasn't afraid."
She was more afraid now seeing her mother like this.

Linda heard the car pull into her driveway. There were no
sirens or whirring lights this time. And why would there be? she
questioned as she got stiffly to her feet to let the police in. This
wasn't a police matter. They knew that nobody had been in her
house tonight. To them she was just a nuisance, a crank caller, a
crazy woman. And obviously they were right.

She opened the door as Officers Saul and Jamison walked up
the porch stairs. "Please go away," she said to them in a voice
that sounded a hundred years old. "I called you in error. There's
nobody here . . . nobody," she whispered again and closed the
door.

Toby was standing across the room looking at her. Her face
was riddled with confusion, but she remembered another time
when her mother had acted like this, and that was a time she
didn't want to think about at all.

"I'm sorry," Linda said again, and shook her head. She reached
out her hand, and Toby took it hungrily. When they touched,
Linda couldn't even tighten her hand around Toby's, afraid that
even the gesture of love would hurt her little girl.

"Aren't you going to turn off the lights downstairs?" Toby asked when they reached the top of the steps.

"Leave them." Linda seemed to croak out the words. She didn't even try to fall back to sleep that night. She paced her bedroom anxiously. Her stomach was churning and palpating with a cold nausea. She didn't know how to escape from the terror inside her that burned like searing metal. She was out of control. She had completely regressed to the state she had been in in Los Angeles—hallucinating sounds and figures, melding reality and unreality without distinction.

chapter 21

It was a little after nine when the intercom buzzed. Thomas picked up the phone—"Yes, Diane?"—and his face furrowed in surprise. "Send her in."

He moved quickly to the door and opened it to Linda. Surprise turned to shock when he saw her; her face was pale, almost a pasty white. It was more than just not made up, it was as if it were completely drained of color. Her eyes were sunken, exhausted, and darkly frightened.

"Oh, Thomas," she cried, and grabbed onto him almost as if trying to make certain that he was real and not just another phantom.

"What's wrong?" he asked quickly. "Is it Toby? Did anything happen?"

"No," she said haltingly. "Toby's fine. She's in school. She doesn't know I'm here."

"What happened, Linda?" he repeated sharply, and led her to the couch. She slumped onto the cushions, bones and muscles refusing to support her. Thomas sat next to her and took her hands, which were so cold he almost pulled away; it was like touching something lifeless. "Tell me, Linda," he pleaded.

She hadn't wanted Thomas to know what was happening to her, hadn't wanted to test his love. She felt she could work it all through herself, but something tragic had almost happened last night—*because of her sickness*—and she could no longer shoulder it alone. That had been one of the four A.M. decisions she had made and remade, so terribly confused, not knowing what to do, where the answers lay. She didn't know what his reaction would be; she just needed to unburden herself to him.

She tried to remain calm and almost dispassionate as she told him what had happened, explained what the doctors had analyzed and why she thought she was regressing into a schizophrenic state again. She fought back tears and tried to keep her voice from breaking. She watched Thomas's face, looking for clues to what he was feeling as he let her speak, not daring to interrupt. His eyes were squinting with confusion, his lips slightly parted. Fine, troubled lines stood vertically on his forehead between his eyebrows, as his face crinkled into a mask of concern and his head shook back and forth.

"I could have killed Toby!" she cried helplessly when she finished, as again the reality of what might have happened last night became evident, and all her fears suddenly erupted like boiling water spilling out of a cauldron. "I don't know what to do!" Her voice was high-pitched and plaintive as she fought for control.

Thomas didn't know either as he struggled to understand and absorb the horror of what she had been through—the details of what had happened to her in Los Angeles. Knowing that she had been sick and hospitalized was so far removed from what she was telling him now. And now it was happening to her again. She had thought it was all behind her, but it wasn't. "Linda . . . Linda . . ." he started, feeling feeble and inadequate. He would have given away all his Harvard business degrees and half his money for the right words to say to her. He searched her face almost as desperately as she searched his. Embarrassed, defeated, she turned away from him, but he tightened his hold on her hand and she snapped back again. She needed him now, and a sudden rush came over him, a surge of love and abject pity. He wanted to just grab hold of her and shake sanity and reason back into her. That was all she really needed, one part of him believed. What was all this talk about hallucinations? What was this thing called mental illness? None of it made any sense, he denied defensively. But he saw the reality of her terror as he looked deeply into her eyes. There was no denying it.

"Maybe if I left West Ledge," she said graspingly. "Maybe it's being back here again. Maybe if I put distance between myself and the tragedy at the well. Maybe that's all I need."

"Listen to me, Linda," Thomas said tenderly, searching for words, not knowing what to say to her, which words were right, which wrong. He took her head in his hands, pulled her close to him, tried to spin a web around her with his arms to shield her from all fears—from herself. Her fingers grabbed at him tightly, pinched his skin as they ran searchingly up and down his arms. Their clutching embrace made him feel as if they were lovers about to be torn apart by coming war. "You've had such a terrible time recently. You've been through so much—more than any person should have to go through in an entire lifetime. You're vulnerable now to incidents from the past, your own painful memories. But we'll get you through this, Linda. You'll get better. I swear it!" And in that one second he understood the near desperation that had been in her voice the day before when she told him she loved him. "I love you, Linda!" he said urgently, trying to allay her fears. "And nothing will ever change that." Then, not wanting her to answer, he continued quickly, "I know an excellent psychiatrist. He'll help you; I know he will. I'll try to get you to see him this morning." He punched his intercom but when Diane clicked on, he thought better of it and dialed the number himself.

Linda walked to the window and stared out at the fall day as Thomas spoke to the psychiatrist, his voice calming as he listened to the doctor. Dark clouds were slowly drifting eastward, the sky was a turgid gray. More rain was expected. The papers had reported it was the wettest fall in three decades. Linda concentrated on the approaching clouds to block out Thomas's conversation with the psychiatrist. She was ashamed of herself, of her illness.

"Thank you for fitting us in," Thomas concluded. "We'll be over in an hour." He hung up the phone. "Dr. Gardner can see you," he said.

Linda still stared blankly out the window. There was a small park across from the bank. The branches of the trees there were barren, undraped—exposed, defenseless. Just as she was feeling now. Inside her she was hearing sounds, remembering faces, cringing from threatening voices, reliving a man on her staircase, a knife stuck in a newel post. She wasn't aware that Thomas had walked over to her, and she stiffened when he touched her arm. He didn't pull away but cupped her elbow and turned her toward him.

"I don't want you to be afraid of me," he said sincerely. "I don't want you to apologize and I don't want you to feel like you've been deceptive. I love you, Linda, and I will never leave you or abandon you. Do you hear me?'' Her expression remained lost, vacant, and it was only the faint nod of her head and the fluttering of her eyelids that answered his question. "Good." He smiled. "And after the doctor we're going back to your house and pack some clothes for you and Toby. You're moving in with me. I'm not going to let you stay alone in that house anymore."

They were halfway out the door when Linda remembered she was expected at work. Fortunately Nancy was busy at the photocopy machine and Helen picked up her call. Helen put her through to Mr. Robinson immediately. "I'm not feeling well today and won't be coming in," Linda explained. "Please don't forget about the mortgage papers that I was going to do this morning. Nancy can finish them. I'm sorry. I'm—" Her voice cracked but she held control of herself long enough to finish the conversation. "Yes, thank you, Mr. Robinson. I hope to be in tomorrow too."

But she had no idea what today, or tomorrow, would bring.

Dr. Gardner was Thomas's age, with a full head of gray hair smartly parted. His clothes were casual—a plaid shirt open at the collar, chino pants, and a well-worn pair of Wallabees, now more brown than the original beige. His manner of dress and easygoing handshake immediately put her at ease—the effect he strove for, she was certain.

He was direct and asked why she was there.

"Because I'm paranoid," she answered, "hearing sounds and seeing people at my window." Then she laughed hollowly, embarrassed that someone new had to see her sickness.

Two hours later she left the office with a prescription for pills. She had talked about her childhood, the deaths of her parents, and then the mugging in Los Angeles. Dr. Gardner asked questions to keep her on track and explained that together they would work to assuage her guilt and feelings of responsibility, ease her fears.

When she saw Thomas as she came out of the doctor's office, her lips turned upward in a tentative smile. "I'm feeling better now," she said. "Calmer. Dr. Gardner's going to help me."

"I know he is," Thomas reassured. "He's a good man."

They drove in silence to Linda's house. Thomas watched her pack a suitcase for herself and Toby. He didn't know what else to say to her so he just suggested items of clothing to be taken along. He was feeling confused, helpless. To look at Linda, there was nothing wrong with her. No broken bones, no open wounds. Just hidden scars. And pain. Emotional pain, but as agonizing as any physical pain. He knew better how to deal with physical pain: with pills, with exercise, with touch. He was at a loss as to how to deal with Linda's kind of pain. Except with words. And love. But his words alone couldn't help her, he suspected. And love was perhaps as abstract and unreal as her private visions and ghosts from the past.

He would do whatever was required to make her whole again, he vowed, just as if she had a broken bone or an open wound.

He was pleased that she offered him her hand as they got out of the car. The underground garage was dark and shadowy and he thought he should have parked on the street. But she showed no fear as they walked to the elevators, their footsteps echoing loudly, hollowly on the cement floor. This time his eyes searched for figures lurking behind the concrete posts and parked cars.

He got Linda settled in his apartment and picked up Toby at school, explaining that they would be staying with him for a while; he didn't want them to be all alone in that house any more.

Linda had started dinner and she shooed Thomas out of the kitchen. Happy that she was occupying herself, he willingly left her alone and watched cartoons with Toby, who was somewhat confused by what was happening.

"Is Mommy all right?" she asked, intuitively sensing that something was wrong.

"Of course," Thomas answered.

"She was sick once before," Toby said. "She was in a hospital. Will she have to go to the hospital again, Uncle Thomas?"

Thomas saw her fear that she might be abandoned by her mother and he shook his head. "Absolutely not."

"Good," Toby said, and turned her attention back to the television. That was what she had wanted him to say. Once she was reassured, she didn't want to dwell on the subject anymore.

Thomas kept up a stream of small talk at dinner—questioning, probing minutae, anything to keep the conversation from lapsing and creating an unfillable void at the table. He hoped he wasn't being too solicitous toward Linda, but suspected the chatter was easier and more beneficial for her than silence. He watched the dynamics between Linda and Toby—the furtive glances the little girl stole toward her mother, to assure herself that she was all right and still there.

As if reading her daughter's mind, Linda said "always" to her as she tucked Toby into the cot set up in the guest room. Where she would be sleeping on the bed. The blinds were open wide, a change from the tightly drawn curtains they had become used to. But they were high atop the apartment building and nothing could possibly appear outside their window tonight. *Nothing real*, that was, Linda chided herself, as she kissed Toby good night and tiptoed out of the room.

"Is she asleep?" Thomas asked as Linda came back into the living room.

"Yes." She settled into the chair in the corner and picked up a magazine.

Thomas was looking at the evening paper but wasn't really concentrating, just using the paper to hide behind so he wouldn't have to look at Linda and perhaps embarrass her.

The silence in the room grew evident. The dinner small talk was over and awkwardness crept in. Linda knew that Thomas didn't know what to do or say next; he was as helpless as she was. She thought back to the afternoon. Dr. Gardner had told her he knew how real the voice and footsteps, the face in the window, had seemed to her. But she knew they weren't real. And she was surprised when he said she should even be happy it had all happened before, because she knew now it had passed— she had gotten better!—and she would get better again this time as well.

"Do you want anything else to eat?" Thomas asked.

"What?" She was distracted. She looked up and saw him watching her. For how long? she wondered. What was he thinking when he looked at her? She shook her head. "No—I'm tired. I think I'll go to bed."

He put down the paper and crossed to her, helped her out of the chair, took her hands, then drew her close to him; hugged her.

"I love you," he whispered into her ear. "And I'm here."

"And I'm grateful," she answered him.

He put his finger to her lips; stopped her from saying anything more. "Remember our rule," he said. "No more thank-yous."

She turned away so he wouldn't see her tears and left the room. She didn't want to fail him, she didn't want to lose what had developed between them. She even considered making love to him, not because she wanted to, but just to hold him, know that he was really there, as Keith had been for her. But that would be cheating them both.

Toby was breathing gently, her hair splashed across her cheeks. Linda undressed quickly in the dark and slipped between the sheets. She remembered suddenly, oddly, how her mother used to tuck her in when she was little. Tuck her in and tell her stories. Then together they would say their nighttime prayers. She had stopped saying prayers after her parents had been killed. But she didn't want to think about her mother now. Not her mother, not her father, not their deaths. Nor about nighttime prayers that didn't protect them. She didn't want those thoughts to linger in her subconscious as she crossed over to sleep, afraid that, despite Dr. Gardner's medication, they might surface again and haunt her dreams.

Thomas watched the door slip shut to the guest room and exhaled. It had been a particularly stressful evening. He had been so afraid of saying the wrong thing. He poured himself a brandy and sat down on the couch, sipping the warming liquid and staring out at the lights of West Ledge, blurred and distorted in the rainswept night. It was a view he now associated with Linda, like a remembered fragrance.

But then, like the fog that swirled in front of the window, his thoughts turned to his visit to his mother that day. Linda had insisted he tell her—she didn't want to keep anything from her.

"I knew it was going to happen, Thomas!" Eleanor cried. "I told you, but you wouldn't listen to me. One is never over those kinds of illnesses, *never*!" She shuddered as if trying to step back from the disturbing news. Then, as if she was trying to work a problem through for herself, she added, "All right, it's happened. We must decide what to do."

But when Thomas told her it had all been worked out, and that Linda and Toby were staying with him, Eleanor shook her head back and forth strongly as if trying to blot out his words. "You can't, Thomas! By all means, help her, get her the best psychiatrist, but you can't have her living with you. She's so very troubled. She's been violent in the past. What if something happens and she becomes violent again?"

"All the more reason I should be with her. She needs me more than ever now."

"But you're not equipped," Eleanor protested. "Knowledgeable. What will you do if . . .? Oh, Thomas, she should be put somewhere where she could be properly cared for."

"You mean in a mental institution again?"

"If that's what's required. And we can take care of the child until she's well again."

"No. She told me what it was like for her and I'm not going to let her go to any such place again. Dr. Gardner doesn't think it's necessary and besides, she shouldn't be alone when she has people who can care for her."

"And she didn't have Keith when those things happened to her in California?" Eleanor challenged. "She could have killed him or Toby."

"Mother, I know what's best—"

"You don't know any such thing, Thomas. What if something happens? What if she thinks she hears something again? Are you safe? Is the child? How can you deal with—"

He cut her off. "Nothing is going to happen!"

"Thomas, you can't say that. Nobody can."

"Mother, she will get better," he pleaded. "Please don't worry."

"But I am worried," Eleanor cried. "Thomas, I am worried to death."

Thomas poured himself another drink and stretched his legs across the coffee table. They were tired, weighty. His entire body was drained from the day's tension, but he knew he wouldn't be able to fall asleep just yet. He was finally alone and able to reflect on what Linda had told him. Everything that had happened to her was all so inconceivable, and the absolute horror of it sent prickly needles up his back. He didn't want to think of the

woman he loved having been tortured so, and he was so utterly
helpless. He was used to being in control, the man in charge of
all situations. All situations, he thought ruefully, except when it
counts the most. He understood why she had been so afraid to
tell him, afraid his feelings for her would change, but his love for
her would never falter! he swore to himself. He was ready to take
vows to love her in sickness and in health, but he knew that now
was not the right time for either of them. As he finished his
brandy and poured another, he thought about the engagement
ring locked in his wall safe at the office—it would have to wait
until she was well again.

And in that way, he thought grimly, Linda's fears had been
realized after all.

Eleanor walked from room to room in the empty, silent house.
For the first time in a long time the grandfather clock refused to
chime, accenting the loneliness she felt. She wandered from
Thomas's bedroom when he was a child, to Keith's bedroom, to
the room they had set aside for storage when the boys had
outgrown their toys. There were sleds there, bicycles, building
blocks, electric trains. Eleanor knelt down and picked up the
miniature Lionel locomotive that had captivated Thomas, then
Keith as well. She spun the wheels with her finger, watching the
connecting arm rotate rhythmically, listened to the clack-clacking
sound the toy made.

She was sixty-five years old and her world was crumbling.
She had led a very comfortable life, virtually pain free, except
for her recent bouts with arthritis. Except for her husband's
death, the only other pain in her life had come when Keith had
moved away.

She had been stubborn, she knew now, had not gone after him
right then, had not apologized and accepted his wife. But he
would have returned home, she was so certain, if not for Linda,
who had kept him from her.

"There will be nothing wrong with Linda's staying with me,
Mother," Thomas had said to her.

But there was something wrong. There was very much wrong.
Things were all wrong!

This was not what she wanted to see happen.

Not at all.

She was afraid of what might happen to her son if that woman moved into his apartment.

But she didn't know what to do about it.

chapter 22

Linda saw Dr. Gardner for an hour every day after work. Her therapy was almost simple in its approach, he told her—accenting the positives in her life and trying to eliminate the negatives that weighed so heavily on her, the traumas she had lived through. Dr. Gardner explored her unforgiving feelings of guilt and responsibility—if they hadn't been celebrating her birthday, her parents would not have been killed; if she hadn't parked in the corner of the mall lot, Toby would not have been jeopardized; if she had covered the well, Carol Ann would not have . . . If . . . If . . . If . . . She felt unworthy of living, he told her. She had contributed to terrible things. Her guilt led her to self-hatred, and because she hated herself she felt she deserved what was happening to her. And she allowed it, welcomed it, in fact created the phantoms that were trying to kill her and right the wrongs she mistakenly thought she had perpetrated on others. Be it the curly-haired man from her distant past, or Beatrice Dailey, psychologically they were one and the same—Linda needed an enemy to torment her.

But she was not a bad person, Gardner stressed over and over, or worthy of the ultimate punishment of death. She was torturing herself wrongfully. She had been a good and faithful wife, a loving and caring mother; now she had a new life with Thomas. She must lay her guilt to rest once and for all.

And she knew that the voices weren't real, because they weren't real the last time. And because she made herself well before, she could draw on her past and make herself well again. "And you will do it, Linda! You've done it before. You've gotten well before!" The almost spiritual light in Dr. Gardner's eyes when he pronounced the words gave her the confidence that she could.

She really didn't have to go to work, Thomas told her. But Dr. Gardner had voiced his approval—to keep some sense of normalcy in her life. And things were indeed normal at the job: She ate lunch as she normally did—alone; and Nancy acted as she normally did—making her life miserable with sly smiles, denigrating comments about her work, and reporting on her evenings spent with the late Suzanne, as Linda referred to the fired receptionist. Her husband still wasn't working, Nancy chattered, and the only employment Suzanne had been able to find was as a check-out clerk at the local supermarket, not a fitting job for someone as frail as Suzanne was. (So she was *frail* now, Linda raged. *Do you want to talk frail?* she wanted to scream at Nancy. I could tell you frail that would knock your socks off!) But she kept silent and did her work the best she could. She would leave this job soon, she resolved. But not until she was better—she didn't want to add job hunting to the list of everything else she had to cope with. Still, it was easier to endure the law office knowing that, like the voices, as Dr. Gardner kept telling her, the job too would eventually pass.

She was concerned about the awkwardness between herself and Thomas and prayed that that would pass as well. It was almost as if they were afraid of each other, Thomas of being overly solicitous and Linda of being overly dependent. She wanted to be held by him, make love to him, but she didn't want him to misinterpret her lovemaking for clutching need. She wanted to tell him how much he meant to her, not because she was frail and hearing voices in the night, but because she loved him. For his part, Thomas treaded cautiously too, trying to maintain an equilibrium, not test or strain the relationship, fearful she might grow resentful of his care. It seemed to Linda as if he worked on his thoughts before voicing them, as if he was afraid of saying or doing something that would frighten her. His movements were careful. He never just came into a room, he entered loudly so he wouldn't inadvertently sneak up on her, set her off again, she suspected. The spontaneity had gone from their relationship.

They found ways to combat the awkwardness, not by confronting it but by avoiding it. Thomas left for work early, before Linda got up. A heavy workload, he complained, but even though he wasn't fooling either of them, they both kept up the charade. That way they didn't have to speak in the morning, or pass closely on the way to the kitchen, or slam doors to announce they were entering the room. Many mornings Linda lay awake in bed, listening to him tiptoe through the apartment (as they were tiptoeing around each other, she mused), waiting for him to leave before getting up. She thought that was how he wanted it. She made dinner and they made small talk—her job, the bank, Toby's school, world news. Neither mentioned therapy or hallucinations or their feelings for each other, for fear of losing what they had. After supper Toby became the center of attention, and they both threw themselves into the child's activities.

On Linda's first nights in Thomas's apartment, she had been almost afraid to go to sleep for fear she would hear Beatrice's threatening voice again and wake up screaming. Lying in the dark, her heart beat so loudly she thought she might wake Toby or summon Thomas from his bedroom (where he was also up, he later told her).

But as the nights passed without incident, she began to sleep more restfully, the voices and her fears growing fainter and slipping further behind her. With each day she saw a lightening in Thomas's eyes—hope! As if he as well finally believed Dr. Gardner's words that this too shall pass.

After a month of therapy, Linda's spirits were lifted. She felt as if she had been pulled put of a pit of depression and she wanted to yell to the world that she was better. Not the world, no—just Thomas. Her love.

She planned it to be a surprise for him.

She arranged for Toby to sleep at Mrs. Green's house for the night. She splurged on champagne, which she placed in the refrigerator to chill, then she bathed and slipped into the dress she had worn on their first real date—the night they first held each other close. Thomas noticed her appearance and the lack of dinner odors as soon as he arrived home.

"Is this a hint to go out to eat tonight?" he asked, smiling.

"No," Linda said, her eyes sparkling. "I've ordered in."

As if on cue the doorbell rang and the delivery man arrived.

"Pizza!" Thomas exclaimed, pleased.

They opened the champagne and ate and drank, but they hurried to finish because the excitement was building up. After eating just half the pizza, they could contain themselves no longer. Weeks of built-up tension and frustration bubbled over. Thomas almost ripped the coral buttons off her dress in his haste to undo them, his mouth hungrily covering hers, his hands touching her skin graspingly as if he was in danger of losing the very sense.

They didn't even get to the bed. They made love in the living room, in front of the window for all of West Ledge to see, surrounded by the pizza box, the champagne, and their clothing strewn all around them, so great was their frenzy to be in each other's arms. And it was as if they had never been separated, as if these last weeks didn't exist. There was nobody else in the world except the two of them and they clung to each other with excitement and bliss that neither had ever experienced before.

Then they talked for hours, about subjects that had been taboo. Of love and therapy and voices that came no more. And of the future and being cured.

The next day Linda told Dr. Gardner what she wanted to do. He listened, frowned, and she saw he did not approve.

"You don't have to, Linda. There is really no reason."

"Yes," she said, not looking directly at him. "I think I do. I have to go back to the house that frightened me so. Like getting back on a horse that threw me, I have to live there again to prove that my being better is not just an illusion. I've got to face my fears, live through them, and finally put them behind me."

Dr. Gardner smiled. "You're sounding a little like me now."

Linda's smile matched his. "All these weeks of therapy and something has to rub off."

"Are you sure you're ready?" he asked seriously.

A simple question, yet a difficult one. She thought about it. She had spent weeks free of voices, visions, sounds, and shadows. She knew she could stay at Thomas's house now without awkwardness between them. But she knew too that they would both always wonder. Would it happen to her again? And when? She felt she had to go back to the house and prove to both of them that it was over, this time forever. "Yes," she answered, she was ready, and she hoped her surety rang in her voice.

"What if you hear voices again?" the psychiatrist asked her, his practiced eyes looking at her.

She avoided his glance when she answered. "Then we'll have

more to talk about." The words came glibly, but both knew it wouldn't be that easy; the setback would be traumatic.

"Let me make a suggestion," the psychiatrist said. "Don't live there alone, not yet. Let Thomas stay with you for at least several days as you reorient yourself. Then, if you still want to, you can try it by yourself."

Thomas wasn't as agreeable. "You shouldn't, Linda," he argued. "Why do you want to expose yourself to . . . to . . ." He searched futilely for the word.

"Myself?" she filled in. "My own subconscious demons?"

"Yes, damn it!" he exclaimed. He seemed genuinely angry. Maybe it was a mistake, she conceded, but after an evening of yelling back and forth about what she hoped to accomplish by returning to the house, Thomas relented. She was convincing and he understood. And he, too, was hoping for a conclusion. "But I'll be with you," he warned.

"Until I ask to try it by myself," Linda said. "That's our deal."

"And after you stay in that house by yourself and nothing happens, what then?" he asked.

Linda smiled and shrugged and repeated his words. "What then?" And Thomas knew the next move would be his.

Beatrice Dailey was knitting in the cane-back rocking chair by her bedroom window. She knitted a lot now, and while she used to knit for Carol Ann—sweaters, halter tops, in a dazzling array of colors—now she knitted for herself, to keep busy, to fill time. And she had to fill a lot of lonely hours. She had never worked, devoting herself to being a full-time mother, explaining to those who thought she should do otherwise that she always wanted to be in the house when Carol Ann came home from school.

But Carol Ann wasn't coming home from school anymore.

Passing cars beneath her window were a pleasant distraction, and she recognized every car on the block—the sight, the sounds, which needed a new muffler, whose brakes squealed. She knew when the Smiths bought a new Toyota Corolla and the Schneiders a Cadillac.

She stiffened as she saw the silver Mercedes driving up the street. They all look alike, she told herself, but still there was something familiar about the car and the three figures inside. She stopped knitting as the car pulled into the driveway. There was no question at all.

They had come back.

Thomas noticed the slight tensing of Linda's body, the increased wariness to her eyes as the evening drew on. He understood she would feel this way, and that was why he never left her alone and kept lights on throughout the house so there would not be a dark or shadowy corner.

They put Toby to sleep and relaxed in front of the fire. They warmed and massaged each other's toes, Linda enjoying his gentle pressure on the balls of her feet. This was what she and Keith had done the night she was released from the hospital. And weren't there similarities between that night and this? Both times she had returned home to the man she loved after being away. Then they sat on the floor in front of the fire and let the flames bathe their faces with light, and they whispered their love and hopes.

Linda never wanted the evening to end, but soon it was bedtime. Thomas took her upstairs first, then returned to douse the fire and stir the ashes, and turn off the lights. She was waiting for him and they quietly made love. They stretched out next to each other, Thomas's arm around her shoulders to hold her next to him. In the safety of his closeness, Linda fell asleep.

She woke an hour later to a car horn sounding beneath her window. Then the bark of a dog. And the swish of a tree branch in the breeze. Night sounds. Normal sounds. And that was all.

She snuggled closer to Thomas and drifted back to sleep.

That was all.

A week passed and decisions had to be made. A week of work and love and undisturbed sleep. And normal creaks of the house, the hum of the water heater, the metallic clang of a pipe, the refrigerator switching itself on and off. But no footsteps on the stairs, no faces at the window, no voices in the dark.

Only if she was really ready to test herself, Dr. Gardner told her. There was no rush and no reason if she wasn't.

But she was. She wanted to know it was over.

And that night, looking out of her window at the smoke spiraling up from Linda Devonshire's chimney, Beatrice Dailey saw Thomas open the front door, carry out a suitcase, and load it into his car. This was the first time he was leaving her alone in the week he had been there. Beatrice knew, because she had been watching.

chapter 23

She usually didn't go to Sammy's for lunch, preferring to put some distance between herself and the other girls for at least some portion of the day. But today she felt in high spirits and didn't care that the others sat in their usual booth right behind her counter seat. She had spent a comfortable night—restful and silent. "A-okay," she said when Thomas called early in the morning.

"That's just what I wanted to hear," he answered.

And she knew that she would soon be leaving the law office to look for something else—so let them eat without me, she thought. I don't need them!

After lunch, Mr. Robinson came bustling into the office. He was harried, speaking before he took his coat off.

"Nancy, are the Donovan contracts typed yet? He's coming by in an hour and I want to read them over."

"Let me ask Linda. I gave them to her this morning."

Linda heard what was transpiring behind her. She knew that Nancy hadn't passed her the Donovan papers.

"Linda?" Robinson was saying.

"Nancy didn't give them to me."

"Of course I did," Nancy snapped. "You were on a personal call and don't remember—"

"I wasn't—" Linda said.

"Here they are," Nancy said. She moved the telephone log on Linda's desk and there were the papers.

And suddenly the months of Nancy's stridency welled up inside Linda. She knew those papers hadn't been there that morning, and she finally had confirmation that Nancy had indeed been setting her up.

"Nancy, I told you those papers were important," Robinson said.

"And that's why I told Linda to hurry with them. You're always telling me to give her more to do so I did. I'm sick and tired of being blamed for her sloppiness. If she can't do the job—"

"That isn't so!" Linda raged, rising from her chair. "I have never seen those papers and Nancy knows it!"

"There they are!" Nancy answered.

"Because you put them there without telling me!"

"Oh, it doesn't matter anymore," Nancy dismissed it. "I'll do them right now, Mr. Robinson. I can finish them in no time."

"Don't you touch those papers!" Linda snapped. "*I'll* do them."

Nancy was leaning across the desk, her hands on the contracts. Linda grabbed her arm below the elbow and pushed her aside. Nancy shrieked and jerked away.

"You saw her!" she screamed. "She attacked me."

"What?" Linda asked blankly.

"She wanted to hurt me!"

"You're out of your mind!" Linda protested.

Robinson rubbed his eyes, tired of the infighting in the office. "Let's talk about all this later, *please*," he said. "Nancy, will you do those papers right now. Linda, would you come into my office for a second." He turned and started for the door.

A sudden storm raged inside Linda. She felt the secretaries' curious glances burn through her as they enjoyed the show, and she saw Nancy's smug expression; the other woman had bested her. Linda's eyes glazed and a red mask covered her face as she blushed deeply in fury. The words came in an involuntary torrent, building as her helpless frustration built as well.

"No, Mr. Robinson, from the very first day I've worked here, Nancy's been trying to get me fired. I have done nothing wrong. None of these disturbances has been my fault and I'm tired of getting blamed for things I didn't do." Her voice thickened. She tried to hurry the words out before the tears flowed and choked off her speech. "I don't want to get fired, but I just can't work here anymore either."

Her lips quivering, she was unable to continue. She grabbed
her purse and coat and stormed out of the office. She didn't see
the shocked, open mouths of Mr. Robinson and the others and the
smile that lanced across Nancy's face.

She drove straight to Dr. Gardner's office and waited until
he was finished with a patient. The ride over and the time
she spent waiting had calmed her, and now she looked down
at her hands as she finished telling him what happened. "I lost
my cool," she said dully. "Part of me wanted to stop myself
but part of me didn't. I felt everything was closing in around
me. Every other time I've been able to ignore Nancy, or at least
not let her get to me. Today I just couldn't." She shook her
head. "But I just don't understand why she would do this to
me. To carry a grudge after all these months when I've done
nothing to her, it's irrational." She stopped, let her shoulders
droop, and smiled wanly. "Look who's talking about being
irrational." She shrugged philosophically. "Well, I've wanted to
get out of there and now I am. I'm sorry it had to happen
the way it did, but I guess I'm more angry at myself for letting
her defeat me. What Mr. Robinson and the others must think of
me!" She sighed.

"Linda," Dr. Gardner said evenly. "I think you know now
that it doesn't matter what anyone thinks of you. It's only you and
Toby and Thomas who matter. Please don't let this affect all the
progress we've made. Too many good things are happening for
this to get in your way. All right?" he asked.

"All right." She nodded, then exhaled and her smile widened.
"Of course all right," she repeated.

"So how was staying alone in the house?" Dr. Gardner asked
her.

"No problems," she said happily.

"Well, that's certainly positive now, isn't it?"

"Yes," Linda agreed. It certainly was. And for that reason then,
the absolute hell with Nancy and the others!

Thomas came to dinner. After he took off his coat, Linda told
him what had happened. "I guess you could say I overreacted a
little, but I'm all right now."

"Good," he said uncertainly.

"I'm sorry if I embarrassed you with the law firm."

"That doesn't matter, Linda. As long as you're all right."

"And I'm going to find my own job this time," she said, then smiled. "But I might have to call on you for a good word. I don't know how well I'll do with Mr. Robinson."

"Whatever you need," Thomas said.

A goulash was simmering on the stove and Thomas helped himself to a taste of gravy off the wooden serving spoon. Out of the corner of his eye, though, he watched Linda, troubled by what had happened to her today, but she seemed calm and over it, and if Dr. Gardner wasn't concerned, he would not let it disturb him either. After supper he threw himself into the game of war that they all played, but not to avoid conversation like at his house. They were laughing, joking. As if they were a family.

At the door he whispered to her, "I could stay over tonight if you want."

Linda shook her head no. No, she didn't want to think that today's incident had sent her reeling backward. What happened in the office had nothing to do with her staying in the house alone, with her getting better.

A cold front had swooped down from Canada. Linda shivered and hung in the room as Thomas buttoned his coat. He kissed her then darted down the steps. Across the street he saw the Dailey house. Framed in a lighted second-floor window was the silhouette of Beatrice. A motionless, almost cardboard figure, flat, one-dimensional. A sentinel. Her presence startled him—was she watching them? he wondered, but shook off the thought. He ducked into the car and drove down the street, not knowing that Beatrice's eyes were following his Mercedes as it disappeared from view. Only her eyes were moving; the rest of her body remained stationary. Then her eyes shifted back and looked across the street toward Linda's house where the downstairs lights were now being switched off, one at a time.

Thomas promised his mother he would stop by after dinner.

"It's cold," she said as she let him into the house.

"It'll be in the twenties tonight." He took off his coat.

"How is she, Thomas?" Eleanor asked.

"Last night, okay. And tonight she's really up. Confident."

"That's good. I'm glad. She's lived through so much, hasn't she, the poor dear?"

"Yes," Thomas said, then added, "Mother, I want to thank

you for all the support you've given Linda these last few weeks. You've really helped her. I know it hasn't been easy for you, but I want you to know how much I—we—appreciate it."

Eleanor waved off the compliment. "I'm just doing what I know you want me to, Thomas, and I really am glad things are working out well for her."

"Tell me," Thomas said suddenly. "How's Elvira's facelift?"

"Oh, still holding," Eleanor said. But she knew that Thomas certainly didn't care about Elvira's facelift. About anything these days it seemed. Except *her*.

"I hope she's all right alone tonight," Eleanor said.

"I'm sure she will be," Thomas answered, praying that his words were not empty ones.

The grandfather clock, now fixed and ticking again, chimed eleven o'clock and seemed to join their conversation. As if supporting Thomas's words, or denying them.

Eleanor watched the sweep of the second hand as it traveled patiently, endlessly about the clock face. It would soon be midnight. Then one. Then two. Then later still.

Things happened to Linda late at night, Eleanor knew. Especially when she was alone and vulnerable to her past.

chapter 24

Linda watched Thomas's car back down the driveway, then turn into the street and be swallowed up by the darkness. Even though things had gone well last night, she still couldn't help but feel uneasy as the evening drew to an end. She turned away from the window and with her hands on her hips faced the quiet room. It's just us now, she thought. And it almost seemed as if the house thumped in response. The fire was dead, the ashes cold at the bottom of the hearth. Linda gathered up the coffee cups and carried them into the kitchen. She hummed a tuneless song as she washed, then dried and put away the dishes, making more noise than she had to. Extra motions to delay going to bed; extra noise to block out sounds and voices that remained teasingly just out of sight. She flipped off the light and walked into the living room, glancing behind her to the kitchen door, now a scrim wall of blackness.

There was something almost forbidding about a house at night, she thought as she climbed the stairs. It had a feel of its own, like a grainy texture, where the grayness is murky and tactile, a fine, choking mist, and shadows flit in and out, separating, coalescing, forming shapes and patterns. She stood at the top of the stairs, her hand resting on the newel post, rubbing the fluted surface. Except for the movement of her fingers, she was motionless, and all was silent. But tonight the silence felt almost alive and predatory. The alert silence of a crouching panther, about to spring, where the only movement is the flutter of whiskers, the flaring of nostrils as it searches the air, targeting a victim. The thick silence of a fog-shrouded lighthouse. The absolute silence of night shadows waiting for the people to go to sleep so they can make the empty rooms their playground.

Linda smiled thinly. Dr. Gardner would not be proud of what she was thinking right now. So she pretended she was talking to him, and listened to what he would say. He would tell her that she had gotten through last night without difficulty and could do it again tonight as well. And the next night, and the next, a hundred nights, a thousand, because she was strong.

She got into bed, pulled the covers up to her eyes to shut out the night, said prayers she hadn't said since she was a child, and let sleep wash over her, repeating to herself in a hypnotizing litany that she was strong, she was better, she was strong . . .

Late that night she awoke suddenly. There was a rush in her ears, as if they were clogged with wax.

Not wax, water!

Running water.

Linda broke the surface between sleep and waking to the distant rumble of a faucet, water rushing out of the spigot and splashing against the porcelain sink. It's Toby, she thought, but then the whispered voice passed through her like an electric shock, tingling arms and legs, jerking her eyes wide as if her lids were attached to marionette strings.

You were responsible!

The words were muffled, as if under water, coming from deep inside her. Faint. A breath of wind. A dream. A memory. A subconscious still haunted by guilt and punishment, unable to let go.

You killed my daughter.

The speech was clipped and taut, the words seemingly vibrating within her, plucked from a bow.

"Stop it!" Her voice caught in her throat, as if she were still asleep. She swallowed, unable to break through to the air. Her eyes were open but sunken into their sockets, staring inwardly as she heard the water pouring out of the faucet, pooling in the sink, the swirl of froth and bubbles as the surface rose.

You killed Carol Ann.

"Stop it!" Her voice harsh now, husky, shakily spit out through a barely opened mouth.

I have to kill Toby too.

It was Beatrice she was hearing, her voice subliminal, almost below the threshold of consciousness.

Kill her like you killed my daughter.

Only a slither of current . . .

Put her head under the water!

But more ominous than the loudest voice.

"No!" Linda cried, her hands to her ears to block out the awful sounds. If she couldn't hear them, they wouldn't be there, wouldn't be there, wouldn't be there . . ,

"Mommee!" A high-pitched child's scream pierced the air and Linda shocked to Toby's voice. She swung out of bed and ran into the hallway—her child was in danger.

Kill her because you killed Carol Ann! Beatrice's voice still raged.

She heard water splash over the rim of the sink and onto the tile floor.

"Stop it!" Linda cried.

And then as if she hit a wall of silence outside the bathroom door, the voices did stop. As did the sound of running water, making her feel she had been thrust into an airless, soundless void. She looked into the bathroom and saw it was empty. Suddenly she felt weak, as if wind and breath had been sucked out of her. She slumped against the wall, her legs slender twigs, brittle, ready to snap off beneath her. She covered her eyes with the thick of her palms and rubbed as a pathetic squeal escaped through her closed lips. Then she heard a step somewhere near her, sensed eyes on her, and jerked her hands away. But no one was there, there were no more sounds, and the inky silence seemed to smile at her victoriously, the voices hidden in the blackness, no longer there, yet not quite gone. Lurking. Waiting. Just around the corner, down the stairs. Just beyond her peripheral hearing. Just out of mind. Her eyes slipped shut again as she tried to regain control, calm her labored, gasping breath, fight the endless mounting terror of her illness. She wasn't strong, she wasn't better. Her own words haunted her, taunted her now. She felt beyond help.

She heard movement from Toby's room, a twist of covers. She hated to turn her back on the stairway and the darkness of the first floor, but Toby was sitting up in bed, her slender body illuminated by the faint light that streamed into the room.

"What's the matter?" the little girl asked. "I heard something. It woke me up."

"Nothing, baby," Linda answered weakly, her voice high in her throat, stripped bare by her terror. "Only Mommy talking to herself."

"Are there burglars?"

"No, dear. There aren't any burglars." Linda looked at her child with a ferocious swelling of love and pity. She wanted to be better for *her*. But she wasn't better. "Were you in the bathroom running the water?" she asked with a hair thickness of hope.

"No, I was sleeping."

"Okay. Why don't you go back to sleep now?"

She helped Toby turn over on her side, and Linda knew that in the morning her daughter wouldn't even remember this conversation.

She backed out of the room, watching the mound of covers that was her sleeping child.

She went into the bathroom. The nightlight was a flickering blue that made her skin look pale, ghostly. She looked into the sink. Droplets of water dotted the sides, but nothing was trickling down into the drainhole, no water pooled at the ledge. No water had run there recently. She turned the faucet on. The familiar grumbling sound rang out and the water poured out. The same sound she had heard a moment before—*thought she had heard*, because she really hadn't heard anything at all. She put both her hands under the running water, brought them up to her eyes, and doused herself.

"God, it still isn't over, is it?" she moaned as she returned to her bedroom. Oddly enough, she was no longer afraid; the blind terror of a moment before had released its grasp on her. She knew she had reached absolute bottom. Therapy alone would not help her; only hospitalization was left. It was almost comforting to confront her worst fears, and a strange calmness settled over her. From rock bottom she could only go up again. Thomas would watch Toby and wait for her, as Keith had. She even managed to smile. Everything was under control. Her child. Her future. *Everything . . . under . . . control*, except her mind, she thought dismally. Now she accepted what would have to be. It was as if the past month had been a prelude to this moment.

She heard the noise beneath her window and automatically

looked outside. She hadn't expected to see anyone and was more than surprised to see a woman. Only a shadow, a shrouded spectre. Beatrice! Her mind reeled. Running away from the house, out of the circle of light beneath the streetlamp and back across the street to her own house.

There was an extended moment of confusion as what Linda saw connected and the implication unscrambled. And then she exploded with anger and hate. She wasn't sick! She hadn't imagined the voices, the sounds, the faces. All of it had been real. All the weeks of therapy and there had been nothing wrong with her! All the torture, all the pain. It was Beatrice! She had to catch her, confront her, prove to everyone—the police, Dr. Gardner, Thomas, herself!—that she had been sane all along.

In her slippered feet she ran downstairs and burst through the front door. Her fists clenched, she raged across the street, a grim smile of triumph on her lips. Beatrice had made a mistake; she had gotten caught.

But now no figure was in sight, and no lights were on in any of Beatrice's windows. The house seemed silent and closed for the night. But Linda knew she was in there, perhaps even hiding behind the door. Linda charged up the porch steps and banged her fist against the wood, a loud, hollow knock, making the door rattle back and forth.

"I saw you!" Linda screamed. "You can't get away with it anymore! Come out here! It's been you all along!" Over and over, her arm made a giant arc as she slammed her fists against the door, first one, then the other, desperate to prove her sanity.

"Come out of there!" she yelled into the night.

She didn't know how long she stood at Beatrice's door, but she became dimly aware of lights and sounds around her—police sirens breaking the night and spinning, flashing red lights. Arms suddenly touched her, and a hand closed around her wrist, stopping her from striking the door further. She looked behind her and saw Officer Saul, his face lined with confusion and concern, but now he had a job to do.

He pulled her away from Beatrice's door. Blood ran down her arms from where she had scraped the flesh from her hands, and only now did she start to feel the pain. But that pain was secondary to Beatrice's having gotten away with what she had done.

"She was in my house tonight! She was in there!" Linda babbled frantically. She tried to break away from the officers, to lunge again at Beatrice's door. She was crying as she slumped to the ground. They half carried, half dragged her down the porch steps and across the street. Behind her she saw Beatrice standing in her doorway, framed in the light, her nightclothes pulled around her. "There she is!" she screamed again. "She wanted to kill my little girl!"

Saul sat her down on the couch. "It was her all along!" Linda repeated. "I saw her at my window that night. I knew I didn't imagine it. And she was in my house tonight!"

Then Jamison was back in the room, closing the door behind him with a slam.

"Bring her in here! Let her face me. I'll prove it!"

The policemen were looking at her. Her eyes traveled from Jamison to Saul. It was as if they were speaking different languages, unable to communicate with each other. Why wouldn't they believe her? What would she have to show them to make them believe—Toby dead! Was that what they needed? Her daughter killed by that woman! Drowned! Were the police part of it too? She wasn't crazy. She knew what she had heard and seen.

"Check for her fingerprints here," she cried, grasping for proof. "That'll prove—"

But still they were looking at her and she heard words. Their words. And words from the past.

"*Your body,*" *the policeman said, pointing to the newel post, where the half-buried knife glistened in the hallway light.*

"I'm not crazy." She sobbed again, her voice breaking, faltering in her dread confusion. She felt as if she were trying to scale a wall of their disbelief, hanging on tenuously by her fingertips, her nails clawing at the concrete, cracking, splitting in her desperation to prove her story, to prove her sanity, to the others and to herself. She no longer knew what was real or unreal. She slipped back down the wall, her nails leaving helpless, bloody scratches on the concrete as again she accepted her sickness.

"Thomas," she cried weakly. "Please help me."

"I would recommend it," Dr. Gardner said.

"No!" Thomas said. "She doesn't need to be, I know it."

"She was capable of killing Mrs. Dailey, who has filed a

complaint. A hearing will be scheduled, although I've talked to the police. We might be able to avoid any of that if—''

"If I have her put away!''

"Only for observation now. It's the best thing for her.''

"But she was getting better,'' Thomas said helplessly, not knowing where to look. There were diplomas on Dr. Gardner's walls, diplomas he had trusted. He thought the therapy had worked. "She *was* better,'' he corrected himself. "If she hadn't gone back to that house . . . I never should have let her. *You* should have known better,'' he accused. "She was still sick—''

Dr. Gardner touched his arm. "It's not either of our fault. If it didn't happen last night, it could tomorrow. Any time. If not in her house, somewhere else. She might mistake a total stranger on the street. She might only have pretended to be better, fooled both of us—''

"No!'' Thomas cried. "She wasn't fooling. She was better! And I won't put her into a hospital again.''

"It may be out of our control. To avoid criminal prosecution.''

"It will devastate her,'' Thomas said weakly, knowing Linda's fears. "She can't go back to the hospital. There's got to be another way.'' Then he brightened. "I've got it. Let me take her away from here. We'll go somewhere. I'll watch her. She'll be away from that house, from Beatrice Dailey, all the influences on her.''

"That isn't a solution, Thomas.''

"But it's a start. Look—I'll talk to the police, a judge. To Beatrice. I'll square it with them. I'll call you every day. I'll find her another psychiatrist wherever we go. I can't let her go to a hospital again.''

He rubbed his hands against each other, suddenly cold, because he knew the worst had happened. Then he raised his eyes slowly and looked directly at Dr. Gardner.

"You know her psychological makeup better than I, Doctor, but if she goes into another institution, I just don't think she'll ever come out.''

chapter 25

It was midafternoon. It had taken Thomas the morning to arrange what he had to. Now he was with his mother, telling her what he planned to do.

He watched her grow stiffer and stiffer—her posture, her expression, her eyes frozen, unblinking, disbelieving. Her body seemed to draw into itself, contract like a crazy shrinking woman as she listened to him. He was babbling, he knew; he wanted to get it all out in one breath, heard only bits and pieces of what he was saying. "Can't let her be institutionalized . . . needs my help and attention . . . I love her . . . I know if she just gets away from West Ledge for a while she'll be better . . ."

"Yes, by all means help her, Thomas," Eleanor said. "Do whatever is in your power, but for God's sake—go away with her! Move away? Just like this! Leave everything? The bank?"

"I'm not leaving the bank, Mother. I'll be in daily contact. And we'll be back soon. All she needs is a little time."

"But you don't know how long. And you don't know what's going to happen to her. She could get worse. Thomas, you're not a psychiatrist. You're not qualified to diagnose and help. Listen to Dr. Gardner. You could be doing her more harm than good by not letting her get the help she needs."

"I know what she needs, Mother. And I love her. And that's what matters to me. I can't watch her be put away."

"Love her?" Eleanor spat out. "*Do* you, Thomas? Really? Might it not just be infatuation? She's a beautiful woman. Maybe it's only—what's the word?— a crush you have on her? Or maybe pity. You were drawn so nobly to the pathetic creature. You still feel guilty about what happened to her—'' She raised her chin, stared at him piercingly. "What *I* did to her."

"It's love," he said with perhaps the strongest tone he had ever taken with his mother.

"What about *me*?" Eleanor asked, a note of desperation woven through her voice. "What's going to happen to *me*? You'll go off somewhere with her, you'll forget me . . ."

"Never. I promise." He moved toward her, to take her hand, reassure her. But Eleanor snapped her hand away.

"Like Keith, Thomas. The same thing will happen. I'll never see you again."

"It's nothing like Keith."

"It's the same! The exact same! It's her. And she's taking you away from me just as she did Keith. What is she—some devil woman who came into our lives?"

"Keith left her because of what—"

"Well, she can't! I won't let her take away my only remaining son."

Thomas's voice was low, controlled. To Eleanor it had as much shock impact as if he had hit her over the head. "You can't stop this, Mother. So please don't try."

Eleanor looked at him, her face contorted with private anguish. Thomas knew what she was feeling and didn't want to hurt her. He wanted to stem her fears, tell her she wouldn't lose him, that Linda wasn't a Siren taking him away forever. But he didn't know how to make her listen.

Suddenly his mother seemed older than she ever had. He remembered how she had aged after his father's funeral and then more so when she received the news of Keith's death. It was almost as if she had died a little bit when Keith left and now he had just dealt her a final blow. Throughout she had tried to remain Eleanor Devonshire—stiff-lipped, regal—but inside he knew she was wasting away. Now he and Linda could both share guilt, he thought glumly.

"Mother, it will be nothing like you think. I swear it."

But Eleanor wasn't listening to him. She was thinking. Everything in her life had gone so wrong because of that woman. Keith went back to California because of her. He would have eventually returned to West Ledge, if not for her. First Keith. Now history was repeating itself with Thomas. After this moment she would never see her son again. Linda would take him, as she had taken Keith. She would kill him as she had killed Keith. Then she would return to West Ledge again—for what? Next time there would be no one left for Linda to take away.

No one left. Except herself.

She would be all alone.

She would die alone. That was Eleanor's one deepest fear, a fear that bordered on terror.

"Please, Mother," Thomas said. He held her hands in his so she couldn't pull away from him. "Please give me your approval."

Eleanor was silent, thoughtful, for a long moment before she spoke. Thomas wasn't really expecting to hear it and was totally surprised when she said, "Yes, Thomas. You have my approval."

Linda and Toby were packing their clothes; Thomas was coming by for them at six. The last sixteen hours had seemed endless, and Linda was exhausted. It was as if she had gone through the day in slow motion, as if walking in her sleep, her head steeped in a vaporous mist. She barely remembered the time she spent in the police station, in Dr. Gardner's office, barely remembered the people who were talking about her, deciding her future, and what she had said to them and they to her. Their voices melded together, becoming a distant, forgotten drone. Her life was out of her control, but thank God Thomas had pulled strings, exerted every bit of Devonshire influence he could muster to keep her out of an institution. Thank God he was willing to go away with her because when she was with him she wasn't tortured by her past. Now they would be away from this house and the traumas that had happened here, and she was optimistic; it was only a matter of time until she was finally and completely well again. Just knowing they were going was making her feel better, less afraid, more in control. But she had felt that way many times before, she knew.

"Where are we going?" Toby asked her.

"I don't know yet, dear," Linda answered dully. "Just on vacation for a little bit. Somewhere nice, okay?"

"Okay," Toby said tentatively, wanting to ask about her friends and school. Yet again she kept silent. The police had been there last night again, and her mother was so quiet today, subdued, *afraid*. It seemed important for them to get away from this house, and while she didn't understand what was happening, she had overheard the words "hospital" and "institution" and knew her mother would have to go away again if they didn't leave. So instinct told her to accept without question whatever they were doing, because that was the only way she would hold on to the tenuous security she had.

But where would they go? Linda wondered. To Vermont? There would be irony in that too, wouldn't there?

Patterns, she thought. Her life was filled with crazy patterns. An inescapable pattern of guilt, and a pattern to her relationships too. She had run away from West Ledge with Keith on the spur of the moment. Now with his brother as well.

Patterns.

"Can I take this?" Toby interrupted her thoughts as she lifted a pair of shorts out of her bottom drawer.

"Of course. And why don't you take some of your heavier clothes too. The new ones. It's going on winter soon and it'll be chilly."

"Okay."

"And don't forget your rainboots. They're in your closet. I'm going to pack my clothes now."

Toby went into the closet. "I can't find them."

"Look on the right side," Linda called from her bedroom. "I think I put them there."

"I see them."

The little girl was bending down, picking up her rubber boots, when she noticed something odd. A thin line of black at the edge of one of the wall panels at the back of the closet. Curious, she pushed against the panel tentatively and was surprised that it moved. She pushed a little more and a small door sprung open. Not much taller than she was. She hadn't noticed it before because she hadn't really been that deep in the closet. She saw the way the door was outlined—it started just above the woodwork on the floor, extended the width of the closet and up to the wood trim midway up. Waist-high for an adult, normal-high from her point of view. It was really hidden; the sliver of black might almost have been mistaken for a painted line. Imagine. A door in the closet.

She pushed the door open all the way. There was a little room

behind, swatched in a bleak gray from where the light filtered in
from her bedroom, black a few feet beyond. But when her eyes
adjusted to the darkness, she saw it wasn't a room at all—rather
it was a staircase stretching down from a landing, into the black
abyss. She wasn't able to see beyond the third step. A stairway in
the closet? she puzzled; that was strange. Then she remembered
something Uncle Thomas had said the very first day they arrived
in West Ledge. He was talking about the house, apologizing for
how old and ugly it was. But in that same conversation he
had mentioned something about secret passageways! At one time
she had thought it might be exciting to explore the house with
Petey and the others, but then she had totally forgotten. She
wasn't sorry; Petey would have wanted to go through this doorway
into the blackness of the staircase, follow it wherever it went.
There must be hidden dangers in there, she decided. Like there
had been hidden dangers in the well. Perhaps there was a punishment room at the bottom of the stairs for a child who once lived
in this house. It was just as well they hadn't gone exploring. She
had been brave enough to go down into the well, but she didn't
think she'd ever be brave enough to go through this secret
doorway. "Mommy." She started to call and ask about the
passageway, but stopped in a moment of adult decision making.
The passageway would remain just one more thing she wouldn't
question her mother about. They were leaving this house and she
wouldn't have to be bothered by it anymore. She pulled the door
shut behind her and resolved to forget about it.

She felt proud of herself for helping her mother by not making
her worry about anything else.

After Thomas left his mother's house, he drove to the bank
and called Jeff Forbes into his office.

"What was the emergency this morning, Thomas? I finished
the Woodstone deal with no difficulty, but is anything wrong?"

"Not wrong exactly, no," Thomas said. "I'm going away
with Linda for a while."

"Hey, that's great. When?"

"Now."

"What do you mean, now?"

"Well, in about two hours."

"That's certainly now."

"I want to pass some things on to you. I'll be away for a little bit."

"Where are you going? Or is that part of the secret?"

"I'll tell you the truth, Jeff. I honestly don't know."

"My kind of traveling."

"I'm picking Linda and Toby up, we're getting into the car and then wherever . . ."

Jeff laughed. "You must have driven the Triple-A people crazy. A Triptik to wherever. When will you be back?"

"I don't know that either. I haven't taken a vacation in years and I'm going to do a blow-out now. Bring your calendar in here. Let me give you my meetings. I'll check in once a day so if you have any questions—"

Jeff held up his hand, stopped him. "Hey, not on your vacation. Things will be all right. I'm competent, remember?"

After finishing with Jeff, Thomas drove home and left his car in the circular drive in front of the building. As he pushed the elevator button he thought briefly about what he was doing. He was repeating what his brother had done ten years before—leaving everything he had ever known for the woman he loved. That made him smile. He felt closer to Keith than he ever had when his brother was alive. Keith would be proud of him now.

He filled two suitcases and tried to devise some sort of plan. They would drive south—toward the Carolina coast. Off-season now, it should be quiet and isolated. He would devote himself to Linda, and with his care and attention she would get well again, he was confident. As she had at his apartment. The mistake was letting her move out, but now the mistake was being corrected. And if she still needed a psychiatrist, he would find her one. Any help that was required. He swore he wouldn't let her out of his sight or arms. Eventually they would be a family.

The phone rang. He picked up on the second ring. "I need an hour," he said.

"Thomas?"

"Yes, Mother."

"I'm not feeling well. I think I'm sick—"

"Mother, please. Don't do this to me," Thomas begged. "You can't keep me here."

"I'm not trying to. I really feel weak. I'm calling the doctor. Can't you come over before you pick them up?"

Thomas checked his watch. He would have barely enough time to go to his mother's house and then get to Linda by six. But he would go and put her at ease, ask the doctor to prescribe tranquilizers. He was certain there was nothing wrong with her. She was desperately trying to stop him from leaving in any way she could. "Please don't do this to me, Mother," he repeated. "Don't make me feel guilty for doing the most important thing I've ever done in my life."

Eleanor hung up the phone first, a soft click.

The rain was starting to fall, bringing on the evening an hour earlier. Winter would soon be upon them. Eleanor couldn't bear the thought of a winter all alone in that big house.

She had few real friends. Many acquaintances from the country club, charity organizations, but few people she could really talk to. There had always been a lot of entertaining in her group, but it had all been for business, never socially. Suddenly she felt very much alone, a tightening in her chest. Perhaps I really am sick, she thought.

She looked above her at the house. Silent now, except for the ever-present ticking of the clock, witness to so many years of life. It had ticked a century before she was born and would probably continue for a century after her death. More. A constant. A credit to good workmanship and care. The house would stand too, survive her for many years.

Perhaps Thomas planned one day to move back in here with Linda, as Thomas, Sr, had with her after his father's death, to continue the Devonshire name in the big, old house.

She didn't know if he planned it, but she knew now that it would not be happening.

Thomas was surprised when she let him into the house. She was wearing one of her dressier outfits and was all made up. As he took off his raincoat and shivered, she anticipated his question.

"I only pretended to be ill, and I'm sure you figured that out. But after we talked, I realized I can't stop you from what you want to do. So as the old cliché goes—if you can't beat 'em, join 'em. So voilà." Stepping aside, she pointed to the bottle of wine on the coffee table and the two glasses filled with the shimmering liquid. "Let's drink to Linda's good health."

Touched by her gesture, Thomas relaxed and said, "I'm grateful,

Mother." He loved her more at that moment than he ever could
remember. "I'm glad you're not upset."

"I'm not, Thomas," she said. "Not anymore. I have accepted
what I have to accept, and know what I have to do." She picked
up the glasses, handed him his. She clinked lightly with him, the
delicate crystal making a soft, pinging sound. "A good life for all
of us," she toasted, "and peace for Linda." And they drank.

"Sit for a minute, will you?"

"Maybe a minute," Thomas said. The hands on the grandfather clock inched toward six. He would stay five more minutes
and then leave to pick up Linda.

"Do you have any idea where you might be going?"

"I thought the Carolina coast for starters. Then we'll see. Take
each day as it comes. But we'll be back here, Mother. Very
shortly, I'm sure. Linda just needs some tender loving care and I
know she'll be as good as new."

"I'm sure." Eleanor smiled.

Thomas blinked. Suddenly his eyes had grown heavy. He
yawned. The day had been a long and tiring one and had taken a
lot out of him. Well, they wouldn't drive far that night. Just to a
motel across the state line in New York where they could sleep,
then start the trip fresh in the morning. They just had to get out
of West Ledge. Linda shouldn't spend another night in that
house.

He yawned again. He hadn't eaten since lunch and had drunk
the wine on an empty stomach. It had traveled right to his head.
Damn!

He was looking at his mother. She was smiling at him, talking
about the different towns in the area, offering her vote for which
they might select to live in when they got back. Which had the
best schools, the best shopping. *Damn!* His mother suddenly
seemed to grow fuzzy. He stood up. His head buzzed. Dizzy, he
sat back down again.

"Are you all right, Thomas?" Eleanor asked as the grandfather clock started to ring six o'clock.

"I'm not sure." He put his hands over his eyes, rubbed them
hard, hoping that when he took his hands away his sight would
be clear again and he wouldn't be woozy. Liquor never affected
him this way.

The grandfather clock bonged again. A second, crisp tone.

Thomas took his hands away from his eyes. "I'm just feeling so tired all of a sudden." He shook his head to try to clear it. That's all it was, he told himself; he wasn't sick. This wasn't a heart attack or stroke, was it?

"Well, you work very hard," Eleanor said.

He stood up, then swayed and sat back down again. "I can't," he said.

"It's just the wine, Thomas. Why don't you rest for a little bit . . .''

The clock sounded again, the deep, rich chime seemingly louder in his ears.

"Just for a few minutes. Let the wine settle. Then you'll feel better."

"So tired . . . so tired. Call Linda, Mother, tell her I'll be a few minutes late. Tell her—''

Eleanor walked to the phone. "Yes, of course. She should know. I'll do that right away."

Bong.

Thomas stood again, tried to take a step forward, then collapsed back onto the couch. His eyelids fluttered for a second. He saw the face of his mother standing above him, talking on the phone. At least Linda knew. Then his eyes fell closed.

He did not hear the last tone of the clock or the slight, slight residual echo that always remained and never really faded away.

Seven o'clock came. The suitcases were packed and standing by the door. Linda and Toby were sitting in the living room waiting for Thomas. The rain was falling steadily now, making the night seem even darker and more desolate. The streetlight struggled to shine through the haze, the raindrops formed a halo of color around the incandescent bulb. It would change to snow before the night was over. For the thirtieth time Linda walked to the window, peered behind the curtain, hoping she would see Thomas's car turn into their driveway. She had phoned him at six thirty and he wasn't home. He must be on his way, she reasoned. Perhaps he'd gotten a late start. It was a twenty-minute trip across town.

Maybe he stopped off to see his mother. She phoned Eleanor but the line was busy. It had been busy now for fifteen minutes. Well, he must be on his way.

At seven fifteen she fixed a light supper for Toby. She could always have dessert with them later. She tried Thomas again—no answer. Eleanor—the line remained busy. At seven thirty, fearing an accident, she phoned the local hospital. No, they reported, no patient by the name of Thomas Devonshire had been brought into the emergency room.

At eight o'clock she understood what had happened.

If he was going to be this late he would have phoned. If he had been in an accident the hospital would have informed her. And she could hardly call the police.

Thomas wasn't coming. He had changed his mind. He had offered to take her away at an emotional moment; now, after having had a chance to think about what he had said he decided no, he didn't want to have to babysit for someone who was out of her mind. So he had left her. He had sworn never to abandon her and now he had. Her worst fears had been realized.

God, give me strength, she pleaded, shuddering as the pain shimmered through her and she choked back bitter tears. But her eyes remained dry and accepting as she stared inwardly and fought the rejection. She had to remain strong for Toby, in control for her little girl who had no one else to watch over her. Keith was dead and Thomas was uncaring. Only she was left. The hurt would come later, she knew, and it would be bad; she had given so much of herself to Thomas, so much love, so much trust. So much of herself these last few months was part of him, bound with him. But she wasn't going to let it blind or paralyze her now. Nor would she even dare to think what his rejection would do to her when it impacted fully. Now there were too many things she had to plan. She had to prepare for the future.

A new strength passed through her, culled from her pain and need; a primal strength born from her desperation and loss. She had survived for more than a year without Thomas and she would again. Recently she had let others control her, make decisions for her; now *she* was in charge. She felt an almost spiritual uplifting. She could be strong when she had to be. They would leave West Ledge first thing in the morning; it was too late and too wet and she was too tired to go anywhere that night. And the police wouldn't know she had gone by herself until she was miles away. She could endure one more night in this house because it had done its worst to her and now the end was in sight. Once out of

West Ledge, *away from this house*, she would be well again. And if that had to be without Thomas, then it would be without Thomas. She even managed to smile for the first time all day, and it was not tentative or hesitant, not a smile clouded by uncertainty. Rather it was a prideful smile, one of resolve and victory. She was a survivor!

"Where's Uncle Thomas, Mommy?" Toby asked, coming in from the kitchen.

Linda turned away from the window where she let the curtain flutter back into place for what would be the last time, she decided. "I don't know, honey. I don't think he's going to be coming with us tomorrow."

"Are we going to stay here tonight?"

"Yes, dear. Is that okay?"

"I guess." Toby nodded. But when the little girl thought about it, she grew uneasy. For some reason she felt uncomfortable about going to sleep in her room where she had discovered that secret passageway.

Because she didn't know what was behind the door.

Or behind other doors in the house, as yet undiscovered.

chapter 26

Linda woke to the mix of sounds. They came in assaulting waves, and louder now than ever before. Booming. More external. No longer teasing phantom noises. The pound of footsteps. Louder. The slam of doors. Louder. Creaks. Clicks. A mushroom cloud of sound in the room with her, discordant, deafening! All real!

And the rush of water, prominent now as the other sounds disappeared suddenly.

Water raged from the bathtub faucet, rumbled up and out of the pipes, filling the tub! Barefoot, Linda raced to the bathroom. The nightlight was off. She was about to put on the overhead light when she paused, shivered, and did a crazy dance step as her feet seemed suddenly thrust into ice. They were wet. Water had overflowed the rim of the tub, coming out faster than the holes at the top could drain it. It covered the floor; the hallway too, swirling past her feet. Standing in the water, turning on the switch—was she in danger of passing current and electrocuting herself. *How did the water get turned on?* only a part of her questioned. But she had to turn it off before the whole house flooded.

The light from the hallway aided her in the bathroom. The mat was soaked through, unpleasant to step on, like a wet forest floor after a storm—heavy, muddy.

The water continued to pulse over the edge of the tub. She twisted off the tap and was pulling her hand away when it brushed against something. Something soft—and soaked through. Matted. Spongy. Reflexively she pulled her hand back. She noticed the odor now as well.

Her eyes had grown accustomed to the dimness of the room,

and when she looked into the tub she didn't have to turn on the lights to see what it was.

With a curious horror she thought she recognized the soft ball of gray fur, the two dead eyes, appearing more black and sunken by the darkness of the room. *Thought* she recognized, because on a conscious level it did not make sense. But a tail was splayed out across the surface of the water. And four stiffened legs, bent and mangled, and a broken spine—

She took a moment to question and absorb. Only a moment before shock registered clear to the marrow, and terror and disbelief riffled through her.

Princess was floating in the bathtub!

What kind of a joke was this? she questioned, but even before the question was raised inside her, she had her answer. This was no joke. *No joke.* She reacted.

"Toby!" she screamed, and ran into her daughter's room.

As she flipped on the light and squinted against the brightness, she first thought that everything was normal, as it should be. Deep down she knew it couldn't be, because Princess was in the bathtub! But right now Toby was okay, asleep under the mound of covers. And that was all that mattered.

Something seemed wrong.

She couldn't see her child's head. The blankets were pulled all the way up—suffocatingly.

She threw the covers back.

Bolsters were underneath, disguised as the sleeping child.

"Toby!"

Was this a mad joke her daughter had concocted? It had to be!

She whipped open the closet door, half expecting Toby to scream out "Boo!" and charge through. Praying that she would. Because that would mean her daughter was there.

The closet was almost empty. Most of the clothes had been removed; Patricia and the other toys as well, packed away earlier that evening. Just some dresses that Toby had outgrown were left, and shoes she would never wear again. And a square of blackness at the edge of the closet that she saw only out of the corner of her eye. But nothing that warranted her attention now.

"Toby!"

With both hands she thrust wide the curtains to look out the windows. She had no idea what she expected to see. Water droplets distorted her face on the snow-soaked glass. But the window was locked and nobody was on the roof of the porch.

She raced downstairs, stomped through the rooms, fighting nausea and panic. *Where was her child?*

She remembered the patch of blackness in the closet, replayed the single frame in her mind that had registered it. The blackness suggested depth. Was it a place to hide? Be hidden? Be taken? She was halfway up the stairs when the telephone rang. Jarringly loud. Startled, she stumbled against a step, lost her balance, pitched forward and jammed her knee. Using the banister, she pulled herself up the stairs and grabbed the phone in her bedroom. *Thomas?*

The message was simple. "This is Beatrice. Toby is mine." Then a disconnect and the buzzing sound of the dead line.

The words impacted and the implication was clear: The threats had all been real. Beatrice had killed Princess, then dug her up from the grave to scare her!

And now she had Toby.

They had spent one night too many in the house. They should have left earlier. This wouldn't have happened. Damn Thomas for what he did to them! Damn the weather for locking them in! Had she only known. But there was no time now for regret. A cornered animal, her head swiveled crazily in eight different directions. She couldn't decide what to do. The police! She started to dial the phone when she slammed the receiver down. They would never believe her. Not after all the false alarms.

But they hadn't been false alarms, had they? Everything had been real. It had been Beatrice's doing all the time! And now she had the proof!

But she felt no triumph, for her realization had come too late. Toby was in terrible danger. And she couldn't take the time to convince the police.

The police wouldn't help her. Thomas couldn't be found. She was all alone.

There were knives in the kitchen.

In a sweep one was in her hand and she was running through the door and out into the wet, cold night. With purpose—to save her child. And for the first time she knew for certain that it wasn't all in her head.

*   *   *

Thomas opened his eyes and quickly closed them, covered them with his hands. He struggled to open them again, but his heavy lids didn't want to comply. He was beyond tired—almost to the point of cold nausea. He felt as if he had just come out of anesthesia. He breathed deeply to try to flush his system. He blinked and squinted, then shook his head to free it of the fog that seemed to hold it trapped.

"Mother?"

The grandfather clock answered him mellifluently. One tone. Like the one he missed when he had fallen asleep. One low hum that oddly suggested knowledge. Otherwise the house was silent and nighttime eerie. His eyes fell first on the coffee table. He saw the bottle of wine, the two glasses. He raised his head and looked at the clock just as it sounded another note. Then it stopped. It was two o'clock.

Next to the phone on the nighttable was an open account book. Thomas's eyes were drawn to it. It was odd because though it wasn't from their bank, still it bore his mother's name. He thought his mother kept all of her money at the bank. He knew nothing about this account. Curiosity made him open the book, though he was aware he was intruding on his mother's privacy. If she wanted a secret account so checks wouldn't have to clear through the bank, that was her business.

He scanned the ledger. The checks for this account were only made out to cash. But on the stubs were notations in his mother's handwriting. And the following names: Nancy Stone. Peter Ehrlich. Ira Perdue. Dres-rich Cleaners.

He knew who Ira Perdue was, but wasn't Nancy Stone the secretary in Linda's office she had complained about? He thought that was her name. Why would his mother be giving her money? And who was Peter Ehrlich? He thumbed through the old entries. The payments to Nancy had been made recently. Peter too. There was just one payment to Ira and Dres-Rich Cleaners, but there were other cash payments made to Peter. They were listed in his mother's neat handwriting on a separate sheet of paper. From years ago. Ten years ago. And an address—a box number in California.

It didn't make any sense, and while it was his mother's business, he would make certain to question her about it. But now he had more pressing problems. He put the ledger back onto the endtable and was getting up when he accidentally knocked the book to the floor. As he reached down to pick it up, a metallic gleam under his mother's bed caught his eye. He reached under and pulled out his old Panasonic cassette recorder. He hadn't seen it in years, not since he had used it to tape college lectures. He didn't know why it should be there now. More than curious, he pushed the playback button.

There was a rush of static, then the gurgle of a sink and a sound—was it running water he was hearing?

A moment of silence followed as the blank tape advanced through the playback heads, then there was another rush of water, slurping down a drain. Then a whisper, almost completely masked by the water. He could have missed it, but he didn't.

You killed her.

Words caught on the wind. Barely an exhale.

Startled, he turned up the volume. There was nothing for several seconds as the tape continued. It was almost as if the machine was playing with him, he thought. Had he really heard those words?

You killed my daughter.

Beatrice Dailey's voice was coming out of the tape recorder. He hadn't been mistaken. He looked at the machine, puzzled. This didn't make any sense.

He turned the volume up on the recorder and the words repeated themselves. But even with the volume on high, some of the speeches were so faint as almost not to be there. Seemingly. Because they were there. At different volume levels, sometimes frightening loud, other times barely audible. As if they were coming from great distances. Or depths.

I have to kill you, Linda. And Toby too.

Thomas shocked to the words. And the new voice. It could have still been Beatrice speaking, but he sensed a change and knew it wasn't. The voice was false. Close—although with a subtle difference. The clarity was the same and the tonal quality— slightly arched, shrill. Almost a flawless impersonation. *But an impersonation.*

With the water!

It hit him. His mother's voice!

Then a child's cry. "Mommeeeeee—"

It was a moment packed with understanding and disbelief.

You go out with her, have dinner with her, whatever you want.

It doesn't matter what other people think; if this is what you want, Thomas, then the issue is closed.

You have my approval, Thomas.

All his mother's words. And all totally uncharacteristic. He had thought she was changing, mellowing. Had wanted to believe it.

What about me! You'll forget me! Just like Keith! Because of her!

But she was really afraid!

And if he hadn't been blinded by hope, he would have known.

He punched Linda's phone number again. "Answer—answer," he pleaded, his fists clenched as if willing the phone to be picked up.

Something was happening.

Right then.

And Linda hadn't gone away!

He raced out of the house and into his car. He was well on his way before he realized he should have phoned the police. He couldn't go back to do it—it would take too much time. He was really only a few minutes from Linda's house. Maybe he'd run into a patrol car on the way.

The snow was falling, drifting across the road.

He prayed he would not be too late.

In her nightgown, Linda ran across the street, slipping on the snowy pavement. Beatrice's house was lighted up—a beacon in the night. Up the porch steps, across the slatted wood. If she was surprised to find the front door open, she didn't think about it now. The knob turned easily to her touch; the door burst wide and she was inside the house.

She heard the sound coming from upstairs. It was the sound of water pouring out of a faucet. She looked down. Her feet were wet again, and not from the snow-covered walk. The water had overflowed the tub and was running down the stairs, pooling in the entranceway, now trickling past her and out the door.

Then she understood.

"Toby!" she screamed, and vaulted for the stairs. A hysterical call, born of the image of her own house and Princess dead in the bathtub. An image of Toby now as well.

"Nooo—" A gurgle of terror, a pained cry of anguish from deep in her soul. Was she too late? Had Beatrice gotten revenge on her daughter for the death of hers? The stairs were slippery from the flowing water. Twice she stumbled and slid down. It took only seconds to get to the second floor, but the seconds, steeped in horror, seemed like hours. And every one counted if her daughter was in the bathtub, being held under the water.

She had never been upstairs in Beatrice's house but knew in an instant where the bathroom was. The corridor was flooded with water. Her feet sloshed on the rug. It would take forever for this house to dry out, she thought with the one tiny part of her mind that could still reason. *What kind of a person would do this?*

"Toby!" she called again. Please God, please let her answer. Let me hear her voice, know that everything is all right.

The bathroom door was closed. Water slapped out through the crack at the bottom. She raced toward it, her hand cramped around the carving knife, ready to use it, the blade beaded with water from the melted snow.

She burst through the door. The tap was open. Water spilled out of the faucet, over the rim. Toby wasn't in the tub, thank God, thank God. She looked for an extra second just to make certain. She had gotten there in time.

Then she gasped, a sudden intake of breath, high in her chest, a choking squeal like an animal about to be slaughtered.

She hadn't seen it when she first came into the room. She was looking at the bathtub, across from the door. The sink was off to the side, partially hidden by the door. She saw it all only when she turned away from the tub to leave the room. First Shana, her tail wagging obediently, although with a puzzled look in her eyes. Then Beatrice, slumped on the floor. She was sitting in a pool of water, her head leaning against the metal leg of the sink.

Dead! Linda shrieked and almost slipped on the bathroom tile as she spun to get away from the figure on the floor.

Beatrice was dead; where was Toby? Had she killed her little girl?

Hysterical, she ran out of the room, into the corridor. There were other rooms, other doors. She tried the next—locked. *None of this makes any sense!* she screamed to herself in her need to understand.

The second door opened. She didn't know why she still held

the knife. She thought she had dropped it in the bathroom, but her fingers seemed paralyzed around the wooden handle. And to drop it would be to use up precious seconds. It preceded her into the room, blade pointing outward, ready to lunge.

A hand struck her forearm—a sharp, stinging blow. Pain radiated from her wrist to her elbow. Her fingers opened and the knife clattered to the floor. That was the mistake. Linda snapped to, alert, her senses heightened. She knew her attacker was there. Out of the corner of her eyes she saw movement. A blunt object, coming toward her head. Prepared now, she jumped aside, and it barely brushed her. She hunched into a ready position, and, breathless, she stared into the barrel of the pistol.

For Linda it was a moment of confusion, then things connected. Eleanor was holding a gun on her.

A thin layer of snow covered the ground—a tentative blanket of white, uncertain in the gusts of wind, like waves slapping against sand. It was too soon for the plows or sanders to come through, but not too soon for the road to be slick. Thomas kept his foot steady on the gas. He was nearing the turnoff from the main road to Linda's sidestreet. Then she was only a few blocks down.

He didn't know what he expected to find when he got there. Nobody had picked up the phone. Most probably she had left earlier that evening when he had failed to show up for her—when he had let her down. Most probably she was miles away right now. In any direction—it didn't matter. And he wouldn't have thought it possible for him to be happy that Linda had left West Ledge without him. Because she would be safe. But deep within him, he knew there was a flaw. Where was his mother? If Linda had left, his mother would have been home when he came to.

In frustration he hit the steering wheel. "Mother, why?" he cried in anguish. "She didn't mean you any harm. She never did."

Thomas sped forward into the night, wondering what his mother—cold-hearted, soulless Eleanor Devonshire—was truly capable of.

But from the tapes he already knew.

Because of his desperation to get to Linda, the car turning onto

the road from the hidden drive did not fully register in time for
him to slow down. Still, his reflexes were good, and it took less
than a second for his foot to jump from the accelerator to clamp
down hard on the brake. But he had forgotten about the slippery
roads. The rear wheels skidded out. He tried to straighten the car,
direct it back into his lane, but he had no control. The car slid
across the wet surface and spun around, colliding with a parked
car. He was propelled into a dip on the side of the road, half
on the pavement, half on the soft shoulder, which sloped downward. He tried forward and reverse but was unable to budge
the car; its front end was wedged into a gulley.

Toby woke up. Her head hurt and felt funny. She tried to raise
herself from the pillow but it was as if a giant clamp held her
neck locked in place. The feeling was odd. And somewhat familiar.
She remembered when she was a little girl and had her tonsils
taken out. She remembered two things from the operation. First,
the doctor had lied to her—rather, misled. He had told her that
afterward she would be able to eat all the ice cream she wanted,
an inducement to the little girl to go through with the operation.
But after it was over, her throat was too sore to even attempt to
swallow the ice cream. The other thing she remembered was
waking up after it was all over. Her mother and father were both
there so she knew everything was all right. But still she felt
funny. Just like this, woozy and unable to move her head. Her
eyes were half closed and everything was fuzzy, and she was
very, very cold. It was only the anesthesia, they told her, and she
would be better in no time. She had been put to sleep with a gas
so the operation wouldn't hurt at all. That was how she felt now.
As if she had been put to sleep with a gas.

And just like the last time, it took only a few minutes for her
to be able to pull herself off the pillow. She hoisted herself up
onto her elbow, wrapped her arms around herself, and rocked
back and forth to get warm. She frowned. The mattress felt
different. It was very firm, while hers was soft—a little too soft
in certain spots. Sometimes she had to angle herself so she wouldn't
sleep in a dip. This mattress had no dips because this wasn't her
mattress.

Gradually her eyes grew accustomed to the darkness in the
room. There was a canopy above her bed. And the frilly lace was

familiar. Across the room was a dresser. Dolls were perched on top of the dresser, on display, watching her.

Then at once everything was familiar and she knew exactly where she was. In Carol Ann's room. In her bed. But that didn't make any sense.

She struggled to sit up, and that was when she smelled the smoke.

The fire started in the kitchen wall, behind the lightswitch. The wires, made wet by the water that had seeped down through the wall, shorted out. The fire fed on the wooden structure of the house and started to spread.

chapter 27

"All I wanted was for you to leave West Ledge. That was all. Either leave or if everyone thought you were sick enough, they would put you away. Away from Thomas. But you wouldn't leave. You stayed. And stayed. And Thomas remained with you. As Keith did. You should have just taken my money. You should have."

Tears were streaming from Eleanor's pained, anguished eyes. Linda saw that her hand was quivering on the trigger of the gun.

"Where's Toby?" she begged, looking from the gun to Eleanor's twisted face. She thought of Beatrice on the floor of the bathroom. "What have you done to her?"

"Even until tonight I kept hoping you would just go away . . . be frightened away. Be put away! But you wouldn't go," Eleanor repeated. "And then when Thomas told me what he planned on doing . . ." She shook her head pitifully. "I couldn't have it. It would happen all over again. You would take him away from me. Just as you did with Keith."

Linda smelled the smoke now too. Faint in her nostrils. Wafting teasingly.

"Where's Toby? Let me just take my daughter and we'll leave here." She started to ease toward the door. "We'll go away. I'll never see Thomas again. I swear it."

Eleanor tightened her hold on the gun, pointed it stiff-armed at Linda, who froze.

"I swear it!" Linda repeated desperately.

"He'll find you," Eleanor said. "He loves you and he'll find you. If you have money you can find anything, do anything. . . ."

She broke off and they both listened. There was the rush of fire. Eleanor's arm twitched and the gun shook.

"I didn't want to have to kill you," she continued as she steadied herself. "All I wanted was for you to go away." A slight, hysterical giggle. Cracking. "But you wouldn't."

"You can't get away with this," Linda breathed, suddenly realizing now that Eleanor had been setting her up, mirroring her illness in California, making everyone think she was sick. But that was wrong, she thought distantly; she hadn't told Eleanor anything until after so much had already happened to her.

"I can!" Eleanor cried. "Nobody knows I'm here and Thomas is out cold. By the time he comes to, I'll be home again. This is what everyone will think happened: Tonight you went out of your mind, thought you heard Beatrice in your house again, came across the street, and tried to drown her because you thought she had done the same to your child." Eleanor's voice built in hysteria. She was far from the cool, unruffled Devonshire that Linda had known. "But she got away, came back into her bedroom, got this gun, and shot you! Then when she was running away, she slipped on the water, banged her head, was knocked unconscious, and eventually drowned. . . ."

"You killed Beatrice too." It was an involuntary statement. She should have realized that already, although she was surprised she was realizing anything at all beyond *it had been Eleanor all along*. How? She raged with questions. But only one mattered. "Where's Toby?"

"I didn't want to kill anyone!" Eleanor cried. "I could have had you killed at any time if I did. Even on that street in Ohio before you got here. If you pay someone enough they will kill for you, and Peter would have! But now I don't have any other option. You'll take Thomas away from me as you did Keith. I'll never see him again. I'll—" Smoke entered the room and Eleanor coughed. The chamber of the gun angled away from Linda for a second. It was her moment, Linda knew, and she had to grab it. She lunged toward Eleanor, seized her arm, pointed it upward. The gun barrel aimed toward the ceiling as Linda tried to wrest it free. It went off, an explosion of sound. Plaster rained down on them. But still Eleanor didn't loosen her grip. Her bones seemed so brittle that Linda thought the older woman's arm would snap as she wrestled her for the gun. That was exactly what she wanted—for Eleanor's arm to snap and drop the gun. Because her grip could not be broken. The older woman's desperation had given her surprising strength; as had her own, Linda reasoned. She had to find her child.

Then they were both coughing and struggling for the gun, which Eleanor still refused to let go of, her fingers frozen around the handle in a rigor mortis grip. Linda's hand closed around Eleanor's fist and thrust downward. Her aged bones were weaker than her hold on the gun. The crack was sudden, like stepping on a twig. Eleanor cried out in pain as her arm shattered.

Linda held the gun triumphantly, pointing it at Eleanor, who, defeated, was slumped next to the bed sobbing hysterically.

She knew she had failed. Lost everything. Now the worst would happen.

Smoke filled the room.

"Mommeeee!"

Toby was coughing too. She smelled smoke and felt the heat. There was fire in the house. She touched the walls; they were warm against her hand. The fire was getting closer!

She had to get out of the room but the door was locked. She had tried it a half-dozen times but the knob wouldn't turn. And there was no bolt to flip. The door was locked from the outside!

She ran to the window and threw it open. The swirling snow hit her in the face, the fresh air washed over her, and she breathed it in. She saw fire raging out of the first-floor windows. The house was ablaze and she was trapped.

"Help!" she screamed out into the night. Across the street was her own house, brightly lighted. Her mother was awake. Was she looking for her? "Here I am, Mommy! Here!" she cried.

But it was hopeless. Her mother wasn't coming for her.

Nobody was home in the first house Thomas tried. He was running up the steps to another when his mind tripped and something registered. The date of the checks sent to Peter Ehrlich in California. That was when Linda and Keith had been there—around the same time as her breakdown and hospitalization.

His mother had hired Peter Ehrlich to stalk Linda in California, he realized.

She hadn't been sick then. Everything she thought she imagined had been real! Then, as now!

The only traumas in Linda's life had occurred when she was young. Everything else was a sham, his mother's doing.

"Help me, please!" he yelled as he pounded on the door to try to wake the people inside.

But he was already too late; he would not be able to affect the outcome.

"Where's Toby?"

Linda shook the woman on the floor as acrid smoke billowed above them, burning her eyes, filling her mouth, her nose. "Where is she?"

"You would leave me all alone . . ." Eleanor was babbling pathetically, hunching into herself. "I would die alone. All alone . . ." She looked up at Linda imploringly. *She had to understand!*

"Where is she?" Linda slapped Eleanor's face roughly to snap her out of her paralysis, but clearly the older woman had come apart.

"I would have taken care of Toby," Eleanor said distantly. "I would have brought her up as a Devonshire. You needn't have worried about her."

She would be no help, Linda knew.

She ran out into the hallway. Smoke engulfed the corridor, and she instinctively dropped to the floor to stay below it. Eleanor would die in the fire, but that wasn't her concern now. She had to find her daughter.

Square of darkness, her subconscious prickled. An opening in her daughter's closet had suggested depth but she hadn't looked inside because the phone had rung and interrupted her. There were passageways in the house, behind the walls and leading to the outside. That's how Eleanor had gotten in and out of the house undetected. And a dream had once tried to warn her of that; her subconscious had known! That's where Eleanor had hidden Toby now—somewhere in her house. At least her daughter wasn't in the fire. At least she was safe. *Unless Eleanor had already killed her!*

She had to get out of this house, find her daughter.

She had just started down the staircase when she heard it.

"Mommy—"

A faint cry. Almost below the threshold of her hearing, swallowed by the crackling of the flames. She almost dismissed it as a residual sound deep within her. Then it came again.

"Mommy—"

"Toby!" she screamed madly. Her daughter *was* there! "Where are you, baby?"

Flames appeared on the walls at the other end of the hallway, disintegrating the paper, spreading. She had only moments to find her daughter before the house went up and all was lost.

"Where are you?"

"In here, Mommy. In Carol Ann's room." A manic pounding on the door led Linda to it. She grabbed the doorknob; twisted. Locked. "Dear God!" The heat was beginning to get to her, the smoke was almost overpowering. She coughed, ducked low to the floor, took a deep breath, and gasped as the hot air entered her lungs. She crashed into the door, trying to shoulder her way past the lock. It couldn't be all that secure. But the door didn't budge.

"The fire, Mommy! There's fire in here!" Toby shrieked. The fire blazed across the outside wall, near the window, cutting off that escape. Even the doorknob was hot now as Toby tugged at it frantically. "Get me out!"

"I am!" Linda cried, but she didn't know what to do.

There had to be a key! Eleanor must have it. Sweat broke out on Linda's face. Down the hall the fire raged. Soon it would spread to the staircase, their only hope.

Back to the bedroom, she faced Eleanor, who was cradling her useless arm.

"The key. Where is it?"

Eleanor looked at her blankly, as if she had slipped into herself.

"The key!" Linda demanded again. A surge of smoke entered her lungs, gripped her chest. She coughed, doubled over. She yanked at Eleanor's pocket. The key had to be in there. The pocket ripped. There was no key.

Linda saw her knife lying on the floor. She would have to use it. Only later would she remember the gun.

"Get out of here, Eleanor!" she called as she left the room. "You'll die!"

But Eleanor never moved. She lay still slumped by the bed, seemingly growing smaller. And Linda didn't care.

Back into the hallway. The other end of the corridor was bright with flame, a pulsing red monster. The heat was almost unbearable, searing her face, bathing it in red-orange light. Linda was acting on pure adrenaline now. By all rights she should already be dead, she knew, consumed by the inferno, like so much more wallpaper.

She held the knife in her closed fist and started to hack at the plasterboard door around the knob. She had to break through it, release the knob. She coughed, dropped the knife into the water that still swirled over her feet, scooped up a handful and splashed her face. The knife started to chip through the plaster.

"Mommy!"

"I'm coming, baby. Hold on!" she cried, stabbing at the door more and more frantically. The door flaked, the knob loosened. She pulled at it. It came off in her hands, flaming hot from conductive heat. But the door sprung wide. Toby ran into her arms.

"Quickly," she said, trying to hold Toby at arm's length. "We have to get out of the house."

The little girl was coughing, her lungs straining. Her skin was blackening from the punishing smoke.

"Low now!" Linda ordered. And low to the floor, splashing water up into their faces, they started back toward the staircase. She glanced behind her for only a second; Eleanor was left to her fate.

They were passing the bathroom door, about to dart down the stairs, when Beatrice leaped.

She had only been stunned by Eleanor's blow. Now she had come to.

She lunged through the doorway, grabbed onto Linda's ankle, tightened her hold around it. Linda plunged forward, crashed to the floor, the knife clattering out of her hands. "What?" She snaked around, saw Beatrice. The shock was fractionally delayed; then it registered. "No!" she screeched, in surprise, in horror, as she understood what Beatrice was doing. She tried to pull out of her grasp, moving her arms and legs spastically, uselessly, like a turtle trying to gain momentum. She tensed her knee, kicked out, tried to catch Beatrice in the face, break her grip, but the other woman eluded her attempts, kept her pinned to the floor.

"Mommy!" Toby screamed. She started to hit at Beatrice.

"Run, baby!" Linda ordered. "Out of the house." There was a moment of hesitation on Toby's part, as she understood many things as she looked at Beatrice Dailey. "Now!" Linda shouted, and the little girl disappeared down the steps, just as the flames converged above the stairway, a canopy of hellish red.

"You killed my daughter!" Beatrice screamed madly above the fire. "You killed Carol Ann! And Keith! You have to die too!"

"We'll both die!" Linda cried. "But we can get out now." A funnel of flame closed elliptically around the staircase. In seconds they'd be trapped with no escape.

"I have nothing to live for! My child is dead! The man I loved!"

"I loved him too!" Linda cried, trying to twist away from the woman whose fingers were digging into her heel. She felt nails break her skin, sensed blood seeping down her leg, but had no time to think about the pain. At least low to the floor she was able to breathe. The water against her clothes felt good. Flames whistled above her as the ceiling caught. She had only a moment. Or less. And there would be no reasoning with this insane woman. She prayed Toby had gotten down the stairs and out of the house. Would she ever know?

Beatrice was coughing—hacking—the bitter smoke starting to consume her lungs, do its worst, then leave the remains to the fire to char and burn. But she seemed to gain new strength as the time grew more desperate and her flesh reddened and blistered from the searing heat. And she was grinning—a crazy, maniacal grin. Monstrous. Victorious. Vengeance was hers.

Linda tried to crawl forward and snap free. Her fingers burrowed painfully into the carpet, searching for handholds. The rug ripped, tufts of thread coming off under her nails. Plaster bits fell on her head from the disintegrating heat. The house was collapsing around them.

One chance.

The knife.

Just out of reach, but her only hope. She lunged forward. Her fingers brushed the handle; seemed to push it infinitesimally farther away. It was teetering on the edge of the steps, seemingly balanced, tauntingly. One more tap against it could knock it

down the stairs, out of reach, useless. She would be doomed.
"Come on . . . come on . . ." she grated through tightened lips.
Water flowed around the knife—a rock in a stream; down the
stairs, a waterfall. Linda stretched to her fullest. She wasn't able
to move Beatrice, whose legs must have been anchored around
the supports of the sink. Beatrice was holding on to her with
inhuman strength. All Linda had was her arm. Shoulder straining
as if it might pop from its socket, she stretched. Carefully. One
chance. She'd either grab it or lose it. One final thrust forward
and she clamped down and had a grip on the knife.

"You were a bad girl and have to be punished," Beatrice said,
and then repeated the words over and over, as if a litany.

Linda had to do it. There was no other option. And no thought
or hesitation. She was sprawled on the floor at full extension, and
as she twisted painfully around, all she could reach with the knife
was Beatrice's hand. Her eyes burned and were almost blinded
by the bitter smoke, but she swung carefully so not to stab
herself. Too late Beatrice saw the blade arcing toward her. The
tip of the knife sank into her forearm, just above the wrist, drove
through the slender bones and pinioned her to the wooden floor.
An unearthly howl rose above the rush of fire and Beatrice's
fingers loosed their grasp on Linda's leg. Blood was spurting,
mingling with the water as Linda struggled to her feet. Alive.

Shana was standing paralyzed by her mistress.

"Come on!" Linda slapped the dog. Shana snapped to and
darted into the inferno. "Get up, Beatrice!" Linda yelled. But
she didn't know if Beatrice was behind her.

A wall of flame engulfed the staircase. Thank God for the
water on the steps. She had one chance. If not for the water she
would have already been consumed by the fire. She threw herself
headfirst down the stairs, rolled to the bottom just like on the
water ride at a carnival, inches beneath the raging flames. Then
she half crawled, half stumbled through the living room, just as
the firemen were coming through the door.

"There are two people up there," she croaked hoarsely; the
smoke had violated her throat.

The firemen looked at the knife still in her hand for only a
second before pushing past. The tip was red with Beatrice's
blood. In her shock Linda didn't even remember pulling it out of
the woman's arm, but now in her inner ear, above the hiss of

the flames, she heard the sound as it yanked free from the floor—the hollow pop a knife makes when it splits a newel post. A sound that would never leave her.

She stumbled out into the freezing night, but after the horror of the inferno, nothing could have been more delicious than the fresh, cold air.

Then she saw Thomas running toward her and understood he had never left her. He grabbed her hand, broke her hold on the knife, and then they were in each other's arms.

"Toby?" she begged.

"Safe. She's in the ambulance."

"Your mother's still inside!" Linda blurted as they watched the house shudder and wheeze and start to collapse upon itself, a disintegrating mass of wooden beams. The firemen came running out; they hadn't been able to get upstairs and save the others.

"I know," Thomas said, with only the slightest bit of emotion. Then he pursed his lips and looked at the house; watched it burn, thinking about his mother, who had died all alone.

Without glancing back, he piled into the ambulance with Linda. Siren on, they sped to the hospital. His mother was dead, but he had to go on with the living—for his wife-to-be and daughter-to-be. Both were still alive and finally free of the past.